Advanced Dungeons & Dragons 2nd Edition

Player's Handbook **Rules Supplement**

The Complete Priest's Handbook

by Aaron Allston

Table of Contents:

Credits

Project Design: Aaron Allston

Editing: Karen S. Boomgarden
Black and White Art by:
Thomas Baxa
Color Art by: Erik Olson, Larry
Elmore and David Dorman
Typography: Gaye O'Keefe
Special Contributions by:
Mark Bennett
Playtesters: Luray Richmond, Mark
Richmond

Since the creation of the ADVANCED DUNGEONS & DRAGONS® game system, the cleric has been one of the most popular character classes. He has been a happy bridge between warriors and mages: Capable of armoring up and wielding heavy weapons, capable of casting useful magics, he was a very versatile adventurer and the favorite choice of countless players.

With the release of the AD&D® 2nd Edition game, none of that has changed. The cleric is the same magic-hurling, mace-wielding hero that he always was. And in *The Complete Priest's Handbook*, we're going to see to it that he's even more than that.

In this supplement, we're going to elaborate on what the priest (including the cleric) *is* to the campaign, to the setting's civilization, and to the adventuring party.

We'll be providing guidelines for the DM to work up the cleric's faith: The god or philosophy he serves, the rules and mores he follows, the duties he practices, the restrictions he suffers, the powers he possesses, and the relations he and the others of his faith have with the followers of other faiths.

We'll show you how to work up priests devoted to specific mythoi. The druid, from the AD&D® 2nd Edition *Player's Handbook*, is one example; this supplement describes many, many more, and provides rules for the DM to create new priesthoods of his own design.

We'll talk about priestly orders. Some priesthoods have soldierly orders, scholarly orders, missionary orders, oracular orders, and many other types. If your priest character belongs to a faith with several orders, he may choose one of them, which will give him special abilities and duties beyond those of ordinary priests.

We'll talk about role-playing the priest character. Certainly, priest characters don't have to have the same sort of identical personality (the kindly father-confessor with the bloody mace in his hand) which many players imagine them all to have.

We'll describe whole campaigns devoted to priests: How to run them, how to give them a purpose, how to determine what goals and interests are most appropriate.

And we'll talk about the sort of equipment that priests use in their devotions and adventures, including weapons, armor, holy symbols, priestly vestments, and other items.

The Complete Priest's Handbook is equally useful if you're a Dungeon Master or a player. It will add depth to the campaign world and the range of NPCs for Dungeon Masters, and add detail to the abilities, backgrounds, and responsibilities of player-character priests.

* * *

In the text, for reasons of simplicity, we normally use masculine nouns and pronouns inclusively. When we say "god," "priest," or "man," we're normally also implying "goddess," "priestess," and "woman."

In order to be able to use this supplement, you must use the Weapon and Nonweapon Proficiencies rules from the AD&D® 2nd Edition game. If you're not yet familiar with them, you ought to read them before continuing in this rulebook.

A special note for those of you who are using this *Complete Priest's Handbook* with your original AD&D® game instead of the new edition: This supplement mentions a lot of page numbers from the *Player's Handbook* and the *DMG*. The page numbers cited are for the newest edition, not the original; they won't be correct for those of you using the old books.

This chapter is for DMs who want to design the mythic history of their campaign world(s). It's not prohibited for the campaign's players to read this. . . but not all of them will find it useful. Players may wish to skip on to the third chapter, "Sample Priesthoods."

* * *

One of the first things the DM can do to add color and detail to his campaign world is to work up that world's *mythic history.* Such a history will help establish, in his mind and those of his players, the relationships between the gods, and between gods and men. It will help set the tone of the campaign and the attitude of the player-characters' culture. It will give the players some idea of what their characters expect from their gods and their future. And once it's done, the DM can then elaborate on it and decide how each individual god relates to other gods and to the sentient races of the world.

In this chapter, we'll discuss some of the common themes that run through myths; the DM can use these topics as a framework for his own mythic history.

Creation

The first place to start is the creation of the universe and the world.

In most creation stories, there was usually some disinteresting, stable condition in effect at the dawn of time. It might have been a formless void, or darkness, or unending ice and snow.

Then, we have the first great being, the one who brings about creation of the world. Note that this great being doesn't have to be the god who is now dominant in the campaign world. The myths are packed with tales of gods who created their worlds, became oppressive, and were then cast down by other gods, even their own children, who now rule in their place.

Nor does the creation have to have been a deliberate event. It might have been an accident; the god could have been dreaming and his dreams became reality.

The creator could be a tremendous monster, one which began the process of creating the world, but was overthrown before it finished making the world to its own satisfaction. . . and one which, legends say, will return some day to finish the job.

It could be a simple creature, one not necessarily deserving of worship, which shapes the world simply by acting as the animal it is. As one example, if the original state of the universe were a giant block of salt, this creature could be a giant cow which licks it into the shape of the world.

In some mythologies, the great being that shapes the world stays around after that task is done; he or she might be the principal deity of the world. More often, that great being perishes, or is cast down by descendants, or settles for a lesser role once creation is accomplished.

Basic Astronomy

What is the shape of the world and the universe once they are created? What are suns, moons, planets and stars?

The entire universe could be a single huge world, with a dome overhead which holds the stars and confines the sun(s) and moon(s). The world could be a disk, a sphere, a bowl, or an unending surface continuing in all directions to infinity.

The sun and moon could be glowing chariots, or bright gods continually flying across the sky (perhaps as a service to the world, perhaps because they're being chased). They could be worlds unto themselves, and the player-characters might someday have the opportunity to visit and walk the bright surface of the sun in search of adventure. They could be the great, glowing eyes of the most powerful deity. They could be gigantic, fiercely-burning lamps created by the craftsman-god, lamps which circle the world on some giant mechanism. (Perhaps, instead of circling the world, they just shut off each day when the time is due; the sun just turns off, and the moons just turn on.) They could even be suns and moons as we understand them, though some of the charm of fantasy lies precisely in making such things *different* from our cold, modern explanations of them.

The planets and stars could be holes in the dome of the sky, suggesting that there is a great brightness beyond. They could be decorations placed in the sky by the gods. They could be worlds unto themselves. They could be glowing creatures forced to trace paths through the sky every night. They could be the suns of distant worlds.

And, of course, the DM can choose for all these astronomic bodies to be one thing, but for the prevailing belief of the people to be different, an incorrect belief; nothing says that the world's deities want the humans and demihumans to know the truth.

Effects of Terrain on Creation

In the real world, the terrain of the human culture to which a mythology belonged often had a strong effect on the myths. Norse mythology started with a huge abyss filled with ice, for instance.

If one race's religion is dominant in the campaign world, the DM should decide whether or not their creation-story has a setting like the land where that race originated.

In a fantasy world, this situation could come about from one of two reasons:

The gods, having emerged from a particular type of terrain, would find similar terrain in the mortal world to be their favorite land for creating new races, exploring, and interacting with humans; or

The sentient races might have erroneously re-interpreted the story of the world's creation as a reflection of the terrain in which they live, and the legend is simply wrong.

Propagation

Once creation of the world and universe are established, the DM can move on to the propagation of the gods. In other words, once the setting is in place, the cast of gods gets larger and larger.

Naturally, the DM can always do this the other way around. Perhaps all the gods were in place before they decided to create the world. There's nothing wrong with this choice; it's simply backward from the way the best-known Earth mythologies operated.

Regardless, unless the DM is creating a monotheistic faith (one dedicated to only one deity), he must now begin creating the other gods of the faith.

These gods could be children of the first great being. They could be that being's creations instead. They could be representations of natural forces brought to awareness and life by the catalyst of Creation. They could emerge from some less wholesome process (for example, they could be created by the decay of the body of the first great being, or could merely spring forth whole from its corpse: One god from the bones, one from the brain, one from the heart, etc.).

Each god should have some special *attribute*, an area where he or she is dominant. Some can have several attributes. Such attributes include Thought, Strength, War, Love, Craftsmanship, Earth, Sea, Sky, Sailing, Farming, Hunting, and many, many others. Any activity that is important to humans (or demihumans) can be an attribute for a god.

Not all these gods need to have been "first-generation," or born to/created by that first great being. Obviously, some should be. But they, too, can create or become parents to other gods.

In some mythoi, the god of a particularly important attribute will have children who bear lesser forms of that attribute. For instance, the god of Love might have children who represent Passion, Marriage, Infatuation, and Unrequited Love. The god of Sleep might have children who represent Dreams and Nightmares. The god of Intellect might have children who represent Memory, Poetry, Song, and Riddles or Puzzles.

Characteristics of the Gods

The DM can create as many gods for his pantheon as his imagination will allow him. He doesn't have to work up an extensive set of legends about every god; even in the real world, many gods of various mythologies were scarcely more than a name and an attribute. As his campaign continues, the DM can flesh out the descriptions of these gods to his heart's content.

Some of the traits which characterize the gods, and can be defined by the DM for each god or pantheon, include:

Immortality: Are the gods immortal? In most pantheons, the gods are certainly *ageless*; that is, they do not grow old. But in some, they are not just ageless, they also cannot be killed; regardless of how severely they might be wounded, with time they will always fully recover from injury. In others, the gods can be killed by sufficient force. For example, in the Greek myths, the gods are undying, while in the Norse myths the gods face eventual certain death at the battle of Ragnarok.

Indestructibility: As a further level of what was just described, some gods which are immortal are also described as indestructible. No force on heaven or Earth can hurt them (except by hurting their feelings, by betraying them). This is sometimes the trait of the greatest god of a pantheon, and is usually the trait of the only god of a monotheistic religion (one which believes in only one god).

Influence on the World: How much influence does the god have on the mortal world, the world of animals, the world of plants? With some gods, there is very little of such influence. A god whose attribute is the unchanging stars, for instance, might exert a little influence on the sailors who navigate

by stars, but could have very little effect on anyone or anything else. On the other hand, gods relating to powerful human emotions or preoccupations (such as love, war, creativity, and so forth) might exert a great deal of influence on the world, especially if it is said that every application of his attribute requires the god's help or permission. For instance, if it requires the aid or permission of the god/goddess of childbirth for every human birth to take place, then that deity is exerting a profound effect on the world.

Interest in the World: Additionally, some gods are very interested in what goes on in the mortal world, while others are entirely disinterested. Naturally, those who are interested are more prone to meddle in mortal affairs than those who aren't. In fact, gods who are disinterested in the world might punish characters who are bold enough to call upon them.

Intentions Toward the World: Finally, there's the question of what the god's intentions are toward the world. . . especially toward the sentient races of the world. Some gods are content just to pursue their attributes and make sure they are properly worshipped and recognized. Others may have more far-reaching plans. This is especially true of evil gods, who wish to bring about the destruction of races, other gods, or the entire world; it is also true of ambitious gods, who wish to cast down the ruling gods, take their place, and reshape the world to their own liking.

Inhibitions: Some gods and pantheons had limitations placed upon them. These might have been limitations placed by some greater power of the universe, or merely enforced by the greatest of the gods. Often, these inhibitions dictate how much aid or hindrance the gods can offer to mortals, whether or not they can help their favorite men and beasts directly or indirectly, etc.

Example

As an example of how a familiar god matches these characteristics, let's look at the Greek goddess Aphrodite.

She was immortal, as were most or all of the Greek gods. She certainly was *not* indestructible, and was in fact once wounded in battle by the Argive hero Diomedes.

She had a very profound influence on the world, for it was she who put all varieties of the emotion of love in the breasts of man and beast. Even the other gods, with the exception of Hestia, Athena, and Artemis, were regularly affected by her power.

Her interest in the world was limited to a couple of areas: Making sure that all humankind respected her (which generally meant that all humans knew love at one time or another, and thus did not deny her); and making sure her special favorites, such as her mortal son Aeneas, survived and prospered. Other than that, she appeared to have no special intentions toward the world.

Aphrodite had a couple of inhibitions restricting her: First, she and all the Olympians were subject to a higher destiny, which not even Zeus could thwart. Second, physically, she and most other gods could be hurt or even defeated in battle by the mightiest Greek heroes. Third, the god-king Zeus obviously preferred for gods to help their favorites indirectly rather than by showing up in person. All these inhibitions affected the way Aphrodite and the other Olympians related to their favorite "player-characters."

Humans, Humanoids, Animals, Plants

At some point in the history of the gods, they probably created all living things. (It's possible for the flora and fauna of the world to have been created by some other factor. For example, they might have just *been* there when the great ice-cap melted. But it's a more common element of the story that the gods created them.)

This creation process might have involved an accident; for instance, the greatest god sneezed, and blew fully-formed living things all over the world.

More commonly, it's a deliberate process, and the gods or one particular god methodically created all the living things known to man.

When working up this aspect of the story for his own campaign world, the DM can use this to help define the way the gods look upon specific forms of life. Was Man created so the gods would have something entertaining to watch? To fulfill a higher destiny? So that his brightest and best might one day add to the ranks of the lesser gods, or accompany the gods on one last, great battle? This kind of decision helps define man's view of the gods and their requirements of mankind.

It can also be used to define mankind's opinions on certain matters. If, for instance, animals in general were created to serve Man, then Man might have little regard for them, except as pets and beasts of burden. However, if each god created one or more animals to serve as totems for the god, then Man might have a lot more respect for certain animals.

If the story of creation says that one sex of the sentient races was created subordinate to the others, then there will be a crushing social pressure to keep that sex "in its place." If the story of creation does no such thing, then any such attitudes will be have been created by mortals and may vary from place to place. Additionally, with the added complication of *several* sentient races around (humans, elves, dwarves, etc.), the DM can make this decision several times and choose a different approach each time. Perhaps, on his world, dwarves are strongly male-

dominated, elves are female-dominated, and humans are more or less equal? Any such arrangement is possible.

Note, however, that when one sex is oppressed, players are less likely to want to play members of that sex. Few players want their escapism to involve this sort of prejudice directed at them.

Fall From Grace

In some stories, humans or sentient races in general start out with an exalted relationship with their deities and then fall out of the deities' favor. In Greek myth, for example, the humans were well-beloved of the gods until the god Prometheus gave them the secret of using fire, which they had

lacked until then; this so offended Zeus that he afflicted mankind with all sorts of ills.

This sort of thing could be a characteristic of your campaign world's story; or, mankind might never have had a closer relationship with its gods.

The Challenge

In many faiths, the gods, deliberately or not, visit a challenge on the humans.

One of the commonest challenges involves the afterlife. In many faiths, the better one lives one's life, the better the afterlife to which he progresses. The usual sorts of afterlives tend to fall into one of the following categories; in some faiths, a character might face

the possibility of reaching more than one of these choices, depending on his actions in life.

Oblivion: No afterlife at all, this is when the human's spirit perishes and becomes nothingness.

Torture: An afterlife where torture, either permanent or temporary (until the spirit repents, recants, or otherwise improves) is the order of the day.

Boredom: An afterlife where there's nothing to do, nothing to see, nothing to entertain.

Rebirth: An afterlife which involves rebirth in the physical world and the living of a new mortal life.

Pleasure: An afterlife where the things man most loves in life are visited upon him in abundance.

Ascension: An afterlife where the best of the best are granted great powers, making them heralds and messengers of the gods. . . or even gods themselves.

In such faiths, humans usually have a good idea of what it takes to get into these specific afterlives. To get into the "good" ones may require strict adherence to a certain life-style, or may require that the human somehow impress the gods with his deeds or personality, or may merely require that the gods like the character. . . which is not something the character can necessarily bring about deliberately.

Other challenges are possible: Humankind as a whole might be challenged to achieve a certain level of civilization by a certain time, to achieve a certain level of artistic or philosophic ability, to defeat a certain spirit of evil, to evolve to a certain enlightened state, etc.

The Future

Some, but not all, faiths make predictions for the future. Sometimes they're grim, such as the Norse belief in Ragnarok, the destruction of the gods and man. They could also be happy and cheerful. . . though this isn't usually the case in a world involving great heroes.

The DM, when deciding whether or not to "predict the future" for his world, should try to figure out what this choice will do to the attitudes of his intelligent races.

A future which is bleak and gloomy will sometimes make the campaign bleak and gloomy. The characters can hope for success and glory in the short-term, but certain death awaits them, and they can't count on the world being there "when they get back." This sort of approach does make for the greatest of heroism, though: It's the greatest hero who strives on knowing that ultimately he must fail, yet fights for his goals anyway.

A future which is happy and bright will sometimes make the campaign a little more goofy and irresponsible. Characters, believing that whatever their mistake, they'll be preserved or rewarded, may behave in a foolish manner. Acts of bravery are often nothing of the sort; they're just short-term sacrifices in anticipation of a long-term reward. This is not to say that such a campaign can't be rewarding. . . it's just harder for it to be serious.

A future which is neither doomed nor excessively happy will tend to have less of an effect on the player-characters. For instance, if holy writings say that a thousand years in the future, the gods will "start over" and reshape the world, populating it with the survivors from the last world and the best spirits in the halls of the afterlife, that's all very interesting. . . but its effects on the current campaign are minimal. On the other hand, if this reshaping is supposed to take place in only ten years, or one, it becomes *very* interesting to the PCs. They'll work very hard to make sure that they're either among the survivors from this world, or among the brighter spirits of the afterlife, so they can experience the new world.

Of course, the DM doesn't *have* to specify future events for his campaign. It's often better if he doesn't, because it makes for more uncertainty in the minds of the PCs.

The Pantheon

Once the DM has created the individual gods, he ought to relate them to one another — that is, establish how they feel about one another. This can affect how their mortal followers, especially priesthoods, feel about one another and work together.

These relationships don't have to be very detailed. It's quite sufficient to say that one god loves another, hates another, likes another, dislikes, respects, holds in contempt, whatever. Then, simply apply that sentiment to the priesthoods of the gods.

And when that sentiment is applied to mortals, it can turn out to be greater or less than the emotion actually felt by the gods in question.

For instance, let us say that two gods dislike one another. Their respective priests may dislike one another with similar intensity. On the other hand, they *might not dislike one another at all*. They might, in fact, recognize that their gods have certain foibles (human-like failings of personality), and might look upon those foibles with amusement and affection but without following them themselves.

However, these priesthoods instead *might loathe one another*. They could hate one another with an intensity which far surpasses that of the gods in question. They could, in fact, start wars on the earth because of their hatred for one another.

So, for many gods, the DM may wish to decide how the gods feel about one another, and then may choose a slightly different view of how their priests react to one another.

Events

Once all the principal characters (i.e., gods) are in place, the DM can create the *events* of the faith.

The creation of the world was one such event; it described "characters" (gods) acting or interacting, and something happening. The fall from grace of the sentient races was another: How did that happen? But these shouldn't be the only events known to the believers. What else has happened?

Do the gods mate with mortals to produce heroic characters who go on adventures? If so, then the conception of these heroes and their adventures in life are all events of the faith. (Note: If this process is still going on, some of the campaign's player-characters could be the mortal children of the world's gods.)

How do specific gods get along

together? Having determined that the DM can next determine *why* two gods hate each other, why? Did one steal from the other, or embarrass him? That's an event.

Have the gods ever warred on one another? If so, that was certainly an event.

The DM can create as few or as many events as he wishes; the more there are, the richer his campaign setting will be for it.

Forces and Philosophies

The mystical history of the world is somewhat different if it is driven by a *force* or a *philosophy*.

As we'll discuss in more detail next chapter, a *force* is a mystical power which strongly affects the world. . . but which probably is not a sentient being like gods are. It has drives, it has a goal, but it probably does not have a mind.

On the other hand, a *philosophy* is a compelling idea or set of ideas which can capture the imagination and influence the actions of communities or whole civilizations. It might exert enough popular appeal that it can support magical powers for priest-philosophers. But it is still not precisely a god, for it has no independent mind.

If your campaign world is driven by a force or philosophy, its mystical history is going to be somewhat different. It will mostly be a history of men or other sentient races and their relationships with the force or philosophy: How they came to recognize it or create it, how they came to believe in it, how they introduced it to others, and so forth.

In short, the DM won't have to create an entire separate history as he would have to do for distinct pantheons of gods. He will, how-

ever, have to decide for himself what effects these forces or philosophies have had on the human and humanoid histories of his world, and take these factors into account for every part of those histories.

Mythic History Creation Sheet

The DM can photocopy and fill in the following sheet to give him a starting-place for the creation of his world's mythic history. The sheet follows the order of subjects from this chapter.

* * *

In this chapter, we discussed creation of the *history* of the campaign's gods. In the next chapter, we'll talk about individual faiths, how they're put together, and what effect they have on priest-characters.

Mythic History Creation Sheet

Creation: How was the universe created?

_____

_____

What is the shape of the world and universe? What are suns, moons, planets and stars?

_____

_____

_____

Characteristics of the Gods: Are the gods immortal? Are the gods indestructible?

_____

_____

_____

How much direct influence do they have?

_____

_____

_____

How much interest do they have in the world?

_____

_____

_____

What are their intentions toward the world?

_____

_____

_____

Does anything inhibit them?

_____

_____

_____

Humans, Humanoids, Animals, Plants: How were they all created?

_____

_____

_____

Fall From Grace: Did sentient races fall from grace? If so, how?

_____

_____

_____

The Challenge: What is the afterlife believed to be like?

_____

_____

_____

The Future: Are they any legends about the future of the world?

_____

_____

_____

The Pantheon: Who are the main gods and what are their attributes?

God	Attribute	God	Attribute
___	___	___	___
___	___	___	___
___	___	___	___
___	___	___	___
___	___	___	___
___	___	___	___
___	___	___	___

Events: What are the main legends known to the player-characters?

_____

_____

_____

_____

_____

_____

This chapter is for DMs who want to design detailed faiths and cults for their campaign worlds. It's not prohibited for the campaign's players to read this. . . but not all of them will find it useful. Players may wish to skip on to the next chapter, "Sample Priesthoods."

* * *

As the *Player's Handbook* points out (page 34, first column), "In the simplest version of the AD&D® game, clerics serve religions that can be generally described as 'good' or 'evil.' Nothing more needs to be said about it; the game will play perfectly well at this point."

That's true enough. But DMs who work to make their campaign settings into interesting, detailed backgrounds for the campaign, won't be satisfied with that simple approach. A big part of the color of any fiction setting, including campaign settings, is the relationship of the supernatural world to the "real" world. . . and gods, with priests as ambassadors to the human world, form a big part of that supernatural element.

So, eventually, most DMs will want to work up at least the basic details of who the gods are in his campaign world, how they relate to one another, and what their goals are (especially those pertaining to the mortal world). This, in turn, will let them enhance the role of cleric, druid and other priest player-characters in the campaign. . . and that's what this chapter is all about.

In this chapter, you'll learn how to create specific faiths (related to specific gods, natural forces, and philosophies); how to create the priests of these specific mythoi; and how to relate the gods together into a full-sized pantheon for your game world. In the next chapter, you'll find many examples of this priesthood creation process.

God, Force, or Philosophy

For each faith you establish in your campaign world, you have to decide what it is that's being worshipped and venerated: A God, a Force, or a Philosophy.

A **God** is a powerful being, usually of human or greater intelligence, usually desiring to impose its will or characteristics upon the world. A god is often devoted to a single attribute or set of attributes (e.g., warfare, love, agriculture, marriage, etc.) and so most of his interactions with the world will deal with the god's promotion of that attribute among humankind. Gods do not have to be anthropomorphic (i.e., manlike in form or personality characteristics), and so one faith's god is often another faith's monster. However, most of the gods worshipped by player-characters are likely to be anthropomorphic and not monstrous.

A **Force** is some sort of natural (or unnatural) process which influences the world. It isn't necessarily intelligent, but it is magically powerful. . . and humans who accept the dictates and goals of this force can become its priests and use spells based on that magical power. Some Forces which can be so worshipped include Entropy, Nature, the Life-Death-Rebirth Cycle, and Magic. Druids tend to be priests of the Force of Nature, instead of specific Gods of Nature. (There are exceptions to that generalization, of course.)

A **Philosophy** is an idea, or set of ideas, which (in these magical worlds) is so compelling that it attracts magical energy and faith to it, much as a Force does. Philosophies are usually created by man or other sentient races, spread throughout cultures, and gain such widespread acceptance and belief that they do become much like Forces. When no one believes in a Philosophy any longer, it can generate no magical power and support no priests, so the priests' duty is to embody its attributes and to teach the philosophy so that it will never die. Sample philosophies include Oneness With Nature, Peace, the Divinity of Mankind, the Sanctity of Life, Nihilism, and so on.

In the AD&D® game, the God, Force, and Philosophy are identical in the way they are treated by the game mechanics. All three provide spells and powers to their priests. All three demand personal requirements and services of their priests and of their non-priest followers. And all three, to a lesser or greater degree, shape the world, both through their own powers and through their agents, the priests.

Ethos and Requirements of the Faith

Each faith requires certain codes of behavior, beliefs, and even abilities of its followers and of its priests. When creating a faith, you have to decide what those requirements are and how they're to be implemented in your campaign.

Goals and Purposes

First, what are the goals and purposes of the god (or force or philosophy), and therefore of the faith?

Often, that's self-evident, because it's usually tied to the attribute of the god, or the explanation of the force or philosophy.

For example, if the faith's god is a God of Love, then the goals and purposes of the faith will probably include:

Promotion of Love, which might include the helping along of lovers, opposition to those who interfere in the development of romantic relationships, punishment of those who defy the god and refuse to love, etc. This could also include "social services" to the community, through the god's temples: Counseling to young lovers, for instance.

Promotion of the God, which includes the building of temples or churches, carrying the word of the god to those who have not heard it, and keeping the stories of the god ever-present in the ears of the population.

Opposition of Enemies, which means subtle or direct opposition to enemy gods and their followers; obviously, a god of Love is likely to be opposed to a god of Hatred, Misanthropy, Misogyny, etc.

Those are some basic goals, but you obviously aren't limited to goals which are that direct and simple.

For instance, a god may represent only a small part of his attribute. A God of War does not have to be just a god of all types and elements of warfare. He could be the God of the Chaos of War, the God of Intelligent Warfare, the God of Naval Warfare (in which he might share traits with a god of Oceans), the God of the Sword (in which case he might share traits with a god of Metalworking), and so forth. If you choose, you can always make a god's personal attribute more specialized, and can choose more specialized goals for the faith based on that choice.

In addition, a god isn't defined just by his attribute. In the campaign history, he also has a personal history, likes and dislikes, relationships with other gods, and ambitions, all of which can provide more goals for the faith.

As one example, Zeus, the king of the gods of Greek mythology, had many attributes and associations. He was the king of the gods, a sky-god, a god whose emblem and weapon was the lightning bolt, a god of Wisdom (he had swallowed and absorbed the wisdom-goddess Metis, mother of Athena), a god of oracles (though he was eventually supplanted by Apollo in this role, he had a major oracle at the city of Dodona), a protector of fugitives, a lover of many goddesses and women. . . In short, he had many characteristics and attributes, and in an AD&D® game campaign his priesthood would embody and promote most or all of them.

Alignment

A faith will often demand that its priests belong to a specific alignment or a limited range of alignments. The DM determines this, usually basing the choice on the attributes and character of the god, force or philosophy in question.

But don't be too restrictive in this regard. Even if, personally, you're opposed to War, the God of War and his followers don't have to be Chaotic/Evil.

Alignment Guidelines for the Priesthood

Here are some general guidelines to go by:

The first, and most important, note is this: The gods usually do not insist that their priests be of *identical* alignment to the god. The alignment may not be so dissimilar that the priest cannot serve the god, but it does not have to be identical.

If the faith does not promote any sort of harm to living beings, or promotes benefits to living beings, then it probably excludes Evil alignments among the priesthood. If the faith allows for harm to living beings but does not promote wanton cruelty, then it can include Good, Neutral, and Evil priests. If the faith does promote cruelty, then it probably excludes Good alignments among its priests.

If the faith demands ordered thinking, strict obedience to laws, and unquestioning acceptance of policy, then it leans toward Lawful behavior. (Now, every faith requires rituals and devotions of its priests, but this *isn't* the same thing, and doesn't require any alignment choice.) If the faith demands more free-willed and spontaneous behavior, defiance of social conventions or restrictions, and so forth, then it leans toward Chaotic behavior. If it promotes neither approach strongly, then it can probably include Lawful, Neutral, and Chaotic choices.

Here are some sample choices:

God of Love: This type of faith usually promotes no harm to living beings, and promotes the benefits of love; it often promotes free-willed and spontaneous behavior, but not strongly. Therefore, its priests will probably be required to be Good, and may be of Lawful, Neutral, or Chaotic alignments, though the tendency is toward Chaotic. However, if the god is a god of passionate affairs and selfish love, regardless of who gets hurt, and if he promotes revenge on romantic competitors and ex-lovers, then the faith could well include Evil and Neutral priests, thus giving its priesthood the full range of alignment choices.

God of War: This faith generally allows for harm to living beings without promoting wanton cruelty; and warfare runs the gamut from carefully-reasoned strategy to wild, bloodthirsty battlefield chaos. Therefore, the faith probably places no restriction on the alignment of its priests. However, a specific god can be devoted to one aspect of war. For example, a god who promotes the bloody destruction of all enemies, including sacrifice of prisoners and innocents, will probably have an Evil priesthood. A god who is the god of military planning will probably have a Lawful, or Lawful and Neutral, priesthood.

Alignments of the Worshippers

Most faiths define various acts and types of behavior as evil and demand that their followers not perform those acts. Some few make those same definitions and demand that their followers *do* perform them. Almost no faiths demand that their followers belong specifically to Lawful or Chaotic alignments.

Therefore, most faiths require of their (non-priest) worshippers that they be anything but Evil. A very few faiths require instead that their worshippers be any sort of Evil (Lawful/Evil, Neutral/Evil, or Chaotic/Evil).

Most priesthoods demand some sort of minimum ability scores of their priests.

The prime characteristic of priests is Wisdom. To be a priest of any sort whatsoever, the character must have at least a wisdom of 9. Some priesthoods will require that the wisdom score be higher, though usually not higher than 13.

Generally, if the priest's Wisdom is 16 or better, he gets a +10% bonus to his earned experience.

Many priesthoods will require a second prime requisite. For example, priests of a god of War may have to have a certain Strength score, while priests of a god of Magic might have to have a certain Intelligence score. Usually, this second prime requisite must have a score of at least 12; up to 15 is not an excessive requirement.

In such cases, the DM may decide that the character, if he has *either* the Wisdom score or the other Prime Requisite at a score of 16, gets a +5% bonus to earned experience, but if he has *both*, he gets a +10% bonus.

In the next chapter, you'll find numerous examples of such priesthoods and recommended minimum ability scores for them.

Races Allowed

The DM may wish to limit certain priesthoods to certain races.

This is almost always a choice based on the history of his own campaign world. There is no game-related reason why most races can't have priests for any god, force or philosophy; but there are often campaign-related reasons why a certain race can't belong to a certain priesthood.

For example, if the halflings of a specific campaign world are pacifists, they'll be excluded from priesthood in the faith of the war-god. If dwarves are pragmatic, un-

romantic sorts who arrange all their marriages and don't conduct affairs of the heart, they'll be excluded from priesthood in the faith of the love-god.

In the next chapter, we provide numerous examples of priesthoods of specific mythoi. With each, there's a recommendation for allowed races. These recommendations are based on the most common and popular conceptions of these races, and the DM is free to change them for his specific campaign.

Players beware: When the *Complete Priest's Handbook* says one thing about allowed races, and the DM says another, the DM is always right.

Experience and Spell Progression

It would be possible to come up with an Experience Levels Chart and Spell Progression Chart for every priesthood of specific mythoi, but it would also be crazy; there's no reason to have the extra complication in your campaign.

All new priesthoods introduced in the next chapter use the Cleric experience progression and the basic Priest spell progression, both from page 33 of the *Player's Handbook*. If your DM, when creating a new priesthood, decides that it is observably less powerful than the Cleric or the priesthoods written here, he can choose to use the Druid experience progression, which allows for faster acquisition of experience levels.

Gender Requirements

In the worlds of the AD&D® game, most priesthoods should allow both priests and priestesses. However, in fantasy worlds and the real world, some faiths have required that all their priesthood be of just one sex. If there is such a restriction on a given priesthood, the DM will make note of it and tell the players.

Nonweapon and Weapon Proficiencies

Various priesthoods will require priests to know certain skills (nonweapon proficiencies) and be able to wield certain weapons (weapon proficiencies). For example, a priest of the god of Agriculture must know the Agriculture proficiency, while a priest of the god of Fire must know Fire-Building.

Every priesthood should require one nonweapon proficiency of its priests and priestesses; it's a sign of their devotion. It's permissible, but not recommended, for them to require more than one.

A priesthood *may* require one or more weapon proficiencies of its priests and priestesses, but we don't recommend this for most priesthoods. Many faiths allow their priests so few weapon choices anyway that it's pointless to *require* they be taken. An exception is when a god is noted for wielding a specific weapon; for instance, it's quite reasonable to require Weapon Proficiency in War-Hammer for priests of the god Thor, whose principal weapon and symbol was the hammer.

Duties of the Priest

Now, we get to a topic which adds a lot of color to the priesthood and the campaign world.

All priesthoods have certain duties to perform, duties to the god and duties to the community or civilization. The DM needs to decide what each priesthood's duties

are, and will often be able to use those duties to tie the priest character in to specific adventures and role-playing situations.

Following are some sample ideas for priestly duties. The DM can use as few or as many of these as he wants when designing a new priesthood; he can also invent new ones to suit his campaign.

Devotions

These are ordinary prayers and rituals which the priest conducts on a regular basis. They might include the saying of prayers at specific times of the day, upon observation of specific incidents or natural phenomena, and so forth.

The DM can decide what these are and when they're undertaken, but the campaign shouldn't devote a lot of time to them; it's annoying and disconcerting to interrupt the adventure every so often so that the priests can pull out their holy symbols, kneel to the sun, and lead the faithful in prayer. Just knowing that they do this sort of thing on a regular basis is enough for most players.

Guidance

In most civilizations, priests are supposed to act as counselors to everyone in need of advice. (This is one reason that Wisdom is a prime requisite.)

Therefore, the priest character should not be surprised when he finds NPCs seeking him out and consulting him on troubling moral and ethical problems. These are good role-playing opportunities; they are often leads to specific adventures; and, with especially knotty problems, they can be difficult puzzles for the players to solve, all without using their

swords and maces.

Often, priests are posted to specific noble leaders in order to be their personal advisors. Naturally, this is only done when those noble leaders desire it, are willing to allow it, or (because of the priesthood's political strength) cannot afford to refuse it. This is a way to establish some sort of bond between new player-characters: The priest player-character could be assigned as advisor to the noble player-character.

Marriage

In many human cultures, only the priest can perform marriages, so the DM may wish for this to be a duty of priests in his campaign.

The DM will need to decide for his campaign whether or not marriages require the ministrations of priests, and might make a different choice for each sentient races. If humans require priests for marriage, do dwarves? (Perhaps they use advocates and notaries instead.) Do elves? (Perhaps their marriages are officiated by bards, who write songs commemorating the event as a sort of "marriage certificate.") Do halflings? (Perhaps they prefer ceremonies presided over by sheriffs or judges.)

Also, the DM can always decide that priests of certain faiths cannot perform marriages. What, for example, does the god of weaponmaking have to do with marriage? On the other hand, it's equally appropriate for priests of *any* god to be able to perform marriages. This is especially true if, in the campaign, marriage constitutes permission or recognition from "higher forces," and any god, including those with attributes unrelated to marriage, may bless a marriage.

Missions

The duties of priesthood often involve going on missions important to the welfare of the god or the priesthood in general.

One of the most common missions involves going somewhere and trying to convert the local population to worship of the priest's god. Usually, this involves religious education and what amount to social services; sometimes, it involves conquering that culture and ruthlessly suppressing all signs of its old religion.

Other, more exciting missions can involve recovery of artifacts, transportation of persons or goods (such as temple money) through dangerous territory, interpretation of phenomena in distant places, and holy war with the followers of another god.

It's important for the DM to remember that the god himself isn't the only one who sends priests out on missions. For most missions, it's the upper ranks of the priesthood who do the assigning, and priests are supposed to follow the orders of their superiors. So it's possible for any priesthood to have a "bad egg," a priest who issues orders which are contradictory to the tenets of the faith or designed to promote only his personal power. This should, however, be a very rare campaign event, unless the campaign revolves around uncovering and purging a corrupt element of the sect.

Omen-Reading

In some campaigns, priests will be charged with the duty of reading omens for the future.

If a campaign's priests have that duty, the DM has to decide how they do it, what it is they're actually doing, and who they're doing it for.

How They Do It

Omen-Reading always requires some sort of ritual, usually a public one.

The priests may sacrifice animals and examine their entrails for clues to the future. They may read tea-leaves. They may inhale dangerous fumes and prophesy while under their influence. They may listen to whispering in the trees, babbling of brooks, or the singing of birds and interpret that noise. They may enter meditative states and wait for inspiration from the gods. Each cult could do it a different way, and the DM can choose the method which he feels will add the most appropriate color to the cult in question.

What They're Doing

Then, the DM has to figure out what it is the priests are actually doing when prophesying. Here are some choices:

They're Receiving the Word of Their God: The priests are actually receiving some inspiration from their deity. Naturally, such omens are usually clouded in imprecise terminology and symbolism, so that it's easy for the recipient of an omen to misinterpret the results.

They're Following Ritual Interpretation: The priests have a set of techniques of interpretation which they follow rigidly. These techniques may or may not have any basis in campaign reality; they might have been granted by the god, or created through ignorance.

They're Analyzing Based On Their Knowledge: The priests aren't actually prophesying at all, but supplying answers based on their understanding of the situation and of the ways of the world. If they are then pretending that their answers come from a higher source, they are obviously being dishonest; only a corrupt branch of a priesthood will do this. However, it's possible for such a method to be very accurate, especially if it concerns itself mostly with questions of warfare and human nature.

They're Telling the Audience What It Wants to Hear: The priests are acting primarily as cheerleaders and telling the people precisely what they want to hear: That they'll win the war, they're always right, they've done no wrong, love conquers all. Again, priests acting in this manner are being dishonest to their flocks, but it will often be difficult to convince the flocks of that.

They're Working for Gain: Some very corrupt sects or branches of sects manipulate their answers to gain in power or money. This usually takes one of two methods.

In the first, the priests supply answers which favor their purposes. If representatives of one city ask, "When we attack our enemies, will we prevail?" the priests then decide whom they want to win that war. If they want the attackers to win, they answer "Yes." Then, the attackers will be encouraged by the reply, and the defenders discouraged, which weighs the war in the attackers' favor. If they want the defenders to win, they answer "No," with precisely the opposite effect; the discouraged attackers might not even launch the attack.

In the second, the priests accept bribes in order to put their god's stamp of approval on the activities of certain men. For instance, a king might secretly pay the priests a lavish amount, then publicly approach the oracle and ask, "Shall I not execute the traitor so-and-so now without benefit of trial?" or "Should I marry so-and-so against her wishes?" or any other such question. The answer he receives, of course, will be the one he paid to get, and because the god has "made his wishes known," the citizens will probably not dispute the choice.

In both these approaches, the god may eventually notice that one branch of his priesthood is corrupt, and set about correcting matters, either through his own intervention or by alerting other branches of the priesthood. On the other hand, a particularly disinterested god might never notice.

But Are They Right?

As part of deciding what they're doing, the DM has to decide how often they're right.

The priests will often be right if they're receiving the word of their god; this word may be misinterpreted, but it's always *correct*.

They could have any sort of accuracy the DM decides if they're following some pattern of ritual interpretation; perhaps the ritual is effective, perhaps it is not.

If they're analyzing the situation based on their current knowledge, then their accuracy depends mostly in their interpretive abilities; a priesthood might have enough knowledge of the world and human nature to be able to supply consistently-correct answers to supplicants.

If they're telling the audience what it wants to hear, they could be very accurate for a time, especially if they're prophesying for a warlike state which is on the rise and mostly asking about upcoming victories. Eventually, however, the tides of

fate will turn and the prophecies will become unreliable, which will disillusion the populace.

If they're working for gain, they could be very successful for quite a while. Eventually, though, the scandal will break, and the population will learn the truth. . . which could be very bad for those greedy prophets.

Who It's For

Finally, the DM has to decide who is able to receive these prophecies. Here are some typical choices:

Anyone: Anyone who asks a question will receive some sort of reply.

Anyone With the Means: Some temples require a sacrifice of animals or wealth in order for the supplicant to receive a prophecy. (This isn't necessarily a sign of corruption; it's often just a means of ensuring the temple's upkeep and the faith's continuing secular, or worldly, power.)

Nobles Only: In this arrangement, only members of noble houses can ask questions of the oracle.

The DM can also make more peculiar choices for specific oracles. An oracle might only be for slaves, for adventurers, for people who have at least once travelled to a specific holy site, for people of specific alignments, for members of one race, etc.

Vigilance

Finally, priests have to be vigilant against powers or elements which threaten their faith or their followers.

These powers and elements don't usually take the direct approach, such as attacks by armies

or monsters. The priest needs to be vigilant against more subtle intrusions, including:

The Agent Provocateur: This is someone who falsely joins the priesthood, spends a long time becoming a trusted member or even a leader of it, and then persuades members of the faith to perform actions which will get the faith into trouble. For example, in times when the priesthood is in conflict with another faith, the Agent Provocateur might encourage outright war with that faith. When a conflict with the local rulers could be sorted out by calm diplomacy, the Agent Provocateur will instead recommend or issue ultimatums and demands. And, naturally, the Agent will keep his true masters apprised of the priesthood's secret movements and activities at all times.

Corruption in Specific Orders: Sometimes priests go bad and use the priesthood for their own gain. In addition to methods mentioned above, they may also secretly defy requirements of their priesthood, steal temple funds, use their duties of guidance to influence others to profit these priests, etc. No such corruption goes unnoticed forever, but the unwillingness of people to believe that they've put their faith in crooks and thieves can ensure that this corruption can go on for a long, long time.

Libels: At times, members of rival priesthoods will persuade their followers that other priesthoods perform acts which are profane and evil. In a culture where religious prejudice is a strong factor, this is often easy to do. For instance, it might prove simple to convince one's flock that the priests of a more despised faith are kidnapping young women (only women of the libeller's faith, of course) to serve as unwilling temple concubines, then killing them. It's especially easy to do when the libeller secretly arranges for the kidnapping and murder of several young women in his own faith. When this sort of thing goes on, it's vital that the priests of the accused faith prove the truth. They can't do it just by giving local authorities a tour of their temple to show there are no unwilling concubines here — and even if they do, a particularly clever enemy will have concealed the body of one of the kidnapped girls there for the authorities to find! It requires capture of the killers and demonstration that they were serving someone else. . . all of which is a good basis for a priest-oriented adventure.

Obviously, it's the duty of faithful priests to combat all these situations these when they're noticed. However, it's a characteristic of the greatest priest-heroes to notice these trends *well ahead of the time that they become critical*, and to deal with them early in their development, before they can result in serious harm to the priesthood.

For the DM, this is a good way to give the PC priest an opportunity for rapid advancement in his priesthood: If he's the first to notice such a trend and is able to spearhead the movement to correct it, he will be well-regarded by his peers. This is also a good way to establish that an NPC priest is a hero of his faith, if he, in the past, has thwarted such situations.

Rights of the Priesthood

At the DM's discretion, priesthoods can have special rights and powers, too. These rights usually depend on the amount of influence the priesthood wields in the campaign setting; a minor priesthood may not enjoy any of these benefits, while a dominant one could have all of them.

Church Trial

In some cultures, the secular (non-priestly) authorities cannot put priests on trial for any sort of crime. That doesn't mean a priest can perform a crime and laugh at the law, however: Most priestly orders police themselves, and will try (or punish without trial) transgressions.

Priestly orders don't ordinarily flaunt this power in order to defy secular authorities. When priests commit crimes, priesthoods usually punish them. Exceptions occur when the priest was acting at the priesthood's behest, particularly when the god requires actions which are against the law of the land. In these cases, the priest sometimes goes unpunished; sometimes he receives a "slap on the wrist" punishment to quiet the secular authorities.

The DM, not the player, gets to decide whether priests have the right to church trial.

Coronation

The most powerful priesthood in a given land will probably have the right to crown kings when they ascend the throne. The DM has to decide whether this is merely an honor bestowed on the priesthood, or whether it is a right which the priesthood can use to influence the throne.

If it's the former, then the chief priest is accorded the right to officiate at the coronation ceremony. However, if the priest refused to officiate, the crowning will take place anyway; the king can choose another priesthood for the honor, or he can be crowned without the priesthood's sanction.

If it's the latter, then the priesthood can deny someone the right to take the throne by refusing to crown him. This is a very powerful right, and through it the priesthood can exert considerable influence on the nation.

That's not to say that, by refusing to crown a certain candidate, the priesthood can stage a bloodless coup and choose the king.

Let's assume a priesthood does such a thing and refuses the chief candidate for the throne, then spreads the word they will support a certain other candidate.

The refused candidate may decide to mount a war against the priesthood. The new candidate, if crowned, may find that none of the other nobles in the nation support his kingship. All of this can result in a bloody civil war which could tear the nation apart and wreck the priesthood's power.

Therefore, when the priesthood decides to exercise this power, it does tend to make compromises, to negotiate secretly with the parties involved, to plan things carefully so that trouble is kept to a minimum. Only the most arrogant of priesthoods would try to take for itself the full right to choose the king. . . and such priesthoods are likely to lead their nation into war or chaos.

Other Confirmations

It could be that confirmations other than coronation are the special province of one priesthood. For example, in one nation, any priest might perform marriages for commoners, but only the priests of a specific god might perform marriages for nobles.

This would give that priesthood great power, because by collectively deciding or refusing to marry certain couples, this priesthood has the power to influence which families unite and which do not.

Again, abuse of this right could lead to harm, but careful application of it would allow the priesthood to affect the growth and development of the nation.

Tithes

Some priesthoods, the most powerful ones in a culture, are able to demand *tithes* of their followers. A tithe is an amount of money, often represented as a fraction of the money-earner's regular wage, which the follower is required to pay to the priesthood. Theoretically, it is used for upkeep of churches and temples, purchase of supplies and equipment for the priests, etc. Some priesthoods also use these moneys for influence with the government; a very few corrupt priests dip into it for personal gain.

In an AD&D® game campaign, only the religion of a monotheistic state, or the state religion, will be able legally to demand tithes of its followers. Such tithes will usually run from 5% to 15% of the character's income, with 10% being most common.

Priesthoods of other faiths will *ask* their followers to tithe a like amount. Naturally, not all their followers will tithe and so such religions bring in less tithed income than those who can demand it.

Player-character priests don't get to see that money; it is recorded by church accountants, stored in church treasures, and

distributed or spent by superior priests.

Separation from the Faith

Some priesthoods can exert considerable influence on their followers by being able to separate them from the faith. If, for instance, all followers are promised a certain role in the afterlife, and separation from the faith would deny them that role (and replace it with something far more frightening or ghastly), then the followers of the faith are likely to obey the priesthood.

Naturally, most priesthoods visit this punishment only on those followers who most flagrantly defy the requirements of the faith. Just as naturally, the occasional corrupt priest would threaten followers with this punishment unless they are blindly, absolutely obedient to him.

However, this punishment doesn't work so well in a culture which worships many gods and which has a separate, independent priesthood for each god. If you threaten a follower of the war-god with separation, he might be just as happy to switch over to worship of the sea-god. This is a balancing factor which helps keep down abuse of this right in many cultures. However, monotheistic cultures (those which worship only one god) don't have this balancing factor; they have to rely on the honesty of the priesthood.

Rule

Some cultures are *theocracies*, which means they are ruled by their priestly classes. Naturally, in such a culture, one priesthood will be dominant; the culture may worship only one god, or may tolerate

other worships but be mainly devoted to one specific god.

In a theocracy, the nation may be ruled by a board of priests from the state religion, but it's more common for it to be ruled by a single king who is also a priest and the head of his priesthood. Such an arrangement may be benevolent, with a wise cleric ruling the land; or it may be particularly nasty, with a power-mad priest or the priest of an evil god in charge.

Many "lost worlds" (i.e., nations hidden away from the rest of the world, secluded in a lost valley or cavern or other distant place) are theocracies ruled by evil priests; adventurer-heroes stumbling into such cultures often find themselves having to stir up revolution and cast down these rulers so that justice can return to these lands.

The State Religion

For any culture, the DM will have to decide if there is a State Religion. The State Religion is the official faith of the nation, as sanctioned by the government.

Its priesthood will have the following rights: Right to church trial, right to coronation (though not necessarily the right to deny coronation to the chief candidate), right to demand tithes. If the culture is monotheistic, the State Religion will also have the right to separate offenders from the faith. The DM can assign other rights to the State Religion as he sees fit.

State Religions are not limited to big nations. Any independent city or city-state could have its own state religion. Thus, cities mere miles apart might have different state religions. This could cause trouble if both are monotheistic, or both belong to enemy priesthoods;

on the other hand, the priesthoods could be neutral or friendly to one another, causing no such trouble.

However, a nation does not have to have a state religion. In fact, the most powerful faith in a nation will not necessarily be a state religion; it will just exert considerable influence.

Restrictions on the Priest

Priesthoods are also restricted, usually by decree of the god himself. Below are examples of many typical sorts of restrictions: Note that most priesthoods will only have a *few* of these restrictions, and each faith may employ different ones.

Gods make these requirements of their priesthoods for four principal reasons: Commemoration, Function, Philosophy, and Sacrifice.

Commemoration means that the action is a reminder of some important event from the history of the faith. For example, the cross and crucifix are symbols of the Crucifixion.

Function means that if the requirement is not met, the priest cannot for some reason function as a priest. For instance, if, in a specific campaign world, clerical magic will not work if the caster has consumed alcohol, then the priesthood will have a requirement that its priests not drink.

Philosophy means that the choice is bound up with other elements of the faith. If certain creatures are held to be unholy, unclean, or otherwise taboo, for instance, there will be many secondary requirements derived from that thought. A priest wouldn't be able to wear armor made from its hide or eat its meat. To be buried in or with its skin might even result in involuntary separa-

tion from the faith!

Sacrifice means that the god requires this behavior to test the mettle of his followers. Those who can't make the sacrifice are obviously not cut out to be his priests.

At his discretion, the DM can make any of these requirements apply to the worshippers of the god in addition to the priesthood. Especially appropriate are restrictions involving Contamination (see below).

Armor

Priests may be limited in the types of armor they wear. Some sample limitations:

May not wear non-metal armor
May not wear metal armor
May not wear magical armor
May not wear *any* armor
May not use shields
May not use certain types of shields
May only wear armor made by priests of the same faith

Any of these restrictions could be made for any of the four reasons given above. If metal armor disrupts clerical magic, then it could not be worn by priests. If the religion's philosophy forbids harm to animals, then leather armor may be forbidden. And so on.

Armor restrictions don't just reflect the god's attributes or prohibitions; they help define the combat roles of priests in the campaign. A priest who can wear full metal armor is more likely to be a combat force in the campaign than one who can't.

You can be more sure that a player who picks a priest-type which is limited to less efficient armor is a player who wants to roleplay a priest, rather than one who

merely wants to play a fighting machine who is efficient in both combat and magic.

Celibacy

Though in modern times the terms Celibacy and Chastity have become confused, here we're only using the older meaning of the word Celibacy: The state of being unmarried. Priests who are required to be celibate must remain unmarried. A DM must decide individually for each celibate priesthood if its priests must also remain chaste (see below).

A priesthood could require celibacy as a sacrifice to the god, because it was philosophically opposed to the state of marriage, or for many other reasons. The fighting priesthood of a war-god might require its priests to stay celibate so that they won't be distracted by thoughts of home and family while engaged in warfare.

Chastity

Chastity involves not engaging in sexual relations. A priest could be celibate but not chaste; one could even be chaste but not celibate, though that would be pretty strange.

Priesthoods require chastity as a sacrifice to the god, or when its priests are supposed in some way to be spouses of the god (either in a symbolic or genuine sense).

In some faiths, chastity is required of its priests except for during specific events or times of the year. For instance, priests of an agricultural deity might be required to remain chaste except during the planting season, when chastity is revoked in order to magically "encourage" the fertility of the fields.

Clothing

Priests are often required to wear distinctive costumes proclaiming their status. They may only have to do so during the performance of their official functions, or might have to wear their priestly vestments during all waking hours.

Such items don't have to be full costumes. A priest might be only required to wear the specific holy symbol of his faith; otherwise, he could wear what he wished.

In some faiths, priests cannot wear certain types of clothing. Historically, some priest-kings of earth-goddess were forbidden to wear clothes with knots in them; if they wore textile garments, they had to have ragged, unknotted hems.

Priests might also be required to conceal certain parts of their bodies by clothing. Beyond restrictions imposed by society for modesty's sake, priests might have to conceal other parts not considered immodest by the general population.

Contamination

Many faiths regard certain items or substances as unholy, unclean, or taboo. Its priests are not permitted to handle such things. If they come in contact with them accidentally, they must undergo holy rituals of purifications to cleanse themselves of the taint.

Some sample items or substances include:

Animals (specific animals or whole classes of animals)
Blood
Gems or Jewels (specific types)
Iron
Plants (specific plants or whole classes of plants)
Water (from specific bodies of water)

Hit Points

Clerics and Druids receive 8-sided dice for hit point progression (see *Player's Handbook*, page 33). The cleric does a lot of fighting, and the druid has a very demanding existence, living as he does in the wilderness; both need to have comparatively high hit point totals.

The DM can, if he wishes, make any priesthood of a specific my-

thos take six-sided dice for hit points (like rogues) or even four-sided dice (like wizards). But this is only appropriate for priestly orders which are not very demanding physically.

Most priesthoods should have eight-sided dice for hit points. If a DM decides that a priesthood will have less robust dice, then he must compensate the priesthood with enhanced access to spells and (especially) numerous Granted Powers (discussed below).

A priesthood should only receive six-sided dice if it has medium to poor combat abilities, and belongs to a deity with very few physical demands.

For example, a god of dawn has no intrinsic orientation toward combat, and "dawn" does not imply any specific physical demands.

A priesthood should only receive four-sided dice if it has poor combat abilities, and belongs to a deity whose attribute implies soft living.

For example, a god of peace or love could have priests with little or no combat abilities and with four-sided dice. However, it's *important* to note that this does not *have* to be the case. . . It is only the case when the DM insists upon it. Priests of the god of peace could be pacifists, but still be good at combat. . . which they may only employ in self-defense. A god of love noted for weapons use, as Eros was noted for his archery, could have priests who specialized in that weapon, and would *not* have to be stuck with a measly 1d4 for hit points.

Magical Items

Priests are already limited to using magical items usable by all classes or by priests only. But they might also be further restricted by their faiths.

For example, priests of a specific faith might be required to use only magical items made by priests of their order, or might be required to use no magical items whatsoever.

Mutilation

Occasionally, a priesthood will demand a sacrifice of mutilation of its priesthood. This is most common among evil priesthoods, but could theoretically occur with any priesthood, regardless of alignment.

For example, devotees of a blind god of prophecy might be forced to blind themselves. (However, it would be more appropriate for them merely to have a Clothing restriction that required them to wear blindfolds when performing official duties.)

When this sort of thing does take place, the priesthood is often compensated for its loss: The god often grants them an extra power (as described below, under "Powers of the Priest"). A priesthood required to be blind, for example, might have an extra power of analysis, identification or prophecy.

Weapons

Many priesthoods require their priests to use only a certain category of weapons. Some only restrict them *from* using a certain narrow category of weapons. Some require their priests to use no weapons at all. Commonly, a god identified with a certain type of weapon will require his priests to use that weapon and a certain number of similar or related weapons.

The DM should assign the priesthood a weapons restriction based on two choices.

First, weapons restrictions rein-force the special attributes and character of the worshipped god; limiting priests of the god of Death to sickle-like weapons certainly establishes flavor for them.

Second, weapons restrictions, like armor restrictions, help define the combat roles of priests in the campaign. If a priest is limited to daggers and creampuffs, he's not going to be the campaign's combat monster, so magic and his priestly duties will be much more important to the character.

Many examples of this are given in the next chapter, "Sample Priesthoods."

Spheres of Influence

As you'll recall (from the **DMG**, pages 33, 34), priest spells are divided into categories called *spheres of influence*. Each spell belongs to one of 16 categories. Those categories include:

All, Animal, Astral, Charm, Combat, Creation, Divination, Elemental, Guardian, Healing, Necromantic, Plant, Protection, Summoning, Sun, and Weather.

Priests can't cast spells from all spheres of influence. Any specific priesthood can have *major access* to one or several spheres, and thus eventually learn to cast spells of any level from that sphere, and can have *minor access* to one or several other spheres, and learn to cast spells from only 1st through 3rd level in that sphere.

When designing a new priesthood, the DM decides which spheres of influence the priesthood has.

All priesthoods should have major access to the All sphere. Beyond that, the DM should choose a number of spheres, and the access to each, based on the attributes of the god being served, and on how combat-efficient the priest is already.

If a priesthood currently has access to good armor and a wide range of weapons, the DM should limit the range of spells available to them. If, however, the priests do not have access to mighty engines of war, the DM may want them to have a greater ability with magic, reflected by access to more spheres, and major access to a greater proportion of them.

Priests should have Major access to just about any sphere that has any bearing on the primary attribute of their god, and at least Minor access to spheres which have a lesser relationship to their god. (For instance, priests of a God of War who is noted for his protectiveness might have minor, or even major, access to the Guardian and Protection spheres.)

Here are some rules of thumb to go by when assigning Spheres of Influence to specific priesthoods:

The Priesthood Has Good Combat Abilities

If a priesthood is allowed to use metal armors and a good range of weapons, we consider that it has good combat abilities. Therefore, it should have less effective magic, including:

Major Access To: The "All" Sphere, and two other Spheres.

Minor Access To: Two Spheres.

The Priesthood Has Medium Combat Abilities

If a priesthood is allowed to use metal armors but restricted to a poor range of weapons, or is not allowed to use metal armors but has access to a good range of weapons, we consider that it has medium combat abilities. It should have a more average access to magic, including:

Major Access To: The "All" Sphere, and four other Spheres.

Minor Access To: Four Spheres.

The Priesthood Has Poor Combat Abilities

If the priesthood is not allowed to use metal armors (or even *any* armors) and has access to a poor range of weapons, we say that it has poor combat abilities. It should have an enhanced access to magic, including:

Major Access To: The "All" Sphere, and six other Spheres.

Minor Access To: Six Spheres.

Some Definitions

"A good range of weapons" is not a very precise definition, but it's harder to be more precise; what is and is not considered a good range varies with each individual DM. In general, if the priesthood is allowed access to five or more different types of weapons (a bow isn't that different from a crossbow for our purposes, but a mace is different from a spear), or if the priesthood is limited to a few efficient and high-damage (1d8 and better) weapons (such as swords), we say that it has a *good* range of available weapons.

"A poor range of weapons" is just as imprecise. In general, if the priesthood is allowed access to four or fewer different types of weapons, or has access to a greater number of weapons which do no more than 1d6+1 damage, we say that it has a *poor* range of available weapons.

If a priesthood doesn't allow the priest access to the full number of spheres appropriate to that type of priesthood, then the DM should supplement the priesthood with extra Granted Powers. For instance, if a priesthood has Good Combat Abilities but is designed with major access to the All sphere and *only* one other sphere, and minor access to two spheres, then the priesthood is receiving less abilities than it should; it should be given some minor Granted Power to compensate.

Now, this valiant effort to keep combat abilities and magical abilities balanced is substantially thwarted by the original Cleric class himself. The Cleric has major access to 12 Spheres, minor access to one, and the ability to wear metal armors. In short, he is more powerful than just about *any* more restrictive priesthood.

If the players in a campaign are likely not to take priests of specific mythoi simply because the original Cleric class is more powerful, the DM may wish to revise the Cleric in his campaign. For more on this, see "Toning Down the Cleric" in the Role-Playing chapter.

Granted Powers

Many types of priests also have special Granted Powers. The basic Cleric, for instance, can turn undead. The Druid starts out with bonuses to specific saving throws and speaks an additional specific language, and gains other granted powers as he gains in levels.

The DM should add at least one Granted Power to the abilities of a priest of a specific mythos; this gives the priest more individual flavor and character. The DM could add several, if this specific priest-class is weak compared to other priests.

Additionally, as with the Druid, the DM can arrange things so that the priest acquires new Granted Powers at certain experience levels, instead of receiving all of them at first level.

Granted Powers come in three levels: High Powers, Medium Powers, and Low Powers.

As with all the priest's special abilities, Granted Powers should be chosen for the priest based on the attributes of the worshipped god. It's not inappropriate to give a water-breathing ability to the priest of an ocean-god, but is quite inappropriate for the priest of a god of the desert winds.

Some Granted Powers may be used any time the priest wishes and when circumstances allow. For example, normal clerics can try to Turn Undead as many times in a day as they wish (but it can only work when they're facing undead, naturally). Other Granted Powers may only be used a certain number of times per day. When the DM first adds a Granted Power to the listing of a priest's abilities, he must define how often and under what conditions the Granted Power may work.

High Powers

High Powers are those which are of great use in situations which arise frequently in the campaign.

Here are some examples of High Powers appropriate to various types of priests:

Charm/Fascination

This power works just like the third-level Wizard spell *suggestion*, except that the priest does not have to use material components to the spell.

The DM may define this Power as working one of two ways. Either it can be used in combat (in which case it can be used against only one target at a time), or it cannot be used in combat (in which it can be used against a number of targets equal in HD to two times the Priest's experience level).

In either case, the Priest can use the ability three times per day. If the target makes his saving throw, he may choose to reject the suggestion, but will not recognize that priestly magic was being used against him.

This power is most appropriate to priests of the gods of love, mischief and trickery, music, and peace, but can be given to any priesthood which has an influential position in the society.

Immunities

This power gives the priest an automatically-successful saving throw against certain types of damage, attacks, or broad classes of spells.

Examples of appropriate categories for immunity:

Certain types of priests might have automatically successful saves against **all Evocation spells**. This is a very powerful ability; it means the priest will automatically take half damage from most damaging spells. (Those spells which don't allow a saving

throw are not stopped or affected by this immunity.)

Others might have automatic success against **all Enchantment/Charm spells**. This is equally powerful; it means that the priest will be completely unaffected by most spells of this sort, as well as other powers such as the vampire's hypnotic gaze.

Immunities may be taken against any one wizardly **School of Magic**, against any one priestly **Sphere of Influence**, or against **all Poisons**, as a High Power. There are other, lesser, immunities, discussed below.

Immunities can work *against* a character, though. Immunity to **all priestly Necromantic spells** means that the character does not benefit as much from Healing spells. He automatically makes his saving throw against them, whether he wishes to or not, and so gets only half the healing value of the spell.

The Immunity must be appropriate to the attributes of the god being served. The priest of a god of healing might have an Immunity to all poisons, while the priest of the god of love might have an Immunity to Enchantment/Charm spells.

The most important thing to remember about Immunity is that it isn't complete protection. It merely gives the character an automatically-successful Saving Throw. In most cases, this means that he will still take half damage from the attack or spell.

There is no limit on the number of times per day a character can use this ability; whenever he is struck with the appropriate attack, his Immunity helps protect him.

Inspire Fear

This power is similar to the wizard's fourth-level *fear* spell, though the cleric does not have to use material components.

A priest with this power can use it twice per day.

This power is most appropriate to priests of gods with dark or fearsome aspects: Death, for example.

Shapechanging

This power is very similar to the druid's shapechanging Granted Power, not to the ninth-level wizard spell; read the description of that power in the *Player's Handbook*.

The power can be used three times per day; it is the DM's decision whether the priest can change into three different types of animal, each once per day, or only into one specific type of animal three times per day.

This power, though it would seem to be most appropriate to priests of gods of nature, is actually appropriate for any priesthood. . . if the god in question has an animal symbol or totem. For instance, if the god of the sky has as his symbol the eagle, it's appropriate for his priests to have this power and turn into an eagle three times per day.

Turning Undead

This is identical to the cleric's ability. It is most appropriate to priests of the gods of birth, dawn, fertility, fire, good, guardianship, healing, light, love, magic, and the sun.

There is no limit to the number of times per day a priest can use this ability.

Medium Powers

Medium Powers are those which are of some usefulness in situations which arise frequently in the campaign, or are of great use in situations which only arise occasionally. Here are some examples of Medium Powers:

Defiance of Restriction or Obstacle

With this power, the priest can simply ignore some aspect of the physical world which normally slows, impedes, or prevents passage.

For example:

The priest of a nature god might be able to ignore heavy underbrush: He can travel through the thickest undergrowth as fast as he could normally walk, while other humans are slowed or even stopped completely.

The priest of the god of winter or the north wind might not find ice slippery; he could move at a normal rate across the slipperiest frozen rivers or glaciers with no chance of falling.

The priest of a god of wind might be able to walk into the fiercest headwind without being slowed.

The priest of the god of mischief might be able to climb walls and hillsides at his normal walking-speed, and without the need to make a roll for success.

There is no limit to the number of times per day a priest can use this ability.

Immunities

You read about Immunities above, under "High Powers." The Medium Powers immunities are not so strong. A single immunity will give a priest an automatically-successful saving throw against:

A narrow category of spells (for example, all Fire spells of the Evocation school);

A narrow category of special powers (all Paralysis, including Hold spells and ghoulish paralysis; or all Energy Drains; or all dragon-breath powers); or

A narrow category of poisons (all snake venoms, for example).

Again, each type of Immunity is appropriate to a different type of priest. Priests of the god of Fire could be immune to Fire spells. Priests of the god of Earth, whose symbol is often the snake, could be immune to all snake venoms.

And, again, Immunity isn't complete protection; it just gives the character an automatically-successful Saving Throw.

Incite Berserker Rage

This power allows a priest to inspire a fighter (anyone belonging to the warrior class) to a state like berserker rage. The warrior must be willing to have this war-blessing bestowed upon him.

It takes one round for a priest to incite a single warrior to berserker rage; the rage last six turns. A priest can use this power on any number of warriors per day, one at a time. A warrior may only be incited to berserker rage once per day; even if a different priest tries it on him, it cannot incite a warrior to a second rage in the same day.

The rage isn't identical to the abilities of the true berserker (see the description for the berserker in *The Complete Fighter's Handbook*). However, it does give the warrior a +2 to hit and damage for the duration of the rage. While enraged, the warrior cannot flee from a fight; he cannot leave the field of battle until no enemies face him. Once he does leave the field of battle, he can choose whether or not he will emerge from the rage or sustain it; a warrior would sustain it if he felt that another fight was likely to take place soon. When he emerges from the rage, the warrior takes no extra damage or ill effects.

This power is most appropriate to priests of the god of war.

Language and Communication

The priest with this power gains one extra language *per experience level* he gains. This power is often granted only after a certain experience level is attained; for example, with the druid, this power is granted at 3rd level.

If nonweapon proficiency rules are used, then the priest gains one *extra* nonweapon proficiency slot each level, and must use that slot to acquire a language.

The types of languages learned with this power should be restricted by the DM. Priests of the gods of nature are limited to learning the languages of woodland creatures, while priests of the gods of the earth are limited to learning the languages of serpents, dragons, and other cthonian reptiles; priests of the gods of the sky are limited to the languages of birds and other aerial creatures, while priests of the gods of the seas are limited to the languages of sea-dwelling creatures.

The number of languages learned with this power may likewise be limited. Six to ten extra languages learned this way is a practical limit.

If the campaign is using the optional weapon and nonweapon proficiency rules, then priests might, instead of being limited to languages, receive proficiency slots limited to certain categories of languages, weapon proficiencies, and nonweapon proficiencies pertinent to their faith.

Example: The priest of a specific war-god might, at third level, start receiving one extra weapon proficiency slot every experience level up to 12th.

Laying On of Hands

This power is identical to the paladin's ability; the priest can, once per day, heal himself or another for 2 hit points per experience level.

This constitutes a little extra healing ability. It's most appropriate to priests of the god of healing. It's also appropriate to priests who don't have access to necromantic spells, but who should have a little bit of healing ability anyway.

A *reversed* version of the power, where the priest lays on his hands and inflicts 2 points of damage per experience level, or 1 point of damage per level if the victim makes a saving throw, is appropriate for priests of the god of disease. A priest cannot have a healing Laying On of Hands that is also *reversible* to a harmful Laying On of Hands; it must be defined as either healing *or* harmful.

Prophecy

With this power, the priest can sometimes see visions of the future. A priest with the Prophecy power can use it two different ways.

First, the priest may sink into a meditative trance and try to receive visions of the future. This trance lasts ten turns; if the priest is interrupted before the ten turns are done (struck with a weapon, shouted at by someone within six feet of him, or knocked over), the trance is prematurely broken and the priest gets no vision.

Second, visions may just come to the priest, at the DM's discretion. When the priest is hit with such a vision, for a single combat round he no longer perceives the real world; he sees, hears and experiences nothing but his vision.

The priest receives no vision of the future if the DM doesn't have one for him to see. Therefore, the priest who deliberately sinks into a receptive trance gets absolutely no vision if the DM doesn't want him to see one. Therefore, this power is only partly an ability which gives the priest an advantage of future sight; it's primarily a tool for the DM to give the priest clues about the future, clues which guide the adventure without giving the priest an overwhelming advantage in the campaign.

The visions which the priest receives should be short and easy to misinterpret. They may be highly symbolic; if he sees a rat fighting a serpent to the death, the animals may represent mighty armies which bear those creatures on their flags, or may represent two characters with traits similar to those animals.

Also, the DM must decide whether, in his campaign, prophetic visions are *changeable* or *unchangeable*. If they're changeable, then the priest will sometimes see events which can be prevented. This tells him which way the winds of fate are currently blowing, but he knows that enough effort can change the future he sees. If they're unchangeable, then nothing he can do will alter this vision; however, it's still possible that the vision is deceptive and not exactly what he thinks it is. (For instance, when he sees his best friend plummeting to his death from a clifftop, he may actually be seeing his friend's twin or doppleganger dying in this manner.)

This is a particularly tricky power to use within the scope of the campaign. Always remember that it's a tool for the DM to give a slight advantage to the character and to guide the story, and not a weapon for the priest character to use against the DM or the story. The priest character can't sink into a trance, receive no vision, and then immediately sink into another one and expect to receive a vision then. The endowing of visions is strictly at the DM's pleasure, just as, in the campaign, visions are granted to characters strictly at the god's pleasure.

This power is most appropriate to priests of the god of prophecy. However, it's appropriate to priests of any god. In Greek mythology, for example, there were famous prophetic temples devoted to the gods Zeus (a god of the sky, lightning, oaks, and wisdom), Apollo (a god of light, the sun, and music), and Gaea (the ancient earth-goddess).

There is no limit on the number of times per day this power may be used. A character can try to entrance himself several times per day, though this is usually fruitless and annoying. However, the DM can supply a priest-character with visions any number of times per day. To keep prophecy from becoming a dominant part of the campaign, it's best to limit the number of visions received, through either of the two methods, to once or twice per *month*.

Low Powers are those which are of some usefulness in situations which arise occasionally in the campaign, or are of great usefulness in situations which hardly ever arise. Here are some examples of Low Powers:

With this power, the priest can identify a category of persons, places, or things. He must be within 10' of the object in order to identify it correctly; he does not have to see it, and the object can be hidden. In some cases, it could even be buried.

If the DM designs it as part of the ability, the priest can also *analyze* the object and get additional details about it. The type of information brought about by this analysis varies from object to object, as we'll discuss below.

Here are some examples:

A priest of the god of **healing** could identify and analyze injury and illness. He could look at an injury and see not just where it hurts, but also if it is infected or poisoned, how long ago it was inflicted, etc. He could look at a sick person and determine which disease afflicts him, what stage of advancement the disease is in, and what the sick person's chances of recovery are.

A priest of the god of **good** could *detect evil*, as per the first-level Priest spell; analysis would let him know whether the evil were lawful, neutral, or chaotic in orientation.

A priest of the god of **goldsmithing** could *detect gold*, including refined gold that has been hidden or unmined gold still under the earth.

Some of these powers of identification and analysis are especially useful, such as those which duplicate *detect good*, *detect evil*, and *detect magic* spells. These may only be used three times per day.

Other powers may be used any number of times per day. These powers are not automatic; the priest must concentrate for a full round in order to use this power.

Immunities

As a Low Power, Immunity can act in one of two ways.

A granted Immunity can give the priest an automatically-successful saving throw against one specific type of poison or magic spell. For example, a priest could automatically save against cobra venom, or against the *fire ball* spell.

Alternatively, such an Immunity could give the priest a +2 bonus to Saving Throws against a narrow category of spells; a narrow category of special powers; or a narrow category of poisons. These are the same categories the Medium Power immunities are broken down into; the difference here is that the Low Power immunity only grants a +2 bonus to saves vs. those attacks, instead of providing an automatically-successful saving throw.

Therefore, a Low Power immunity could give a priest automatic success against the *charm* spell; a different one could give the priest automatic success against the paralysis brought on by the ghoul's touch; a different one could provide a +2 bonus to all saving throws vs. all enchantment spells; another one would provide a +2 bonus to all saving throws vs. any sort of paralysis ability or spell.

As a Low Power, the priest receives one extra language appropriate to the priesthood. If the campaign uses the nonweapon proficiency rules, this power consists of an extra nonweapon proficiency slot which must be used to take one specific extra language.

Soothing Word

With this power, the priest can remove the effects of the *fear* spell or can sway the attitude of a hostile crowd or mob.

The priest can use this power three times per day. A single use can either: Dispel one application of the *fear* spell on one victim; eliminate one warrior's berserker rage; or momentarily calm down a number of characters or monsters (equal to 2x the priest's experience level in hit dice; therefore an 8th level priest could momentarily calm 16 HD of angry mob, for instance).

This power is primarily useful for getting the attention of an angry group of people and allowing the priest to address them. The combination of the *soothing word*, the respect that many cultures have for their priests, and the speaking abilities of many priests can often defuse an angry mob.

As described above, this power is most appropriate to priests of the gods of healing, love, music, peace, and wisdom.

If the DM limits this power still further, it becomes appropriate to other classes of priest. For instance, if the *soothing word* only works on animals, it becomes appropriate for priests of the gods of animal protection, the earth, fertility, and hunting. If it only works on dwarves, it is appropriate for priests of the god of the dwarven race.

Other Powers

Just about any spell can be adapted to a priest's Granted Power.

Which Spells Can Be Used

Priest Granted Powers may not be derived from every spell on the books. Some wizard schools and priest spheres are not permitted for adaptation to granted powers. Normally, when a spell belongs to two schools or spheres, where one is permitted and the other is not, the spell can still be adapted to a granted power; but some exceptions are noted below.

Priest Granted Powers may be derived from wizard spells of the schools of Abjuration, Alteration, Charm, Greater Divination, Invocation, Lesser Divination, and Necromancy. They may also be derived from priest spells from the spheres of All, Animal, Charm, Creation, Divination, Guardian, Healing, Plant, Protection, Sun, and Weather.

Priest Granted Powers may *not* be derived from wizard spells of the schools of Conjuration, Summoning, or Conjuration/Summoning; from Enchantment (spells listed as Enchantment/Charm are permissible, but those listed as belonging to Enchantment and any other school are not; for instance, *Leomund's Secure Shelter*, usable by Alteration and Enchantment, is not allowed); from Illusion or Illusion/Phantasm; from Evocation (if a spell can belong to the school of Evocation, it cannot be taken as a granted power even if it can be used by other schools; for instance, *Melf's Minute Meteors*, usable by evocation and alteration, cannot be taken as a granted power).

Neither may they be derived from priest spells of the spheres of Astral, Combat (even if a spell belongs to Combat and one other sphere, as *shillelagh* belongs to Combat and Plant, it cannot be used to make a Granted Power), Elemental, Necromantic, or Summoning.

Note that priest spells are listed with wizard-school designations *and* with spheres of influence (for example, Animal Friendship is shown as an Enchantment/Charm school and of the Animal sphere). When making granted powers from priest spells, ignore the wizardly school and pay attention only to the sphere of influence.

Maximum Levels

Granted Powers may not be derived from wizard spells of fifth level or higher, or from priest spells of fourth level or higher.

Limitations on Use

The DM must determine limitations on the use of the Granted Power. (There's no call for a priest to be using his power all the time, every day.)

If it's a power which is very useful in a lot of situations (for example, a healing ability), it should be usable once, twice, or three times per day. The more useful it is, the less a priest should be able to use it; thus, a healing power would be usable once per day, while a detection ability might be usable three times per day.

The DM can also choose for the power to take considerable time to use; special powers should take a minimum of one round to use; more commonly, they should take a complete turn.

High, Medium, or Low

Once the DM knows which spell the power is derived from and how often and easily it may be used, he can decide whether it is a High, Medium, or Low Power.

High Powers are those which frequently can dramatically affect the course of a combat or otherwise affect an adventure. The examples of High Powers listed above (charms, major immunities, the ability to inspire fear, shapechange, or turn undead) can all have dramatic and powerful effects on an adventure in progress.

Medium Powers are those which frequently give an advantage to the priest, or which occasionally will dramatically affect the course of a combat or adventure. The examples of Medium Powers listed above (defiance of obstacles, medium immunities, inciting berserker rages, enhanced language abilities, laying on of hands, and prophecy) all do these things.

Low Powers are those which only occasionally give an advantage to a priest, but which are also very much in character for the priest and his god. The examples of Low Powers listed above (detection and analysis, minor immunities, minor enhancements to language abilities, soothing word) all meet that definition.

So, when a DM creates a new granted power, he must decide which of these three sets of criteria the power meets, and define the power as High, Medium, or Low.

In any case, this definition is only a rule-of-thumb guideline to how powerful the granted power is. It helps the DM when he's assigning powers to priests of specific mythoi. For instance, if he has created a description of a priest-

hood and decides that it's just almost powerful enough, and only needs a little bonus (a Low Power) to make it just right, he'll be able to choose from his list of available Low Powers and can ignore his listings of High and Medium Powers, which would make that priesthood too powerful.

Followers and Believers

At a certain level, priests receive *followers and believers*, men and women of the same faith who serve the priests.

To receive their followers and believers, priests must achieve a certain experience level (8th or above, with 9th as the most common level). Soon after (the same experience level or during the next-higher level), the priests must assume the duties of a church leader by building a church or temple (whatever is appropriate to the faith) and ministering over a specific geographic area. At that time, their followers begin showing up, and arrive over a period of several weeks.

What Are They?

Followers and Believers are non-player characters who are supposed to help promote the priest's faith. But *what* they are in terms of character classes, levels, and duties varies from faith to faith.

The DM decides what character classes the followers belong to (based on the needs and orientations of the player-character priests and the beliefs he promotes).

For example, let us say that the priest serves the God of Strength. The followers are likely to be all Warriors and Priests of the same god.

If the priest serves the God of

Mischief, the followers are likely to be primarily Rogues and priests of the same god. There may be some Warriors and Wizards among the followers, men and women who are particular admirers of this god and his attributes as they pertain to combat and magic.

If the priest serves the God of Agriculture, the followers could be Normal Men and Women who don't belong to a specific class, with a few priests of the same god among them.

Now, it could be that the priest player-character is trying to create a specialized *order* within the more generalized faith. A priest of the God of Everything might want to create a militant order. Though the broad worship of the god includes every subject and attribute possible, this priest is devoted to the god's warrior-aspect. Therefore, with the permission of the elders of his faith (and, by inference, the permission of the DM), all this priest's followers would be warriors and some priests, probably at higher than first level, whose mission is to bring war to the enemy and then religious enlightenment to the conquered.

This sort of thinking is to be encouraged among player-characters. A player who's thinking of creating a specific religious order is thinking in character and within the scope of the campaign rather than just thinking about how to acquire more spells and magical items.

Who Are They, and How Do They Know to Arrive?

The answers to these questions vary from faith to faith. The DM has at least three ways to approach this:

(1) The followers are local people who are already worshippers of the priest's god. When they hear that there will be a new priest of that god in their area, they arrive and offer him their services.

(2) The followers already belong to another church or temple of the same faith. When the PC announces his intent to build his own temple, his faith's superiors send him followers and believers to help him.

(3) The god subtly inspires people from near and far to journey to the new temple and offer their services to the priest.

How Many and How Strong Are They?

As a general rule of thumb, the priest should receive anywhere from 10 to 100 experience levels worth of followers, with the average being around 30. The DM should decide how many levels of followers show up rather than having the priest-character roll a die.

These followers can all be of the same level, or can be of differenc experience levels. Zero-experience characters (i.e., normal men and women) count as ½-level characters. No follower can be of higher level than three levels below the priest (thus, an 8th-level priest cannot have a follower higher than 5th level).

Here are some examples of arrangements of followers that different types of priests can have. With each arrangement, we're presuming 30 levels' worth of followers.

The priest-leader of a militant or-der could have 24 first-level fighters, one second-level fighter, and two second-level priests.

The priest-leader dedicated to the common man could have 56 normal men and women, and two first-level priests.

The priest-leader who is part of a bureaucratic hierarchy could have five fifth-level priests and five first-level priests.

The priest-leader of a temple which is supposed to guide, protect, and teach a community could have one fifth-level priest, one second-level priest, three first-level priests, ten first-level warriors, two second-level warriors, and sixteen normal men and women.

The DM can assign even more esoteric followers to a priest. The priest of a woods-god might have nymphs and centaurs among his followers, in which case the HD of the monster corresponds to its level (a 2HD monster corresponds to a second-level character, while a 2d6 + 2HD monster corresponds to a third-level character).

All these followers constitute priests, warriors, and workers (the normal men and women) belonging to or assigned to the priest's temple or church. Their entire job is serving the temple or church; they are housed, fed, and sometimes paid by the temple or church. They aren't the "flock" or whatever you choose to call the populace of the area the priest is supposed to serve.

How Much Control Does the Priest Have?

The priest's command over these followers varies from faith to faith. A player-character priest cannot assume that he has a tyrant's powers of life and death over this followers and believers. The DM decides what sort of command the priest has over them based on the nature of the campaign's culture and on the dictates of the faith.

In a normal faith, the priest will be able to order his followers to work and effort like any employer (and, in a medieval or fantasy setting, employers have more power over their employees than in contemporary society). He can advise them and (if he chooses) put considerable pressure on them regarding the people they associate with or even marry.

Punishments

When he is displeased with their actions or performances, he can punish them by restricting their activities and movements, applying corporal punishments (beatings which may not reduce them below three-fourths their starting hit points), and assigning them particularly nasty tasks and duties. If their offenses are sufficiently great, he can fire then from service in his church or temple, or even separate them from the faith (as described earlier in this chapter).

Customarily, he cannot incarcerate them for any great length of time (i.e., over a week), seriously injure them (perform any punishments which reduce them below three-fourths their starting hit points), kill them (killing them and restoring them to life is still forbidden), or use harmful magic on them, including magic which denies them free choice.

Spells which are normally forbidden for purposes of punishment or even "guidance" include *create light wounds, magical stone, shillelagh, charm person or mammal, enthrall, flame blade, heat metal, produce flame, spiritual hammer, call lightning* (except when used to frighten instead of damage), *cause blindness or deafness, cause disease, curse, summon insects* (except when used to frighten instead of damage), *cause serious wounds, poison, produce fire, cause critical wounds, flame strike, insect plague, quest* (except when the target willingly undertakes the quest to atone for his misdeeds), *spike stones, wall of fire, fire seeds, harm, creeping doom, earthquake, fire storm, wither, energy drain, destruction,* or *symbol.*

Spells like *command, entangle, cause fear, hold person,* and *confusion* are permissible, because they last only a short time, or do not change a character's belief about any subject.

However, in evil faiths, the priest may be able to order the execution of followers for anything which displeases him. In particularly bureaucratic faiths, a priest may not be able to assign any punishment without a process of trial and conviction, or without permission from a higher-ranking priest at the faith's main temple or church. The DM will decide whether or not a particular faith has these characteristics. . . but most don't.

Important Followers

The DM should create many of these followers as fully-developed NPCs, including names, personalities, ability scores, equipment, etc.

When a large group of followers are "identical" in class and level (for example, if you have sixteen Normal Men and Women), one or two should be singled out and fully developed. When followers are already more individual (for instance, if you only have two second-level priests or one fifth-level fighter), such followers should be fully developed.

When possible, it's a good idea to role-play the arrival of such characters within the temple, the better to give the priest PC an idea of what his followers are like.

All of this work will make the temple and its inhabitants more immediate and real to the priest character (and the other player-characters).

What If They Die or Gain Experience?

When followers die, they are replaced by whatever means brought them to the temple in the first place. A new local will volunteer his service, or the church hierarchy will send a replacement, or the god will inspire a new NPC to volunteer his service.

It's all right for followers to gain in experience. A soldier who defends his temple from attackers can be expected to gain experience points; a follower who accompanies his priest on adventures can, too.

Only followers who have been given individual names and personalities should gain in experience. An anonymous first-level fighter guard can be expected to remain so; but a named character could rise through levels and become guard-lieutenant, guard-captain, personal bodyguard to the priest, etc.

Named followers gain experience at normal rates based on what they do in their adventures. The only limits placed on all this personal growth are these: No follower can be higher than three experience levels below the level of the priest; and the levels of all followers of a specific temple or church cannot add up to more than 100.

If a group of followers becomes so experienced that it adds up to more than 100 levels, the DM can take steps to reduce the number of levels. For instance, a senior guard-captain may leave the temple when offered captaincy of a guard-unit in another temple (one closer to his family, one more prestigious, etc.). He'd be replaced by a captain of lower level, thus adjusting the available experience levels downward.

Whenever a follower dies or leaves, he is replaced by a follower who was at the experience level the original character held *when he first became a follower.*

For instance, let us say that a temple starts with a third-level wizard who acts as the priest's advisor. Through adventuring, this wizard rises to sixth level, and then is killed in an adventure. He will be replaced by a third-level wizard.

If a guard-captain rises from second to sixth level in the course of adventuring, and then leaves for service elsewhere, he'll be replaced by a second-level fighter. This doesn't mean that the new fighter is the guard-captain. The priest may prefer for some other follower, who is higher than second-level, to be the new guard-captain. But the replacement character always arrives at the experience level the original character held when he first became a follower.

What If The Priest-Character Is Scum?

Inevitably, some campaign priests, including some player-character priests, will see their followers as a resource to be exploited and abandoned for the priest's amusement. For example, a priest might seduce and cruelly abandon attractive followers, or might send soldierly followers into certain-death situations in order to enhance his own glory.

If the faith is not an evil one, the priest is not following the dictates of his faith and will eventually suffer for it. The first few followers who perish or feel compelled to leave will be replaced normally. After twenty experience levels' worth of followers have left in this manner, however, the other temples of the faith and the local population will "catch on" and the priest will find replacements slowing.

At that point, the priest will receive one experience level of replacement follower for every *two* he loses. (This doesn't even count experience levels gained by followers through adventuring. If a second-level guard-captain rises to sixth level and then is wasted in this manner, he'll be replaced by a soldier half his *original* experience level, i.e. a first-level fighter.)

If the priest loses another twenty levels through neglect or maliciousness, he will receive one experience level of replacement follower for every *five* he loses. If he loses another ten levels through neglect or maliciousness, he will receive one experience level of replacement follower for every *ten* he loses. If he loses any more through his misbehavior, they are not replaced.

That isn't the only result of evil behavior. The higher-ranking priests of the faith will launch an investigation, assigning a priest of level equal to the offending priest to his temple to conduct the investigation. If it is this priest's conclusion that the priest has behaved badly, he could find himself punished; he could have his temple taken away and could even lose experience levels (if his god is offended by his misbehavior and decides to punish him).

Also, the other followers and the flock could become disillusioned. Surviving followers could leave or even betray the priest. The local population could gradually cease to attend the priest's church, and seek their spiritual fulfillment elsewhere.

How long does all this take? That's a role-playing consideration. A priest can be corrupt and hide his behavior from the faith and from his following for years. If he does "waste" followers, but does so at a very slow rate, it could be years or decades before the population catches on. If he's overt, and flaunts his corruption or wastes his followers at a more advanced rate, he could find himself in trouble mere weeks or months after first attracting his followers.

However, if the faith is an evil one, such behavior is normal. Wasted followers will be replaced normally. (They are not, however, likely to be *loyal* followers, and may conspire to eliminate and replace the priest.)

Role of the Faith

The DM must decide what role an individual faith has within the campaign's culture. This role breaks down into four parts:

How the faith relates to other faiths;

How the faith relates to the aristocracy;

How the faith relates to the people; and

How the faith relates to foreign faiths.

Relations With Other Faiths

Most fantasy cultures tends to fall into one of the following categories:

> Monotheistic By Demand
> Monotheistic By Dogma
> Pantheistic, Chief Faith Dominant By Charisma
> Pantheistic, Chief Faith Dominant By Strength
> Pantheistic, No Chief Faith

Here's what those terms mean within a campaign.

Monotheistic By Demand: The faith's god acknowledges that there are other gods, but demands that everyone worship him or her alone and not those other gods. If a culture is Monotheistic By Demand, it means that this one faith is the only one legally permitted within the culture. This faith is able to demand a tithe (discussed earlier in this chapter) of its followers.

Monotheistic By Dogma: Whether it is true or not, the faith claims that there is only one god or goddess and that everyone must worship that one being. If a culture is Monotheistic By Dogma, only the one faith is permitted within the culture. Typically, the worshippers are sufficiently inflexible in their belief that they often participate in religious wars in order to extend the domination of their own faith or suppress faiths they consider dangerous or heretical. This faith is able to demand a tithe of its followers.

Pantheistic, Chief Faith Dominant By Charisma: This culture concedes that there are several gods with individual faiths or cults associated with them. One, however, is the special favorite of the population, because they consider that god's attribute, personality, or blessings superior to any other god's. Most citizens of the culture worship this chief god and any other gods they choose. In this type of culture, the dominant faith typically asks but is unable to demand a tithe of its followers.

Pantheistic, Chief Faith Dominant By Strength: This culture concedes that there are several gods with individual faiths or cults associated with them. One, however, is supreme in power, either because it has a strong hold on the culture's ruling aristocracy or because the chief god has a power or promises rewards that make his worship necessary. (For example, even in a culture where many gods are worshipped, the god who decides how each person's afterlife is to be spent could be the dominant god; or the king of the gods, who rules the god of the afterlife, could instead be dominant.) In this type of culture, the dominant faith is able to demand a tithe of its followers.

Pantheistic, No Chief Faith: This culture concedes that there are several gods with individual faiths or cults associated with them. Though individual cults may be stronger or weaker than each other, none is dominant throughout the culture. Each faith can only ask, not demand, a tithe of its worshippers. Within the culture, individual *communities* may have dominant gods; and within those individual communities only, the chief god's worship will correspond to one of the "Pantheistic, Chief Faith Dominant By Charisma" or "Pantheistic, Chief Faith Dominant By Strength" categories. Some cities will not have dominant gods, or may have two or more dominant gods who have joint worship here but not elsewhere. All the gods worshipped within the culture will be perceived to belong to the same family, or pantheon, of gods.

Relations With the Aristocracy

Once the DM makes the decision about the sort of hold the faith has on the culture, he can decide what sort of relations the faith has on the country's rulers. This was discussed earlier in this chapter, under the heading "Rights of the Priesthood."

Relations With the People

Then, the DM can determine what sort of relationship the faith has with the population. All faiths exert some control over the flock, by helping interpret or define what the flock believes; some faiths exert more power, some less. Some abuse that power, and some don't. Some faiths rule the people, while others *are* the people.

The DM needs to ask himself these questions:

Is There A Priestly Caste?

That is, is Priest the full-time job of the priest, making priesthood something a little distant from ordinary humanity; or do most priests only act as priests part-time, having other occupations most of the time, and making priesthood something that any ordinary person can attain?

Just because Priest is a character class in the AD&D® game doesn't mean that the campaign culture has a priestly caste. In a specific culture, a character could be a blacksmith and also priest of the god of metalwork, or a soldier and also priest of the god of the sun, or a scribe and also priest of the god of death. The character's profession does not have to have any bearing on his priestly role. . . though it would be inappropriate

to be a soldier and a priest of the god of peace, for instance.

In such an arrangement, the character lives in his home, works to make his living, and is an everyday fellow. On occasion, he puts on his priestly vestments and attends to his priestly duties (performing marriages, arranging and performing rituals, giving guidance to those who ask it of him, praying to the god for favors). Most of these events take place at the god's temple or church, but most of the faith's priests do not live there; only priests with no other quarters, and followers of the chief priest, would live there. (A priest could live in his own home while his followers lived in the temple!) With this sort of arrangement, priests are very definitely men and women of the people. They are not supported by tithes (though tithes probably led to the building of the temple), and just about anyone in the culture can become a priest.

However, if priests are a distinct caste in the society, then priesthood is (in addition to everything else) a *job*. It is the priest's principal occupation. Most priests live in the temple or in properties owned by the faith. It may be considerably more difficult to become a priest; someone intending to become a priest may have to go through years of education and enlightenment before becoming a priest. (This isn't all that important from a campaign perspective; player-character priests still start out at first level, but with the understanding that they've gone through all this teaching and training before the enter the campaign.)

Can The Faith Inflict Serious Punishments On Non-Believers?

This is a reflection of the faith's political power in the campaign culture. Does the faith have the power to inflict punishment on those who do not follow the faith's principals? Can they imprison, interrogate, or even torture or execute non-believers or worshippers of other faiths?

If they can, they're a very powerful faith in the culture, and one which can guide the culture into periods of religious terror (whenever they try to purge the land of heretics, or to conceal elimination of political enemies by pretending they're heretics and purging them) or into all-out wars with cultures of different faiths.

Giving a faith this right in a campaign means that there's always the danger of religious persecution in the campaign. If it's the campaign's main setting where a faith has this power, the player-characters may find themselves hired to oppose or even to help such an effort of persecution. If it's a foreign power, the heroes may find themselves helping fugitives escape that land, or may even face the oncoming juggernaut of an army when that faith decides it's time for a holy war.

Is The Faith Indigenous To This Population?

Did the faith in question spring from this culture, or was it introduced to this culture by immigration or war?

If it sprang from this culture, that's fine.

However, if it was introduced into this culture and supplanted an earlier faith, the DM has the opportunity to introduce some interesting story elements because of friction between the two faiths.

If the new faith conquered and eliminated the old faith almost completely, then there will be hidden, secret sects of the old faith still in existence. . . sects which plan to re-establish the preeminence of their god.

If the new faith has dominated and absorbed the old faith without destroying it, you can deal with changes to the culture resulting from that absorption. What if, in the old culture, female priestesses and their goddesses were dominant, while in the new faith male gods and their priests are in power? Or, what if the reverse is true? Or, what if the old faith oppressed one gender and the new faith treats them as equals? In any case, there will be ongoing struggles, especially struggles of politics and traditions, where believers in the old faith try to keep things traditional and familiar while believers in the new faith try to impose their own beliefs on the population.

As a variant of that, a campaign setting, or even an entire campaign, can be built around a missionary situation, where priests of one faith have been introduced into a setting where a different faith reigns. . . and have appeared with the intent of converting the local population to their beliefs. This is especially interesting where missionaries of a more sophisticated culture are sent to a more primitive region.

The priests of the new, intruding faith are sent with the purposes of educating the "natives," challenging and defeating their priests (if any), and converting the native population to the new belief. The priests might have to oppose sol-

diers of their own land, who are raiding and exploiting the natives, or may cooperate with them for the glory and profit of their own temples, depending on whether the DM considers this a "good" or a "bad" faith and cause.

In such a setting, player-characters could take on any number of tasks. They could be the new priests, spreading the new faith. They could be enemies of the new priests (perhaps they're priests of another faith altogether!) working to defeat the missionary efforts of the new priests. They could be warriors or foreign defenders of the native population, fighting the soldiers who steal the native culture's treasures and take natives as slaves. They could be those exploitative soldiers. In as complicated a situation as this one is, there are many opportunities for adventure. . . and for tough ethical questions for the DM to introduce into the campaign.

What Secondary Roles Does The Faith Fill?

The DM also needs to decide if a faith fills one or more cultural niches which are not intrinsically religious.

For example, a faith could be the principal educator of a society. Each temple would then also serve as a school, and all priests would have nonweapon proficiencies which allowed them to teach subjects or preserve knowledge. A faith with this privilege will be a powerful one in the culture, because it influences the thinking of each new generation.

A faith might have a secondary function as a shelterer of travellers. Each temple would have a wing or annex which was a sort of

hotel for travellers, with many of the brothers and sisters of the faith "running the hotel." This makes this faith a principal waystation for rumors, and the church would be the first place that people would turn to for news.

The faith of the god of Wisdom might be the only one which could supply judges and advocates in trials. The faith of the god of Strength might supply all judges and marshals to athletic events. Perhaps only priests of the god of metalwork can mint coins.

It's extra work to introduce these small cultural elements into a campaign setting, but they add a depth of detail to a campaign for the DM who is willing to do that extra work.

Relations With Foreign Faiths

Once he's decided how the campaign's chief culture is arranged, the DM can make the same decisions about all the other, foreign, cultures in his world.

Then, if he wishes, he can add still more detail to the religious fabric of his campaign setting by defining how different cultures regard one another's religious practices.

Some cultures avidly welcome the introduction of new religious elements into their own. Pantheistic cultures, especially those which have no dominant faith, are likely to welcome worship of each foreign god that is encountered.

Some cultures violently oppose such an introduction. For example, a culture might be pantheistic, worshipping many gods, and yet still believe that its pantheon is the only true pantheon. . . and that all foreign gods and foreign pantheons are lies or demons.

Foreign cultures often worship some of the same gods as the campaign's principal culture, but do so under different names, with different rites, and believing in different stories about those gods. A tolerant culture will welcome new interpretations of their gods. An intolerant one will, at best, seek to educate the foreign culture to "correct its misunderstandings"; at worst, it will insist that the foreign land be conquered and forcibly "corrected."

This, then, is another way to add detail and texture to a campaign: By deciding how foreign faiths regard one another, and what effect that regard has on the cultures involved. These effects range all the way from increased trade and exchange of knowledge through war, conquest, and even genocide.

Rites and the Calendar

Most faiths have regular rites and rituals tied in to the calendar. This is discussed more fully in the "Role-Playing" chapter later in this supplement.

Hierarchy of the Faith

Most faiths have a definite organization, with more experienced priests leading less experienced ones. In some faiths, bribery and corruption can allow a less experienced priest to gain power and influence over more experienced ones, but this is uncommon.

In the AD&D® game, most faiths are organized based on the experience levels of their priests. The higher in level a priest is, the higher he may be in the faith's organization.

But the DM needs to note a couple of important facts.

First, most NPC priests start at first level and never rise any higher than second. The player-character priest, who gains levels throughout a career that is mostly characterized by *adventure* is an exception to the usual rule.

Second, the PC priest, with his (comparatively) meteoric rise through levels, may not wish to or may not be able to enjoy the benefits and responsibilities of most priests. Many priest PCs will wish to forego the duties of running a temple and stay on the road, acting as a mobile agent for their faith. This is a viable option for a priest in a campaign.

More on this subject is discussed in the "Role-Playing" chapter.

Experience Levels and Hierarchy

Below is the usual arrangement of priesthoods in a campaign. First is the organizational structure which NPC priests usually follow; then, we'll talk about player-characters and their place in the structure.

Level Zero (Normal Men and Women)

A "level-zero" priest is someone who has just been accepted into a priestly order and is receiving his initial training. Player-characters do not have to start out at zero-level; the only zero-level priests that the PCs will ever encounter will be NPCs undergoing training.

Level One-Level Two

First-level priests are typically assigned as aids, clerks, and assistants to higher-level priests, and keep that assignment through second experience level. During this time, the low-level priests will be getting practical field experience in the execution of their duties, in the way the priesthood works with the population, and in the way the priesthood's organization works in the real world.

Most first-level priests are assigned to priests of third to fifth level, but some few (especially very capable ones) will be assigned to much more powerful priests.

Level Three-Level Five

At third level, the priest will be assigned to a single community (a village, a small town, a broad tract of land containing many scattered farms, or a single small neighborhood in a large city).

If he asks for one, and the faith's leaders (i.e., the DM) agree that he needs one, he will be assigned a first-level priest as an assistant. This priest isn't a follower in the same fashion as the followers he receives at a higher level, and might wish to be re-posted elsewhere if his superior is unlikable or difficult. (However, if this assignee is still with the priest when that priest reaches eighth or ninth level, the DM might decide for him to become one of the priest's official followers.) If he doesn't ask for a subordinate priest, he won't receive one.

The priest is assigned a small building to serve him as a temple or church. (This is not the same as a stronghold.) The priest is supposed to finance repairs to the building, food and supplies for himself and any assistants, and salaries for any servants he chooses to hire through tithes and donations. Half of all tithes and donations are sent on to the superiors, and the rest go to the priest's own temple for these purposes. If the priest doesn't receive enough tithes and donations, the faith will probably not help him; his mission is to inspire his flock, and inadequate tithes and donations are merely evidence that he needs to work harder at it.

Level Six-Level Seven

At around sixth level, if the priest has done a good job of maintaining his church and seeing to the needs of his flock, he may be given a more important assignment. He could become the chief priest of a large town (one with more than one church; the third-level priests operating those churches would report to him), or the central church authority over several villages.

He may keep any subordinate he has had previously. He will automatically be assigned two additional first-level priests as subordinates. Again, they do not precisely constitute ''followers,'' though those specific characters could become followers when the priest reaches the appropriate level.

If the priest's work does not merit a better posting, he won't lose his experience levels or his subordinate, but he'll be stuck in the little church that he has been operating all this time. When a priest reaches sixth or seventh level and is still the priest of a one-horse town, it's often a sign that he is not held in high regard by his superiors. It may merely be a sign that there are too many priests in the priesthood and advancement is slow.

Naturally, a higher-level priest can *ask* to be posted to or remain posted to such a small community.

Some people will snicker at his lack of ambition while others will admire his dedication and his care for the common man.

Level Eight-Level Nine

At around eighth or ninth level, again assuming that the priest has done well in his priestly career so far, he will be allowed to build a stronghold. The faith will finance half its cost, and it remains the property of the faith when the priest retires his post.

However, the stronghold is semi-autonomous; the priest's superiors seldom interfere in its operations. They might interfere, especially by sending another priest to investigate, if they receive rumors of incompetence, greed, or trouble from the stronghold. Otherwise, the priest is free to operate it much as he pleases.

The priest's assigned area may remain the same. He might continue to be chief priest over a large town or collection of villages. At his request and with his superiors' permission, or solely at his superiors' wish, he may instead build his stronghold in some other place: In a frontier where he is supposed to defend the peace, in a wilderness area where he and his subordinates are supposed to work undisturbed by the secular world, etc.

At this same time, the priest will receive his followers, as we have discussed earlier this chapter. The followers manage the stronghold and its duties under the priest's administration. As discussed earlier, the levels, classes and goals of these followers will depend on the attributes of the faith and on the specific goals of the priest for his stronghold. If it's to be a military post manned by holy warriors, the

followers will mostly be capable fighters; if it's to be an educational monastery, most of the followers will be Normal Men and Women or first-level priests with appropriate scholastic talents.

During this time, the priest's progress and efficiency will be carefully measured by his superiors, who are considering what role the priest will play in the higher-level politics of the faith.

Level Ten-Level Twelve

Sometime between tenth and twelfth levels, the priest may find himself promoted to prominence over a much larger area; he will be administering a bigger chunk of the religious "map." Priests of numerous cities and regions in his vicinity (at least a fifty-mile radius) will be reporting to him, and of course he will still be reporting to his superiors. By twelfth level, he may be the high priest over an entire nation (assuming that the faith spans several nations, as many faiths do).

He does not, however, receive any more followers.

Level Thirteen-Level Fifteen

The most powerful of a faith's leaders belong to these experience levels: The high priest of the faith and his immediate advisors. If the DM wishes, politics or the god's preference alone may decide who the high priest is, and the high priest might then not have to be the highest-level priest of the faith. The faith's high priest might be chosen by vote or omen, and could be a thirteenth-level priest while all his immediate advisors are of higher level.

Level Sixteen-Level Twenty

These experience levels don't have any effect on the priest's ranking within his faith. They are reflections of additional knowledge that he has learned. . . but don't grant any additional benefits within the structure of the faith.

PC Priests and the Hierarchy

Now, just how do player-character priests relate to this whole organization? Many campaigns are set "on the road;" the player-characters spend much of their time travelling from place to place in search of adventure, and it's hard to keep a church-bound priest active in such a campaign. So, here's how to keep the priest in the campaign.

In a campaign, it's often not appropriate for **first and second level** priests to be assigned as scribes to some small-time village priest. If the DM wants to avoid this, he can assign the character to a third-level priest (especially a physically harmless one, who won't contribute much combat ability to a PC party) who travels. This third-level priest may be a friend and travelling companion of one of the PCs, or may be an unusual priest who prefers to train his subordinates by life on the road.

When the PC reaches **third level** and is supposed to be assigned his own village, he may instead be given a special mission which will keep him on the road and with the other PCs. For instance, if the PC party typically encounters new monsters or magic, the faith may want the PC priest to stay with them to benefit himself (and the faith as a whole) with these new experiences and knowledges. The PC priest could keep this assignment all the way from **third to seventh levels**.

At **eighth or ninth level**, when the PC is supposed to be "settling down" and building a stronghold, he should do so. The DM should work up a whole series of adventures centered around the stronghold, its construction and defense. After the stronghold is built and settled with followers, if the PC priest wants to remain on the road with his allies, he should be able to do so. He must leave most of his followers at the church to operate it, and should take no more than two followers with him. Naturally, the stronghold was built and organized with this in mind, and the priest will still have to return to the stronghold a few times per year in order to sign important papers and set new policies. . . but for the rest of the year he's doing the temple's business on the road.

This can remain the situation for the rest of the priest's career in the campaign. Alternately, as the priest reaches higher levels, the DM may wish to orient the campaign around him and the concerns of his faith; we discuss this in the "Role-Playing" chapter.

Finances of the PC's Temple

We mentioned tithes and donations above, and there's always a temptation to provide some sort of lengthy and involved money-management scheme for the campaign, so that the DM can keep track of every copper piece that flows through the temple coffers.

But that doesn't contribute to the spirit of adventure that AD&D® game campaigns are supposed to promote. So we're going to provide you with a much simpler system for keeping up with a temple's tithes and donations.

When the priest character is first assigned a temple or church, the DM decides, entirely arbitrarily, whether the faithful who attend that temple contribute enough for the priest to lead a mean, average, or comfortable existence.

"Mean" indicates that he gets barely enough to eat and cannot afford repairs or salaries for servants; "Average" means that he and one subordinate get an ample diet and can afford one servant; "Comfortable" means that the temple can house more than just its one or two priests (it can, for example, house one or two horses per priest) and can afford two or more servants per priest.

Then, the DM decides whether or not this economic condition is one that will change with the priest's management. If the local population isn't contributing as much as it could, the new priest might be able to inspire them to a better performance. If the last priest was a very charismatic leader, then perhaps the new priest will start out with a Comfortable or Average existence but then see it start to slip away.

Then, from time to time, the DM can confront the priest with situations which can affect his standing.

Example: An unpopular man seeks sanctuary in the priest's church; if the priest denies sanctuary, he'll be more popular with the locals, but will not have done his priestly duty; if he provides sanctuary, he'll have done his duty, but will see contributions slip or dry up altogether.

Example: A young man of the area asks the priest's advice on a difficult problem: Should he marry the girl of his choice, and alienate his father, or acquiesce to his father's arranged marriage, and wed the wealthy girl he does not love? If the priest answers one or the other, it has no effect on his standing in the community. But if he can suggest and implement a plan which will allow the youth to marry his love, keep his father's affection, and not alienate the family of the spurned girl, the priest's standing will be improved, and so will the economics of his temple.

Later Assignments

As the priest is given larger and more important postings and assignments, the DM should assign him to temples which are always compromises for him. The DM decides how many men and women these temples have on their staffs, what the standard of living is for the temple-dwellers (usually modest, though not uncomfortable, etc.). And these temples simply do not receive enough from tithes and donations normally to live up to all his expectations, much less to build up a large treasury of available coins.

Example: If the priest dreams of having a body of soldiers decked out in full plate and riding trained warhorses, what he has is a squadron of foot soldiers in chain.

Example: If the priest wants to live a luxurious existence, with expensive furnishings and many servants and a hedonistic lifestyle, what he gets is dull stone walls, used furnishings, and one scruffy servant (or none).

In all situations like this, the priest must either:

(1) Re-structure the temple's budget, which results in shortages elsewhere in the temple's existence (taking from the kitchen to pay the armory results in poorer food and worse cooking; taking from the armory to redecorate makes for brighter and less-defensible temples; taking from the repair fund to improve the kitchen makes for better meals and buildings which start to fall apart; etc.);

(2) Finance the changes from his adventuring treasures (which means that the priest will find it hard to save up a "retirement fund" of any consequence); or

(3) Tap into the monies which are supposed to be sent on to the higher ranks of the faith (which will work for a time, perhaps a very long time, but will eventually result in a temple investigation. . . which is very bad for the faith as a whole, as it causes disillusionment among the populace when the true facts emerge).

Notes on Economics

By presenting temple economics as choices of lifestyle ethics, rather than numbers on a column-sheet, the DM encourages role-playing within his campaign and doesn't have to devote a lot of time to keeping track of silver pieces.

Non-Priests Working For the Faith

One last note about levels of priests within the faith: There are many non-priest characters who belong to the administrative organization of any faith in a campaign world.

Most are Normal Men and Women who work in individual temples, as servants, messengers, grooms, and sometimes as teachers, scribes, and consultants.

Many are warriors hired to protect temples in dangerous areas, to act as bodyguards for travelling priests, and to train priests in the finer points of combat.

Some are mages, bards, and even thieves hired as consultants and specialists.

PCs, Forces and Philosophies

Some players will eventually ask themselves, "If the gods are sentient but forces and philosophies are not, then if I become priest of a force or philosophy, I don't have some god dictating what I can and can't do. I can do anything I want to."

The DM needs to step on this sort of foolishness when it crops up. Though forces and philosophies are not sentient beings, they can still enforce their ethos and tenets on their priests.

For example, if a priest of the Philosophy of Good does evil things, the natural power of the philosophy will abandon him (denying him all his priestly until he repents, makes amends, and again follows the restrictions of the priesthood).

Sample Priesthoods

The next chapter contains more than sixty individual priest classes. Each has been built according to the guidelines discussed in this chapter, and can be introduced as written or with modifications into most DMs' campaigns.

Faith Design Sheet

On page *39* is the Faith Design Sheet, a worksheet which will help the DM design his own faiths. You can use any of the Sample Priesthoods from the next chapter as a template, or create a faith from the ground up.

The Faith Design Sheet is arranged to follow, more or less in order, the subjects of this chapter.

Faith Design Sheet

Name of Worshipped Being:

_____

Is it (check one): _____ a God _____ a Force

_____ a Philosophy

Goal and Purpose of the Faith:

_____

_____

_____

Requirements of the Priesthood:

Alignment Choice(s) _____

Minimum Ability Scores: _____

For +5% exp: _____ For +10% exp: _____

Races allowed: _____ Gender: _____

Nonweapon and Weapon Proficiencies Required:

_____

_____

_____

Duties:

_____

_____

_____

_____

_____

Rights:

_____

_____

_____

_____

_____

Restrictions: _____

_____

_____

Spheres of Influences: (major) All,

_____

_____

_____

Granted Powers: _____

_____

_____

_____

Followers (How Many): _____

When: _____

Their Class and Level: _____

_____

Relations: Other Faiths, Aristocracy,

People, Foreign Faiths: _____

_____

_____

_____

Hierarchy of the Faith: _____

_____

_____

_____

Requirements of the Followers:

Alignment Choice(s): _____

_____

Races Allowed: _____

Restrictions: _____

_____

Here, we're providing examples of what we described in such detail in the previous chapter.

In the pages that follow, you'll find more than sixty priesthoods. Each of these priesthoods constitutes a complete character class of the "priest of a specific mythos" type. The *druid* presented in the *Player's Handbook* is one type of a priest of a specific mythos, and is written up there in greater detail than the priesthoods presented here. But each of these priesthoods can be fine-tuned by your DM and adapted more fully to the campaign world.

Each of these priesthoods follows the normal Priest rules (*Player's Handbook*, page 33) for experience level progression and spell progression. Most follow the normal Priestly eight-sided dice progression for hit points; those which don't will be singled out in the text.

For each of these priesthoods, your DM will ultimately have to supply the campaign-specific details of what the deity's name is, what his family and relationships are, what his history is, etc. However, players don't have to know all these details in order to create priest characters; just use the priesthood class descriptions below, and, when options are provided (for skills, requirements, powers, etc.), the players can ask the DM which options they should take.

This section supplements the material from the "Weapons Allowed" chart from the *Player's Handbook*, page 34.

Priesthoods

Below are the priest character classes. The description of each is arranged in this fashion:

Sample Faith Writeup

We start out with a quick explanation of the god's attribute. The first paragraphs talk about what the god's goals may be, what his priest's goals will be.

Next, we discuss what kinds of variations there may be to his attribute. (Example: A god of the arts may be devoted to only one specific kind of art — painting, for instance).

Sometimes these variations on the god's attribute might change your opinion of what the god's nature and alignment are. (Example: A god of death might be a frightening Grim Reaper sort of deity, or might be a gentle god of a cheerful sort of afterlife.)

We also describe the gender that gods of this attribute usually belong to. *This isn't a limitation for your campaign.* Any attribute shown below can be represented by a god or goddess, or even by a sexless deity. However, in real-world mythologies, various godly attributes are usually represented by one sex or the other, and so here we describe which one that is.

We also talk about the other types of priests this priesthood is on especially good terms with. (Just because a priesthood isn't mentioned here doesn't mean that there is bad feeling between them, however.)

Alignment: This paragraph describes the usual alignment of such a god, and the alignment choices available to his priests.

Minimum Ability Scores: This text explains what minimum ability scores (always Wisdom, and often one other) the priest must possess to be a priest in the first place.

Races Allowed: This paragraph describes which player-character races may belong to this priesthood.

Nonweapon and Weapon Proficiencies: This paragraph describes which nonweapon and weapon proficiencies a priest *must* have, and which additional nonweapon proficiencies are recommended for him. The proficiencies required of the priest must be taken from the normal proficiency slots he starts play with; he does not receive *extra* slots with which to take these proficiencies. Also listed here are the "Nonweapon Proficiency Group Crossovers" for this specific priest-class (see Table 38, *Player's Handbook* page 55 for more on the Proficiency Group Crossovers).

Duties of the Priest: This talks about the duties typically demanded of this sort of priest. Almost all priests are supposed to provide Guidance to the flock; generally, that guidance is related to the god's attribute. (In other words, members of the flock come to the priest of the god of love for questions of love, to the priest of the god of justice on questions of revenge, etc.) All priests except for the priests of the god of Death can perform the marriage ceremony, and this is a duty most don't mind performing. Many priesthoods have other duties as well.

Weapon and Armor Restrictions: Here, we talk about which weapons and armor the priest can and cannot use. Mentioned in these paragraphs are some weapons which do not appear in the *Player's Handbook*. The belaying pin, bo stick, cestus, chain, daikyu, lasso, main-gauche, net, nunchaku, sai, shuriken, stiletto, and swords such as cutlass, katana, rapier, sabre, and wakizashi appear in *The Complete Fighter's Handbook*. The bill, lasso, maul, net, nunchaku, and scythe appear later in this supplement, in the "Equipment" chapter (note that the bill is the same as the gaff/hook from *The Complete Fighter's Handbook*; "gaff" and "hook" are its nautical names). Of the armors mentioned, banded mail, brigandine, bronze plate mail, chain mail, field plate, full plate, plate mail, ring mail, scale mail, splint mail, and studded leather constitute metal armor (not all of them are all-metal, but all of them have metal elements); hide armor, leather armor, and padded armor constitute non-metal armor.

Other Limitations: Here, we discuss other limitations and restrictions which are typically placed on this type of priest.

Spheres of Influence: This paragraph describes the priest's access to spells of different spheres of influence. You'll remember from the previous chapter that priesthoods which have Good Combat Abilities tend to get three major accesses (including All) and two minor, that those which have Medium Combat Abilities tend to get five major accesses (including All) and four minor, and that those which have Poor Combat Abilities tend to get seven major accesses (including All) and six minor. In the examples below, not all priesthoods follow those guidelines *exactly*; some have one major access to few and a couple of minor accesses to many, for instance. But if a priesthood comes up notably short on the number of spheres it can access, it is given extra Granted Powers.

Powers: This paragraph talks about which Granted Powers the priest receives, and when this oc-

curs during the course of his career. Most priesthoods have at least one; some have several. Unless the text says otherwise, each Granted Power is available to the priest at first experience level; some, specifically listed, will become available at other levels.

Followers and Strongholds: Here, we talk about how many followers the priest receives, what they are, when he receives them, and when he is allowed to build his own stronghold. We also describe how many and which of his followers can take with him when adventuring "on the road." Normally, most of the followers are supposed to stay at the priest's temple and operate it for him; in spite of many priest-PCs' preferences, the priest can't just bring along all his followers with him on every adventure. The numbers given here are for the maximum number of followers the priest can take with him on adventures; naturally, he can always take fewer.

Possible Symbols: This is a set of recommendations for the symbols that the priesthood uses. Usually, they're representations of the god's attribute. They are also used upon the priesthood's Holy Symbol.

Notes: Finally, if there are any further items important to the description of this character class, we place them in this paragraph.

Important Notes

Most godly attributes (Love, War, Agriculture, etc.) don't specifically say that they are enemies of Evil. This just means that these attributes are not of themselves distinctly opposed to Evil; some have no relationship with Evil whatsoever (for example, Agriculture).

You can assume, unless the text lists Evil among the friends of an attribute, or says that priests of this other god can be evil, that the priests of the other god don't care for the Philosophy of Evil.

We haven't included a paragraph which discusses the rights the priesthood has in the culture. That's because we don't know what sort of culture the DM will be placing the priesthood within. The DM determines what special rights the priesthood has; special rights, as discussed last chapter, include Church Trial, Coronation, Other Confirmations, Tithes, Separation from the Faith, Rule, and being the State Religion.

Also, the guidelines we're providing in this chapter are based on the most common views of these sorts of gods, priests, and races. Any campaign may have a different view of these topics, and so the DM may change these limitations and requirements to suit his campaign. Especially prone to reinterpretation are: races allowed, proficiencies required or forbidden, rights, weapon and armor restrictions, other limitations, and spheres of influence.

Agriculture

Agriculture concerns Man harvesting Nature. The god has shown man how to plant, grow, reap, and utilize crops; man, in turn, worships the god as thanks for this bounty. The gods of agriculture is different from the other gods of nature and natural forces in that he represents the elements of growing that man utilizes and can control.

The priesthood of this god is principally interested in making sure that mankind continues to appreciate the agricultural god. An angry god of this sort can decide that crops fail, either on a local level or even worldwide, resulting in mass starvation and (eventually, if the god is not appeased) a destruction of civilization; man would return to a hunter-gatherer culture, living in small nomadic tribes and following herds of beasts, if this were to take place.

A god of Agriculture doesn't have to be the god of all agriculture. He could be the god of a specific crop (especially wheat, barley, corn, vines, olives, and other principal crops) or of a specific, lesser attribute of agriculture (sowing, reaping, brewing, etc.).

Most agricultural deities are female.

The priests of this god are on good terms with Druids and the priests of Community, Earth, Fertility, Fire, Life-Death-Rebirth Cycle, Nature, Seasons, and Vegetation.

Alignment: The deity is true neutral. His priests may be true neutral or neutral good; most are neutral good. The flock may be of any alignment.

Minimum Ability Scores: Wisdom 11, Constitution 12. Wisdom or Constitution 16 means +5% experience; Wisdom *and* Constitution 16 means +10% experience.

Races Allowed: Gnomes, half-elves, halflings, humans.

Nonweapon and Weapon Proficiencies: Nonweapon Proficiencies Required: Agriculture. Nonweapon Proficiencies Recommended: Local History, Reading/Writing, Religion. Weapon Proficiencies Required: None. Nonweapon Proficiency Group Crossovers: Priest, General.

Duties of the Priest: Guidance, Marriage. Observation of annual celebrations at the start of winter and start of spring. Vigilance against any threat to the community's ability to grow its food, including magical blights and droughts brought on by evil magicians or priests, artifacts or enemy gods.

Weapon and Armor Restrictions: Weapons Permitted: Bill, flails (both), hand-throwing axe, scythe, sickle. Armor Permitted: All non-magical non-metal armor, all non-magical (non-metal) shields. Oriental Campaigns: Also nunchaku. All together, these constitute Poor combat abilities.

Other Limitations: None.

Spheres of Influence: Major Access to All, Creation, Divination, Plant, and Summoning (can only use *wall of thorns*, *weather summoning*, and *creeping doom* from this sphere). Minor Access to Animal, Healing, Protection, Sun, and Weather. This does not give the priest all the spheres indicated for a priest with Poor Combat Abilities, so he'll also have more than one Granted Power.

Powers: *Analysis, Detection, Identification* (as described in the Designing Faiths chapter) of any sort of domesticated grain or garden plant; the priest can look at a field and tell what's being grown, how far along it is in the harvest year, what the state of the crop is (healthy, diseased, drought problems, etc.), and even what species is growing it (this can be handy when the party is sneaking up on the dwelling of an unknown monster and there is a garden nearby, for instance). *Create Food & Water:* The Priest can cast this spell once per day in addition to all other spells that he can cast. *Immunity:* The Priest is immune to the harmful effects of spoiled vegetable or fruit substances; he will never be laid low by normal food poisoning. (He's not immune to deliberate poisoning of food, or of food poisoning in meats.) *At 8th Level:* The Priest can cast the *heroes' feast* spell once per day in addition to all other spells that he can cast.

Followers and Strongholds: The followers are received at 8th level, and consist of one fifth-level priest, one third-level priest, one second-level priest, and ten first-level priests, all of the same god, plus one second-level warrior and eight first-level warriors to act as guards. The priest may take the following on adventures: Three priests and two warriors of his choice. The priesthood will pay for half of the cost of stronghold construction at 8th level. The stronghold must act as a central source of information about agricultural techniques for the farmers of the area; the priests must not turn away farmers who come for advice.

Possible Symbols: Sickle, scythe, sheaf of wheat.

Notes: The weapons chosen for this priesthood are those which have some bearing in agriculture.

Ancestors

This is a god devoted to man's communion with and honoring of his dead ancestors. As such, this is a god of civilization and learning, even of courtesy.

The priests of this god keep the deeds of ancestors and heroes in the minds of the population. They commune with and honor the dead, and are also devoted to learning from them — not just reading their writings, but communicating with them magically, even exploring alternate planes to understand the meaning of life and death.

They are also devoted to the protection of new generations, whom they teach to appreciate the previous generations of this race.

This priesthood places a high value on truth.

Priests of the god of ancestors *hate* the undead, regarding them as a mockery of true and noble death. These priests seek to eradicate the undead whenever encountered.

Lesser gods of this attribute would be devoted to subsets of the broad field of Ancestors. Such subsets include: Ancestors of a particular race, of a particular city, of a particular extended clan; all male ancestors, all female ancestors, all warrior ancestors, all scholar ancestors, etc. It would be appropriate for a civic deity (see **Community**, below) also to be a god of the city's ancestors, for instance.

Ancestor deities are not inclined toward either sex.

The priests of this god are on good terms with the priests of Birth/Children, Community, Divinity of Mankind, Fate/Destiny, Race, and Sites. The priests of this god dislike the priests of Disease.

Alignment: The deity is neutral good. His priests may be chaotic good, neutral good, or lawful good. The flock may be of any neutral or good alignment.

Minimum Ability Scores: Wisdom 12. Wisdom 16 means +10% experience.

Races Allowed: Dwarves, elves, gnomes, half-elves, halflings, humans.

Nonweapon and Weapon Proficiencies: Nonweapon Proficiencies Required: Local History.

Nonweapon Proficiencies Recommended: Reading/Writing, Heraldry, Religion. Weapon Proficiencies Required: None. Nonweapon Proficiency Group Crossovers: Priest, General.

Duties of the Priest: Guidance, Marriage. Education: These priests must teach new generations the value of veneration of ancestors, and are therefore also repositories of a lot of historical knowledge. Missions: To investigate old mysteries, find out what really *did* happen to famous ancestors who disappeared or perished mysteriously, sort out the truth from old legends of the city's heroes, etc. Prophecy: Listening to the omens whispered by the dead.

Weapon and Armor Restrictions: Weapons Permitted: Club, dagger/dirk, dart, knife, quarterstaff. Armor Permitted: None; no shields. Oriental Campaigns: Also bo stick. All together, these constitute Poor combat abilities.

Other Limitations: None.

Spheres of Influence: Major Access to All, Astral, Creation, Divination, Guardian, Necromantic, Protection. Minor Access to Charm, Healing. This does not give the priest all the minor accesses to spheres indicated for a priest with Poor combat abilities, so he'll also have some Granted Powers.

Powers: *Detection* (as described in the Designing Faiths chapter) of graves and undead. The priest can detect graves where remains lie, and the presence of undead, within 60'; he can tell the difference between the truly dead and the undead, but has no other analytical ability (i.e., he cannot tell that the undead detected is a vampire); through wooden or thin stone walls, he can only detect

them at a distance of 30', and through thick stone or the earth can only detect them at 10' distance. (Therefore, when he walks over a grave, he will only detect its presence if it is 10' or less down.) *Immunity* (as described in the Designing Faiths chapter) to the charm abilities of undead creatures such as the vampire. *Turn undead* (same as the Cleric ability). *At 8th level: Prophecy* (as described in the Designing Faiths chapter); the priest cannot actively try to prophesy; when receiving prophecies, he is hearing the voices of the dead advising him.

Followers and Strongholds: The followers are received at 8th level, and consist of five third-level priests and fifteen first-level priests, all of the same priesthood. The priest may take the following on adventures: Five priests, no more than two of whom may be chosen from the third-level priests. The priesthood will pay for half of the cost of stronghold construction at 8th level. The stronghold must also act as a genealogical library for the surrounding communities, and will constantly be visited by scholars looking for information on families and ancestry (or who come with information to contribute).

Possible Symbols: Tree.

Animals

This god is the protector of animals. He could intend to protect animals from all harm, and thus be the enemy of all hunters, rangers, and carnivores of all descriptions. Most often he's primarily interested in keeping animal species intact, not allowing them to be hunted to extinction, etc., and thus allows a reasonable amount of hunting and trapping to take place.

The priests of this god also work hard to keep excess hunting and trapping in check, and to remind the flock that the god will avenge abuses. Typically, this god is content to be counted as one of many gods and almost never insists on being the primary deity worshipped by the flock.

A lesser type of animal-god is one who is the protector of a single species or group of species. Such a deity might be the lion-god, or the god of all felines, or the god of elephants, or the god of porpoises and dolphins. In a primitive society, all members of a nomadic tribe might worship the god of the herd animal the tribe hunts (bison, for example).

Animal deities are often male.

The priests of this god are on good terms with Druids and the priests of Earth, Fertility, Hunting, Life-Death-Rebirth Cycle, Nature, Oceans/Rivers (only if priesthood has some association with aquatic animals), and Race (Elven).

Alignment: The deity is true neutral. The priests may be neutral evil, true neutral, or neutral good; evil priests have their own sect and the other priests don't have to tolerate them. The flock may be of any alignment.

Minimum Ability Scores: Wisdom 9, Charisma 13. Wisdom or Charisma 16 means +5% experience; Wisdom *and* Charisma 16 means +10% experience.

Races Allowed: Elves, gnomes, half-elves, halflings, humans.

Nonweapon and Weapon Proficiencies: Nonweapon Proficiencies Required: Animal Handling. Nonweapon Proficiencies Recommended: Animal Training, Riding (either or both), Reading/Writing, Religion, Animal Lore, Tracking. Weapon Proficiencies Required: None. Nonweapon Proficiency Group Crossovers: Priest, General, Warrior.

Duties of the Priest: Guidance, Marriage. Vigilance: Protection of animal life against unnecessary slaughter, especially by humans and other sentient races. Missions: Acts of war against those who do harm to the animal world or to the priest's totem animal. (Normal and recreational hunters do not incur this sort of attack, but those who hunt or trap in mass quantities and threaten the survival of whole species in an area *do*.)

Weapon and Armor Restrictions: Weapons Permitted: Bill, cestus, club, dagger/dirk, knife, mace, main-gauche, stiletto, swords (all), warhammer. Armor Permitted: all non-metal armor; no shields. Oriental Campaigns: Also katana, sai, wakizashi. All together, these constitute Medium combat abilities.

Other Limitations: None.

Spheres of Influence: Major Access to All, Animal, Charm, Divination, Protection. Minor Access to Combat, Creation, Healing, Plant.

Powers: *Identification* (as described in the Designing Faiths chapter) of any natural monster or animal the priest sees. (A "natural" monster or animal is one which exists as a species, within an ecological niche, spawns and rears its young, and has so existed as a species for at least five years. Newly-created animal species, demons, devils, constructs, and similar monsters do not fall into this category; when the priest sees them, he will only be able to identify them if he has encountered them before.) *Language/ Communication* (as described in the Designing Faiths chapter): The priest can communicate with three specific animal species (for example, lion, raven, wolf) *or* one category of animals (for example, all felines, all canines); the DM decides which ones based on the god's attributes, but if the god's attributes do not dictate specific choices the DM can give the choice to the player. *Soothing Word* (as described in the Designing Faiths chapter, but only usable on "natural" monsters or animals). *At 5th Level: Shapechanging* (as described in the Designing Faiths chapter; again, the DM decides which shape or shapes are changed into according to the god's attributes, or can give the choice to the player).

Followers and Strongholds: The followers are received at 9th level, and consist of one fifth-level priest, one third-level priest, and twelve first-level priests, all of the same order, plus one third-level ranger and seven first-level rangers. The priest may take the following on adventures: Three priests and two rangers of his choice. The priesthood will pay for half of the cost of stronghold construction at 9th level. The temple acts as an animal hospice, a "hospital" for sick or injured animals brought in by the rangers; many scholars also visit these strongholds in order to learn, from the rangers, more about animals and monsters in their natural habitat.

Possible Symbols: Any animal; claws.

Notes: The weapons allowed for this priesthood were chosen for their similarity to animal attacks. That's why there are lots of weapons with piercing and slashing attacks, but no ranged weapons or cleaving attacks.

Arts

This god celebrates the arts, particularly the visual arts (such as painting and sculpture).

The priests of this god are devoted to encouraging the visual arts of every sentient race; and though they seem to be devoted to a non-violent cause, they have to learn so many different types of magic (especially Divination, to learn, and Creation, to create), they are very powerful magically, even in combat situations.

Lesser gods of this attribute would be devoted to specific arts: A God of Sculpture, for example.

Gods of the arts are equally likely to be of either sex.

The priests of this god are on good terms with the priests of Community, Crafts, Culture, Divinity of Mankind, Light, Literature/Poetry, Metalwork, Music/Dance, and Sun.

Alignment: The deity is good; at the DM's discretion, he may be chaotic good, neutral good, or lawful good, but tends to be neutral good. Regardless of his alignment, his priests may be of any good alignment. The flock may be of any neutral or good alignment.

Minimum Ability Scores: Wisdom 13, Intelligence 12. Wisdom or Intelligence 16 means +5% experience; Wisdom *and* Intelligence 16 means +10% experience.

Races Allowed: Dwarves, elves, gnomes, half-elves, halflings, humans.

Nonweapon and Weapon Proficiencies: Nonweapon Proficiencies Required: Artistic Ability (DM can choose which art form, or can let player choose). Nonweapon

Proficiencies Recommended: Reading/Writing, Religion. Weapon Proficiencies Required: None. Nonweapon Proficiency Group Crossovers: Priest, General.

Duties of the Priest: Guidance, Marriage. Encouragement of people, even those not in the flock, who exhibit artistic abilities. Participation in semiannual events where artists' works are displayed (in shows, or before the local rulers, or in displays in the marketplace). Punishment of those who defile or destroy great works of art. Vigilance: Art often shocks the sensibilities of those who do not appreciate certain of its forms, so these priests must be vigilant against censorship.

Weapon and Armor Restrictions: Weapons Permitted: Bows (all). Armor Permitted: None; no shields. Oriental Campaigns: Also daikyu. All together, these constitute Poor combat abilities.

Other Limitations: Priests of the Arts gain only 6-sided hit dice, not 8-sided.

Spheres of Influence: Major Access to All, Astral, Creation, Divination, Elemental, Plant, Protection, Sun. Minor Access to Healing, Necromantic. This gives the priest one extra major access and four too few minor accesses, for a priest with Poor Combat Abilities; this is nearly balanced, but he'll also have some Granted Powers.

Powers: *Identification* of and *Immunity* vs. (as described in the Designing Faiths chapter) certain spells. Because of the priest's superior insight into creativity and art, he is Immune (receives an automatically-successful saving throw) to all first-level wizard Illusion spells for which a saving throw is possible, and gets a +2

saving throw vs. all other Illusion spells for which a saving throw is possible (he can't make a saving throw against someone else's *invisibility*, for instance). Additionally, even when he fails a saving throw or a saving throw doesn't apply, he can still tell when the following spells are being used (if he can see the area affected by the spell): *change self*, *spook*, *Leomund's trap*, *fear*, *hallucinatory terrain*, and *vacancy*. This ability does not allow the priest to tell which spell is being used. Also, this does not make the priest immune to the effects of the spell (for example, he'll still be scared by *spook*), but he'll know it was an illusion.

Followers and Strongholds: The followers are received at 8th level, and consist of five third-level priests and five first-level priests, all of the same order, plus twenty Normal Men and Women with artistic Nonweapon Proficiencies. The priest may take the following on adventures: Four priests (no more than two of whom may be third-level) and four Normal Men and Women. The priesthood will pay for half of the cost of stronghold construction at 8th level. The priest must act as a patron of the arts for the surrounding area, and must work to make his stronghold a center for the teaching of those who show artistic promise.

Possible Symbols: Chisel, pallet, paint brush.

Notes: The bow, the only weapon allowed for these priests, was chosen because it is a symbol representing inspiration.

Birth, Children

This god's interest is in the safe and successful birthing of children and, subsequently, their protection and nurturing.

His priests take those interests to heart, and, because of the god's protective aspects, tend to learn fairly powerful combat magics.

One lesser god of this attribute would be the god of Youth, representing children and youths of all ages from birth to the verge of adulthood.

Gods of birth, children, and youth tend to be female.

The priests of this god are on good terms with the priests of Ancestors, Community, Fertility, Healing, Love, Marriage, and Race. The priests of this god dislike the priests of Death, Disease.

Alignment: The deity is neutral good. The priests may be any sort of good alignment. The flock may be of any neutral or good alignment.

Minimum Ability Scores: Wisdom 10. Wisdom 16 means +10% experience.

Races Allowed: Dwarves, elves, gnomes, half-elves, halflings, humans.

Nonweapon and Weapon Proficiencies: Nonweapon Proficiencies Required: Healing. Nonweapon Proficiencies Recommended: Herbalism, Reading/Writing, Religion. Weapon Proficiencies Required: Nonweapon Proficiency Group Crossovers: Priest, General.

Duties of the Priest: Guidance, Marriage. Education: Teaching medicine, especially the arts of midwifery, to the flock. Vigilance, in some areas of the world, against the type of monsters who prey on babies and children: Dark elves, who sometimes steal human children and leave *changelings* (baby dark elves) in their place to be raised in their steads; or night-spirits who snatch away the breath of babies and kill them (treat as vampires).

Weapon and Armor Restrictions: Weapons Permitted: Lasso, net. Armor Permitted: None; no shields. All together, these constitute Poor combat abilities.

Other Limitations: None.

Spheres of Influence: Major Access to All, Astral, Charm, Creation, Elemental, Healing, Protection, Summoning, Sun. Minor Access to Animal, Combat, Divination, Guardian, Necromantic. This priesthood has two *extra* major accesses and is only short one minor access; therefore, it is far superior in magical power.

Powers: *Turn undead* (same as the Cleric ability); the priests of this faith, which is symbolic of life, are therefore enemies of and have some power over the undead.

Followers and Strongholds: The followers are received at 8th level, and consist of one fifth-level priest, three third-level priests, and six first-level priests, all of the same order, plus one third-level paladin and seven first-level fighters to act as guards and soldiers. The priest may take the following on adventures: Two priests and two fighters of his choice, and the paladin. The priesthood will pay for half of the cost of stronghold construction at 8th level. The stronghold must act as a maternity hospital for the local community, and may turn away no woman who is close to having her child.

Possible Symbols: Cradle.

Notes: This is a nonviolent order, which is why no damaging weapons were included in its choices.

Community

When a god's principal interest is in one city (its growth, defense, and prosperity), he's called a god of community or, more commonly, a *civic deity*.

The priests of the civic deity are responsible for making sure that the god receives worship from the city's inhabitants, and promote all sorts of plans and efforts to improve the city: Civic improvement plans, improvement of the city walls and army, etc.

One god may be the civic deity of several cities, or each city could have its own, lesser god.

The DM may not wish for there to be so many gods in his campaign world. If this is the case, then a civic deity should also (and primarily) be the god of some other attribute, and would be a given city's civic deity in addition. For example, in Greek mythology, Athena was primarily the goddess of wisdom, and had secondary attributes as a goddess of war, of crafts, and of the city of Athens.

Civic deities are just as commonly male as female.

The priests of this god are on good terms with the priests of Agriculture, Ancestors, Arts, Birth/Children, Death, Guardianship, Marriage, Messengers, Peace, Prosperity, Race, Rulership/Kingship, Sites, Trade, and War.

Alignment: A deity whose sole attribute is that he is the protector/patron of a single community has an alignment appropriate to that community. Most are true neutral; their interest is in the survival of the community by any means, whether by law, chaos, good, or evil. Their priests may be of any alignment, but evil priests gather in one cult, neutral priests in another, and good priests in a third; at the DM's discretion, they don't have to get along. The flock may be of any alignment. The DM can decide that a particular civic deity is neutral good, in which case there will be no evil priests or flock; or that he is neutral evil, in which case there will be no good priests or flock.

Minimum Ability Scores: Wisdom 10, Charisma 12. Wisdom or Charisma 16 means +5% experience; Wisdom *and* Charisma 16 means +10% experience.

Races Allowed: Dwarves, elves, gnomes, half-elves, halflings, humans. If a community has only one type of sentient race inhabiting it (or is principally devoted to one race), then the priests may be only of that race; if the population consists of several types of sentient races, then the priests of the community god may be of any race.

Nonweapon and Weapon Proficiencies: Nonweapon Proficiencies Required: Local History. Nonweapon Proficiencies Recommended: Etiquette, Heraldry, Ancient History, Reading/Writing, Religion. Weapon Proficiencies Required: None. Nonweapon Proficiency Group Crossovers: Priest, General.

Duties of the Priest: Guidance, Marriage. Education: The priest must preserve the history of the city, teach it to the young of his flock, and never let it be forgotten. Vigilance: Against any threat to his city. This is why priests of community deities often wander the wider world: They are acting as an intelligence network for the city, keeping their ears open for any hint of threat or danger to the city from outside.

Weapon and Armor Restric- **tions:** Weapons Permitted: Dagger/dirk, knife, and any *two* from the following list (the DM decides based on which weapons are most representative of the city in question; at least one weapon should be in the 1d8 or greater damage range): Battle axe, bows (all), crossbow, flails (both), harpoon, lance, mace, morning star, net, polearm, quarterstaff, spear, sword/bastard, sword/cutlass, sword/long, sword/rapier, sword/sabre, sword/short, sword/two-handed, trident, warhammer. Armor Permitted: All armor and shields. Oriental Campaigns: Also added to choices list: Bo stick, daikyu, katana. All together, these constitute Good combat abilities.

Other Limitations: Priests of a civic deity must always wear clothing indicating their priestly status when appearing in public.

Spheres of Influence: Major Access to All, Creation, Healing. Minor Access to Combat, Protection. These choices don't give the priest access to very many spells, so this priesthood will have good Granted Powers. Note that the DM may wish to substitute some other choice for the Major Access to Creation and the Minor Access to Combat if the civic deity that he has created has secondary attributes not reflected in this listing.

Powers: *Incite Berserker Rage* (as per the Designing Faiths chapter). *Soothing Word* (as per the Designing Faiths chapter). *Turn Undead* (the Community is a gathering of the living, and so priests of this sect are no friends to the undead).

Followers and Strongholds: The followers are received at 7th level, and consist of three third-level priests and six first-level priests, of the same order, and one third-level fighter and twelve first-level fighters to act as guards. The priest may take the following on adventures: Two priests and three fighters of his choice. The priesthood will pay for half of the cost of stronghold construction at 7th level. The stronghold must be built within the city, and it must act as a library specializing in the history of the city and the arts and literature created by important artists and writers from the city.

Possible Symbols: Whatever is used as the symbol for the community also serves as the symbol for this priesthood; if the civic symbol is a lion, so is the god's.

Competition

This is the god of competition, especially of athletic competition. This god stresses fairness, impartiality, and truth in his followers. He is also a proponent of health, exercise, and physical self-improvement.

His priests follow the same goals, and support these goals by conducting regular athletic exercises and games, and by acting as impartial judges for those games.

Gods of lesser parts of the Competition attribute might be gods of specific events; for example, to be the god of Boxing or Wrestling might be a very honorable thing. It would be far less dramatic to be the god of the Broad Jump or the god of Synchronized Swimming, however.

Gods of competition are usually male.

The priests of this god are on good terms with the priests of the Divinity of Mankind, Fortune/Luck, Justice/Revenge, Peace, and Strength.

Alignment: The deity is lawful

good; so must be his priests. The flock, who tend to turn to the god only in times or events of competition, may be of any alignment.

Minimum Ability Scores: Wisdom 12, Intelligence 10. Wisdom or Intelligence 16 means +5% experience; Wisdom *and* Intelligence 16 means +10% experience.

Races Allowed: Dwarves, elves, gnomes, half-elves, halflings, humans.

Nonweapon and Weapon Proficiencies: Nonweapon Proficiencies Required: Endurance. Nonweapon Proficiencies Recommended: Reading/Writing, Religion, Gaming. Weapon Proficiencies Required: None. Nonweapon Proficiency Group Crossovers: Priest, General, Warrior.

Duties of the Priest: Guidance, Marriage. Judgement: Priests of this god are asked to be judges at all athletic events, to help ensure fairness in the sport. (A given event won't necessarily have *only* priests of this god as judges, but the later rounds of events, and especially the finals, will be judged only by these priests.) Vigilance: Against unfairness. Priests of this god loathe unfairness and dishonesty above all other human traits. This isn't just unfairness in the sports arena: They also oppose unjust rule. Additionally, when two forces of basically equal honor and righteousness clash, these priests, if they choose to become involved, tend to support the weaker side, the underdog.

Weapon and Armor Restrictions: Weapons Permitted: Bows (all), crossbow, dagger/dirk, hand/throwing axe, javelin, knife, lance, spear, sword (DM chooses *one* sword type from following list; choice should be the type of sword most commonly used in organized competitions in the campaign culture: Bastard, cutlass, khopesh, long, rapier, sabre, short, two-handed). Armor Permitted: All non-magical armor and non-magical shields. Oriental Campaigns: Also daikyu; katana would automatically be the sword choice. All together, these constitute Good combat abilities.

Other Limitations: A priest of the god of competition may use magical items in normal combat and warfare *but* he may not use them in competition matches, and he may not use them in challenge matches with enemies unless he declares their presence to the enemy in question. If he violates this rule, he offends his god; this is an "inappropriate weapon and armor use" from the "Priests and Punishment" section of the "Role-Playing" chapter, later in this book.

Spheres of Influence: Major Access to All, Divination, Elemental. Minor Access to Combat, Healing.

Powers: *Analysis, Detection, Identification* (as per the Designing Faiths chapter) of cheating in athletic competition and challenge fights. If the competition is set up with rules in advance, the priest of this sect, if he is watching the fight or competition from within 60', will always be able to detect when the rules are broken, and be able to tell whether it was deliberate or accidental; they are also 100% accurate when telling whether someone stepped out of a boundary, telling who reached the finish line first, etc. (This power is the principal reason that these priests are always asked to judge events.) *Bless:* The priest can cast this spell three times per day in addition to all other spells he can cast. At eighth level, he can cast it six times per day in addition to all other spells he can cast.

Followers and Strongholds: The followers are received at 8th level, and consist of one fifth-level priest, three third-level priests, and sixteen first-level priests, of the same order. The priest may take the following on adventures: Three priests of his choice. The priesthood will pay for half of the cost of stronghold construction at 8th level. The stronghold must include athletic fields, and youthful athletes from the local communities must be admitted regularly so that they might use those fields.

Possible Symbols: Laurel wreath.

Crafts

This god represents the crafting and creation of all sorts of non-metal goods: Wooden art objects, furniture, textiles, clothing, leather goods, glassware, porcelain ware, and so forth. He may also be the god of engineering and stonemasonry.

This god's priests try to support and aid young craftsmen, to encourage the exchange of ideas and techniques between different cities and different guilds, and to improve the state of sophistication of all crafts and related arts.

Lesser gods of this attribute would be gods of specific craftsman arts. One might be the God of Woodworking; one might be the God of Leatherworking.

Gods of crafts are equally likely to be male or female.

The priests of this god are on good terms with the priests of Arts, Community, Culture, Divinity of Mankind, Light, Literature/Poetry, Metalwork, Music/Dance, Race (Dwarven), Race (Elven), Sun, and Trade.

Alignment: The deity is good; at the DM's discretion, he may be chaotic good, neutral good, or lawful good, but tends to be neutral good. Regardless of his alignment, his priests may be of any good alignment. The flock may be of any neutral or good alignment.

Minimum Ability Scores: Wisdom 10, Dexterity 12. Wisdom or Dexterity 16 means +5% experience; Wisdom *and* Dexterity 16 means +10% experience.

Races Allowed: Dwarves, elves, gnomes, half-elves, halflings, humans.

Nonweapon and Weapon Proficiencies: Nonweapon Proficiencies Required: Any one from this list — Carpentry, Cobbling, Engineering, Leatherworking, Pottery, Seamstress/Tailor, Stonemasonry, Weaving, Appraising, Gem Cutting, Bowyer/Fletcher. Nonweapon Proficiencies Recommended:Reading/Writing, Religion. Weapon Proficiencies Required: None. Nonweapon Proficiency Group Crossovers: Priest, General, Rogue.

Duties of the Priest: Guidance, Marriage. Education: Teaching of craftsmanship to the flock; promotion of all sorts of craftsmanship in the community and society. Must participate in semiannual events where crafts are displayed and promoted (before the throne or in market). Investigation: These priests are keen on history and seek to re-discover lost craftsman techniques and arts; this often leads them into old ruins and lost cities on expeditions of discovery. Vigilance against any enemy, ruler or private enterprise who seeks to suppress learning, especially of craftsman learning. (However, these priests encourage competitive thinking between guilds, or between the craftsmen of different cities; though this results in hard feelings sometimes, it does advance the state of craftsmanship.)

Weapon and Armor Restrictions: Weapons Permitted: Bows (all), club, crossbow, quarterstaff, sling, staff sling. Armor Permitted: All non-metal armor, all shields. Oriental Campaigns: Also bo stick, daikyu, nunchaku. All together, these constitute Medium combat abilities.

Other Limitations: None.

Spheres of Influence: Major Access to All, Creation, Divination, Healing. Minor Access to Combat, Elemental, Guardian, Plant, Protection, Sun. This priesthood has one too few major accesses, and two extra minor accesses; we'll consider it balanced.

Powers: *Analysis* (as per the Designing Faiths chapter) of workmanship quality in crafted goods. The priest will be able to tell whether a crafted good is of poor, average or superior quality. This gives him a +2 to his Appraising proficiency check if he has that nonweapon proficiency, but does not give him the ability to rate crafted goods as to their gold piece value of he does not have that nonweapon proficiency. *Detect Secret Doors* (same as Elf ability: Success on roll of 1 on 1d6 when passing within 10′, 1-2 on 1d6 to find secret doors and 1-3 on 1d6 to find concealed portals when actively searching; elven priests of this order have success on a roll of 1-2 when passing within 10′, 1-3 to find secret doors and 1-4 to find concealed portals when actively searching).

Followers and Strongholds: The followers are received at 7th level, and consist of three third-level priests and six first-level priests of the same order, one third-level fighter and two second-level fighters to act as guards, and twenty Normal Men and Women, each with a craft-related Non-weapon Proficiency. The priest may take the following on adventures: Three priests, only one of whom may be third-level); plus two fighters, and four Normal Men and Women of his choice. The priesthood will pay for half of the cost of stronghold construction at 7th level. The stronghold must provide workshops for its craftsmen, including the Normal Men and Women.

Possible Symbols: Loom, Pottery Wheel, Drop-Spindle, Needle.

Notes: The weapons chosen for this priesthood were chosen because they are weapons that can be made by craftsmen instead of smiths, especially by woodcraftsmen.

Culture (Bringing Of)

This god's interest is in the education and "improvement" of other cultures... especially those considered "lesser" cultures by the principal culture of the campaign.

The priests of this god are charged with the education of the population in whatever subjects the god espouses. If the god wants everyone to be literate, the priests teach Reading/Writing, free of charge, to as many students as they can teach at a time.

However, if the god is simply of the opinion that one whole culture is the best culture of all, then his priests are charged with turning every other culture into this best culture. Consequently, the priesthood invades other nations, peacefully if possible, setting up missions and trying to convert the population wholesale to the worship of this god, and to the cultural behavior of the god's favorite civilization.

When peaceful intrusion is not possible, the priesthood agitates for war with the other civilization; if the civilization can be conquered, they move in to convert is population by force. In these situations, we see mass destruction of the temples and sanctuaries of the "lesser" gods of this culture, elimination of their priesthoods, and ruthless suppression of the cultural elements which the culture-god's priesthood wants to change.

Not all culture-gods have to be racist or contemptuous of other cultures. Sometimes they're just education-minded gods who want to bestow *godly* cultural elements on the human population; in such cases, the priesthood is not one that proposes war or holds inquisitions to suppress other sects.

Culture-gods are most likely to be male.

The priests of this god are on good terms with the priests of Arts, Crafts, Literature/Poetry, Marriage, Metalwork, Music/Dance, Race, Rulership/Kingship, Trade, and War.

Alignment: The deity is lawful neutral. His priests can be of any lawful alignment. The lawful evil priests' sect is separate from the sect of lawful good and lawful neutral priests. The flock may be of any alignment.

Minimum Ability Scores: Wisdom 12. Wisdom 16 means +10% experience.

Races Allowed: Dwarves, elves, gnomes, half-elves, halflings, humans.

Nonweapon and Weapon Proficiencies: Nonweapon Proficiencies Required: Reading/Writing. Non-

weapon Proficiencies Recommended: Ancient History, Religion. Weapon Proficiencies Required: None. Nonweapon Proficiency Group Crossovers: Priest, General.

Duties of the Priest: Guidance, Marriage. Missions: Conquest of new lands and education of the conquered population in the one true way to think and behave. Vigilance: The priests must be ever alert to the sign that old, bad ways and customs are re-emerging in the conquered population (or, if conquest was not involved, in the flock).

Weapon and Armor Restrictions: Weapons Permitted: Dagger/dirk, javelin, knife, lance, polearm, spear, stiletto. Armor Permitted: All armor; no shields. All together, we consider that this priesthood has Good combat abilities.

Other Limitations: None.

Spheres of Influence: Major Access to All, Charm, Divination. Minor Access to Combat, Creation.

Powers: *Inspire Fear* (as per the Designing Faiths chapter). *Soothing Word* (as per the Designing Faiths chapter).

Followers and Strongholds: The followers are received at 9th level, and consist of one fifth-level priest, three third-level priests, and six first-level priests, of the same order, and one fifth-level fighter and five second-level fighters to act as soldiers. The priest may take the following on adventures: Two priests and two fighters of his choice. The priesthood will pay for half of the cost of stronghold construction at 9th level.

Possible Symbols: Book, Quill, Scroll.

Darkness, Night

This god is a god of some forces that humans fear. However, this

doesn't mean the god is evil. Generally, he's not. He's just the embodiment of darkness, including all its benefits and all its dangers. The god of Darkness and Night would be the god of sleep, of dreams, of nightmares, and of nocturnal predators; some of these traits are considered good, some ill.

The priests of this god are interested in making sure that man regards Darkness and Night with a reverential awe — making sure that the sentient humanoid races appreciate the virtues of night while still respecting or fearing its more frightening aspects. These priests tend to be more aloof from the common man than priests of many other gods.

Lesser gods of this attribute would be gods of only one of these factors. One might be the god of Sleep, and another the god of Nightmares. In these cases, the DM can choose to vary the god's alignment; the god of Sleep, much beloved of men, could be lawful good, while the god of Nightmares, hated by men, could be chaotic evil.

Gods of darkness or night are most likely to be female.

The priests of this god are on good terms with the priests of Dawn, Death, Elemental Forces, Hunting, Light, Magic, Moon, Oracles/Prophecy, and Sun. Some DMs may be surprised that the gods of Darkness and Night are not listed here as being opposed to those of light and sun. It's because they don't have to be; in Greek mythology, for instance, the sun-god, moon-goddess, and dawn-goddess were all siblings who never opposed one another. Naturally, the individual DM can decide for his campaign that the deities of darkness and light, moon and sun are enemies.

Alignment: The deity is true neutral. The priests may be neutral evil, true neutral, or neutral good; evil priests have their own sect and the other priests don't have to tolerate them. The flock may be of any alignment.

Minimum Ability Scores: Wisdom 11, Intelligence 11. Wisdom or Intelligence 16 means +5% experience; Wisdom *and* Intelligence 16 means +10% experience.

Races Allowed: Elves, gnomes, half-elves, halflings, humans.

Nonweapon and Weapon Proficiencies: Nonweapon Proficiencies Required: Astrology. Nonweapon Proficiencies Recommended: Reading/Writing, Religion, Spellcraft. Weapon Proficiencies Required: None. Nonweapon Proficiency Group Crossovers: Priest, General.

Duties of the Priest: Guidance, Marriage.

Weapon and Armor Restrictions: Weapons Permitted: Bows (all), crossbow, dagger/dirk, dart, knife, stiletto, sword/rapier, sword/short. Armor Permitted: All non-metal armor; no shields. Oriental Campaigns: Also shuriken. All together, we consider this priesthood to have Medium combat abilities.

Other Limitations: None.

Spheres of Influence: Major Access to All, Charm, Divination, Necromantic, Summoning, Sun. Minor Access to Animal, Elemental, Guardian, Protection. This priesthood has one extra major access.

Powers: *Infravision* (same as the Elf ability; an elven or half-elven priest of this faith has Infravision of doubled range, to 120'). True neutral and neutral good priests can *turn undead*; neutral evil priests can *control undead* (same as the Cleric ability).

Followers and Strongholds: The followers are received at 8th level, and consist of three third-level priests and twelve first-level priests of the same order, and one third-level fighter and six first-level fighters to act as guards. The priest may take the following on adventures: Three priests, only one of whom may be third-level; plus three fighters of his choice. The priesthood will pay for half of the cost of stronghold construction at 8th level.

Possible Symbols: Black banner, owl, wolf.

Dawn

The god of dawn represents the border between Night and Day, Darkness and Light, Moon and Sun. He's a friend of mankind, a bringer of inspiration, an enemy of dark things.

The priests of this god work mostly to keep the flock appreciating the god's virtues. These priests, like their allies, the priests of the god of the Sun, are also enemies of the undead.

Deities of the dawn are mostly likely to be female.

The priests of this god are on good terms with the priests of Darkness/Night, Elemental Forces, Fire, Healing, Hunting, Light, Magic, Moon, Oracles/Prophecy, and Sun.

Alignment: The deity is lawful good. Priests may be of any good alignment; the flock may be of any good or neutral alignment.

Minimum Ability Scores: Wisdom 10, Charisma 13. Wisdom or Charisma 16 means +5% experience; Wisdom *and* Charisma 16 means +10% experience.

Races Allowed: Elves, gnomes, half-elves, halflings, humans.

Nonweapon and Weapon Proficiencies: Nonweapon Proficiencies Required: Direction Sense. Nonweapon Proficiencies Recommended: Reading/Writing, Religion, Spellcraft. Weapon Proficiencies Required: None. Nonweapon Proficiency Group Crossovers: Priest, General.

Duties of the Priest: Guidance, Marriage. Vigilance against evil creatures of the night, especially undead.

Weapon and Armor Restrictions: Weapons Permitted: Bows (all). Armor Permitted: None; no shields. Oriental Campaigns: Also daikyu. All together, these constitute Poor combat abilities.

Other Limitations: Priests of the god of Dawn earn 6-sided, not 8-sided, dice for hit points.

Spheres of Influence: Major Access to All, Charm, Divination, Elemental (only spells involving heat, fire, or air; earth and water spells may not be used), Healing, Summoning, Sun. Minor Access to Animal, Creation, Necromantic, Plant, Protection, Weather.

Powers: *Charm/Fascination* (as per the Designing Faiths chapter, cannot be used in combat). *Immunity* (as per the Designing Faiths chapter) to experience level drain from undead creatures. *Turn Undead* (same as the Cleric ability). *At 10th level, chariot of Sustarre*; the priest can use this spell once per day in addition to his other spells.

Followers and Strongholds: The followers are received at 9th level, and consist of one fifth-level priest, three third-level priests, and six first-level priests of the same order, plus one third-level mage and two first-level mages to act as consultants and one third-level ranger and two first-level rangers to act as guards and soldiers. The priest may take the following on adventures: Three priests, one mage, and one ranger of his choice. The priesthood will pay for half of the cost of stronghold construction at 9th level.

Possible Symbols: Chariot; pattern of rosy colors.

Notes: The bow was chosen as this order's only weapon because it is representative of light (shafts of light being equivalent to arrowshafts).

Death

The God of Death is, naturally, a terrifying figure whom man regards as an enemy, an unavoidable doom.

But this doesn't mean that death-gods are evil. Most, in fact, are true neutral. A death-god can be the King of the Land of the Dead, the Grim Reaper who cuts down the living, or the Guide of the Souls who helps the departed spirit on to its reward or next existence.

Priests of the death-god are often agents who must "help" people on to the afterlife, especially if such people have successfully thwarted Death in the past. This duty may take the form of assassination, or of mercy-killing. In some campaigns, spirits sometimes escape the afterlife and return to the land of the living; the death-god's priests must hunt them down and capture them for return to their proper place.

Death-gods are equally likely to be male or female.

The priests of this god are on good terms with the priests of Ancestors, Community, Darkness/Night, Disease, Justice/Revenge, Life-Death-Rebirth Cycle, and Time. Priests of this god are sometimes (at individual DM discretion) allies of the priests of the philosophy of Evil, but this is actually not common, regardless of how scary the god of Death might be. The priests of this god dislike the priests of Fertility and Healing, and (at the DM's discretion) Strength.

Goal and Purpose: The deity is true neutral. The priests may be neutral evil, true neutral, or neutral good; evil priests have their own sect and the other priests don't have to tolerate them. The flock may be of any alignment.

Alignment: The deity is usually completely neutral. His priests may be of *any* alignment: Some will be evil-doers who serve him by sending souls to him as fast as possible, while others could be good priests guiding their followers to their inevitable destiny. The flock can be of any alignment, but the evil ones will specifically be followers of evil priests.

Minimum Ability Scores: Wisdom 9. Wisdom 16 means +10% experience.

Races Allowed: Dwarves, elves, gnomes, half-elves, halflings, humans.

Nonweapon and Weapon Proficiencies: Nonweapon Proficiencies Required: Religion. Nonweapon Proficiencies Recommended: Reading/Writing. Weapon Proficiencies Required: Scythe. Nonweapon Proficiency Group Crossovers: Priest, General.

Duties of the Priest: Guidance. Vigilance against any being which is unnaturally keeping Death at bay. The key word here is *unnaturally*, meaning in defiance of the gods. Wizards using *potions of longevity* are okay, until they reach an age of three hundred or so, at which time these priests become their enemies. Healers who cure injury and disease are accepted, unless they stumble onto some technique or magic that allows them to imbue immortality. Even priests who can *resurrect* or *reincarnate* are acceptable, because if the gods didn't want them to be able to, they wouldn't have given them the ability to do this.

Weapon and Armor Restrictions: Weapons Permitted: Battle axe (usually styled as a headman's axe), dagger/dirk, knife, lasso (often tied in the fashion of a noose), scythe, sickle, stiletto, sword/khopesh, sword/short. Armor Permitted: None; no shields. All together, these constitute Medium combat abilities.

Other Limitations: Priests of the god of Death must remain celibate. They need not remain chaste.

Spheres of Influence: Major Access to All, Astral, Charm, Divination, Protection. Minor Access to Guardian, Necromantic, Sun, Weather. Option: Evil priests can substitute major access to Healing for major access to Protection, but can only use the reversed versions of the Healing spells.

Powers: *Inspire Fear* (Designing Faiths chapter). *Command Undead* (same as the evil Cleric ability). The priest of the Death-god does *not* have to be evil in order to use this power. This is a rare exception to the rule that only evil priests can command undead.

Followers and Strongholds: The followers are received at 8th level, and consist of three third-level priests and six first-level priests of the same order, plus special agents whose class is determined by the specific aspect of the god; these agents consist of one fifth-level character, two third-level characters, and four first-level characters. If this is a fearsome, terrifying god of death, these agents will be thieves who act as assassins. If it is a god of the collection of the dead, one who escorts the dead souls to their final rewards, the agents will be specialist wizards: Necromancers. If it is a god of rulership, one who presides over the afterworld, they will be fighters. The priest may take the following on adventures: Two priests and three agents of his choice. The priesthood will pay for half of the cost of stronghold construction at 8th level.

Possible Symbols: Gates, Gravestone, Scissors, Scythe, Shroud, Skull.

Disease

This is an evil god which dislikes mankind and other sentient races. It creates new and ever-more-terrifying illnesses to inflict upon the sentient races.

The priests of this god spread illness and ignorance. They carry infected victims and rats infested with disease-bearing insects to new ports. Through their actions, they deny their victims an honorable death and can sometimes topple entire civilizations. This is not a character class for PCs to take unless the campaign is very unusual.

Lesser gods of disease would be gods of specific ailments. It's entirely appropriate, for instance, for the Black Plague to have its own representative god.

Gods of disease are just as likely to be male as female.

The priests of this god are on good terms with the priests of Death and Evil. The priests of this god dislike the priests of Birth/Children, Fire, Healing, and Strength.

Alignment: The deity is neutral evil. So must be his priests and their flock.

Minimum Ability Scores: Wisdom 9, Constitution 15. Wisdom or Constitution 16 means +5% experience; Wisdom *and* Constitution 16 means +10% experience.

Races Allowed: Dwarves, elves, gnomes, half-elves, halflings, humans.

Nonweapon and Weapon Proficiencies: Nonweapon Proficiencies Required: Herbalism. Nonweapon Proficiencies Recommended: Reading/Writing, Religion, Ancient History. Weapon Proficiencies Required: None. Nonweapon Proficiency Group Crossovers: Priest, General.

Duties of the Priest: Missions: To bring illness to communities which are too healthy and joyous.

Weapon and Armor Restrictions: Weapons Permitted: Bows (all), dart, scourge, scythe, sickle, whip. Armor Permitted: All non-magical armor, all non-magical shields. All together, these constitute Medium combat abilities.

Other Limitations: Priests of the god of Disease must remain celibate and chaste.

Spheres of Influence: Major Access to All, Animal, Healing (reversed forms of spells only), Summoning, Weather. Minor Access to Combat, Divination, Necromantic (reversed forms of spells only), Protection (reversed forms of spells only, where applicable).

Powers: *Immunity* (as per the Designing Faiths chapter) to all diseases. *Laying On of Hands* (same as the Paladin ability, but reversed — it does damage, rather than curing damage).

Followers and Strongholds: The followers are received at 9th level, and consist of one fifth-level priest, three third-level priests, and six first-level priests of the same order, and ten first-level fighters. The priest may take the following on adventures: Three priests (only one of whom can be third-level) and three fighters of his choice. The priesthood will pay for half of the cost of stronghold construction at 9th level. In most cultures, to keep the priesthood safe from the wrath of the people, the priests will have to keep the location of the stronghold secret; it must either be built in the wilderness, or may be built in a community if it is disguised as some other facility (for example, the front rooms may ironically be a healer's guild, while the back rooms are where the real temple activities take place).

Possible Symbols: Mice, Rats.

Divinity of Mankind (Philosophy)

This is not a god, but a philosophy, and one so compelling that it generates magical energy which priests of the philosophy can tap like a true god's priests are granted energies by the god.

This philosophy states that mankind (specifically, the human race, including half-elves reared among humans, but excluding dwarves, elves, gnomes, halflings) is nearly a divine being, and should do as much as he can to achieve perfection — physical, mental, and emotional perfection, always and in all ways. The philosophy encourages men to strive for the physical ideal and to learn as much as possible of the world.

So that's the idea that the priests promote. They cooperate in all sorts of educational, artistic, and competitive enterprises, seek to counsel people in every aspect of living their lives, and provide sanctuaries for people to meditate on the priesthood's teachings.

The priests of this philosophy are on good terms with the priests of Ancestors, Arts, Competition, Crafts, Literature/Poetry, Metalwork, Music/Dance, Good, Love, Race (Human), Strength, and Wisdom. The priests of this philosophy dislike the priests of Evil.

Alignment: The philosophy is true neutral. Priests may be lawful good or lawful neutral. The flock may be of any Good or Neutral alignment.

Minimum Ability Scores: Wisdom 12, Strength 12. Wisdom or Strength 16 means +5% experience; Wisdom *and* Strength 16 means +10% experience.

Races Allowed: Half-elves, humans.

Nonweapon and Weapon Proficiencies: Nonweapon Proficiencies Required: Reading/Writing. Nonweapon Proficiencies Recommended: Religion. Weapon Proficiencies Required: None. Nonweapon Proficiency Group Crossovers: Priest, General.

Duties of the Priest: Guidance, Marriage. Encouragement of the flock (and of mankind in general) always to improve itself spiritually and physically.

Weapon and Armor Restrictions: Weapons Permitted: Dagger/dirk, knife, stiletto, swords (all). Armor Permitted: All armor, all shields. Oriental Campaigns: Also katana, wakizashi. All together, these constitute Good combat abilities.

Other Limitations: None.

Spheres of Influence: Major Access to All, Charm, Healing. Minor Access to Combat, Creation, Divination, Protection. This priesthood has two extra minor accesses

and so will not have especially strong Granted Powers.

Powers: *Soothing Word* (as per the Designing Faiths chapter).

Followers and Strongholds: The followers are received at 8th level, and consist of one third-level priest and seven first-level priests of the same order, one third-level paladin and seven first-level paladins, and one third-level and seven first-level bards. The priest may take the following on adventures: Two priests, two paladins, and two bards of his choice. The priesthood will pay for half of the cost of stronghold construction at 8th level. The stronghold must include large discussion rooms or halls, where priests and those interested in debating the subject may convene and discuss their philosophy, and meditation chambers where visitors may meditate in peace.

Possible Symbols: Human silhouette.

Druid

The Druid, too, is a priest of a specific mythos. It has been worked up in more detail than the priests presented here, but is still counted one of their number. The Druid priesthood has much in common with those of the gods of Agriculture, Animals, Earth, Fertility, Life-Death-Rebirth Cycle, Nature, and Vegetation.

Earth

This deity is the manifestation of the world in all its aspects. He's not just a god of growing things, plants and animals; he also represents weather, volcanoes, earthquakes, flood, and many other powerful natural forces. Many earth-gods are also makers of monsters.

This god's priests are a vigorous sect who insist that everyone worship the god, for without the god all creatures on the face of the world could not exist.

Lesser gods of this attribute would represent only one aspect of the earth. One might be a god of earthquakes, one a god of stony mountains, one a god of caves and caverns. The gods of Agriculture, Animals, Nature and Vegetation can also be considered lesser gods of the Earth attribute.

Lesser gods are as likely to be male as female, but the comprehensive god of all the earth is probably female.

The priests of this god are on good terms with Druids and the priests of Agriculture, Animals, Fertility, Life-Death-Rebirth Cycle, Nature, Seasons, Sky/Weather, and Vegetation.

Alignment: The deity is true neutral. The priests may be true neutral or neutral good; most are true neutral. The flock may be of any alignment.

Minimum Ability Scores: Wisdom 12. Wisdom 16 means +10% experience.

Races Allowed: Dwarves, elves, gnomes, half-elves, halflings, humans.

Nonweapon and Weapon Proficiencies: Nonweapon Proficiencies Required: Any one from the following list — Agriculture, Brewing, Mining, Stonemasonry. Nonweapon Proficiencies Recommended: Ancient History, Ancient Languages, Reading/Writing, Religion. Weapon Proficiencies Required: None. Nonweapon Proficiency Group Crossovers: Priest, General.

Duties of the Priest: Guidance, Marriage.

Weapon and Armor Restrictions: Weapons Permitted: Club, dagger/dirk, knife, mace, maul, morning star, picks (all), scythe, sickle, sling, staff sling, stiletto, warhammer. Armor Permitted: All non-magical non-metal armor, all non-magical non-metal shields. Oriental Campaigns: Also nunchaku. All together, these constitute Medium combat abilities.

Other Limitations: None.

Spheres of Influence: Major Access to All, Creation, Elemental (the priest may only use spells dealing with dust, stone, rock, mud, and earth, plus *transmute metal to wood*), Plant, Summoning. Minor Access to Animal, Divination, Healing, Protection.

Powers: *Detect grade or slope* in passage on 1-5 on 1d6 (same as Dwarf ability; dwarf-priests and gnome-priests of this faith will detect slopes automatically when they try). *Determine approximate depth underground* on 1-3 on 1d6 (same as Dwarf ability; dwarf-priests and gnome-priests of this faith succeed on a 1-5 on 1d6). *Immunity* (as per the Designing Faiths chapter) to all snake venoms.

Followers and Strongholds: The followers are received at 8th level, and consist of one fifth-level priest, three third-level priests, and six first-level priests of the same order, plus one third-level fighter and seven first-level fighters to act as guards. The priest may take the following on adventures: Three priests (only one of whom can be third-level), plus two fighters of his choice. The priesthood will pay for half of the cost of stronghold construction at 8th level.

Possible Symbols: Snakes; stones.

Notes: The weapons chosen for this order come in three types: Agricultural/harvesting type weapons (such as the scythe), those which sometimes use stones (such as slings, or primitive maces and axes), and those which simply suggest heavy beating, pounding, or the earth (picks and mauls, for example).

Elemental Forces (Force)

This force is a representation of all pure, natural power, including forces of nature (such as waterfalls) and magical energies.

The priests of this force learn as much as they can of magic and try to pass that learning along. They also don't like to see natural forces extensively channelled by man; they often destroy dams, for instance.

Because they are devoted to powerful natural forces, priests of this force tend to be magically powerful.

Lesser attributes of the Elemental Forces could be represented by actual gods. The gods of Darkness, Fire, Light, and Lightning might be considered lesser gods of this attribute.

The priests of this god are on good terms with the priests of Darkness/Night, Dawn, Fertility, Fire, Light, Lightning, Love, Magic, Seasons, Sky/Weather, Sun, Thunder, and Time.

Alignment: The forces being worshipped and protected are chaotic in nature, so all its priests must be chaotic; they may be chaotic good, chaotic neutral, or chaotic evil. Each branch has its own cult, so good priests don't have to be friends with evil ones. The flock may be of any alignment.

Minimum Ability Scores: Wisdom 10, Intelligence 13. Wisdom or Intelligence 16 means +5% experience; Wisdom *and* Intelligence 16 means +10% experience.

Races Allowed: Dwarves, elves, gnomes, half-elves, halflings, humans.

Nonweapon and Weapon Proficiencies: Nonweapon Proficiencies Required: Spellcraft. Nonweapon Proficiencies Recommended: Fire-building, Astrology, Reading/Writing, Religion. Weapon Proficiencies Required: None. Nonweapon Proficiency Group Crossovers: Priest, General, Wizard.

Duties of the Priest: Guidance, Marriage. Education: These priests help in the education of the flock in both priestly doings and magical learning. Missions: These priests often go on voyages to observe phenomena and learn more about the forces that bring them about. Vigilance against any beings that might interrupt, divert, or channel great natural forces for those beings' own gain.

Weapon and Armor Restrictions: Weapons Permitted: Battle axe, bows (all), cestus, club, hand/throwing axe, harpoon, javelin, mace, net, picks (all), scourge, scythe, sickle, spear, trident. Armor Permitted: All armor and shields. Oriental Campaigns: Also daikyu. All together, these constitute Good combat abilities.

Other Limitations: None.

Spheres of Influence: Major Access to All, Combat, Elemental. Minor Access to Creation, Sun, Weather. This priesthood has access to many powerful spells and to one extra minor access, so it will not have much in the way of Granted Powers.

Powers: *Immunity* (as per the Designing Faiths chapter — +2 to all saving throws) to all priest spells of the Elemental sphere.

Followers and Strongholds: The followers are received at 9th level, and consist of one fifth-level priest, three third-level priests, and six first-level priests of the same priesthood, plus one third-level mage and two first-level mages to act as consultants, and five first-level fighters to act as guards. The priest may take the following on adventures: Two priests, one mage, and two fighters of his choice. The priesthood will pay for half of the cost of stronghold construction at 9th level. Part of the stronghold must be a library devoted to elemental magics and the elemental planes, and scholars interested in these subjects will visit the stronghold in order to learn from the library or contribute to it.

Possible Symbols: Fire, Lightning.

Everything

This deity represents all godly attributes. He is usually the god of a monotheistic culture, and is either (a) the creator of all the world and the only true god in existence, or (b) a powerful god who demands that everyone accept him as the only real god and intends to demote all other gods to the status of lesser demons, devils, or servants-beings.

Priests of this god seek to convert all the world to the worship of this god. They persuade whole populations that all other gods are false, or lesser beings. They sometimes agitate for and initiate wars so that conquered populations may be reeducated in this doctrine. In such times, they are much like priests of Culture.

This god is just as likely to be male as female. If male, he'll probably have some sort of sky aspect; if female, she'll have an earth aspect.

The priests of this god can, at the DM's discretion, be on good terms with the priests of the philosophies of the Divinity of Mankind and Good, for these are philosophies and not gods. The priests of this god dislike the priests of all other gods, and also hate priests of the philosophy of Evil.

Alignment: The deity is lawful good. The priests may be any sort of good alignment. The flock may be of any neutral or good alignment.

Minimum Ability Scores: Wisdom 10. Wisdom 16 means +10% experience.

Races Allowed: Dwarves, elves, gnomes, half-elves, halflings, humans.

Nonweapon and Weapon Proficiencies: Nonweapon Proficiencies Required: Religion. Nonweapon Proficiencies Recommended: Reading/Writing, Ancient History. Weapon Proficiencies Required: None. Nonweapon Proficiency Group Crossovers: Priest, General.

Duties of the Priest: Guidance, Marriage. Missions of conversion and education in populations which don't belief in this god's supremacy. Vigilance against evil and decadence.

Weapon and Armor Restrictions: Weapons Permitted: Belaying pin, club, flails (both), mace, mancatcher, maul, morning star, net, quarterstaff, sling, warhammer. Armor Permitted: All armor and shields. Oriental Campaigns: Also bo stick, chain, nunchaku. All together, these constitute Good combat abilities.

Other Limitations: Priests of the God of Everything must wear their priestly vestments whenever they appear in public.

Spheres of Influence: Major Access to All, Creation, Healing. Minor Access to Divination, Protection.

Powers: *Soothing Word* (as per the Designing Faiths chapter). *Turn Undead* (same as the Cleric ability).

Followers and Strongholds: The followers are received at 8th level, and consist of one third-level priest and two first-level priests of the same priesthood, plus one fifth-level fighter, two third-level fighters, and twelve first-level fighters to act as soldiers, plus four Normal Men and Women with the Reading/Writing nonweapon proficiencies to act as scribes and recorders. The priest may take the following on adventures: One priest, three fighters, and two Normal Men and Women of his choice. The priesthood will pay for half of the cost of stronghold construction at 8th level.

Possible Symbols: Staff, Sceptre.

Notes: This priestly order is very similar to clerics (though with reduced magic); if you decide to remove clerics from your campaign, based on the advice from the Role-Playing chapter, you may wish to recommend that players who still want to play clerics take this priest-class instead.

Evil (Philosophy)

All evil thoughts and deeds generate negative energies, and priests of the Philosophy of Evil can tap into those energies, much as a "real" priest receives energies from his god.

The goal of these priests is to spread as much evil as possible throughout the universe. They especially delight in causing suffering among the sentient races (humans, elves, dwarves, etc.). They kidnap, torture, murder, steal, humiliate, and degrade in the name of their philosophy.

The priests of this philosophy are on good terms with the priests of Disease. They are sometimes (at the DM's discretion, based on the nature of his campaign) allies of the priests of Death and Mischief/Trickery. The priests of this philosophy dislike the priests of Divinity of Mankind, Everything, Fortune/Luck, Good, Healing, Love, Redemption, and Wisdom.

Alignment: This philosophy is evil, and its priests may be of any evil alignment (chaotic evil, neutral evil, lawful evil). All belong to the same sect, so the lawful, neutral, and chaotic priests have to cooperate. Members of the flock may be of any evil alignment.

Minimum Ability Scores: Wisdom 9. Wisdom 16 means +10% experience.

Races Allowed: Dwarves, elves, gnomes, half-elves, halflings, humans.

Nonweapon and Weapon Proficiencies: Nonweapon Proficiencies Required: Religion. Nonweapon Proficiencies Recommended: Reading/Writing. Weapon Proficiencies Required: None. Nonweapon Proficiency Group Crossovers: Priest, General, Warrior.

Duties of the Priest: Missions: These priests are dedicating to spreading evil and misery across the world, and their whole lives are spent in missions against happiness, goodness, contentment, and beauty. Vigilance against the do-ings of any good priests, especially priests of the Philosophy of Good.

Weapon and Armor Restrictions: Weapons Permitted: Bill, crossbow, dagger/dirk, dart, knife, net, picks (all), polearm, scourge, scythe, sickle, stiletto, sword/long, sword/rapier, sword/sabre, sword/short, whip. Armor Permitted: All armor and shields. Oriental Campaigns: Also katana, shuriken, wakizashi. All together, these constitute Good combat abilities.

Other Limitations: None.

Spheres of Influence: Major Access to All, Charm, Necromantic. Minor Access to Animal, Protection (may only use reversed forms of the spells).

Powers: The priest can cast the *detect good* spell (the reversed *detect evil*) three times per day in addition to all other spells. *Inspire Fear* (as per the Designing Faiths chapter). *Control Undead* (same as the evil Cleric ability).

Followers and Strongholds: The followers are received at 9th level, and consist of one third-level priest and two first-level priests of the same order, plus one fifth-level fighter, three third-level fighters, and six first-level fighters to act as soldiers, and one third-level thief and two first-level thieves to act as special agents; all will be of the exact same alignment as the priest they follow. The priest may take the following on adventures: Two priests, two fighters, and one thief of his choice. The priesthood will pay for half of the cost of stronghold construction at 9th level. Temples of Evil typically have torture chambers and dangerous, trapped dungeons as part of their construction, but this is a tendency, not a requirement of the order.

Possible Symbols: Skeleton.

Notes: It is easy to make this into the priesthood of a specific *god* of evil. You don't need to change any of the requirements and abilities of the priest; the only difference is that the priest of a god of evil will receive orders from the deity all the time, instead of being always able to cook up his own schemes of destruction.

Fate, Destiny

This god cautions the mortal races to accept whatever fate that the gods or even a higher Destiny have in store for them. This is the god of acceptance, of resignation, of coping without struggling.

Priests of this faith believe that everything that happens is predestined. They preach a doctrine of acceptance of the will of the gods, including gods other than their own. When two gods are in opposition, these priests do not interfere in the mortal doings resulting from that struggle (unless one of the gods is the god of fate/destiny, in which case they support him); but when a single god is pursuing a goal and mortal beings are trying to oppose him, these priests work on behalf of the god and against the mortals. This takes place even when the god is evil; these priests take the side of gods against mortals regardless of the god's motives. In short, this is a very strange priesthood, one that is philosophical but joyless.

Lesser gods of this attribute might be gods of specific future events: The war that destroys all the gods, for instance. Such gods will strive to make sure that the events they represent do take place, and their priests will dutifully help.

The god of this attribute is as likely to be male as female.

The priests of this god are on good terms with the priests of Ancestors, Fortune/Luck, Oracles/Prophecy, and Time.

Alignment: The deity is true neutral. The priests may be true neutral or neutral good; most are true neutral. The flock may be of any alignment.

Minimum Ability Scores: Wisdom 13. Wisdom 16 means +10% experience.

Races Allowed: Dwarves, elves, gnomes, half-elves, halflings, humans.

Nonweapon and Weapon Proficiencies: Nonweapon Proficiencies Required: Astrology. Nonweapon Proficiencies Recommended: Ancient History, Reading/Writing, Religion. Weapon Proficiencies Required: None. Nonweapon Proficiency Group Crossovers: Priest, General.

Duties of the Priest: Guidance (doctrine of acceptance of the will of the gods). Missions against those who defy the gods. Vigilance against those who defy the gods.

Weapon and Armor Restrictions: Weapons Permitted: Dagger/dirk, knife, lasso, mancatcher, net. Armor Permitted: All armor and shields. Oriental Campaigns: Also chain. All together, these constitute Medium combat abilities.

Other Limitations: None.

Spheres of Influence: Major Access to All, Divination, Guardian, Protection, Summoning. Minor Access to Combat, Necromantic, Sun, and Weather.

Powers: The priest can cast the *commune* spell once per month, even at first level, in addition to all other spells (obviously, at first level, he can only ask one question per application of the spell). *Soothing Word* (Designing Faiths chapter).

Followers and Strongholds: The followers are received at 8th level, and consist of one fifth-level priest, three third-level priests, and 16 first-level priests of the same priesthood. The priest may take the following on adventures: Three priests (only one of them may be third-level) of his choice. The priesthood will pay for half of the cost of stronghold construction at 8th level.

Possible Symbols: Book, Pen/Stylus, Chains.

Notes: This order uses the net and lasso because those weapons represent the inevitability of fate and destiny.

Fertility

This god represents the fertility of beasts, crops, and sentient races. He represents new generations of each species, defiance of death, and sexuality.

Priests of this god conduct rituals which are supposed to interest the god in the fertility of the celebrants, their fields and animals. Through the rituals of the priests, childless couples pray for children, farmers pray for good crops, ranchers and animal handlers pray for their herds to grow fast and strong. In addition to routine prayers, the priests conduct great, semiannual celebrations (usually at the start of the planting and the harvesting season).

Lesser gods of this attribute would be gods of the fertility of specific species or groups of living things; one might be the god of cattle fertility, one of human fertility, one of elf fertility, one of wheat fertility. The god of Agriculture could be considered a deity of one specific part of the fertility attribute.

Fertility gods are as likely to be male as female. Those representing animal life are more likely to be male, those representing plant life more likely to be female.

The priests of this god are on good terms with Druids and the priests of Agriculture, Animals, Birth/Children, Earth, Elemental Forces, Life-Death-Rebirth Cycle, Nature, Seasons, Sky/Weather, and Vegetation. The priests of this god dislike the priests of Death.

Alignment: The deity is true neutral. The priests may be true neutral or neutral good. The flock may be of any alignment.

Minimum Ability Scores: Wisdom 12, Charisma 12. Wisdom or Charisma 16 means +5% experience; Wisdom *and* Charisma 16 means +10% experience.

Races Allowed: Dwarves, elves, gnomes, half-elves, halflings, humans.

Nonweapon and Weapon Proficiencies: Nonweapon Proficiencies Required: Herbalism. Non-weapon Proficiencies Recommended: Agriculture, Animal Handling, Brewing, Dancing, Musical Instrument, Reading/Writing, Religion. Weapon Proficiencies Required: None. Nonweapon Proficiency Group Crossovers: Priest, General.

Duties of the Priest: Guidance, Marriage. These priests are bound to conduct ceremonies which celebrate and promote fertility in all living beings; these ceremonies occur at the start of spring and at harvesttime, and in some places are characterized by orgiastic behavior. Vigilance against the doings of the priests of death, whom they regard with suspicion and dislike.

Weapon and Armor Restrictions: Weapons Permitted: Javelin, polearm, spear. Armor Permitted: Hide armor and leather armor (normal or magical), all non-metal shields. All together, these constitute Medium combat abilities.

Other Limitations: Priests of the god of Fertility *are not allowed* to remain chaste.

Spheres of Influence: Major Access to All, Healing, Necromantic, Plant, Summoning. Minor Access to Animal, Charm, Creation, Divination, Protection, Weather. This priesthood has two extra minor accesses; it will not have very strong Granted Powers.

Powers: *Charm/Fascination* (as per the Designing Faiths chapter, but never in combat, and only once per day). *Incite Berserker Rage* (as per the Designing Faiths chapter). *Language/Communication* (as per the Designing Faiths chapter): The priest may choose one species of animal with whom he can communicate, from the following list: Cattle, goats, horses, rabbits, sheep, snakes. (This does not give him any control over the animal; he may merely talk with it.)

Followers and Strongholds: The followers are received at 9th level, and consist of one fifth-level priest, three third-level priests, and six first-level priests of the same alignment, plus fifteen first-level fighters. These fighters act as guards during the more somber of the god's rituals but participate in the more chaotic rituals. The priest may take the following on adventures: One priest (it may not be the fifth-level priest) and six fighters. In some sects, the fighters are all women of any chaotic alignment, and they are called *maenads*. For others, the DM can substitute intelligent wood-beings such as satyrs, centaurs, dryads, and nymphs, up to 10 HD of them, and they can accompany the priest on woodland adventures. (*Nymphs* are identical to dryads

with these exceptions: They are not bound to specific trees, and can voyage in any forested realm; and when they *charm* victims, there is no chance that the victims will disappear forever; after a day in the company of the nymph, the victim can choose to stay as long as he and the nymph collectively wish, or to leave whenever he wants.) The priesthood will pay for half of the cost of stronghold construction at 9th level.

Possible Symbols: Bull, Corn, Cow, Goat, Pine-cone, Ram, Snake, Wheat.

Fire

This god is the deity of fire in all its aspects: The spark of civilization, the cleanser of sickness and evil, the terrifying natural force, the special gift of the gods to man, the principal force behind some sorts of magic.

The priesthood is devoted to celebrating fire and honoring the god of this most useful gift. They make burnt sacrifices to the god and learn as much as they can of fire-magic.

Lesser gods of this attribute will be gods of just one aspect of fire. One might be a god of forest-fires, one a god of the fires used by metalworkers and pottery-makers, one a god of the hearth-fire that represents home and shelter.

Fire-gods are as likely to be male as female.

The priests of this god are on good terms with the priests of Dawn, Elemental Forces, Justice/Revenge, Light, Lightning, Magic, Metalwork, Race (Dwarf), and Sun. They are not that fond of, but also not *enemies* of, the priests of Oceans/Rivers. The priests of this

god dislike the priests of Disease.

Alignment: The deity is true neutral. The priests may be neutral evil, true neutral, or neutral good; evil priests have their own sect and the other priests don't have to tolerate them. The flock may be of any alignment.

Minimum Ability Scores: Wisdom 10, Intelligence 10. Wisdom or Intelligence 16 means +5% experience; Wisdom *and* Intelligence 16 means +10% experience.

Races Allowed: Dwarves, elves, gnomes, half-elves, halflings, humans.

Nonweapon and Weapon Proficiencies: Nonweapon Proficiencies Required: Fire-building. Nonweapon Proficiencies Recommended: Reading/Writing, Religion, Spellcraft. Weapon Proficiencies Required: None. Nonweapon Proficiency Group Crossovers: Priest, General, Wizard.

Duties of the Priest: Guidance, Marriage.

Weapon and Armor Restrictions: Weapons Permitted: Bill, dagger/dirk, knife, stiletto, swords (all). Armor Permitted: All metal armor, all metal shields. Oriental Campaigns: Also chain, katana, shuriken, wakizashi. All together, these constitute Good combat abilities.

Other Limitations: None.

Spheres of Influence: Major Access to All, Elemental (the priest may only use the spells whose names include the words Fire, Flame, Heat, Pyrotechnics, and the spell *chariot of Sustarre*), Sun. Minor Access to Charm, Divination, Healing, Necromantic, Protection, Weather. This priesthood receives extra minor accesses because its two major accesses are limited in significant ways: Its Elemental sphere is limited to fire-spells and the Sun sphere has only six spells to start with.

Powers: *Defiance of Restriction/Obstacle* (as per the Designing Faiths chapter): The priest can pass unharmed through any *wall of fire* spell. *Immunity* (as per the Designing Faiths chapter): The priest gets a +2 saving throw vs. all priest spells of the Elemental sphere and vs. all wizard spells of the Alteration and Evocation schools with the words *fire, burning, flaming, pyrotechnics,* and *incendiary*.

Followers and Strongholds: The followers are received at 8th level, and consist of three third-level priests and six first-level priests of the same order, plus five first-level fighters to act as guards, one third-level mage and two first-level mages acting as consultants, and ten Normal Men and Women, half with Reading/Writing proficiency and half with Fire-Starting proficiency, who act as temple functionaries. The priest may take the following on adventures: Two priests (only one of whom may be third-level), two fighters, one mage, and two Normal Men and Women of his choice. The priesthood will pay for half of the cost of stronghold construction at 8th level.

Possible Symbols: Torch.

Fortune, Luck

This is a god of the good fortune and good luck that all sentient beings hope will come their way. This is not a god of bad luck or ill fortune.

The priests of this god are practical, common-sense people. They'll help the flock pray for luck. But they also recognize that a lot of luck is self-made. They try to analyze the situations of supplicants who seem to have bad luck all the time, and suggest ways for them to change their lives so that good luck is more likely to shine on them. They even meddle to give luck a little push; they'll contrive so that two people who can help each other accomplish a mutual goal will meet, for example.

Lesser gods of this attribute will be gods of one particular type of luck. The most popular gods of this type would be gods of gambling luck or luck with romantic affairs.

Gods of luck are most likely to be female.

The priests of this god are on good terms with the priests of Competition, Fate/Destiny, Mischief/Trickery, and Trade. The priests of this god dislike the priests of Evil.

Alignment: The deity is true neutral. The priests may be true neutral or neutral good; most are true neutral. The flock may be of any alignment.

Minimum Ability Scores: Wisdom 12, Charisma 12. Wisdom or Charisma 16 means +5% experience; Wisdom *and* Charisma 16 means +10% experience.

Races Allowed: Dwarves, elves, gnomes, half-elves, halflings, humans.

Nonweapon and Weapon Proficiencies: Nonweapon Proficiencies Required: Astrology. Nonweapon Proficiencies Recommended: Gaming, Reading/Writing, Religion. Weapon Proficiencies Required: None. Nonweapon Proficiency Group Crossovers: Priest, General, Rogue.

Duties of the Priest: Guidance, Marriage. Missions to bring luck to the unlucky: Priests are often required to go to communities and places which seem to be suffering a series of bad-luck events and improve matters there. (Some priests of this sect adopt a "fairy godmother" attitude and try to improve peoples' lot through mischievous meddling.) Vigilance against the deeds of priests of disease or the philosophy of evil, who are always bringing bad fortune to the people.

Weapon and Armor Restrictions: Weapons Permitted: Club, lasso, net, quarterstaff, sling, staff sling. Armor Permitted: None; no shields. Oriental Campaigns: Also bo stick. All together, these constitute Poor combat abilities.

Other Limitations: None.

Spheres of Influence: Major Access to All, Charm, Divination, Elemental, Healing, Protection, Summoning. Minor Access to Animal, Creation, Guardian, Plant, Sun, Weather.

Powers: *Charm/Fascination* (as per the Designing Faiths chapter).

Followers and Strongholds: The followers are received at 7th level, and consist of one fifth-level priest, three third-level priests, and sixteen first-level priests of the same order. The priest may take the following on adventures: Three priests (only one of whom may be third level) of his choice. The priesthood will pay for half of the cost of stronghold construction at 7th level.

Possible Symbols: Cornucopia, Rudder, Wheel of Fortune.

Notes: This order's weapon choices reflect "weapons of opportunity," the sort of weapons characters can make from things found on the road. A priest of this order doesn't have to find his weapons on the road, but the weapons permitted him are the sort of things he could make from found items.

Good (Philosophy)

Just as evil thoughts and deeds create evil energies (see Evil, p. 57), good thoughts and deeds create good energies, resulting in priests of the philosophy of Good.

The goal of these priests is to counter the spread of evil throughout the universe. They work primarily to anticipate the deeds of evil beings, head them off, and counter them whenever possible. They may or may not believe in Law; some of them, chaotic good priests, break all sorts of laws and restrictions of society in order to realize their good intentions.

The priests of this philosophy are on good terms with the priests of Divinity of Mankind, Everything, Peace, Race, Redemption, and Wisdom. The priests of this philosophy especially dislike the priests of Evil.

Alignment: This philosophy is good. Its priest may be of any good alignment (chaotic good, neutral good, and lawful good); they all belong to the same sect, so the chaotics, neutrals, and lawfuls must all get along together. The flock may be of any good alignment.

Minimum Ability Scores: Wisdom 9. Wisdom 16 means +10% experience.

Races Allowed: Dwarves, elves, gnomes, half-elves, halflings, humans.

Nonweapon and Weapon Proficiencies: Nonweapon Proficiencies Required: Religion. Nonweapon Proficiencies Recommended: Reading/Writing. Weapon Proficiencies Required: None. Nonweapon Proficiency Group Crossovers: Priest, General, Warrior.

Duties of the Priest: Guidance, Marriage. Missions: Priests of this philosophy spend most of their lives in ongoing missions against priests of the philosophy of evil, not to mention the plots of evil men, priests of the god of disease, etc.

Weapon and Armor Restrictions: Weapons Permitted: Bows (all), dagger/dirk, hand/throwing axe, javelin, knife, lasso, polearm, spear, staff sling, stiletto, swords (all). Armor Permitted: All armor and shields. Oriental Campaigns: Also daikyu, katana, wakizashi. All together, these constitute Good combat abilities.

Other Limitations: None.

Spheres of Influence: Major Access to All, Healing, Protection. Minor Access to Charm, Divination.

Powers: The priest can cast the *detect evil* spell three times per day in addition to all other spells. *Turn Undead* (same as the Cleric ability). *Permanent +1 to hit and damage* vs. all evil enemies, above and beyond all other bonuses.

Followers and Strongholds: The followers are received at 9th level, and consist of one third-level priest and two first-level priests of the same order, plus one fifth-level paladin, three third-level paladins, and six first-level paladins to act as soldiers, and one third-level mage and two first-level mages to act as special agents; the priests and mages will be of the exact same alignment as the priest they follow, while the paladins will automatically be lawful good. The priest may take the following on adventures: One priest, two paladins, and one mage of his choice. The priesthood will pay for half of the cost of stronghold construction at 9th level. Such strongholds are often built with hospitals and libraries as part of their construction, but this is not a requirement of the order.

Possible Symbols: Ray of light, Ankh.

Guardianship

This god is the protector of causes and endangered individuals. He's an appropriate deity for bodyguards, other guardsmen, martyrs, and heroes who espouse lost causes.

Priests of this god meddle in politics, stand up for noble causes, aggravate kings and viziers, supply troops to the underdogs of certain fights and wars, and often provide bodyguards for famous public figures (especially those who are championing causes) who need them. (This is a great way to get priest-PCs into interesting adventures.)

Whether or not this god is more likely to be male or female depends on the culture; if there are few women warriors, then the god is probably male, while if women are often warriors, the god is just as likely to be female as male.

The priests of this god are on good terms with the priests of Community, Healing, Strength, and War.

Alignment: The deity is neutral good; at the DM's discretion, he may be chaotic good or lawful good. His priests may be of any good alignment. The flock may be of any neutral or good alignment.

Minimum Ability Scores: Wisdom 10, Strength 12. Wisdom or Strength 16 means +5% experience; Wisdom *and* Strength 16 means +10% experience.

Races Allowed: Dwarves, elves, gnomes, half-elves, halflings, humans.

Nonweapon and Weapon Proficiencies: Nonweapon Proficiencies Required: Set Snares. Nonweapon Proficiencies Recommended: Riding Land-Based, Healing, Reading/Writing, Religion, Blind-fighting. Weapon Proficiencies Required: None. Nonweapon Proficiency Group Crossovers: Priest, General, Warrior.

Duties of the Priest: Guidance, Marriage. Missions: A priest of this god is almost always on some sort of mission, a simple one — to protect a specific person, place, or thing. The priest might have chosen his current mission, or might have been assigned to it by his priesthood. That mission might change between adventures, but he's almost always on one. Note: Priests of this sort do not maintain temples for small communities; they spend most of their time on mission. Only when they reach eighth level do they build their own temples and send subordinate priests out on missions.

Weapon and Armor Restrictions: Weapons Permitted: Battle axe, dagger/dirk, javelin, knife, polearm, spear, swords (all). Armor Permitted: All armor and shields. Oriental Campaigns: Also katana, wakizashi. All together, these constitute Good combat abilities.

Other Limitations: None.

Spheres of Influence: Major Access to All, Necromantic, Protection. Minor Access to Guardian, Healing.

Powers: *Infravision* (same as the elf ability; an elven or half-elven priest of this faith has Infravision of doubled range, to 120′). *Laying On of Hands* (same as the Paladin ability).

Followers and Strongholds: The followers are received at 8th level, and consist of three third-level priests and six first-level priests of the same order, plus five third-level fighters to act as temple guards. The priest may take the

following on adventures: Three priests (only one of whom may be third-level) and two fighters. The priesthood will pay for half of the cost of stronghold construction at 8th level. The stronghold *must* be built in the fashion of a castle or fortress, even if it is in a city: It must be constructed so that it can easily repel invasion.

Possible Symbols: Crossed Swords; Crossed Polearms; Shield.

Notes: This priesthood represents a god who is a defender, not an aggressor; therefore, the priesthood can use or make no ranged weapon attacks. The priests may not even throw their spears, javelins, daggers or knives.

Healing

This god is the champion of doctors, medicine and other healing functions. He cures the sick and passes on his healing knowledge to his mortal doctor/priests. He is the enemy of disease and injury, and no admirer of war.

The priesthood is devoted to healing and are not allowed by their order to turn away a patient in need; if they can help him, they must.

Lesser gods of this attribute are gods of specific types of healing. One might be a god of combat injuries, one a god who heals illnesses of the mind. The god of childbirth could be considered a lesser god of healing.

Healing gods are as likely to be male as female.

The priests of this god are on good terms with the priests of Birth/Children, Dawn, Guardianship, Light, Love, Peace, and Sun. The priests of this god dislike the priests of Death, Disease, and Evil.

Alignment: The deity is lawful

good. The priests may be any sort of good alignment. The flock may be of any neutral or good alignment.

Minimum Ability Scores: Wisdom 10, Intelligence 10. Wisdom or Intelligence 16 means +5% experience; Wisdom *and* Intelligence 16 means +10% experience.

Races Allowed: Dwarves, elves, gnomes, half-elves, halflings, humans.

Nonweapon and Weapon Proficiencies: Nonweapon Proficiencies Required: Healing. Nonweapon Proficiencies Recommended: Herbalism, Reading/Writing, Religion. Weapon Proficiencies Required: None. Nonweapon Proficiency Group Crossovers: Priest, General.

Duties of the Priest: Guidance, Marriage. Curing the sick and injured. Education: Teaching the flock, indeed anyone who is interested, the arts of medicine, sanitation, and healing. Missions to sickness-infested lands to help in the healing process. Vigilance against the activities of the priests of the god of disease.

Weapon and Armor Restrictions: Weapons Permitted: Lasso, mancatcher, net, quarterstaff. Armor Permitted: All non-metal armor; no shields. Oriental Campaigns: Also bo stick. All together, these constitute Poor combat abilities.

Other Limitations: Priests of the god of Healing must wear a symbol indicating their calling whenever they appear in public. They may not ever deliberately take sentient life. (If they do, it constitutes a "betrayal of goals" from the "Priests and Punishment" section of the "Role-Playing" chapter.)

Spheres of Influence: Major Access to All, Creation, Divination, Healing, Necromantic, Protection, Summoning. Minor Access to Animal, Charm, Guardian, Plant, Sun, Weather.

Powers: *Immunity* (as per the Designing Faiths chapter) to all poisons and diseases, but the priest only gets a +2 to his saving throw. *Laying On of Hands* (same as the Paladin ability). *Soothing Word* (Designing Faiths chapter). *Turn Undead* (same as the Cleric ability). *At 3rd Level: Analysis, Identification* (as per the Designing Faiths chapter) of diseases and poisons; on a Intelligence check (which the DM may modify according to the commonness or rarity of the ailment), the priest will know what sort of disease or poison afflicts his patient.

Followers and Strongholds: The followers are received at 7th level, and consist of three third-level priests and six first-level priests of the same priesthood, plus thirty Normal Men and Women, all of whom must have the Healing nonweapon proficiency, who act as chirurgeons (doctors) and nurses. The priest may take the following on adventures: Two priests (only one of whom may be third-level) and two Normal Men and Women. The priesthood will pay for half of the cost of stronghold construction at 7th level. The stronghold must act as a hospital for the nearest community, and may turn away no patient who has suffered a life-threatening injury or disease.

Possible Symbols: Snakes, Staff.

Notes: Priests of this order are supposed to use nondamaging weapons. However, since the staff is their symbol, many of them end up learning how to use one as a weapon, and the god gives his assent to this knowledge by not punishing them for using the staff in a damaging way.

Hunting

This god is a patron of the hunter, and is a provider of foods and furs; thus he is a god much loved of woodsmen. Though he hunts animals and encourages his flock to do likewise, he is usually a wise hunter; like the god of Animals, he is often a patron of animals and their protector from needless destruction at the hands of too-greedy hunters and poachers.

The god's priests, too, are hunters, and their mission is to teach the flock sound principles of hunting: Not killing mothers with young, not depopulating the wilderness of whole species, etc.

An alternate aspect of the god would be a god of Fishing.

The god of hunting is as likely to be male as female.

The priests of this god are on good terms with the priests of Animals, Darkness/Night, Light, Moon, and Sun.

Alignment: The deity is true neutral. The priests may be true neutral or neutral good; most are true neutral. The flock may be of any alignment.

Minimum Ability Scores: Wisdom 10, Dexterity 12. Wisdom or Dexterity 16 means +5% experience; Wisdom *and* Dexterity 16 means +10% experience.

Races Allowed: Elves, gnomes, half-elves, halflings, humans.

Nonweapon and Weapon Proficiencies: Nonweapon Proficiencies Required: Hunting. Nonweapon Proficiencies Recommended: Direction Sense, Fishing, Reading/Writing, Religion, Animal Lore, Mountaineering, Running, Set Snares, Survival, Tracking. Weapon Proficiencies Required: Bow. Nonweapon Proficiency Group Crossovers: Priest, General, Warrior.

Duties of the Priest: Guidance, Marriage.

Weapon and Armor Restrictions: Weapons Permitted: Blowgun, bows (all), crossbow, harpoon, javelin, lasso, net, sling, spear, trident. Armor Permitted: All non-metal armor; no shields. Oriental Campaigns: Also daikyu. All together, these constitute Medium combat abilities.

Other Limitations: None.

Spheres of Influence: Major Access to All, Divination, Guardian, Protection, Summoning. Minor Access to Animal, Healing, Plant, Weather.

Powers: Permanent +2 to hit with bows, above and beyond all other bonuses.

Followers and Strongholds: The followers are received at 9th level, and consist of one third-level priest and two first-level priests of the same priesthood, plus one fifth-level ranger, three third-level rangers, and six first-level rangers to act as "forest rangers," and ten Normal Men and Women, all of whom have the Veterinarian nonweapon proficiency. (This proficiency doesn't appear in the *Player's Handbook*. It is identical to the Healing proficiency, except it can only be used to heal animals and monsters.) The priest may take the following on adventures: One priest and two rangers of his choice. The priesthood will pay for half of the cost of stronghold construction at 9th level. The stronghold can be built in a city or in the wilderness, but *must* work principally to protect the animal-life of the surrounding wilderness. (This does not mean to stop hunters if the hunting is carried out at a level that does not threaten the animal population. But any factor which does endanger animal species — such as drought, excess hunting, deforestation, etc. — will bring on the wrath of the priesthood.)

Possible Symbols: Bow and arrow crossed.

Notes: The harpoon and trident may only be used by priests whose god includes attributes of the sea or fishing. If the god is devoted to land-hunting, the priests cannot use the harpoon or trident.

Justice, Revenge

This god brings revenge on those who deserve it, rights wrongs, punishes the wicked, and avenges those who cannot avenge themselves.

Normally, the god acts through his priests. Priests of this god are approached by those who have been wronged, and must learn what they can of the situation, decide who's right and who's wrong, and take steps to punish the guilty party. They must make the punishment fit the crime (a theft does not warrant the killing of the thief in most cases, for instance).

Since these priests are often approached to punish those whom ordinary laws can't touch (for instance, to punish a rich man who can bribe his way out of any charge or punishment), they frequently have to perform their missions secretly, so that the local authorities cannot learn of them. These vigilante priests are not appreciated by local governments.

Lesser gods of this attribute could be devoted to only one kind of crime or revenge. One might be the god of the Revenge of Spurned Lovers. One might be a god of Lawful Trials, and must always go through the legal system. One might be the god who punishes those who forswear themselves, and another a god who punishes those who kill their own kin.

The deity of revenge is more likely to be female than male.

The priests of this god are on good terms with the priests of Competition, Death, Fire, and War. (Individual DMs might consider this priesthood to belong to Good or Evil camps. But Good sects consider this one to be too "tainted" to be truly good, while Evil sects don't like the fact that this sect punishes the wicked.) The priests of this god dislike the priests of Peace.

Alignment: The deity is lawful neutral. His priests may be of any alignment but lawful good. The flock may be of any alignment.

Minimum Ability Scores: Wisdom 12, Strength 12. Wisdom or Strength 16 means +5% experience; Wisdom *and* Strength 16 means +10% experience.

Races Allowed: Dwarves, elves, gnomes, half-elves, humans.

Nonweapon and Weapon Proficiencies: Nonweapon Proficiencies Required: Tracking. Nonweapon Proficiencies Recommended: Reading/Writing, Religion. Weapon Proficiencies Required: None. Nonweapon Proficiency Group Crossovers: Priest, General, Warrior.

Duties of the Priest: Guidance, Marriage. Missions to achieve justice when justice has been thwarted. Vigilance: The priests must keep their ears open and keep track of those who try to avoid the consequences of their actions.

Weapon and Armor Restrictions: Weapons Permitted: Dagger/dirk, knife, lasso, scythe, sickle, spear, stiletto, sword/bastard, sword/khopesh, sword/long, sword/rapier, sword/sabre, sword/short. Armor Permitted: All armor and shields. Oriental Campaigns: Also katana, sai, wakizashi. All together, these constitute Good combat abilities.

Other Limitations: Priests of this god may not refuse to investigate when the story of an injustice is brought to them (unless they've already investigated this same complaint). To do so is to constitute a "betrayal of goals" from the "Priests and Punishment" section of the "Role-Playing" chapter. To investigate, find that there has been an injustice, and then to refuse to act on it is a similar betrayal. However, it is not a betrayal to discover an injustice and then take the time to make sure the priest has enough influence and force to effect revenge; he does not have to effect revenge *immediately.*

Spheres of Influence: Major Access to All, Divination, Necromantic. Minor Access to Elemental, Guardian.

Powers: The priest, even at first level, can cast the *detect lies* spell three times per day in addition to all other spells. *At 3rd Level: Inspire Fear* (as per the Designing Faiths chapter).

Followers and Strongholds: The followers are received at 9th level, and consist of three third-level priests and six first-level priests of the same order, plus one third-level fighter, one third-level mage, one third-level illusionist, one third-level thief, and one third-level bard who act as consultants. The priest may take the following on adventures: Three priests (only one of whom may be third-level), the fighter, the mage, the illusionist, the thief, and the bard. The priesthood will pay for half of the cost of stronghold construction at 9th level. In the construction of the stronghold, its builders must include a courtroom and an execution chamber or field (the method of execution is up to the priests).

Possible Symbols: Scales (of Justice); Headsman's Axe.

Life-Death-Rebirth Cycle (Force)

This cycle is most likely to exist in campaigns which *don't* have gods of birth, death, fertility and rebirth. In campaigns which do feature such gods, the forces of fertility and death are opposed, while in campaigns where this cycle is the primary force, fertility and death are part of the overall cycle. Therefore, if the DM has gods of death and fertility in his campaign, he may not have this cycle; if he has this cycle, he may not have those gods.

Followers of this force believe that living things are born, live, and die, and then reincarnate in a continuing cycle. Perhaps the cycle is endless; perhaps its purpose is to give the soul of the living thing enough experience that he can achieve a greater level of being.

In campaigns where this cycle does exist, it provides enough magical energy for its priests to cast spells. The priests' duties include education of the flock in the beliefs of the cycle, comforting the flock with the knowledge that death is merely a point in the cycle and not the end, and protection of the world from forces which might disrupt the cycle. Because undead beings have been removed or removed themselves from this natural cycle, the priests are their sworn enemies.

The priests of this force are on good terms with Druids and the priests of Agriculture, Animals, Death, Earth, Fertility, Nature, Seasons, Sky/Weather, and Vegetation.

Alignment: This force is true neutral in alignment; its priests must also be true neutral. The flock may be of any alignment.

Minimum Ability Scores: Wisdom 10. Wisdom 16 means +10% experience.

Races Allowed: Dwarves, elves, gnomes, half-elves, halflings, humans.

Nonweapon and Weapon Proficiencies: Nonweapon Proficiencies Required: Religion. Nonweapon Proficiencies Recommended: Herbalism, Reading/Writing, Animal Handling. Weapon Proficiencies Required: None. Nonweapon Proficiency Group Crossovers: Priest, General.

Duties of the Priest: Guidance, Marriage. These priests conduct ceremonies at summer and winter solstice, spring and autumn equinox, in celebration of the cycle. Vigilance against any beings who wish to tamper with this cycle (i.e., priests of the philosophy of evil, or, if appropriate, against mad gods of death who won't rest until everything is dead forever); vigilance against despoilers of nature.

Weapon and Armor Restrictions: Weapons Permitted: Dagger/dirk, knife, scythe, sickle. Armor Permitted: All non-metal armor; no shields. Oriental Campaigns: Also nunchaku. All together, these constitute Poor combat abilities.

Other Limitations: Priests of this sect may not eat animal flesh; they are vegetarian. To violate this limitation is a minor offense from the "Priests and Punishment" section of the "Role-Playing" chapter.

Spheres of Influence: Major Access to All, Divination, Healing, Necromantic (Special Note: These priests cannot use *resurrection* spell; they use *reincarnate* instead), Plant, Summoning, Weather. Minor Access to Animal, Charm, Creation, Elemental, Protection, Sun.

Powers: *Incite Berserker Rage* (as per the Designing Faiths chapter). *Turn Undead* (same as the Cleric ability).

Followers and Strongholds: The followers are received at 8th level, and consist of one fifth-level priest, three third-level priests, and sixteen first-level priests of the same order. The priest may take the following on adventures: Three priests of his choice. The priesthood will pay for half of the cost of stronghold construction at 8th level.

Possible Symbols: Unbroken circle; snake swallowing its tail.

Light

This is the god of all forms of light: Sunlight, moonlight, firelight, etc. The god is a friend of life, a patron of magic, a proponent of logical thought, and an enemy of the undead.

The priesthood of the god is devoted to celebrating these aspects of the god and to promoting positive forces such as healing.

Lesser gods of this attribute would be gods of one aspect of light. One god might be the god of Reason, another the god of Inspiration, etc.

This deity is as likely to be male as female.

The priests of this god are on

good terms with the priests of Arts, Crafts, Darkness/Night, Dawn, Elemental Forces, Fire, Healing, Hunting, Literature/Poetry, Magic, Metalwork, Moon, Music/Dance, Oracles/Prophecy, and Sun.

Alignment: The deity is neutral good. His priests may be of any good alignment. The flock may be of any neutral or good alignment.

Minimum Ability Scores: Wisdom 12, Intelligence 12. Wisdom or Intelligence 16 means +5% experience; Wisdom *and* Intelligence 16 means +10% experience.

Races Allowed: Elves, gnomes, half-elves, halflings, humans.

Nonweapon and Weapon Proficiencies: Nonweapon Proficiencies Required: Direction Sense. Nonweapon Proficiencies Recommended: Healing, Navigation, Reading/Writing, Religion, Spellcraft. Weapon Proficiencies Required: None. Nonweapon Proficiency Group Crossovers: Priest, General, Wizard.

Duties of the Priest: Guidance, Marriage. Vigilance against dark, evil forces such as undead.

Weapon and Armor Restrictions: Weapons Permitted: Bows (all), crossbow, dagger/dirk, dart, javelin, knife, sling, spear. Armor Permitted: All non-metal armor; no shields. Oriental Campaigns: Also daikyu, shuriken. All together, these constitute Medium combat abilities.

Other Limitations: None.

Spheres of Influence: Major Access to All, Charm, Divination, Healing, Sun. Minor Access to Animal, Creation, Necromantic, Plant.

Powers: *Infravision* (same as the elf ability; an elven or half-elven priest of this faith has Infravision of doubled range, to 120'). *Turn Undead* (same as the Cleric abil-

ity). *At 3rd Level: Laying On of Hands* (same as the Paladin ability). *At 5th level: Charm/ Fascination* (as per the Designing Faiths chapter). *At 9th level: Prophecy* (as per the Designing Faiths chapter).

Followers and Strongholds: The followers are received at 9th level, and consist of one fifth-level priest, three third-level priests, and six first-level priests of the same order, plus one third-level mage and two first-level mages to act as consultants and one third-level fighter and two first-level fighters to act as guards. The priest may take the following on adventures: Three priests (only one of whom can be third-level), one mage, and one fighter of his choice. The priesthood will pay for half of the cost of stronghold construction at 9th level.

Possible Symbols: Light-rays.

Notes: The weapons chosen for the sun-god's priest are all weapons which can be used at range, representing the god's ability to strike from afar with inspiration... or stroke.

Lightning

This is a bold, powerful, primitive god whose aspect is the thunderbolt. He represents the destructive power of the sky and is a favorite god of warriors. Because lightning sometimes hits trees and sets them ablaze, he has some minor associations with fire and trees (especially oaks). He is also a god of storms.

However, the god himself is little concerned with the doings of mortals; he has no objection to them worshipping him, and does grant some of his power to his priests, but otherwise does not meddle

much in mortal affairs.

His priests promote worship of the lightning-god for his power and his indomitability. They encourage worshippers to emulate the god and his strength.

The lightning-god is male.

The priests of this god are on good terms with the priests of Elemental Forces, Fire, Nature, Race (Dwarf), Sky/Weather, Strength, and (especially) Thunder.

Alignment: The deity is true neutral. The priests may be neutral evil, true neutral, or neutral good; evil priests have their own sect and the other priests don't have to tolerate them. The flock may be of any alignment.

Minimum Ability Scores: Wisdom 10, Strength 12. Wisdom or Strength 16 means +5% experience; Wisdom *and* Strength 16 means +10% experience.

Races Allowed: Dwarves, half-elves, humans.

Nonweapon and Weapon Proficiencies: Nonweapon Proficiencies Required: Weather Sense. Nonweapon Proficiencies Recommended: Reading/Writing, Religion. Weapon Proficiencies Required: Warhammer *or* Hand/ Throwing Axe (player choice). Nonweapon Proficiency Group Crossovers: Priest, General, Warrior.

Duties of the Priest: Guidance, Marriage.

Weapon and Armor Restrictions: Weapons Permitted: Battle axe, dagger/dirk, dart, hand/ throwing axe, javelin, knife, spear, warhammer. Armor Permitted: All armor and shields. All together, these constitute Good combat abilities.

Other Limitations: None.

Spheres of Influence: Major Access to All, Elemental (the priest may only use the spells whose names include the words Air, Wind, Fire, Flame, Heat, Pyrotechnics, and the spell *chariot of Sustarre*), Weather. Minor Access to Divination, Plant.

Powers: The priest can cast a *call lightning* spell once per day, in addition to all other spells, even at 1st level (of course, at 1st level, the spell lasts only 1 turn and does 2d8 damage). *Inspire Fear* (as per the Designing Faiths chapter).

Followers and Strongholds: The followers are received at 8th level, and consist of three third-level priests and six first-level priests of the same priesthood, and one fifth-level warrior, two third-level warriors, and four first-level warriors. The priest may take the following on adventures: Three priests (only one of whom may be third-level) and two warriors of his choice. The priesthood will pay for half of the cost of stronghold construction at 8th level.

Possible Symbols: Bolt of Lightning; Double-Bitted (Battle) Axe.

Literature, Poetry

This god is very much like the deity of arts (see Arts, above), but concerns himself with reading, writing, recitation, the chronicling of history, and the teaching of youth. Lesser gods of this attribute would involve themselves with only one of the above aspects.

The god's priesthood is primarily interested in the education of the young in reading and writing, and the promotion and support of writers and poets in their culture.

The god of literature and poetry is as likely to be male as female.

The priests of this god are on good terms with the priests of Arts, Community, Crafts, Culture, Divinity of Mankind, Light, Metalwork, Music/Dance, Sun, and Wisdom.

Alignment: The deity is neutral good. Regardless of his alignment, his priests may be of any good alignment. The flock may be of any neutral or good alignment.

Minimum Ability Scores: Wisdom 10, Charisma 12. Wisdom or Charisma 16 means +5% experience; Wisdom *and* Charisma 16 means +10% experience.

Races Allowed: Elves, gnomes, half-elves, halflings, humans.

Nonweapon and Weapon Proficiencies: Nonweapon Proficiencies Required: Reading/Writing. Nonweapon Proficiencies Recommended: Artistic Ability (Composition), Religion. Weapon Proficiencies Required: None. Nonweapon Proficiency Group Crossovers: Priest, General.

Duties of the Priest: Guidance, Marriage. Education: These priests must encourage and support members of their flock (or of the general population) who show signs of talent with prose or poetry. Vigilance: Literature and Poetry often offend those who do not understand them or those who disagree with the attitudes expressed in those works of art, and so these priests must be vigilant against the very human forces of censorship and repression.

Weapon and Armor Restrictions: Weapons Permitted: Bows (all), dart. Armor Permitted: None; no shields. Oriental Campaigns: Also daikyu. All together, this constitutes Poor combat abilities.

Other Limitations: These priests receive six-sided dice for hit points, not eight-sided.

Spheres of Influence: Major Access to All, Charm, Creation, Divination, Protection, Summoning, Sun. Minor Access to Animal, Elemental, Guardian, Healing, Necromantic, Plant.

Powers: *Charm/Fascination* (as per the Designing Faiths chapter). *Language/Communication* (as per the Designing Faiths chapter): Every level from 1st to 8th, the priest receives one extra language which he may choose (if you prefer, he receives an extra nonweapon proficiency slot which may only be used for languages); the languages chosen may only be those of sentient humanoid races. *Soothing Word* (as per the Designing Faiths chapter).

Followers and Strongholds: The followers are received at 8th level, and consist of three third-level priests and six first-level priests of the same order, plus one third-level fighter and two first-level fighters to act as guards, and twenty Normal Men and Women, each of whom has either Reading/Writing or an appropriate Artistic Ability nonweapon proficiency. The priest may take the following on adventures: Three priests (only one of whom may be third-level), one fighter, and four Normal Men and Women of his choice. The priesthood will pay for half of the cost of stronghold construction at 8th level. The stronghold must act as a meeting-place for writers and poets to exchange ideas; therefore it must be built with meeting rooms or even lecture halls dedicated to these, instead of priestly, doings.

Possible Symbols: Books, Scrolls, Pens.

Love

This god is the patron of love in all its aspects: Romantic love, desire, affection, lust, infatuation, the love between husband and wife, the love shared between close friends, and so on.

Priests of the god of love are charged with promoting love whenever possible — especially by removing obstacles to it. When star-crossed youths wish to marry, priests of this sect interfere to convince their families of the rightness of it. When a marriage collapses under the weight of distrust or disinterest, the priests try to counsel the spouses into a reconciliation. When one of the faithful falls in love with someone who doesn't reciprocate that love, the priests use every means at their disposal (from trickery to *charm* spells) to make the disinterested party fall in love with the more devout character.

Lesser gods of this attribute will be gods of only one of the above aspects. One god might be the god of Desire, another the god of Romance, a third the god of Infatuations.

A god of all the aspects of love is likely to be female. A god of just one of the aspects is as likely to be male as female.

The priests of this god are on good terms with the priests of Birth/Children, Divinity of Mankind, Elemental Forces, Healing, Marriage, and Peace. The priests of this god dislike the priests of Evil.

Alignment: The deity is good; at the DM's discretion, he may be chaotic good, neutral good, or lawful good, but tends to be chaotic good. Regardless of his alignment, his priests may be of any good alignment. The flock may be of any neutral or good alignment.

Minimum Ability Scores: Wisdom 10, Charisma 13. Wisdom or Charisma 16 means +5% experience; Wisdom *and* Charisma 16 means +10% experience.

Races Allowed: Dwarves, elves, gnomes, half-elves, halflings, humans.

Nonweapon and Weapon Proficiencies: Nonweapon Proficiencies Required: Herbalism. Nonweapon Proficiencies Recommended: Reading/Writing, Religion, Dancing. Weapon Proficiencies Required: None. Nonweapon Proficiency Group Crossovers: Priest, General.

Duties of the Priest: Guidance, Marriage. Vigilance: Priests of this sect believe in marriages of love, not of convenience or politics, and so conspire to keep young lovers together when those lovers might be parted by their families' wishes or by the prejudices and responsibilities of their social classes.

Weapon and Armor Restrictions: Weapons Permitted: Bow (small), club, lasso, mancatcher, net. Armor Permitted: None; no shields. Oriental Campaigns: Also daikyu. All together, these constitute Poor combat abilities.

Other Limitations: Priests of this sect receive four-sided dice for hit points, not eight-sided. Also, unless (at DM's discretion) this god is a deity of pure and platonic relationships, a priest of this sect may be unmarried when he enters the priesthood (1st level) but must have been wed by the time he reaches 8th experience level — to do otherwise is to deny the god his due, and constitutes a betrayal of goals from the "Priests and Punishment" section of the "Role-Playing" chapter.

Spheres of Influence: Major Access to All, Animal, Charm, Healing, Necromantic, Protection, Summoning. Minor Access to Creation, Divination, Guardian, Plant, Sun, and Weather.

Powers: *Charm/Fascination* (as per the Designing Faiths chapter). *Incite Berserker Rage* (as per the Designing Faiths chapter). *Inspire Fear* (as per the Designing Faiths chapter). *Soothing Word* (as per the Designing Faiths chapter). *Turn Undead* (same as the Cleric ability).

Followers and Strongholds: The followers are received at 7th level, and consist of three third-level priests and six first-level priests of the same order, plus one third-level mage and two first-level mages who act as consultants, one third-level fighter and two first-level fighters who act as guards, and ten Normal Men and Women, each with a Nonweapon Proficiency which is of use to the temple's functions (Etiquette, Local History, and Reading/Writing especially). The priest may take the following on adventures: Three priests (only one of whom may be third-level), one mage, one fighter, and four Normal Men and Women of his choice. The priesthood will pay for half of the cost of stronghold construction at 7th level. The stronghold *must* act as a sanctuary for young lovers who come here fleeing the retribution of angry families. For this reason, these strongholds are often built with secret chambers and quarters for those who take sanctuary.

Possible Symbols: Girdle (the woman's belt of the ancient world, not the modern accoutrement).

Notes: The weapons chosen for this order were chosen based on the appearance of these weapons in stories about mythological love-gods, or because of their usefulness in capturing mates.

Magic

This god is the patron of magic in all its forms. At the DM's discretion, he could be the source of all magical energies used by the world's mages; or, he could just be the god responsible for teaching the most important spells and rituals to mortal mages. Either way, he is as beloved of mages as of any other class of characters.

Priests of this god, in addition to encouraging worship of the god, act as scholars of magic. They help preserve libraries of magical information and encourage correspondence and the exchange of ideas (and spells) between mages.

Every school of magic or priest sphere of influence could have its own, lesser god: There could be a god of Necromancy, a god of Enchantment, etc.

Gods of magic are as likely to be male as female.

The priests of this god are on good terms with the priests of Darkness/Night, Dawn, Elemental Forces, Fire, Healing, Light, Moon, Oracles/Prophecy, and Sun.

Alignment: The deity is true neutral. The priests may be neutral evil, true neutral, or neutral good; evil priests have their own sect and the other priests don't have to tolerate them. The flock may be of any alignment.

Minimum Ability Scores: Wisdom 12, Intelligence 13. Wisdom or Charisma 16 means +5% experience; Wisdom *and* Intelligence 16 means +10% experience.

Races Allowed: Elves, half-elves, humans.

Nonweapon and Weapon Proficiencies: Nonweapon Proficiencies Required: Spellcraft. Nonweapon Proficiencies Recommended: Reading/Writing, Religion, Ancient Languages. Weapon Proficiencies Required: None. Nonweapon Proficiency Group Crossovers: Priest, General, Wizard.

Duties of the Priest: Guidance, Marriage. Education: These priests cooperate with magicians to educate in the ways of magic.

Weapon and Armor Restrictions: Weapons Permitted: Belaying pin, dagger/dirk, dart, knife, quarterstaff, sling. Armor Permitted: None; no shields. Oriental Campaigns: Also shuriken. All together, these constitute Poor combat abilities.

Other Limitations: Priests of this sect receive four-sided dice for hit points, not eight-sided.

Spheres of Influence: Major Access to All, Astral, Charm, Divination, Elemental, Healing, Protection, Summoning. Minor Access to Animal, Guardian, Necromantic, Plant, Sun, Weather. This priesthood has an extra major access, which helps make up for its reduced hit points.

Powers: *Inspire Fear* (as per the Designing Faiths chapter). *Language/Communication* (as per the Designing Faiths chapter); from 1st level to 8th, the priest receives one extra language per level (or one extra nonweapon proficiency slot which may only be used for languages); the priest may choose the language of any sentient race known to him, or may choose to communicate with any animal species, with each of these choices. *Turn Undead* (same as the Cleric ability; if evil, Control Undead instead). *At 3rd level: Infravision* (same as the elf ability; an elven or half-elven priest of this faith has Infravision of doubled range, to 120'). *At 8th level: Shapechanging* (as per the Designing Faiths chapter).

Followers and Strongholds: The followers are received at 9th level, and consist of three third-level priests and six first-level priests of the same order, plus one fifth-level mage who acts as consultant, and one third-level fighter and seven first-level fighters to act as guards. The priest may take the following on adventures: Three priests (only one of whom may be third-level), one mage, and two fighters of his choice. The priesthood will pay for half of the cost of stronghold construction at 9th level.

Possible Symbols: Brazier, Book.

Notes: This priest is close in aspect to mages, so the weapons permitted him are similar to those permitted to mages.

Marriage

This god is a deity of the bond of matrimony. Whether marriage is considered to be a holy alliance or merely an important contract, this god represents marriage in all its aspects: Affection, love, jealousy, argument, home, children, development, and compromise.

The priesthood of this god promotes marriage as a way of life. They approve of lovers, but not lovers *staying* lovers without ever being wed. They act as "marriage counselors" for any couple who asks their help in working out marital problems.

The god of marriage is as likely to be male or female.

The priests of this god are on good terms with the priests of Birth/Children, Community, Culture, Love, and Race.

Alignment: The deity is neutral good. The priests may be any sort of good alignment. The flock may be of any neutral or good alignment.

Minimum Ability Scores: Wisdom 9. Wisdom 16 means +10% experience.

Races Allowed: Dwarves, elves, gnomes, half-elves, halflings, humans.

Nonweapon and Weapon Proficiencies: Nonweapon Proficiencies Required: Religion. Nonweapon Proficiencies Recommended: Local History, Reading/Writing. Weapon Proficiencies Required: None. Nonweapon Proficiency Group Crossovers: Priest, General.

Duties of the Priest: Guidance, Marriage.

Weapon and Armor Restrictions: Weapons Permitted: Club, lasso, mace, net, quarterstaff, warhammer. Armor Permitted: All non-magical armor, all non-magical shields. Oriental Campaigns: Also bo stick. All together, these constitute Medium combat abilities.

Other Limitations: Priests of this sect must be married by the time they are fourth level; otherwise they are guilty of betrayal of the god's goals, as described in the "Priests and Punishment" section of the "Role-Playing" chapter.

Spheres of Influence: Major Access to All, Charm, Divination, Healing, Protection. Minor Access to Combat, Elemental, Guardian, Sun.

Powers: *Laying On of Hands* (same as the Paladin ability). *Soothing Word* (Designing Faiths chapter). *Turn Undead* (same as the Cleric ability).

Followers and Strongholds: The followers are received at 8th level, and consist of one fifth-level priest, three third-level priests, and sixteen first-level priests of the same order. The priest may take the following on adventures: Three priests (only one of whom may be third-level) of his choice. The priesthood will pay for half of the cost of stronghold construction at 8th level. The stronghold must be built with a large hall or chapel where very large weddings may take place.

Possible Symbols: Finger-Ring, Short Length of Cord.

Notes: The weapons chosen for this order represent capturing, as in capturing one's mate, and weapons often used in the sudden defense of one's home.

Messengers

This god is the messenger of the gods. When the rulers of the gods want an order conveyed to lesser gods, it is given to this deity.

And so this god's priests are also messengers. They are trained in diplomacy and are often charged with the duty of conveying important messages (whether letters, verbal messages, codes, or threats) from one person to another... usually from one ruler or nobleman to another. The priests take great pride in their role as neutral conveyers of information, and for the reputation for accuracy and honesty they enjoy.

This god is also a favorite god of heralds, spies, and bards, all of whom have to perform messenger-duties at one time or another.

Messenger-gods are as likely to be male as female.

The priests of this god are on good terms with the priests of Community, Mischief/Trickery, Peace, Rulership, Trade, and War.

Alignment: The deity is true neutral. The priests may be true neutral or neutral good; most are true neutral. The flock may be of any alignment.

Minimum Ability Scores: Wisdom 12, Charisma 10. Wisdom or Charisma 16 means +5% experience; Wisdom *and* Charisma 16 means +10% experience.

Races Allowed: Dwarves, elves, gnomes, half-elves, halflings, humans.

Nonweapon and Weapon Proficiencies: Nonweapon Proficiencies Required: Reading/Writing. Nonweapon Proficiencies Recommended: Etiquette, Heraldry, Modern Languages, Navigation, Religion. Weapon Proficiencies Required: None. Nonweapon Proficiency Group Crossovers: Priest, General.

Duties of the Priest: Guidance, Marriage. Missions: These priests are often asked by rulers and required by their temples to go on missions of communication, where they are supposed to convey important letters or verbal messages to others. Often, they are asked to act as negotiators between two warring groups or nations.

Weapon and Armor Restrictions: Weapons Permitted: Club, javelin, mace, maul, polearm, quarterstaff, spear, trident. Armor Permitted: All non-metal armor and all shields. Oriental Campaigns: Also bo stick, sai. All together, these constitute Medium combat abilities.

Other Limitations: None.

Spheres of Influence: Major Access to All, Charm, Divination, Protection, Sun. Minor Access to Elemental, Guardian, Necromantic, Plant.

Powers: *Language/Communication* (as per the Designing Faiths chapter): From 1st level to 8th, each level the priest receives crafted goods as to their gold piece one additional language (or a nonweapon proficiency slot which may only be used for languages); the language chosen must be of a sentient humanoid race. *Soothing Word* (as per the Designing Faiths chapter). At 8th level: *Charm/Fascination* (as per the Designing Faiths chapter).

Followers and Strongholds: The followers are received at 8th level, and consist of five third-level priests and five first-level priests of the same order (most act as messengers, too), one third-level bard and one third-level thief (who act as factfinders and agents), and eight Normal Men and Women, all of whom have the Reading/Writing nonweapon proficiency. The priest may take the following on adventures: Two priests, the bard, the thief, and two Normal Men and Women of his choice. The priesthood will pay for half of the cost of stronghold construction at 8th level. The stronghold must be built with a large library, where the accumulated correspondence and diplomatic writing of the order accumulates.

Possible Symbols: Winged Creatures, Wings.

Notes: When on duty, priests of this order must always carry sceptres, staves, poles, or banners/flags on poles indicating their status. When carrying messages in their official capacity, these priests carry no obvious weapons at all. However, they can use a sceptre as a club and a staff or pole as a quarterstaff if they are attacked.

Metalwork

This god is the forger of weapons and armor, and also the craftsman of gold and silver treasures. He is worshipped by metal-craftsmen across the world, and sometimes visits inspirations for beautiful metal goods upon lucky craftsmen.

The priests of the god try to advance the art of metalwork at the mortal level. They do this by acquiring as much information as they can about smithcrafting and other metalwork, collecting it in libraries, and distributing it to students and metalworking apprentices.

Lesser gods of this attribute will be gods of specific types of metalworking. One might be the god of armoring, another the god of swordmaking.

The god of metalworking is male.

The priests of this god are on good terms with the priests of Arts, Crafts, Divinity of Mankind, Fire, Literature/Poetry, Music/Dance, Race (Dwarf), Strength, and War.

Alignment: The deity is good; at the DM's discretion, he may be chaotic good, neutral good, or lawful good, but tends to be neutral good. Regardless of his alignment, his priests may be of any good alignment. The flock may be of any neutral or good alignment.

Minimum Ability Scores: Wisdom 10, Constitution 12. Wisdom or Constitution 16 means +5% experience; Wisdom *and* Constitution 16 means +10% experience.

Races Allowed: Dwarves, elves, gnomes, half-elves, halflings, humans.

Nonweapon and Weapon Proficiencies: Nonweapon Proficiencies Required: Any one from the following list — Artistic Ability (Jewelwright, Goldsmith, Silversmith), Blacksmithing, Armorer, Weaponsmithing. Nonweapon Proficiencies Recommended: Any of the others from the above list, plus Fire-building, Reading/Writing, Religion. Weapon Profi-

ciencies Required: Warhammer. Nonweapon Proficiency Group Crossovers: Priest, General, Warrior.

Duties of the Priest: Guidance, Marriage. Education: Teaching of metalworking to the flock; promotion of weaponmaking, armormaking, goldsmithing, jewelrymaking, and all other sorts of metalwork in the community and society. Must participate in semiannual events where metal goods of all sorts are displayed and promoted (before the throne or in market). Investigation: These priests seek to re-discover lost metalwork techniques; this often leads them into ancient sites on expeditions of discovery. These priests also encourage competitive thinking between guilds, or between the metalworkers of different cities.

Weapon and Armor Restrictions: Weapons Permitted: Club, mace, maul, morning star, warhammer, whip. Armor Permitted: All metal armor; all shields. All together, these constitute Good combat abilities.

Other Limitations: None.

Spheres of Influence: Major Access to All, Elemental (the priest may only use the spells whose names include the words Fire, Flame, Heat, Pyrotechnics, and the spell *chariot of Sustarre*), Sun. Minor Access to Combat, Divination.

Powers: *Analysis* (as per the Designing Faiths chapter) of workmanship quality in metal goods. The priest will be able to tell whether a metal craft-good is of poor, average or superior quality. This gives him a +2 to his Appraising proficiency check if he has that nonweapon proficiency, but does not give him the ability to rate per the Designing Faiths chapter).

value of he does not have that nonweapon proficiency. *Defiance of Restriction/Obstacle* (as per the Designing Faiths chapter): The priest can pass unharmed through the *wall of fire* spell. *Inspire Fear* (as per the Designing Faiths chapter). Permanent +2 to hit and damage with Warhammer, above and beyond all other bonuses.

Followers and Strongholds: The followers are received at 7th level, and consist of two third-level priest and four first-level priests of the same order, one third-level fighter and seven first-level fighters to act as temple guards, and twenty Normal Men and Women, each of whom has an appropriate and helpful nonweapon proficiency (especially Blacksmithing, Fire-building, Mining, and Reading/Writing). The priest may take the following on adventures: One priest, one fighter, and four Normal Men and Women of his choice. The priesthood will pay for half of the cost of stronghold construction at 7th level. The stronghold must be built with numerous smithies and workshops, enough at least for the priests who do metalwork, as well as the temple's Normal Men and Women.

Possible Symbols: Anvil, Hammer.

Mischief, Trickery

This god delights in trickery for trickery's sake. He loves fooling people, animals, other gods — to show them how much more clever he is, just to see the looks on their faces, for just about any reason.

Naturally, this god is the favorite of rogues, especially thieves. But don't think that he's a god of cowards: To pull off the best tricks and plots, his followers must be brave indeed. However, many cowardly rogues do worship this god anyway, in admiration of his ability to get out of rough spots without resorting to combat.

His priests, in addition to extolling this god's virtues, also love demonstrating cleverness. Some perform harmless pranks for comic relief. Others become polished military tacticians for armies. Others learn nonweapon proficiencies that let them become proficient trapsters or stage magicians.

To be a priest of this god, a character does not have to be nasty or mean to others. The priest might demonstrate his cleverness through sleight of hand or by executing clever plots that straighten out problems rather than cause them. On the other hand, some priests of this god are just sly troublemakers who create problems for everyone. That's a choice left to the player of this type of priest.

The god of mischief is male.

The priests of this god are on good terms with the priests of Fortune/Luck, Messengers, Race (Gnome), Race (Halfling), Trade, War, and Wisdom. Priests of this god are sometimes allies of the priests of the philosophy of Evil; this decision is up to the DM, based on how he perceives his campaign world. The priests of this god dislike the priests of Strength.

Alignment: The deity is chaotic neutral. The priests may be chaotic evil, chaotic neutral, chaotic good, neutral evil, neutral, or neutral good; evil priests have their own sect and the other priests don't have to tolerate them. The flock may be of any alignment.

Minimum Ability Scores: Wisdom 12, Intelligence 12. Wisdom or Intelligence 16 means +5% experience; Wisdom *and* Intelligence 16 means +10% experience.

Races Allowed: Dwarves, elves, gnomes, half-elves, halflings, humans.

Nonweapon and Weapon Proficiencies: Nonweapon Proficiencies Required: Disguise. Nonweapon Proficiencies Recommended: Dancing, Etiquette, Modern Languages, Reading/Writing, Religion, Forgery, Reading Lips, Set Snares, Ventriloquism. Weapon Proficiencies Required: None. Nonweapon Proficiency Group Crossovers: Priest, General, Rogue.

Duties of the Priest: Guidance, Marriage, Missions: Priests often choose to go on adventures where they will have the opportunity to participate in some great plot or caper; it can be a deadly serious mission, so long as the priest gets to be involved in intricate planning and clever tactics. Vigilance against forces (mostly of society) that make people too responsible too young, that mature them too quickly.

Weapon and Armor Restrictions: Weapons Permitted: Blowgun, bows (all), crossbow, dagger/dirk, javelin, knife, lasso, net, quarterstaff, spear, stiletto, sword/bastard, sword/long, sword/rapier, sword/sabre, sword/short. Armor Permitted: All non-magical non-metal armor; no shields. Oriental Campaigns: Also bo stick, chain, daikyu, sai, shuriken, wakizashi. All together, these constitute Medium combat abilities.

Other Limitations: None.

Spheres of Influence: Major Access to Charm, Divination, Protection, Summoning. Minor Access to Animal, Elemental, Guardian, Plant.

Powers: *Charm/Fascination* (as

Detect Secret Doors (same as Elf ability: Success on roll of 1 on 1d6 when passing within 10', 1-2 on 1d6 to find secret doors and 1-3 on 1d6 to find concealed portals when actively searching; elven priests of this order have success on a roll of 1-2 when passing within 10', 1-3 to find secret doors and 1-4 to find concealed portals when actively searching). *At 8th level: Shape-changing* (as per the Designing Faiths chapter; DM chooses the three animal forms, or can allow the player to make the choice).

Followers and Strongholds: The followers are received at 9th level, and consist of one third-level priest and seven first-level priests of the same order, one fifth-level thief and one fifth-level bard (who act as assistant mischief-makers and accompany the priest everywhere), and one third-level fighter and seven first-level fighters who act as guards. The priest may take the following on adventures: One priest, the thief, the bard, and one fighter of his choice. The priesthood will pay for half of the cost of stronghold construction at 9th level.

Possible Symbols: Fox.

Moon

This deity is a god of inspiration, magic, and mystery, and is closely related to the god of Darkness (see above).

His priests celebrate the magics and light granted by the moon.

In a fantasy setting, there could be numerous gods of the moon... one for each of several moons the planet possesses.

Most moon-gods are female.

The priests of this god are on good terms with the priests of Darkness/Night, Dawn, Hunting, Light, Magic, Oracles/Prophecy, and Sun.

Alignment: The deity is true neutral. The priests may be neutral evil, true neutral, or neutral good; evil priests have their own sect and the other priests don't have to tolerate them. The flock may be of any alignment.

Minimum Ability Scores: Wisdom 10. Wisdom 16 means +10% experience.

Races Allowed: Elves, gnomes, half-elves, halflings, humans.

Nonweapon and Weapon Proficiencies: Nonweapon Proficiencies Required: Navigation. Nonweapon Proficiencies Recommended: Astrology, Reading/Writing, Religion, Spellcraft. Weapon Proficiencies Required: Nonweapon Proficiency Group Crossovers: Priest, General.

Duties of the Priest: Guidance, Marriage. Education: These priests help in the promotion and teaching of magic. These priests must participate in celebrations of the god, which take place once each moon (different temples may celebrate on the full moon or the new moon, at the DM's option).

Weapon and Armor Restrictions: Weapons Permitted: Bows (all), dagger/dirk, dart, javelin, knife, sling, spear. Armor Permitted: All non-metal armor; any shield that is circular or crescent-shaped. Oriental Campaigns: Also daikyu, katana, shuriken. All together, these constitute Medium combat abilities.

Other Limitations: None.

Spheres of Influence: Major Access to All, Charm, Divination, Summoning, Sun. Minor Access to Animal, Elemental, Healing, Necromantic.

Powers: *Charm/Fascination* (as per the Designing Faiths chapter).

Infravision (same as the elf ability; an elven or half-elven priest of this faith has Infravision of doubled range, to 120'). *At 5th level: Inspire Fear* (as per the Designing Faiths chapter). *At 10th level, chariot of Sustarre*; the priest can use this spell once per day in addition to his other spells.

Followers and Strongholds: The followers are received at 9th level, and consist of one fifth-level priest, three third-level priests, and six first-level priests of the same order, one third-level mage and two first-level mages who act as consultants, and one third-level fighter and two first-level fighters who act as guards. The priest may take the following on adventures: Two priests, one mage, and one fighter of his choice. The priesthood will pay for half of the cost of stronghold construction at 9th level.

Possible Symbols: Chariot, Moon (in any phase but new).

Notes: The bow, chosen as the weapon for this order, represents the inspiration of light-shafts.

Music, Dance

This god represents the performing arts — vocal and instrumental music, traditional and interpretive dance, even stage tragedy and comedy. He is closely related to the gods of arts and of literature/poetry, and is the favorite god of bards.

His priests are devoted to the advancement of music and dance in the population. They organize events where music is played, dances are performed, and plays are enacted. Sometimes they tour as part of theatrical companies, among bards and other performers. Their quest is to bring light to others through the performing arts.

Lesser gods of this attribute concentrate on only one of his aspects. One god might be the deity of vocal music, another the deity of wild, frantic dances, another the god of ballet.

A god who encompasses all the aspects of music and dance is probably going to be male. Gods of individual aspects are more likely to be female.

The priests of this god are on good terms with the priests of Arts, Community, Crafts, Culture, Divinity of Mankind, Light, Literature/Poetry, Metalwork, and Sun.

Alignment: The deity is good; at the DM's discretion, he may be chaotic good, neutral good, or lawful good, but tends to be neutral good. Regardless of his alignment, his priests may be of any good alignment. The flock may be of any neutral or good alignment.

Minimum Ability Scores: Wisdom 12 and *either* Charisma or Dexterity 14. If Wisdom or second ability is 16, character gets +5% experience. If Wisdom *and* second ability are both 16, character gets +10% experience.

Races Allowed: Dwarves, elves, gnomes, half-elves, halflings, humans.

Nonweapon and Weapon Proficiencies: Nonweapon Proficiencies Required: Any one from the following list — Dancing, Singing, Musical Instrument. Nonweapon Proficiencies Recommended: Any of the others from the list above, plus Artistic Ability/Composition, Ancient History, Local History, Reading/Writing, Religion, Juggling, Jumping, Tumbling. Weapon Proficiencies Required: None. Nonweapon Proficiency

Group Crossovers: Priest, General, Rogue.

Duties of the Priest: Guidance, Marriage. Education: These priests must encourage and support members of their flock (or the general population) who show signs of talent with dance or music.

Weapon and Armor Restrictions: Weapons Permitted: Dagger/dirk, javelin, knife, lasso, quarterstaff, spear, stiletto, sword/long, sword/rapier, sword/sabre. Armor Permitted: None; no shields. Oriental Campaigns: Also bo stick, chain, katana. All together, these constitute Medium combat abilities.

Other Limitations: Priests of this sect receive six-sided dice for hit points, not eight-sided.

Spheres of Influence: Major Access to All, Animal, Charm, Summoning, Sun. Minor Access to Divination, Elemental, Healing, Plant.

Powers: *Charm/Fascination* (as per the Designing Faiths chapter). *Soothing Word* (as per the Designing Faiths chapter, but at 5th level can use the power six times per day instead of three). *Turn Undead* (same as the Cleric ability).

Followers and Strongholds: The followers are received at 7th level, and consist of three third-level priests and six first-level priests of the same order, plus five first-level fighters to act as temple guards and twenty Normal Men and Women, each of whom has a Nonweapon Proficiency appropriate to the temple (Artistic Ability, Dancing, Singing, Musical Instrument). The priest may take the following on adventures: Three priests (only one of whom may be third-level), two fighters, four Normal Men and Women. The priesthood will pay for half of the cost of

stronghold construction at 7th level. One of the elements of the stronghold must be a hall, including a stage, where musicians and dancers from the surrounding area may congregate to practice their arts.

Possible Symbols: Any musical instrument.

Notes: The weapons permitted to this priesthood are the weapons best suited to inclusion in dances.

Nature

This deity is related to the gods of agriculture and fertility. He's most similar to the gods of the Earth, but is less concerned with earthly powers (like volcanoes) and more with weather and its effects on all living things.

The priesthood teaches the population to worship the deity of nature, and to fear him. It stresses the fact that man is a small, insignificant thing next to the grandeur of nature and must recognize that the sentient species are just elements, ingredients, of nature. This philosophy doesn't sit well with most of the sentient species, except the elves, who are in accord with it.

Nature-gods may be male or female.

The priests of this god are on good terms with Druids and the priests of Agriculture, Animals, Death, Earth, Fertility, Life-Death-Rebirth Cycle, Lightning, Race (Elf), Seasons, Sky/Weather, Thunder, and Vegetation.

Alignment: The deity is true neutral. The priests may be true neutral or neutral good; most are true neutral. The flock may be of any alignment.

Minimum Ability Scores: Wisdom 9. Wisdom 16 means +10% experience.

Races Allowed: Dwarves, elves, gnomes, half-elves, halflings, humans.

Nonweapon and Weapon Proficiencies: Nonweapon Proficiencies Required: Agriculture. Nonweapon Proficiencies Recommended: Animal Handling, Firebuilding, Fishing, Weather Sense, Healing, Herbalism, Reading/Writing, Religion. Weapon Proficiencies Required: None. Nonweapon Proficiency Group Crossovers: Priest, General.

Duties of the Priest: Guidance, Marriage. Vigilance against any forces, gods, or mortals that threaten nature: If a god of fire has gotten too happy and is burning up great tracts of plain or forest during an overlong summer, if a mortal civilization is destroying wilderness by exploiting it or expanding into it, priests of the god of nature are commanded (by their temple or by their god) to go forth and do something about it.

Weapon and Armor Restrictions: Weapons Permitted: Club, scythe, sickle. Armor Permitted: All armor and shields. Oriental Campaigns: Also nunchaku. All together, these constitute Medium combat abilities.

Other Limitations: Temples operated by these priests must be built outside city walls. Such priests can sleep within city walls (especially when travelling, when the city is under siege, etc.), but his permanent residence must be outside the city limits. To have permanent residence elsewhere is a minor offense, as described in the "Role-Playing" chapter under "Priests and Punishment."

Spheres of Influence: Major Access to All, Animal, Elemental, Plant, Protection. Minor Access to Divination, Healing, Sun, Weather.

Powers: *Analysis, Identification* (as per the Designing Faiths chapter): The priest has no special detection powers, but when he sees a plant or animal he can identify its species and whether or not it is normal for this area. He can only identify non-magical animals and plants; those with any magical powers, including breath weapons, are beyond his power. *Turn Undead* (same as the Cleric ability). *At 5th level: Inspire Fear* (as per the Designing Faiths chapter). *At 8th level: Shapechanging* (as per the Designing Faiths chapter); the DM can decide whether the priest can turn into one animal or three, and what species he may turn into. He may opt to let the player make that choice.

Followers and Strongholds: The followers are received at 8th level, and consist of one fifth-level priest, three third-level priests, and six first-level priests of the same order, plus two third-level rangers and four first-level rangers to act as guards. The priest may take the following on adventures: Two priests and two rangers of his choice. The priesthood will pay for half of the cost of stronghold construction at 8th level.

Possible Symbols: Mistletoe.

Oceans, Rivers

This god is a god of large bodies of water. He doesn't concern himself much with mortal doings; sailors pray to him for mercy, and he shows them mercy when he feels like it, and shows them death when he prefers. He is also a storm-god, the deity of storms upon the sea, and sailors fear him.

His priests pray to him for good winds and good harvests of the sea, and make sacrifices to him to keep him happy and calm. They also use their powers to save the creatures of the sea, especially creatures such as mermen and dolphins, from needless death at the hands of overzealous fishermen. They are also great explorers of the sea, and when a priest of the ocean-god decides to hide from other men, only another priest of the same order or an experienced mage can find him in his underwater haven.

Lesser gods will be gods of individual rivers, lakes, and seas. In some lands, each of the continent's thousands of rivers will be the domain of a lesser god or goddess.

Sea-gods are just as likely to be male as female.

The priests of this god are on good terms with the priests of Animals (aquatic animals only) and Sky/Weather.

Alignment: The deity is true neutral. The priests may be true neutral or neutral good; most are true neutral. The flock may be of any alignment.

Minimum Ability Scores: Wisdom 9. Wisdom 16 means +10% experience.

Races Allowed: Elves, gnomes, half-elves, halflings, humans.

Nonweapon and Weapon Proficiencies: Nonweapon Proficiencies Required: Swimming. Nonweapon Proficiencies Recommended: Fishing, Rope Use, Seamanship, Weather Sense, Navigation, Reading/Writing, Religion. Weapon Proficiencies Required: None. Nonweapon Proficiency Group Crossovers: Priest, General.

Duties of the Priest: Guidance, Marriage.

Weapon and Armor Restric-

tions: Weapons Permitted: Belaying pin, bill, harpoon, javelin, net, scourge, spear, sword/cutlass, trident. Armor Permitted: None; all shields permitted. All together, these constitute Medium combat abilities.

Other Limitations: None.

Spheres of Influence: Major Access to All, Animal, Divination, Elemental, Weather. Minor Access to Charm, Combat, Plant, Protection. Special Notes: Within his Animal sphere, the priest can only cast spells dealing with sea animals; he can only make friends with, become invisible to, charm, speak with, hold, or summon sea-life, and cannot use the insect-related spells at all. Within his Elemental sphere, the priest can only use spells with the word "water" in the name; he can also use the *earthquake* and *transmute rock to mud* spells; additionally, he can take a spell identical to the 6th-level *conjure fire elemental* spell which conjures water elementals instead.

Powers: The priest can cast the *water breathing* spell on himself only, once per day, in addition to all other spells; at eighth level, the duration of the spell when cast on himself becomes 24 hours, and he is then able to cast an extra *water breathing* on others (as per the normal rules for the spell) in addition to all other spells; the *water breathing* spell he casts on himself may not be *dispelled*, and at 8th level automatically renews itself at the end of the 24-hour period if the priest is still underwater and asleep, unconscious, etc. *Determine approximate depth underwater* on 1-4 on 1d6 (similar to the Dwarf ability concerning depth underground). *Infravision* (same as the elf ability, but only works underwater; an elven or half-elven priest of this faith has

Infravision of doubled range, to 120′, only underwater). *At 5th level: Language/Communication* (as per the Designing Faiths chapter); from 5th to 8th levels, the priest receives one extra language or communication (or nonweapon proficiency slot usable only for languages) which can only be taken for aquatic beings (aquatic elves, porpoises, mermen, etc.). *At 8th level: Shapechanging* (as per the Designing Faiths chapter); the DM may choose for this to be one animal or three, and which animals it is (or can give those choices to the player), but they must be marine animals.

Followers and Strongholds: The followers are received at 8th level, and consist of one fifth-level priest, three third-level priests, and six first-level priests from the same order, plus five mermen and mermaids (total). (The DM may substitute any other intelligent aquatic race, as appropriate, anywhere from 5 to 10 total HD of them: aquatic elves, water-nymphs, etc.) The priest may take the following on adventures: Two priests of his choice. On water-borne adventures, he can take three of the mermen and mermaids (or up to 6 HD of the substituted aquatic races). The priesthood will pay for half of the cost of stronghold construction at 8th level.

Possible Symbols: Dolphin, Fish, Octopus, Trident, Ship, Wave.

Notes: The weapons usable by this priesthood are the weapons of sailors and sea-gods.

Oracles, Prophecy

This is a god who delivers broad statements about the future to his followers. He's distinct from the god

of Fate/Destiny in that he doesn't preach a doctrine of acceptance; he just passes on the visions he has of the future, and lets his followers and those who beg his visions act on them accordingly.

Priests of this god act as intermediaries between the oracular god and visitors who come to receive his prophecies. See the paragraph below on **Followers and Strongholds** for more on this.

The oracular god is as likely to be male as female.

The priests of this god are on good terms with the priests of Darkness/Night, Dawn, Fate/Destiny, Light, Magic, Moon, Sun, and Wisdom.

Alignment: The deity is true neutral. The priests may be true neutral or neutral good; most are true neutral. The flock may be of any alignment.

Minimum Ability Scores: Wisdom 9, Charisma 11. Wisdom or Charisma 16 means +5% experience; Wisdom *and* Charisma 16 means +10% experience.

Races Allowed: Dwarves, elves, gnomes, half-elves, halflings, humans.

Nonweapon and Weapon Proficiencies: Nonweapon Proficiencies Required: Astrology. Nonweapon Proficiencies Recommended: Ancient History, Ancient Languages, Local History, Reading/Writing, Religion. Weapon Proficiencies Required: None. Nonweapon Proficiency Group Crossovers: Priest, General.

Duties of the Priest: Guidance, Marriage, Omen-Reading. Missions: Having passed on a prophecy, the priest may choose to accompany those who received the prophecy. The priest may just want to see how reality matches the vision he received; however, if the prophecy included options, visions of different ways the situation could resolve itself, the priest may be tagging along to help the preferred outcome take place.

Weapon and Armor Restrictions: Weapons Permitted: Choose two from the following list (DM chooses based on other attributes or characteristics of the oracular god): Bows (all), crossbow, dagger/dirk, dart, hand/throwing axe, harpoon, javelin, knife, lasso, net, sling, spear, staff sling, stiletto, whip. Armor Permitted: None; no shields. Oriental Campaigns: Also included among choices are daikyu, shuriken. All together, these constitute Poor combat abilities.

Other Limitations: None.

Spheres of Influence: Major Access to All, Divination, Elemental, Healing, Summoning. Minor Access to Charm, Creation, Necromantic, Sun.

Powers: *Language/Communication* (as per the Designing Faiths chapter); from 1st level to 8th, the priest receives one extra language per level (or one extra nonweapon proficiency slot which may only be used for taking languages); these languages may only be those of sentient humanoids. *Prophecy* (as per the Designing Faiths chapter).

Followers and Strongholds: The followers are received at 9th level, and consist of one fifth-level priest, three third-level priests, and six first-level priests of the same order, plus five second-level fighters who act as guards. The priest may take the following on adventures: Three priests (not including the fifth-level priest, and may only include one third-level priest) and two fighters of his choice. The priesthood will pay for

half of the cost of stronghold construction at 9th level. Part of the stronghold must be an oracular chamber or area where visitors may meet with the priests and receive oracles; the temple may charge a fee of money or goods for this service, so the stronghold must also have large, commodious storerooms for these goods.

Possible Symbols: Bow, Brazier.

Peace

This god is devoted to the cause of peace. He prefers for all conflicts to be settled non-violently.

His priests, in turn, work to keep things peaceful. They intercede between nations which are on the brink of war. They suggest compromises and nonviolent ways of settling important issues. They do their best to keep things calm and civil.

Remember, though, when roleplaying such priests, that they don't have to be played as stupid. Nor do they have to presume that *every* fight can be avoided; when it's obvious that a situation will descend into violence regardless of their best efforts, they don't have to continually badger other players into not fighting. They *do* have to try to preserve peace when it *can* be preserved, and to prevent unnecessary violence when possible. A player who takes a peace-priest character would do well to become party spokesman; this will allow him to do all the party's negotiations and thus head off combat situations on a more frequent voice.

A god of peace is as likely to be male as female.

The priests of this god are on good terms with the priests of

Community, Competition, Good, Healing, Love, Messengers, Prosperity, Race (Halfling), and Rulership/Kingship. The priests of this god dislike the priests of Justice/Revenge and War.

Alignment: The deity is lawful good. The priests may only be lawful good. The flock may not be chaotic or evil, but may be of any alignment not including those elements.

Minimum Ability Scores: Wisdom 10, Charisma 12. Wisdom or Charisma 16 means +5% experience; Wisdom *and* Charisma 16 means +10% experience.

Races Allowed: Elves, gnomes, half-elves, halflings, humans.

Nonweapon and Weapon Proficiencies: Nonweapon Proficiencies Required: Etiquette. Nonweapon Proficiencies Recommended: Modern Languages, Singing, Local History, Musical Instrument, Reading/Writing, Religion. Weapon Proficiencies Required: None. Nonweapon Proficiency Group Crossovers: Priest, General.

Duties of the Priest: Guidance, Marriage. Missions: The priest often accompanies parties of war or groups of adventurers to try to bring about peaceful solutions to as many situations as possible. (Note to the DM: You don't want this priest as a player-character in your campaign unless most of the other players, too, prefer peaceful resolutions to various situations. If they prefer fighting things out, they'll resent the priest of peace and it will result in major annoyances in your campaign.) Vigilance against forces or individuals who seem to stir up trouble continually and needlessly.

Weapon and Armor Restrictions: Weapons Permitted: Lasso, net. Armor Permitted: All non-magical armor and shields. All together, these constitute Medium combat abilities.

Other Limitations: Priests of this sect receive six-sided dice for hit points, not eight-sided. Whenever they appear in public they must wear clothing or badges which display their status as priests of the god of peace.

Spheres of Influence: Major Access to All, Charm, Creation, Divination, Protection. Minor Access to Animal, Guardian, Healing, Necromantic.

Powers: *Charm/Fascination* (as per the Designing Faiths chapter). *Language/Communication* (as per the Designing Faiths chapter); from 1st level to 4th, the priest receives one extra language per level (or one extra nonweapon proficiency slot which may only be used for languages); the language chosen must be that of a sentient humanoid race. *Soothing Word* (Designing Faiths chapter). *At 5th level: Laying On of Hands* (same as the Paladin ability).

Followers and Strongholds: The followers are received at 8th level, and consist of one fifth-level priest, three third-level priests, and sixteen first-level priests of the same order. The priest may take the following on adventures: Two priests of his choice. The priesthood will pay for half of the cost of stronghold construction at 8th level.

Possible Symbols: Dove, Olive Branch.

Prosperity

This is a god of riches and wealth. He may be a god of rich treasures from under the ground, or of riches of herds, or of any sort of prosperity.

The god's priests spend a lot of time dabbling in trade and teaching the children of noble families how to manage their money wisely, to build businesses from the ground up, to improve their communities through the careful, studied application of money. They are not priests of greed and avarice, though the occasional priest will end up being a greedy man.

The god of prosperity is male.

The priests of this god are on good terms with the priests of Community, Peace, Race (Halfling), and Trade.

Alignment: The deity is good; at the DM's discretion, he may be chaotic good, neutral good, or lawful good, but tends to be neutral good. Regardless of his alignment, his priests may be of any good alignment. The flock may be of any neutral or good alignment.

Minimum Ability Scores: Wisdom 11. Wisdom 16 means +10% experience.

Races Allowed: Dwarves, elves, gnomes, half-elves, halflings, humans.

Nonweapon and Weapon Proficiencies: Nonweapon Proficiencies Required: Appraising. Nonweapon Proficiencies Recommended: Mining, Modern Languages, Reading/Writing, Religion, Gaming, Gem Cutting. Weapon Proficiencies Required: None. Nonweapon Proficiency Group Crossovers: Priest, General, Rogue.

Duties of the Priest: Guidance, Marriage. (Note: The priests of this sect do not encourage members of their flock to marry for love if it means alienating the families and living in poverty.)

Weapon and Armor Restrictions: Weapons Permitted: Bill, harpoon, javelin, lasso, mancat-cher, net, picks (all), spear, trident. Armor Permitted: All non-magical armor and non-magical shields. Oriental Campaigns: Also chain. All together, these constitute Medium combat abilities.

Other Limitations: None.

Spheres of Influence: Major Access to All, Animal, Creation, Plant, Summoning. Minor Access to Guardian, Healing, Necromantic, Protection.

Powers: *Detection* (as per the Designing Faiths chapter) of treasure and objects of value; the priest can detect treasure when he is within 10' of it, even when it is concealed (5' if it is behind a thin wall, or 2' if it is behind a heavy wall or buried); however, he cannot divine its direction through this power, and must move around to get a fix on the treasure. The power does not tell him what sort of treasure it is, and even if it's of a type he does not desire (such as a small bag of coins) it will alert him to the treasure's presence. The power is next to useless when the character is among allies (their coin-pouches will set it off), so he must walk alone to be able to use it. *Determine approximate depth underground* on 1-3 on 1d6 (same as Dwarf ability; dwarf-priests and gnome-priests of this faith succeed on a 1-5 on 1d6).

Followers and Strongholds: The followers are received at 8th level, and consist of one fifth-level priest, two third-level priests, and four first-level priests of the same order, plus one fifth-level fighter (bodyguard), one fifth-level bard (the priest's personal bard), and ten Normal Men and Women (good-looking, high-charisma men and women with no perceivable skills or source of income who are attracted to the priests of fortune and luck). The priest may take the following on adventures: Two priests, the fighter, the bard, and all the Normal Men and Women. The priesthood will pay for half of the cost of stronghold construction at 8th level.

Possible Symbols: Bull, Chest.

Notes: The weapons chosen for this priesthood were chosen based on association with the earth, as the source of precious metals, and those which can grab, capture, harvest the bounty of the seas, etc.

Race

This god is the mentor of a specific sentient race (dwarf, elf, gnome, halfling, and human, and even half-elf if there enough half-elves that they are recognized as being an actual species). Usually, the god is the one who, in the legends, created the race in question — or at least nurtured and educated the race in difficult years.

Naturally, there is a separate race-god for each race.

The gods' priesthoods are dedicated to staving off threats against the race, persuading members of the race to achieve their maximum potential and destiny, and to preventing members of the race from betraying the race (or, for that matter, the world, or all life on the world).

A race-god is as likely to be male as female.

The priests of this god are on good terms with the priests of Ancestors, Birth/Children, Community, Culture, Good, and Marriage. Also: (Dwarves) Crafts, Fire, Lightning, Metalwork, Thunder. (Elves) Animals, Crafts, Nature, Race/Half-Elven. (Gnomes) Mischief/Trickery. (Half-Elves) Race/Elven, Race/Human. (Halflings) Mischief/Trickery, Peace, Prosperity. (Humans) Divinity of Mankind, Race/Half-Elven.

Alignment: The deity is good; at the DM's discretion, he may be chaotic good, neutral good, or lawful good, but tends to be neutral good. Regardless of his alignment, his priests may be of any good alignment. The flock may be of any neutral or good alignment.

Minimum Ability Scores: Wisdom 12. Wisdom 16 means +10% experience.

Races Allowed: Only dwarves can be priests of the god of the dwarven race, only elves can be priests of the god of the elven race, etc. The only exception to this pattern is the half-elf. A half-elf can be a priest of the god of the elven race, of the god of the human race, or of the god of the half-elven race (assuming that the DM even *has* a god of the half-elven race). If a half-elf is the priest of the god of the elven race, he follows all the guidelines (in this priest description) for those priests instead of half-elven priests; if he is the priest of the god of the human race, he follows all the guidelines for those priests instead of half-elven priests.

Nonweapon and Weapon Proficiencies: Nonweapon Proficiencies Required: Ancient History. Nonweapon Proficiencies Recommended: Local History, Reading/Writing, Religion, (Dwarves) Blacksmithing, Armorer, Mountaineering, Weaponsmithing, (Elves) Animal Handling, Animal Lore, Bowyer/Fletcher, Dancing, Running, Tracking, (Humans) Riding Land-Based, Navigation, Heraldry. Weapon Proficiencies Required: None. Nonweapon Proficiency Group Crossovers: Priest, General, Warrior.

Duties of the Priest: Guidance, Marriage. Vigilance against enemies of the race and their plots.

Weapon and Armor Restrictions: Naturally, Weapon and Armor Restrictions vary from race to race. Broken down by race, they include:

Dwarves: Weapons Permitted: Battle axe, club, crossbow, flails (both), hand/throwing axe, mace, maul, morning star, picks (all), warhammer. Armor Permitted: All armor and all shields. All together, these constitute Good combat abilities.

Elves: Weapons Permitted: Bows (all), dagger/dirk, javelin, knife, lance, quarterstaff, spear, sword/short, sword/long. Armor Permitted: All non-metal armor; any metal armor *made by elven craftsmen*; all shields. Oriental Campaigns: Also bo stick, daikyu. All together, these constitute Good combat abilities.

Gnomes: Weapons Permitted: Bows (all)/short, crossbow/light, hand/throwing axe, javelin, sling. Armor Permitted: All armor and shields. All together, these constitute Good combat abilities.

Half-Elves: Weapons Permitted: Bows (all), dagger/dirk, knife, lance, lasso, swords (all). Armor Permitted: All armor and shields. All together, these constitute Good combat abilities.

Halflings: Weapons Permitted: Club, dagger/dirk, dart, hand/throwing axe, javelin, knife, sling, staff sling. Armor Permitted: All armor; no shields. All together, these constitute Medium combat abilities.

Humans: Weapons Permitted: Bows (all), dagger/dirk, knife, lance, spear, sword/long. Armor Permitted: All non-magical armor and shields. All together, these constitute Good combat abilities.

Other Limitations: Whenever they appear in public, these priests must wear clothing or badges which indicate their status as priests of the race. Important Note: There is *no* limitation on whom these racial priests can heal. A dwarf-race priest can heal anyone he chooses — humans, half-elves, gnomes, halflings, even elves. Of course, racial prejudice might prompt the priest to deny healing to those of another race... but that's his individual choice, not a requirement of his faith.

Spheres of Influence:

Dwarves: Major Access to All, Combat, Protection. Minor Access to Divination, Healing.

Elves: Major Access to All, Plant, Summoning. Minor Access to Healing, Sun. The DM may, at his sole discretion, substitute Major Access to Animal sphere for the Major Access to Summoning sphere; alternatively, he may give the player the option of choosing Animal or Summoning.

Gnomes: Major Access to All, Plant, Protection. Minor Access to Divination, Healing.

Half-Elves: Major Access to All, Healing, and player's choice of *one* from the following list: Animal, Plant, Protection, or Summoning. Minor Access to Divination, Necromantic.

Halflings: Major Access to All, Creation, Divination, Guardian, Protection. Minor Access to Charm, Healing, Necromantic, Sun.

Humans: Major Access to All, Divination, Healing. Minor Access to Necromantic, Sun.

Powers: *Incite Berserker Rage* (as per the Designing Faiths chapter). *Inspire Fear* (as per the Designing Faiths chapter). *Soothing Word* (as per the Designing Faiths

chapter). *At 5th level: Laying On of Hands* (same as the Paladin ability). *At 8th level: Turn Undead* (same as the Cleric ability).

Followers and Strongholds: The followers are received at 8th level. The priesthood will pay for half of the cost of stronghold construction at 8th level.

For *Dwarf* priests, the followers consist of: One fifth-level priest, one third-level priest, and two first-level priests of the same order; two fifth-level dwarf-fighters who act as bodyguards; and twenty first-level dwarf-fighters, each with a Nonweapon Proficiency appropriate to the temple (blacksmithing and mining especially). The priest may take the following on adventures: Two priests and two first-level fighters of his choice, and his fifth-level bodyguards.

For *Elf* priests, the followers consist of: One fifth-level priest, one third-level priest, and two first-level priests of the same order; two fifth-level elf-fighters who act as bodyguards; and ten first-level elf-fighters, each with a Nonweapon Proficiency appropriate to the temple (animal lore, bowyer/fletcher, hunting, set snares, and tracking especially). The priest may take the following on adventures: Two priests and two first-level fighters of his choice, and his fifth-level bodyguards.

For *Gnome* priests, the followers consist of: One fifth-level priest, one third-level priest, and two first-level priests of the same order; two fifth-level gnome-fighters who act as bodyguards; and ten first-level gnome-fighters, each with a Nonweapon Proficiency appropriate to the temple (mining, set snares, and tracking especially). The priest may take the following on adventures: Two priests and two

first-level fighters of his choice, and his fifth-level bodyguards.

For *Half-Elf* priests, the followers consist of: One fifth-level priest, one third-level priest, and two first-level priests of the same order; two fifth-level half-elf-fighters who act as bodyguards; and ten first-level half-elf-fighters, each with a Nonweapon Proficiency appropriate to the temple (reading/writing especially). The priest may take the following on adventures: Two priests and two first-level fighters of his choice, and his fifth-level bodyguards.

For *Halfling* priests, the followers consist of: One fifth-level priest, one third-level priest, and two first-level priests of the same order; two fifth-level halfling-fighters who act as bodyguards; and ten first-level halfling-fighters, each with a Nonweapon Proficiency appropriate to the temple (agriculture and reading/writing especially). The priest may take the following on adventures: Two priests and two first-level fighters of his choice, and his fifth-level bodyguards.

For *Human* priests, the followers consist of: One fifth-level priest, one third-level priest, and two first-level priests of the same order; two fifth-level human fighters who act as bodyguards; and ten first-level human fighters, each with a Nonweapon Proficiency appropriate to the temple (ancient history, local history, and reading/writing especially). The priest may take the following on adventures: Two priests and two first-level fighters of his choice, and his fifth-level bodyguards.

Possible Symbols: (Dwarf) Axe, Warhammer, Anvil; (Elf) Tree, Bow; (Gnome) Throwing Axe; (Half-Elf) Crossed Bow & Sword; (Halfling) Low Hill With Windows;

(Human) Crossed Sword & Shield or Spear & Shield.

Notes: The DM can create many more racial priesthoods based on the above examples, to reflect variations within races. He could have a racial priesthood for the Aquatic Elf, similar to that of the Elf but using the weapons which the priests of oceans and rivers can use. He could have another for the desert-dwelling human where sabres, horse-back riding, desert survival and no armor are the order of the day.

The DM should be careful when letting race-oriented priests in his campaign. It's not difficult for new or inexperienced players to misinterpret this class as a priesthood of prejudice, which is not the intent at all. These priests are supposed to support and celebrate the virtues of their own race, but *not* to be nasty to other races, contribute to stereotypes about them, exalt in jokes about them, etc. There may be priests like that in any order, but they should be NPCs who are not liked or appreciated by their fellows.

Redemption

This god takes the stand that all opponents to a specific cause are evil and must be converted, redeemed... or destroyed. There could be more than one god of redemption, one for each different cause sufficiently important to warrant one. In this respect, they are much like the gods of Culture (and their priests much like priests of the gods of Culture), but are primarily soldiers for their cause.

The god of redemption is male.

The priests of this god are on good terms with the priests of Good. The priests of this god dislike the priests of Evil.

Alignment: The deity is neutral good. The priests may be any sort of good alignment. The flock may be of any neutral or good alignment.

Minimum Ability Scores: Wisdom 9. Wisdom 16 means +10% experience.

Races Allowed: Dwarves, elves, gnomes, half-elves, halflings, humans.

Nonweapon and Weapon Proficiencies: Nonweapon Proficiencies Required: Religion. Nonweapon Proficiencies Recommended: Reading/Writing. Weapon Proficiencies Required: None. Nonweapon Proficiency Group Crossovers: Priest, General.

Duties of the Priest: Guidance, Marriage. Missions: These priests are often dispatched on missions to persuade sinners and evildoers to repent their misdeeds. Therefore, on adventures, these priests prefer to capture the chief evil-doers alive and give them the opportunity to recant and make reparations. When the evildoers are unwilling to do so, the priests are perfectly willing to let normal or even vigilante justice take its course.

Weapon and Armor Restrictions: Weapons Permitted: Lasso, mancatcher, naul, net, polearms, scourge, whip. Armor Permitted: All armor; no shields. All together, these constitute Good combat abilities.

Other Limitations: Priests of this sect must always wear clothes or badges indicating their priesthood when appearing in public.

Spheres of Influence: Major Access to All, Charm, Combat. Minor Access to Divination, Healing.

Powers: *Inspire Fear* (as per the Designing Faiths chapter). *At 5th level: Turn Undead* (same as the Cleric ability).

Followers and Strongholds: The followers are received at 9th level, and consist of three 3rd-level priests and six 1st-level priests of the same order, plus five 3rd-level fighters who act as guards. The priest may take the following on adventures: Three priests (only one of which may be third-level) and two fighters of his choice. The priesthood will pay for half of the cost of stronghold construction at 9th level.

Possible Symbols: Silhouette of kneeling supplicant.

Rulership, Kingship

This god is a god of authentication: He bestows his blessings on the kings of various cities or countries so that all will know the god supports that king and his family. Usually, the god provides the king with some artifact indicating his approval... and magically takes back the artifact when he withdraws his approval. (The artifact is usually a crown or a sceptre; these are two near-universal symbols of kingship.)

The god's priests are advisors to kings. They analyze politics and make recommendations. They intensively research the genealogy and history of the king's families, the better to authenticate his hold on the throne. At their god's behest, they may participate in the overthrow of a king. Many of these priests do travel, in order to acquire more information about the king or to head off plots against him.

In a male-dominated society, this deity will be male. In a female-dominated society, this deity will be female. In a more equal society, the god may be of either sex.

The priests of this god are on good terms with the priests of

Community, Culture, Messengers, Peace, and War.

Alignment: The deity is true neutral. The priests may be neutral evil, true neutral, or neutral good; evil priests have their own sect and the other priests don't have to tolerate them. The flock may be of any alignment.

Minimum Ability Scores: Wisdom 10, Charisma 11. Wisdom or Charisma 16 means +5% experience; Wisdom *and* Charisma 16 means +10% experience.

Races Allowed: Dwarves, elves, gnomes, half-elves, humans.

Nonweapon and Weapon Proficiencies: Nonweapon Proficiencies Required: Etiquette. Nonweapon Proficiencies Recommended: Heraldry, Ancient History, Ancient Languages, Local History, Reading/Writing, Religion. Weapon Proficiencies Required: None. Nonweapon Proficiency Group Crossovers: Priest, General.

Duties of the Priest: Guidance, Marriage. Missions: When a ruler sees opportunities to strengthen his throne or eliminate problems that might endanger his throne, he often asks for priests of this sect to accompany the adventurers he dispatches; the local temples usually cooperate and provide adventurer priests to accompany those parties. Vigilance: These priests are required to stay alert against forces which threaten the local thrones. This includes foreign intrigue and even internal problems; if a local king has become corrupt and tyrannical, and the local population is edging toward rebellion, these priests may put pressure on the king to shape up... or may even oppose or depose him, so that the throne will remain strong under a new, better ruler.

Weapon and Armor Restrictions: Weapons Permitted: One type of bludgeoning weapon (the DM chooses one from the following list, choosing the preferred bludgeoning weapon of the culture: Club, flails (both), mace, morning star, warhammer), and one type of sword (DM chooses one type from following list, choosing the preferred sword of the culture: Bastard, cutlass, khopesh, long, rapier, sabre, short, or two-handed). Armor Permitted: All metal armor, all shields. Oriental Campaigns: Also katana and wakizashi added to the list of sword choices. All together, these constitute Good combat abilities.

Other Limitations: None.

Spheres of Influence: Major Access to All, Charm, Elemental. Minor Access to Healing, Protection.

Powers: *Soothing Word* (as per the Designing Faiths chapter). *Incite Berserker Rage* (as per the Designing Faiths chapter). *At 8th level: Inspire Fear* (as per the Designing Faiths chapter).

Followers and Strongholds: The followers are received at 9th level, and consist of one fifth-level priest, one third-level priest, and two first-level priests of the same order, plus three third-level fighters and six first-level fighters to act as guards; each fighter must have one of the following Nonweapon Proficiencies: etiquette or heraldry. The priest may take the following on adventures: Two priests and three fighters (only one of whom may be third-level) of his choice. The priesthood will pay for half of the cost of stronghold construction at 9th level.

Possible Symbols: Crown, Sceptre.

Seasons

This god celebrates the changing seasons, and so is related to the gods of agriculture and time. His priests maintain the calendar and are often find astronomers.

Lesser gods of this attribute would be gods of individual seasons: the god of spring, the god of summer, the god of winter, and (where applicable) the god of autumn (not all regions recognize an autumn season).

The gods of seasons are usually female.

The priests of this god are on good terms with Druids and the priests of Agriculture, Earth, Elemental Forces, Fertility, Life-Death-Rebirth Cycle, Nature, Sky/Weather, Time, and Vegetation.

Alignment: The deity is true neutral. The priests may be true neutral or neutral good; most are true neutral. The flock may be of any alignment.

Minimum Ability Scores: Wisdom 10. Wisdom 16 means +10% experience.

Races Allowed: Elves, gnomes, half-elves, halflings, humans.

Nonweapon and Weapon Proficiencies: Nonweapon Proficiencies Required: Weather Sense. Nonweapon Proficiencies Recommended: Astrology, Agriculture, Navigation, Reading/Writing, Religion. Weapon Proficiencies Required: None. Nonweapon Proficiency Group Crossovers: Priest, General.

Duties of the Priest: Guidance, Marriage.

Weapon and Armor Restrictions: Weapons Permitted: Club, quarterstaff, maul, polearms, scythe, sickle. Armor Permitted: All non-metal armor; no shields.

Oriental Campaigns: Also bo stick, nunchaku. All together, these constitute Medium combat abilities.

Other Limitations: None.

Spheres of Influence: Major Access to All, Creation, Elemental, Protection, Weather. Minor Access to Animal, Divination, Healing, Plant.

Powers: *Immunity* (as per the Designing Faiths chapter, automatically successful saving throws) vs. all priest spells of the elemental sphere, and all wizard spells with coldness and heat (not fire!) as one of their components or effects.

Followers and Strongholds: The followers are received at 8th level, and consist of three third-level priests and eleven first-level priests of the same order, plus ten first-level fighters who act as guards. The priest may take the following on adventures: Three priests (only one of whom may be third-level) and four fighters. The priesthood will pay for half of the cost of stronghold construction at 8th level.

Possible Symbols: (Spring) Sapling, (Summer) Sheaf of Wheat, (Autumn) Leaf, (Winter) Leafless Tree, (Entire Year) All of the Above.

Sites

These gods are much like gods of communities, but the sites they represent don't have to be occupied. A site-god could be the deity of a mountain, a cave, a plain, or a valley. These are usually minor gods, one god to a site. Generally, the sites are famous *because* they are the dwellings of gods; however, the gods seldom let themselves be seen.

Priests of these gods are protectors of the sites, and all living things which dwell there. Because of this, the priests seldom leave those sites, and so this is not usually a good choice for a player-character. Only when the site is threatened by distant powers is the priest allowed to leave the site for adventures.

Site gods are as likely to be male as female.

The priests of this god are on good terms with the priests of Ancestors and Community.

Alignment: A deity who is the patron of a single site will probably be true neutral; his interest is in the survival and veneration of the site, with little interest in the doings of men. Their priests may be of any neutral alignment, but neutral evil priests gather in one cult, while true neutral and neutral good priests gather in a second; they won't be friendly to one another. The flock may be of any alignment. The DM can decide that a particular site deity is neutral good, in which case there will be no evil priests or flock; or that he is neutral evil, in which case there will be no good priests or flock.

Minimum Ability Scores: Wisdom 12, Strength 10. Wisdom or Strength 16 means +5% experience; Wisdom *and* Strength 16 means +10% experience.

Races Allowed: Dwarves, elves, gnomes, half-elves, halflings, humans.

Nonweapon and Weapon Proficiencies: Nonweapon Proficiencies Required: Local History. Nonweapon Proficiencies Recommended: Religion, Reading/Writing. Weapon Proficiencies Required: None. Nonweapon Proficiency Group Crossovers: Priest, General.

Duties of the Priest: Marriage. Missions: If the site is threatened, the priest will be dispatched to help straighten out the situation.

Weapon and Armor Restrictions: Weapons Permitted: One lesser weapon from the following list (Club, dagger/dirk, hand/throwing axe, javelin, light crossbow, mace, short bow, warhammer) and one greater weapon from the following list (Battle axe, heavy crossbow, long bow, morning star, polearm, quarterstaff, spear, sword/long). (The DM makes this choice based on the history and attributes of the holy site; often, the choices will be paired, such as dagger and long sword or throwing axe and battle axe.) Armor Permitted: All non-magical armor and shields. All together, these constitute Good combat abilities.

Other Limitations: None.

Spheres of Influence: Major Access to All, Healing, Protection. Minor Access to Animal, Plant.

Powers: *Inspire Fear* (as per the Designing Faiths chapter); this power is granted by the god to help the priest keep the site clear of those who would harm or despoil it.

Followers and Strongholds: The followers are received at 8th level, and consist of three third-level priests and six first-level priests of the same order, plus one fifth-level fighter, two third-level fighters and four first-level fighters who act as guards for the site and the chief priest. The priest may take the following on adventures: Three priests (only two of whom can be third-level) and one fighter of his choice. The priesthood will pay for half of the cost of stronghold construction at 8th level.

Possible Symbols: A silhouette representing the site; if it's a mountain, it would be the silhouette of the mountain, for instance.

Sky, Weather

This is a god of the atmosphere in all its manifestations, from the most clear and still to the most stormy and tumultuous. It is this god that determines how much rain will reach the soil; it is this god that occasionally goes a little crazy and storms until all the living things in the area are terrified. He is a wild and powerful god, and a very necessary one.

His priests primarily work to ensure that he receives the worship that he is due. Beyond that, they may do much as they please, serving individual communities or adventuring as they choose.

Lesser gods of the sky attribute simply embody one aspect of the sky or weather. The gods of Lightning, Thunder, and Wind described in this section can be considered lesser sky- and weather-gods.

The sky-god is almost always male.

The priests of this god are on good terms with Druids and the priests of Agriculture, Earth, Elemental Forces, Fertility, Life-Death-Rebirth Cycle, Lightning, Nature, Oceans/Rivers, Seasons, Thunder, Vegetation, and Wind.

Alignment: The deity is true neutral. The priests may be true neutral or neutral good; most are true neutral. The flock may be of any alignment.

Minimum Ability Scores: Wisdom 10, Constitution 12. Wisdom or Constitution 16 means +5% experience; Wisdom *and* Constitution 16 means +10% experience.

Races Allowed: Elves, gnomes, half-elves, halflings, humans.

Nonweapon and Weapon Proficiencies: Nonweapon Proficiencies Required: Weather Sense. Nonweapon Proficiencies Recommended: Religion, Reading/Writing. Weapon Proficiencies Required: None. Nonweapon Proficiency Group Crossovers: Priest, General.

Duties of the Priest: Guidance, Marriage.

Weapon and Armor Restrictions: Weapons Permitted: Battle axe, bows (all), club, hand/throwing axe, javelin, spear, warhammer. Armor Permitted: All non-metal armor, all shields. All together, these constitute Medium combat abilities.

Other Limitations: None.

Spheres of Influence: Major Access to All, Astral, Elemental (the priest can only use spells with the words Water, Air, and Wind in their names, and the spell *chariot of Sustarre*), Protection, Weather. Minor Access to Combat, Divination, Plant, Sun.

Powers: *Inspire Fear* (as per the Designing Faiths chapter).

Followers and Strongholds: The followers are received at 8th level, and consist of one fifth-level priest, three third-level priests, and sixteen first-level priests of the same order. The priest may take the following on adventures: Any three priests of his choice. The priesthood will pay for half of the cost of stronghold construction at 8th level.

Possible Symbols: Dome, Cloud, Raincloud.

Strength

This god celebrates physical strength, and nothing but strength.

His priests promote physical fitness, contests of strength (such as weight-throws and wrestling, in association with priests of the god of competition) and war.

The strength-god is male.

The priests of this god are on good terms with the priests of Competition, Divinity of Mankind, Guardianship, Lightning, Metalwork, Thunder, and War. The priests of this god dislike the priests of Death, Disease, and Mischief/Trickery.

Alignment: The deity is true neutral. The priests may be neutral evil, true neutral, or neutral good; evil priests have their own sect and the other priests don't have to tolerate them. The flock may be of any alignment. don't like priests of the god of disease, which is a god of weakness.

Minimum Ability Scores: Wisdom 9, Strength 15. Wisdom or Strength 16 means +5% experience; Wisdom *and* Strength 16 means +10% experience.

Races Allowed: Dwarves, elves, half-elves, humans.

Nonweapon and Weapon Proficiencies: Nonweapon Proficiencies Required: Endurance. Nonweapon Proficiencies Recommended: Reading/Writing, Religion, Charioteering. Weapon Proficiencies Required: None. Nonweapon Proficiency Group Crossovers: Priest, General, Warrior.

Duties of the Priest: Guidance, Marriage. Missions: The priest is not required to, but is almost always allowed to go on adventures where he will be able to display his personal strength and demonstrate the attributes of his god.

Weapon and Armor Restrictions: Weapons Permitted: Battle axe, cestus, club, mace, maul, morning star, picks (all), polearm, sword/two-handed, warhammer. Armor Permitted: All armor and shields. All together, these constitute Good combat abilities.

Other Limitations: None.

Spheres of Influence: Major Access to All, Combat, Healing. Minor Access to Elemental, Necromantic.

Powers: *Immunity* (as per the Designing Faiths chapter); the priest is immune to undead life-draining and paralysis, and to the spells *chill touch, energy drain, enervation, ray of enfeeblement,* and *vampiric touch. Turn Undead* (same as the Cleric ability). *At 5th level: Incite Berserker Rage* (as per the Designing Faiths chapter). *At 8th level: Inspire Fear* (as per the Designing Faiths chapter).

Followers and Strongholds: The followers are received at 8th level, and consist of three third-level priests and six first-level priests of the same order, plus one fifth-level fighter, two third-level fighters, and four first-level fighters, all with a Strength score of 16. The priest may take the following on adventures: Three priests (only one of whom may be third-level) and four fighters of his choice. The priesthood will pay for half of the cost of stronghold construction at 8th level.

Possible Symbols: Human Silhouette Holding Up Mountain or Temple.

Sun

This god is a god of magic, healing, inspiration, and life, sometimes of madness and heatstroke. He is an enemy of dark creatures, especially the undead.

The priesthood of this god exists to promote all those traits among the flock, and to celebrate the daily blessing that the sun-god shines down upon the world.

The sun-god is usually male.

The priests of this god are on good terms with the priests of Arts, Crafts, Darkness/Night, Dawn, Elemental Forces, Fire, Healing, Hunting, Light, Literature/Poetry, Magic, Metalwork, Moon, Music/Dance, and Oracles/Prophecy.

Alignment: The deity is good; at the DM's discretion, he may be chaotic good, neutral good, or lawful good, but tends to be neutral good. Regardless of his alignment, his priests may be of any good alignment. The flock may be of any neutral or good alignment.

Minimum Ability Scores: Wisdom 12, Intelligence 12. Wisdom or Intelligence 16 means +5% experience; Wisdom *and* Intelligence 16 means +10% experience.

Races Allowed: Elves, gnomes, half-elves, halflings, humans.

Nonweapon and Weapon Proficiencies: Nonweapon Proficiencies Required: Healing. Nonweapon Proficiencies Recommended: Herbalism, Navigation, Reading/Writing, Religion, Spellcraft. Weapon Proficiencies Required: None. Nonweapon Proficiency Group Crossovers: Priest, General, Wizard.

Duties of the Priest: Guidance, Marriage. Education: Priests of this sect promote the study of magic. Vigilance: The sun-god is a god of observation, of keen eyesight, of vigilance in general. Therefore, all his priests are commanded to keep their eyes open and learn as much as possible about what is going around them at all times. What they do with that knowledge, outside the context of helping their temple and preserving the worship of the god, is up to them.

Weapon and Armor Restrictions: Weapons Permitted: Bows (all), crossbow, dagger/dirk, dart, javelin, knife, spear. Armor Permitted: All metal armor and all shields. Oriental Campaigns: Also daikyu, shuriken. All together, these constitute Medium combat abilities.

Other Limitations: None.

Spheres of Influence: Major Access to All, Divination, Healing, Necromantic, Sun. Minor Access to Charm, Elemental (the priest can only use spells with the words fire, flame, heat, and pyrotechnics in the names), Plant, Protection.

Powers: *Detect Secret Doors* (same as Elf ability: Success on roll of 1 on 1d6 when passing within 10′, 1-2 on 1d6 to find secret doors and 1-3 on 1d6 to find concealed portals when actively searching; elven priests of this order have success on a roll of 1-2 when passing within 10′, 1-3 to find secret doors and 1-4 to find concealed portals when actively searching). *Infravision* (same as the elf ability; an elven or half-elven priest of this faith has Infravision of doubled range, to 120′). *Turn Undead* (same as the Cleric ability). *At 5th level: Laying On of Hands* (same as the Paladin ability). *At 8th level: Prophecy* (Designing Faiths chapter). *At 10th level, chariot of Sustarre*; the priest can use this spell once per day in addition to his other spells.

Followers and Strongholds: The followers are received at 9th level, and consist of three third-level priests and six first-level priests of the same order, plus one third-level fighter and two first-level fighters to act as guards, one third-level mage and two first-level mages to act as consultants, one third-level bard and two first-level bards to act as personal bards. The priest may take the following on adventures: Three priests (only one of whom may be third-level), plus one fighter, one mage, and one bard of his choice. The priesthood will pay for half of the cost of stronghold construction at 9th level.

Possible Symbols: Sun (With or Without Rays); Chariot.

Notes: The weapons permitted for this order are those which strike from afar, like the inspiration (or heatstroke) of the sun.

Thunder

The thunder-god is very similar to the lightning-god; in campaigns where they both exist, they will probably be related, even brothers. He represents the fearsomeness of nature, natural forces at their most frightening, and so is a god of terror and fear as well. Like the lightning-god, he is also a god of storms.

Also as with the lightning-god, the thunder-god is not very concerned with the affairs of mortals; he lets them worship him and grants power to his priests, but otherwise doesn't interfere much in mortal affairs. His priests promote worship of his power and fearsomeness, especially as traits which the followers wish to use against their enemies.

The thunder-god is male.

The priests of this god are on good terms with the priests of Elemental Forces, Lightning (especially), Nature, Race (Dwarven), Sky/Weather, and Strength.

Alignment: The deity is true neutral. The priests may be neutral evil, true neutral, or neutral good; evil priests have their own sect and the other priests don't have to tolerate them. The flock may be of any alignment.

Minimum Ability Scores: Wisdom 10, Strength 12. Wisdom or Strength 16 mean +5% experience; Wisdom *and* Strength 16

mean +10% experience.

Races Allowed: Dwarves, elves, gnomes, half-elves, humans.

Nonweapon and Weapon Proficiencies: Nonweapon Proficiencies Required: Weather Sense. Nonweapon Proficiencies Recommended: Reading/Writing, Religion. Weapon Proficiencies Required: Warhammer. Nonweapon Proficiency Group Crossovers: Priest, General, Warrior.

Duties of the Priest: Guidance, Marriage.

Weapon and Armor Restrictions: Weapons Permitted: Club, mace, maul, morning star, warhammer. Armor Permitted: All armor and shields. All together, these constitute Good combat abilities.

Other Limitations: None.

Spheres of Influence: Major Access to All, Combat, Weather. Minor Access to Divination, Protection.

Powers: *Incite Berserker Rage* (as per the Designing Faiths chapter). *At 5th level: Inspire Fear* (as per the Designing Faiths chapter).

Followers and Strongholds: The followers are received at 8th level, and consist of three third-level priests and six first-level priests of the same order, plus three third-level fighters and six first-level fighters to act as guards. The priest may take the following on adventures: Two priests and two fighters of his choice. The priesthood will pay for half of the cost of stronghold construction at 8th level.

Possible Symbols: Warhammer; Warhammer Across Mountain.

Time

This god is the deity of the march of time. He represents inevitability — not destiny based on

the will of individual gods, but the inevitability of change brought on by time.

His priests preach the philosophy of patience to the flock, and help all the members of the flock adapt themselves to their changing bodies, lifestyles, and needs as they go through life.

The time-god is male.

The priests of this god are on good terms with the priests of Death, Elemental Forces, Fate/Destiny, Seasons, and Wisdom.

Alignment: The deity is true neutral. The priests may be true neutral or neutral good; most are true neutral. The flock may be of any alignment.

Minimum Ability Scores: Wisdom 12. Wisdom 16 means +10% experience.

Races Allowed: Dwarves, elves, gnomes, half-elves, halflings, humans.

Nonweapon and Weapon Proficiencies: Nonweapon Proficiencies Required: Ancient History. Nonweapon Proficiencies Recommended: Local History, Reading/Writing, Religion. Weapon Proficiencies Required: None. Nonweapon Proficiency Group Crossovers: Priest, General.

Duties of the Priest: Guidance, Marriage.

Weapon and Armor Restrictions: Weapons Permitted: Scythe, sickle. Armor Permitted: All non-magical armor; no shields. All together, these constitute Medium combat abilities.

Other Limitations: None.

Spheres of Influence: Major Access to All, Astral, Divination, Healing, Necromantic. Minor Access to Plant, Protection, Sun, and Weather.

Powers: *Identification* (as per the Designing Faiths chapter) of the current time and day; regardless of how long the priest has been underground, unconscious, or otherwise unable to observe the passage of time, he'll know roughly what time it is (within the hour) and exactly what day of the year it is. *At 3rd level: Laying On of Hands* (same as the Paladin ability). At *5th level: Turn Undead* (same as the Cleric ability).

Followers and Strongholds: The followers are received at 8th level, and consist of one fifth-level priest, five third-level priests, and ten first-level priests of the same order. The priest may take the following on adventures: Two priests of his choice. The priesthood will pay for half of the cost of stronghold construction at 8th level.

Possible Symbols: Hourglass, Scythe.

Trade

This god loves bargaining, and loves characters who bargain well. He also promotes the exchange of ideas between cultures through trade. And these, too, are the traits of his priests, who try to keep trade routes between nations open, free from excessive taxes, and mutually profitable.

The god of trade also likes the god of mischief and trickery, and he is a suitable deity for the worship of thieves and bards.

The trade-god is male.

The priests of this god are on good terms with the priests of Community, Crafts, Culture, Fortune/Luck, Messengers, Mischief/Trickery, and Prosperity.

Alignment: The deity is true neutral. The priests may be neutral evil, true neutral, or neutral good; evil priests have their own sect and the other priests don't

have to tolerate them. The flock may be of any alignment.

Minimum Ability Scores: Wisdom 12, Charisma 13. Wisdom or Charisma 16 means +5% experience; Wisdom *and* Charisma 16 means +10% experience.

Races Allowed: Dwarves, elves, gnomes, half-elves, hafllings, humans.

Nonweapon and Weapon Proficiencies: Nonweapon Proficiencies Required: Appraising. Nonweapon Proficiencies Recommended: Etiquette, Modern Languages, Riding Land-Based, Reading/Writing, Religion. Weapon Proficiencies Required: None. Nonweapon Proficiency Group Crossovers: Priest, General.

Duties of the Priest: Guidance, Marriage.

Weapon and Armor Restrictions: Weapons Permitted: Bill, dagger/dirk, dart, hand/throwing axe, javelin, knife, main-gauche, stiletto, sword/rapier, sword/sabre, sword/short. Armor Permitted: All non-metal armor; no shields. Oriental Campaigns: Also shuriken, wakizashi. All together, these constitute Medium combat abilities.

Other Limitations: None.

Spheres of Influence: Major Access to All, Charm, Divination, Guardian, Protection. Minor Access to Combat, Healing, Sun, Weather.

Powers: *Immunity* (automatically successful saving throw, as per the Designing Faiths chapter) vs. all spells with the word *charm* in the name. Language/Communication (as per the Designing Faiths chapter); from 1st level to 4th, the priest receives one extra language per level (or one extra nonweapon proficiency slot which can only be used for languages);

the languages chosen must be those of sentient humanoids. *Soothing Word* (as per the Designing Faiths chapter).

Followers and Strongholds: The followers are received at 8th level, and consist of three third-level priests and six first-level priests of the same order, plus three second-level bards and two second-level thieves to act as agents (eyes and ears) and one fifth-level fighter (to act as guard). The priest may take the following on adventures: Two priests, one bard, and one thief of his choice, and the fighter. The priesthood will pay for half of the cost of stronghold construction at 8th level.

Possible Symbols: Ships, Coins.

Vegetation

This is a god of nature who is devoted specifically to plant-life. He is an admirer of vast forests and plains and all sorts of plant growth, especially that which is wild and not fettered or trimmed or tamed by mankind.

Priests of the god try to make sure that there are always tracts of wilderness in abundance for the god to admire. They work hard to keep civilization from making inroads too deep into wilderness. They do this by spreading tales of the forest as a deep and dangerous place. They often sneak around in the wilderness using their spells on travelling city-folk, or stock the forest with dangerous animals, in order to reinforce this impression. They do not impede those who know the forest (elves, gnomes, rangers, hunters, trappers, woodsmen), but will terrorize innocents and city-soft travellers.

Vegetation-gods are as likely to be male as female.

The priests of this god are on good terms with Druids and the priests of Agriculture, Earth, Fertility, Life-Death-Rebirth Cycle, Nature, Seasons, and Sky/ Weather.

Alignment: The deity is true neutral. The priests may be true neutral or neutral good; most are true neutral. The flock may be of any alignment.

Minimum Ability Scores: Wisdom 9. Wisdom 16 means +10% experience.

Races Allowed: Elves, gnomes, half-elves, halflings, humans.

Nonweapon and Weapon Proficiencies: Nonweapon Proficiencies Required: Herbalism. Nonweapon Proficiencies Recommended: Agriculture, Reading/ Writing, Religion, Mountaineering, Survival, Tracking. Weapon Proficiencies Required: None. Nonweapon Proficiency Group Crossovers: Priest, General, Warrior.

Duties of the Priest: Guidance, Marriage.

Weapon and Armor Restrictions: Weapons Permitted: Club, quarterstaff, scythe, sickle. Armor Permitted: No armor; all wooden shields (no metal or leather). Oriental Campaigns: Also nunchaku. All together, these constitute Poor combat abilities.

Other Limitations: Priests of this sect may not wear leathers or furs in their clothing.

Spheres of Influence: Major Access to All, Divination, Healing, Plant, Protection, Summoning, Weather. Minor Access to Animal, Combat, Creation, Guardian, Necromantic, Sun.

Powers: *Analysis, Identification* (as per the Designing Faiths chapter); the priest can identify plants of any sort with perfect accuracy. *Defiance of Obstacle* (as per the Design-

ing Faiths chapter); the priest can pass through overgrown areas like the druid, but can do so at 1st level.

Followers and Strongholds: The followers are received at 8th level, and consist of one fifth-level priest, three third-level priests, and sixteen first-level priests of the same order. The priest may take the following on adventures: Two priests of his choice. The priesthood will pay for half of the cost of stronghold construction at 8th level.

Possible Symbols: Single plant of any sort (except domestic grains).

War

This god is the deity of combat and warfare. He exists only to promote and participate in bloody battle.

Each nation has priests of this god, and in each nation the priests constitute a separate cult; they do not cooperate with one another in times of war, especially when their armies are opposed. They help train new warriors, teach battlefield tactics, and make records of the most valiant fights of any war or battle.

In painful times of peace, these individual sects may cooperate with one another. However, they usually only do so to conspire and start up another war.

Lesser gods of war will be gods of some secondary aspect. One might be the god of Berserker Rages, another the god of Battlefield Terror, another the god of Confusion, another the god of Tactics, another the god of Cavalry... and so on.

The chief war-god is male, but lesser war-gods are as likely to be female as male.

The priests of this god are on good terms with the priests of

Community, Culture, Guardianship, Justice/Revenge, Messengers, Metalwork, Mischief/ Trickery, and Rulership/Kingship. The priests of this god dislike the priests of Peace.

Alignment: The deity is true neutral. The priests may be neutral evil, true neutral, or neutral good; evil priests have their own sect and the other priests don't have to tolerate them. The flock may be of any alignment.

Minimum Ability Scores: Wisdom 9, Strength 13. Wisdom or Strength 16 means +5% experience; Wisdom *and* Strength 16 means +10% experience.

Races Allowed: Dwarves, elves, gnomes, half-elves, halflings, humans.

Nonweapon and Weapon Proficiencies: Nonweapon Proficiencies Required: Blind-fighting. Nonweapon Proficiencies Recommended: Animal Training, Heraldry, Riding Land-Based, Healing, Reading/Writing, Religion, Armorer, Bowyer/Fletcher, Charioteering, Hunting, Running, Tracking. Weapon Proficiencies Required: No specific weapon required, but priest must choose one weapon from the list of weapons available (below) and *specialize in that weapon according to normal weapon specialization rules.* He is the only priest who can take any weapon specialization. Nonweapon Proficiency Group Crossovers: Priest, General, Warrior.

Duties of the Priest: Guidance, Marriage. Missions: The priests want to and are required to accompany armies on the march of war. At every war, priests of this sect will be in attendance on the officers and rulers of both sides. Vigilance: The priests of this sect must keep their eyes open against complacency and the tide of philosophies of peacefulness; if a land is too peaceful for too long, they must shake things up and get a war, even a small one, going.

Weapon and Armor Restrictions: Weapons Permitted: Battle axe, bows (all), dagger/dirk, knife, lance, mace, maul, polearm, spear, swords (all), warhammer. Armor Permitted: All armor and shields. Oriental Campaigns: Also katana, wakizashi. All together, these constitute Good combat abilities.

Other Limitations: None.

Spheres of Influence: Major Access to Combat, Healing. Minor Access to Necromantic, Protection.

Powers: *Incite Berserker Rage* (as per the Designing Faiths chapter). *At 5th level: Inspire Fear* (as per the Designing Faiths chapter).

Followers and Strongholds: The followers are received at 8th level, and consist of one fifth-level priest, three third-level priests and six first-level priests of the same order, plus two fifth-level fighters who act as guards. The priest may take the following on adventures: Three priests of his choice, and one fighter. The priesthood will pay for half of the cost of stronghold construction at 8th level. The stronghold must include a large armory chamber.

Possible Symbols: Sword Across Banner; Polearms In Formation.

Wind

This god is related to the god of sky and weather, but he is devoted only to winds. Sailors, especially, pray to these gods, praying for good winds to take them in the direction they wish to go. Wind-gods are playful and sometimes malicious, and may choose to blow

ships wildly off-course.

The priesthood of the god of winds makes these prayers for friendly winds, and tries to make sure that the wind-god gets his due of worship; but these priests otherwise are left much to their own devices, and many are adventurers and hero-sailors.

Lesser wind-gods will be gods representing specific types of winds: The cold north wind, the balmy southern wind, the terrifying typhoon or hurricane, the incredibly destructive tornado.

Wind-gods are male.

The priests of this god are on good terms with the priests of Sky/Weather.

Alignment: The deity is true neutral. The priests may be true neutral or neutral good; most are true neutral. The flock may be of any alignment.

Minimum Ability Scores: Wisdom 9, Dexterity 12. Wisdom or Dexterity 16 means +5% experience; Wisdom *and* Dexterity 16 means +10% experience.

Races Allowed: Elves, gnomes, half-elves, halflings, humans.

Nonweapon and Weapon Proficiencies: Nonweapon Proficiencies Required: Weather Sense. Nonweapon Proficiencies Recommended: Riding Airborne, Reading/Writing, Religion. Weapon Proficiencies Required: None. Nonweapon Proficiency Group Crossovers: Priest, General.

Duties of the Priest: Guidance, Marriage.

Weapon and Armor Restrictions: Weapons Permitted: Blowgun, bows (all), crossbow, dagger/dirk, dart, hand/throwing axe, javelin, knife, lasso, mace, net, scourge, sling, spear, staff sling, whip. Armor Permitted: All armor; no shields. Oriental Cam-

paigns: Also chain, daikyu, shuriken. All together, these constitute Good combat abilities.

Other Limitations: None.

Spheres of Influence: Major Access to All, Elemental (the priest can only use the spells *dust devil, air walk, chariot of Sustarre,* and *wind walk*), Protection, Weather. Minor Access to Divination, Guardian. The priest gets an extra major access to make up for the severe limitation imposed on his Elemental sphere access.

Powers: *At 3rd level: Shapechanging* (as per the Designing Faiths chapter), into one bird form of the DM's choice (the DM may allow the player to choose the bird form, if the DM so wishes). *At 8th level:* The priest can cast one *aerial servant* spell per day, in addition to all his other spells.

Followers and Strongholds: The followers are received at 8th level, and consist of one fifth-level priest, three third-level priests, and six first-level priests of the same order, plus ten first-level fighters to serve as guards. The priest may take the following on adventures: Any three priests and four fighters of his choice. The priesthood will pay for half of the cost of stronghold construction at 8th level.

Possible Symbols: Birds; Sails Filled With Wind.

Wisdom

This is a god of common sense. Wisdom is distinct from, though normally compatible with, formal education and conventional learning; but it is not the same. It consists merely of having sense enough to know what it otherwise takes experience or an education to learn. The learned man knows from experience when his words will provoke a fight; the wise man knows it intuitively, instinctively.

The priests of this god promote sensible solutions and actions on the part of the flock. They suggest compromises and alternatives. They plan future events. The look for trouble in upcoming events and try to head it off. But this isn't a god of peace, and so the priests of wisdom will often be advisors to military officers, helping them plan effective strategies.

The god of wisdom will be female.

The priests of this god are on good terms with the priests of Divinity of Mankind, Good, Literature/Poetry, Mischief/Trickery, Oracles/Prophecy, and Time. The priests of this god dislike the priests of Evil, whom they do not consider sensible.

Alignment: The deity is good; at the DM's discretion, he may be chaotic good, neutral good, or lawful good, but is probably neutral good. Regardless of his alignment, his priests may be of any good alignment. The flock may be of any neutral or good alignment.

Minimum Ability Scores: Wisdom 13. Wisdom 16 means +10% experience.

Races Allowed: Dwarves, elves, gnomes, half-elves, halflings, humans.

Nonweapon and Weapon Proficiencies: Nonweapon Proficiencies Required: Religion. Nonweapon Proficiencies Recommended: Modern Languages, Ancient History, Ancient Languages, Local History, Reading/Writing. Weapon Proficiencies Required: None. Nonweapon Proficiency Group Crossovers: Priest, General.

Duties of the Priest: Guidance, Marriage. Education: Priests of

this sect believe in education for its own sake, and work to provide teaching to all the flock and even the general population (when possible). Vigilance: These priests try to act as advisors to rulers, in order to keep them from making decisions in a too-hasty or foolish fashion. Local rulers often *do* give them posts as advisors.

Weapon and Armor Restrictions: Weapons Permitted: Bows (all), dagger/dirk, javelin, knife, picks (all), quarterstaff, spear, sword/long, sword/short. Armor Permitted: All armor and shields. Oriental Campaigns: Also bo stick, daikyu, katana, nunchaku, sai, wakizashi. All together, these constitute Good combat abilities.

Other Limitations: None.

Spheres of Influence: Major Access to All, Charm, Divination. Minor Access to Healing, Sun.

Powers: *Immunity* (as per the Designing Faiths chapter) to *confusion* and *feeblemind* spells. *Soothing Word* (as per the Designing Faiths chapter). *At 5th level: Inspire Fear* (as per the Designing Faiths chapter). *At 8th level: Prophecy* (as per the Designing Faiths chapter).

Followers and Strongholds: The followers are received at 9th level, and consist of two third-level priests and four first-level priests of the same order, plus one fifth-level fighter, one third-level fighter, and two second-level fighters to act as guards, and one third-level mage, one third-level bard, one second-level thief, and one second-level illusionist to act as consultants. The priest may take the following on adventures: Two priests (only one of whom may be third-level), plus two fighters of his choice, and two from the following list: mage, bard, thief, and illusion-

ist. The priesthood will pay for half of the cost of stronghold construction at 9th level.

Possible Symbols: Owl, Raven, Vulture.

Combining Traits in One Priesthood

It may be that one god has several different attributes. In real-world mythologies, many, many gods possessed many different traits all at the same time.

Which leads to the question: When one god possesses several attributes, which priest class do you use for his priests?

There are two ways to answer that.

Multiple Priest Classes

One way to do this is to let the god simultaneously have several appropriate priesthoods. They would actually constitute a single "priesthood" with several different "orders" in it, each order dedicated primarily to one of the god's attributes.

That way, if a specific god (let's call him Kyros the Storm-Shaker) is a god of both War and Sky, two characters becoming his priests could do so in different ways. One character can become a priest of the war-god; another is a priest of the sky-god. But they belong to the priesthood of Kyros, each serving the god in a different way.

Let's take an example from real-world mythology. In Greek myth, the god Zeus was a deity of many, many different attributes. These were some of those attributes:

Fertility
Lightning
Oracles/Prophecy

Rulership/Kingship
Sky/Weather
Strength
Wisdom

Therefore, in a campaign where Zeus is a god, a character created to be a priest of Zeus could be any one of those seven types of priests.

In your own campaign, you can define any god as having two or more attributes, and therefore two or more different classes of priests can serve that god.

That's the simple way to do this.

Revised Priest Classes

The hard way to do this is to create an entirely new priest-class. Use the Faith Design Sheet from the previous chapter to work such a thing up.

First, look over the priest class rules for all the classes related to the attributes you want the god to contain. Then, choose the elements from each you like. Remember to balance your choices of the priest's combat abilities with those of his available spheres of influence so that he will not end up significantly stronger or weaker than any other priest class.

Let's create such a class as an example. Let's say the goddess Melebeth is the goddess of Love, but in the city of Askarth she is also the civic deity and is known as "The Girder-On" because she is said to arm the city's warriors for combat; she is therefore a goddess of Love, Community, and War. What does her priesthood look like?

Alignment

The goddess of Community is probably true neutral, but may be of any alignment. The goddess of Love is any sort of good alignment,

and the goddess of War is any sort of Neutral alignment. Therefore, our combined Community/Love/War goddess averages out to be neutral good. Her priests should also be neutral good.

Minimum Ability Scores

The goddess of Community requires W10, Ch12. The goddess of Love requires W10, Ch13. The goddess of War requires W9, S13. Wisdom and Charisma are obviously the leaders here; the priests of this goddess must have Wisdom 10, Charisma 13, and receive +5% experience if either ability is 16 or better, or +10% if both abilities are 16 or better.

Races Allowed

None of the three priest classes (Community, Love, War) excludes any race. Therefore, this combined class allows priests who are dwarves, elves, gnomes, half-elves, halflings, and humans.

Nonweapon and Weapon Proficiencies

Community requires Local History. Love requires Herbalism. War requires Blind-Fighting. None of these seems to apply especially appropriately to this combined goddess; since she was originally a goddess of Love, with the other attributes added in this one city, the default should be Herbalism.

Taking the most appropriate Nonweapon Proficiencies Recommended, we get Heraldry, Reading/Writing, Religion, Riding Land-Based, Healing, Blind-Fighting, and Local History.

Most of the three original classes require no specific Weapon Proficiencies, so we'll follow that pattern here.

Nonweapon Proficiency Group Crossovers are obviously Priest, General, and Warrior.

Duties of the Priest

Taking the duties from the three types of priesthoods which are most appropriate to this combined class, we get:

Guidance, Marriage.

Education in the history of the city.

Vigilance: Trying to preserve the opportunities for romantic love-matches and marriages in the community, but also recommending marriages which will ally strong families and benefit the city.

Missions of defense when the city is threatened by attackers.

Weapon and Armor Restrictions

The Community goddess' priests can use dagger and knife, and two weapons representing the city. The Love goddess' priests can use bow (small), club, lasso, man-catcher, and net. The War goddess' priests can use battle axe, dagger/dirk, knife, lance, mace, maul, polearm, spear, swords (all), war-hammer.

These are three pretty incompatible sets of permitted weapons. But since this combined-attribute goddess will be using weapons mainly to defend her city, we can eliminate the comparatively weak weapons of the pure love-goddess; let us settle on the weapons of the Community goddess' priesthood. This will include dagger and knife, and (for the city of Ashkarth) bows (any) and long sword.

As for armor: The Community goddess' priests could use all armor and shields, the Love Goddess' priests could use no armor or shields, and the War Goddess' priests could use all armor and shields. It sounds, by weight of numbers, as though the priests should be able to use all armor and shields. Between the superior armor and the two good weapons they can use, these priests have Good combat abilities. This means they will have very limited magic.

Other Limitations

Priests of the civic goddess must always wear priestly garments in public; priests of the love goddess get four-sided hit dice and must be wed by the time they reach 8th level; priests of the war-goddess have no other limitations.

The combined-goddess' priests should retain the limitation of wearing priestly garments whenever they're in public; these priests are still priests of a civic deity, after all.

And since the goddess is still a deity of love, the marriage restriction should remain.

But since this goddess is a fighter, let's drop the four-sided hit dice limitation; priests of this priesthood receive eight-sided hit dice like most fighting priests.

Spheres of Influence

The priests of the community-goddess get: Major Access to All, Creation, Healing. Minor Access to Combat, Protection.

The priests of the love-goddess get: Major Access to All, Animal, Charm, Healing, Necromantic, Protection, Summoning. Minor Access to Creation, Divination, Guardian, Plant, Sun, and Weather.

The priests of the war-goddess get: Major Access to Combat, Healing. Minor Access to Necromantic, Protection.

Since this priesthood, as we de-cided above, has Good Combat Abilities, the priesthood will have Major Access to the All sphere and two other spheres, and Minor Access to two spheres. Let's choose the most appropriate ones.

Therefore, the priests of this combined-trait goddess get: Major Access to All, Charm, Healing. Minor Access to Combat, Protection.

Powers

Priests of the community-goddess get *Incite Berserker Rage*, *Soothing Word*, and *Turn Undead*.

Priests of the love-goddess get *Charm/Fascination*, *Incite Berserker Rage*, *Inspire Fear*, *Soothing Word*, and *Turn Undead*; these priests received extra powers partly because they had only four-sided hit dice, a condition that the priests of this combined goddess do not share.

Priests of the war-goddess get *Incite Berserker Rage*; At 5th level: Inspire Fear.

Taking the common threads from these three goddesses, we decide that priests of the combined-attribute goddess receive:

Incite Berserker Rage, *Turn Undead*, and, *at 5th level, Inspire Fear*.

Followers and Strongholds

The goddesses of Community and Love both get their followers at 7th level, the goddess of War at 8th; so we'll settle on 7th level, and also at 7th level the priesthood will pay for half of the stronghold con-structions.

The goddess of community gets 15 levels of priests and 15 levels of fighters.

The goddess of love gets 15 levels of priests, five levels of mage/consultants, five levels of fighter/

guards, and five levels of Normal Men and Women with appropriate Nonweapon Proficiencies.

The goddess of war gets 20 levels of priests and 10 levels of fighter/guards.

Averaging this out somewhat, the priest of our combined-aspect goddess should get 15 levels of priests (three third-level priests and six first-level priests), 10 levels of fighters (two third-level fighters and four first-level fighters to act as guards), and five levels of mage/consultants (one third-level mage and two first-level mages). On adventures, he can take three priests (as usual, only one can be third-level; the remaining two third-level priests run the temple in the character's absence), three fighters (ditto), and one mage of his choice.

Multi-Class Characters

It's possible for demihumans to be multi-class combinations including the priest character classes above.

On the chart of the *Player's Handbook*, page 44, showing the possible multi-class combinations, substitute the word "priest" wherever you see "cleric." Those are the possible combinations.

The only limit the character possesses on which type of priest he may be is the racial limitation posed for each priest-class above. If a priest-class says that elves can't belong to it, then obviously an elf can't be a multi-class fighter/priest of that type of priesthood.

Multi-class priest characters follow all the rules for multi-class characters, from pages 44 and 45 of the *Player's Handbook*.

In the last chapter, you were confronted with over sixty different priest character classes to choose from. Certainly, that range of choices will make it easy for your to individualize your priest character — to make him different from the rest of the campaign's clerics.

In this chapter, we'll make that even easier.

You can further customize your priest by taking a *priest kit* for him. A *kit* is a collection of skills, proficiencies, restrictions, benefits and hindrances which give the priest more background and personality, further define his role in the campaign and in the campaign's cultures, and give him advantages and disadvantages to make him more colorful.

Kits and the Priest Classes

A kit is more of a cultural description than anything else. Therefore, *most* kits are allowed to priests of *most* faiths. There are exceptions, of course; for example, a priest of the god of Peace may not take the Fighting-Monk kit. Wherever such an exception occurs, it will be mentioned in the text.

Kits and Character Creation

No priest character *has* to take any priest-kit. It's not necessary, it's not required: It's just a way of adding detail to the character.

A priest character may only take one priest-kit. He should take it when he is first created. In campaigns which began before you got *The Complete Priest Handbook*, the DM should allow characters to take priest-kits, but only ones which are appropriate to the characters' actions and deeds so far.

(For example, if a character has been a perfectly ordinary priest until now, he should not take the Outlaw Priest kit; it's not appropriate.)

Once a character has taken a Priest Kit, he cannot change it to another Priest Kit. He can, however, eventually *abandon* it (see "Abandoning Kits" later in this chapter); having abandoned a kit, he will not be able to take another one.

If you want to inject the choice of the Priest Kit into the character creation process, you'll first want to determine your character's Ability Scores (*Player's Handbook* Chapter 1), Race (Chapter 2), Class (Cleric or Druid from Chapter 3 of the *Player's Handbook*, or one of the priest classes from the previous chapter of this book), and Alignment (Chapter 4).

It's at this point that you choose your priest kit.

After that's done, and the information recorded on your character sheet, you can proceed to Proficiencies (Chapter 5), Money and Equipment (Chapter 6), etc.

The Priest Kits

Each priest kit consists of the following elements:

Description: This paragraph talks about what this type of priest is to the culture. It also lists any requirements necessary for the character to take the kit; for instance, to be a Savage Priest, the character must have been born among or adopted by a savage tribe.

Barred: This paragraph details which priest classes (plus cleric and druid) may *not* take this priest kit.

Role: This kit describes the role of this priest in his society and campaign. For example, an Outlaw Priest of the God of Love would have a very different campaign role than the Amazon Priestess of the same god.

Secondary Skills: If you're using the Secondary Skills rules from the AD&D® 2nd Edition game rule books, then your kit may require your priest to take a specific skill instead of choosing or random-rolling his Secondary Skill. However, even more so than in *The Complete Fighter's Handbook*, we're recommending that you use the Weapon and Nonweapon Proficiency rules instead of the Secondary Skill rules.

Weapon Proficiencies: The priest-kit could require the priest to take a specific weapon proficiency. This is one of the factors that makes it impossible for some priest classes to take some priest kits; obviously, no priest class which cannot use a weapon required by a kit could take that kit.

Nonweapon Proficiencies: A given priest kit may require the priest to have a specific nonweapon proficiencies; however, unlike the situation above with Weapon Proficiencies, these are *bonuses*. If a kit requires that the character know Riding (Horse), then the character gets that proficiency free, above and beyond the slots he is normally granted. Some proficiencies might be granted from other than the Priest or General groups, but this doesn't matter; if a proficiency is given free, then it is free.

If the Priest Kit grants a proficiency that the priest has already had granted to him because of his specific priesthood, the character, instead of receiving that proficiency again, receives one extra free nonweapon proficiency slot

which he may spend as he pleases.

Some proficiencies will merely be recommended, not required. When this is the case, the proficiency is *not* given to the character, and the character doesn't have to take it if he doesn't want to. If the character decides to take this nonweapon proficiency, he uses up the appropriate number of his available nonweapon proficiency slots.

Equipment: Some priest kits limit the way their priests acquire or use certain types of equipment; when there is such a limitation, this paragraph will deal with it.

Special Benefits: Most priest kits include special benefits that the priest-character receives. Often, they're defined as special reaction bonuses among certain classes of society, special rights in certain cultures, etc.

Special Hindrances: Likewise, each priest kit carries certain disadvantages which hinder the priest. Outlaw priests are sought by their own orders and perhaps the authorities, for example.

Wealth Options: Some priest kits have special rules regarding their wealth. Generally, these rules don't affect the amount of gold he'll have when he is created (with all clerics and priests, this amounts to 3d6x10gp). However, different priest-kits have variations on the way the money is to be spent. Some insist that it all be spent at the beginning, and the remainder of starting gold returned to the priest's superiors. Others let the priest "keep the change;" still others have limits on the amount that can be spent initially.

Races: If a particular priest-kit discriminates among the demihuman races (for example, if an elf can't take a specific kit), that will be noted here.

DM Choices

Before allowing his players to choose kits for their priests, the DM should look over the priest-kits and make some decisions.

For each Priest Kit, the DM has to choose:

(1) If he will even allow this Kit in his campaign. (It could be that the kit is inappropriate. If there are no Amazons in his world, he shouldn't allow the Amazon priest-kit.)

(2) What additional information he needs to give the players about each Kit. (DMs will probably want to elaborate on the priest-kits to fit them better into his campaign.)

(3) What changes he might wish to make to each Kit. (If, for example, our conception of the Barbarian doesn't match the DM's, he might wish to change the benefits, hindrances, or other factors to match his conception.)

An Important Note

Several Priest Kits get reaction bonuses and penalties as part of their Special Benefits and Special Hindrances.

In the AD&D® game, when a character has a very high or low charisma, he gets what is called a "reaction adjustment." (See the *Player's Handbook*, page 18.) When the character has a high charisma and receives a bonus, it's expressed as a plus: For example, +2. When he has a low charisma and receives a penalty, it's expressed as a minus: For instance, -3.

But here's a special warning: When you roll the 2d10 for Encounter Reactions (see the *Dungeon Master's Guide*, page 103, *don't add the bonus (+) or subtract the penalty (−) from the die roll*. Do it the other way around: Subtract the bonus (+) and add the penalty (−). If the character has a Charisma of 16, and thus gets a +5 reaction adjustment, you *subtract* that number from the 2d10 die roll. Otherwise the more charismatic or appealing a PC is, the more vigorously all the NPCs and monsters would dislike him!

Amazon Priestess

Description: Amazons are women warriors in a world where most cultures are male-dominated or ruled more or less equally by men and women. The Amazon civilization is different from the cultures of the rest of the world in that women occupy all the most important occupations and positions in their society; men are either second-class citizens, or are all kept as slaves, or are exiled from the culture altogether. Amazons continually have to defend themselves from the efforts of surrounding civilizations to "return them to normal," and therefore they are very good at war.

Such civilizations often have one or two specific patron gods. (The deity does not have to be female; in classical mythology, for instance, the Amazons' patron was Ares, the very male god of war.)

The priestesses of this god interpret the god's will for the Amazons, fight alongside them in times of combat, perform the usual service of guidance (and even marriage, if this is still a function of this specific Amazon society); and sometimes travel through the outer world in an effort to learn what they can of the world of men—in order to protect themselves from it, or to educate themselves and the outer-worlders to reduce misunderstandings between the cultures.

There are no special ability-score requirements to be an Amazon.

To abandon this kit, the character would have to renounce her Amazon citizenship... meaning that she would have to identify herself more strongly with another culture.

Barred: The DM will decide which gods act as patrons for the Amazon civilization; most Amazon priestesses will serve those specific gods. However, not all Amazon priestesses *have* to serve those specific gods. An Amazon culture could have as its patron the gods of War and Moon, for instance, but a specific Amazon priestess could serve another god. (Since each attribute has its own role to play in any civilization, few gods are really inappropriate.) Note, though, that no Amazon priestess can serve the gods of Disease or Peace. Also, since Amazon warriors must know the use of the spear and long bow, an Amazon priestess who cannot use those weapons will be looked down upon, and won't command the respect of priestesses who can. Therefore, an Amazon will command less respect *unless she is a priestess of one of the following gods*: Community, Competition, Elemental Forces, Good, Hunting, Light, Mischief/Trickery, Moon, Oracles/Prophecy, Race (Human), Sky/Weather, Sun, War, Wind, Wisdom.

Role: Among the Amazons, the priestess-types listed immediately above are as highly-regarded as the warrior, and the warrior is the most-admired type of Amazon. Outside the Amazon lands, among male-dominated civilizations, the priestess is looked on as an even more unnatural sort of unnatural woman. In cultures where men and women are approximately equal in influence, the Amazon is looked on as a curiosity, and may even (at the DM's discretion) be looked down on as a representative of a race that hasn't yet come to the conclusion that neither gender should oppress the other.

Among player-character adventurers, the Amazon-priestess is likely to prove herself to be a doughty fighter and an effective spellcaster. If the priestess character starts out suffering a bit of discrimination when she's introduced into the campaign, that may be normal according to the culture but the DM shouldn't encourage this attitude, especially after she's proven herself in dangerous situations. Even if the campaign's main culture is discriminatory, the PCs should demonstrate a little more flexibility in their attitudes based on their adventuring experiences.

Secondary Skills: Required: Groom.

Weapon Proficiencies: Required: None. Recommended: Spear, long bow; if possible, various axes and swords.

Nonweapon Proficiencies: Bonus Proficiencies: Riding (Land-Based), Animal Training. Recommended: (General) Animal Handling, (Warrior) Animal Lore, Armorer, Bowyer/Fletcher, Hunting, Running, Survival, Tracking.

Equipment: When an Amazon character is first created, she must buy her armor from among the fol-lowing choices only: Shield, leather, padded, studded leather, brigandine, scale mail, hide, banded mail, bronze plate mail. Once she has adventured elsewhere in the world, she may purchase other types of armor according to her priest-class limitations.

Special Benefits: Male opponents from cultures where women fighters tend to be rare will be amused, rather than cautious, the first time they confront an Amazon. Therefore, in a fight where such a warrior runs up against an Amazon for the first time, the Amazon gets a +3 to hit and +3 damage on her *first blow only*. This reflects the fact that her opponent's guard is down.

This bonus doesn't work on any Warrior character of fifth level or higher, or a character of any other class at 8th level or higher; in spite of any prejudices he might bear, this character is too seasoned an adventurer to let his guard down that way.

At the DM's discretion, he can give a wary, suspicious NPC an Intelligence check; on a successful check, he will see the attack coming and deny the Amazon the bonus.

The bonus won't work on any male fighter who comes from a culture where women do regularly fight, or who has had fighting-women comrades or faced fighting-women opponents before, or even who has seen the Amazon hit someone else with this bonus earlier.

It doesn't work on player-characters unless the player is role-playing honestly enough to admit that his character would underestimate the Amazon.

Once the Amazon hits a character with this bonus, the target (if he survives) will never fall for it again. It can only be used successfully once per victim, ever. But if the Amazon misses a target with this blow, she continues to receive it against this target until she hits him once.

Special Hindrances: The Amazon receives a −3 reaction roll adjustment from NPCs from male-dominated societies. Player-characters do not have to demonstrate this hostility unless they want to do so for role-playing purposes, and even then it should fade as they come to respect her.

Wealth Options: The Amazon gets the ordinary 3d6x10 gp as starting money.

Races: None are excluded. Humans, elvish, and half-elvish Amazons are most appropriate. Dwarves would substitute battle axe and warhammer for their weapons and swine for their preferred mounts. Gnomes would substitute throwing axe and short sword, and would ride ponies, and would have Tracking and Survival as their Bonus Nonweapon Proficiencies. Halflings would substitute javelin and sling for their weapons, and Endurance and Set Snares for their Bonus Nonweapon Proficiencies.

Barbarian/Berserker Priest

Description: This priest is the priest of a culture halfway between what we think of as civilized and savage. His people live at the very edge of or beyond the borders of the edges of the campaign's main civilization. They tend to be very warlike, fighting battles with neighboring tribes and with intruding imperial troops. Their fighters aren't soldiers; they are warriors, and tend to be deadlier in

one-on-one fighting but poorer at formation combat than those of the "civilized" nations. These warriors may, in fact, be berserkers (see *The Complete Fighter Handbook*). They are still more in touch with nature and the world than the people of civilized lands. They may have very different customs from civilized folk.

Priests of this community perform the same functions as priests of civilized lands. However, barbarians have more respect for the gods than civilized folk, and priests also are well-respected. Kings and war-chiefs of their culture listen to their counsel. In their culture, those who disagree with them do not insult them or their guidance, and it is forbidden for a warrior to attack a priest of his culture (though defending himself from attack is all right... if he can prove that it was defense, not aggression).

There are no ability requirements to be a priest of a barbarian or berserker tribe. The warriors of the tribe must have Strength 15, and priests will be most impressive if they can approximate or match that score... but it's not a requirement of the kit.

As with the Amazon, abandonment of this kit means that the character renounces his allegiance to his tribe or clan and accepts citizenship in some other culture. This means that he must now perform his priestly duties in the fashion of the priests of that culture.

Barred: Barbarian tribes tend to have one or two patron gods, and most of their priests will serve those gods. These tend to be gods of natural forces (Agriculture, Animals, Darkness/Night, Earth, Elemental Forces, Fertility, Hunting, Lightning, Metalwork, Nature,

Sky/Weather, Thunder) or other barbarian attributes (Strength, War). Gods of the "softer" attributes (Arts, Love, Music, etc.) would be represented but their priests would be much rarer. No priesthood is barred among the barbarians, however scarce.

Role: In the campaign, the barbarian priest is a spooky, dangerous figure. Like barbarian warriors, he'll be grim and a little alien to his allies from civilized lands. First and foremost, he's a defender of his people, and he'll most often be found wandering in lands other than his own because of some quest set him by the gods or some mystery he's encountered that requires him to travel in order to solve it. When he finds his own tribesmen captured or enslaved in the outer world, which might be a common occurrence, he must do his utmost to free them and return them to his own land, which can imperil other goals he and his player-character allies have. . . but as a leader and protector of his culture, this is a duty he cannot refuse. (If he were to do so, the god would take it as a betrayal of goals; see the Role-Playing chapter.)

Secondary Skills: The main occupation of the barbarian's tribe determines what sort of secondary skill he knows. If the tribe raises and sells horses, then the Groom secondary skill will be known by all tribesmen. Ask the DM what the tribe's main occupation is and that will determine the required Secondary Skill.

Weapon Proficiencies: Required: None. Recommended: Battle axe, sword/bastard, bow (any), sling, warhammer. Naturally, the priesthood may limit the priest's choice of weapons and not allow him to learn all these.

Nonweapon Proficiencies: Bonus Proficiency: Endurance. Recommended: (General) Animal Handling, Animal Training, Direction Sense, Fire-Building, Riding (Land-Based), Weather Sense, Blind-Fighting, Hunting, Mountaineering, Running, Set Snares, Survival, Tracking, Herbalism, Jumping. (Some of these are outside the priest's Nonweapon Proficiency Group Crossovers and will cost twice the listed slots if taken; see the description of the priest class, and the chart at the bottom of the *Player's Handbook*, page 55, for more details.) The DM may require this priest to take a proficiency in the tribal specialty (Fishing, Agriculture, etc.).

Equipment: With his starting gold, the barbarian priest cannot buy armor heavier than splint mail, banded mail, or bronze plate mail. Once he has adventured in the outer world, he can buy any type of armor his priestly requirements allow him to use. With his starting gold, he can buy only weapons appropriate to his tribe (usually battle axe, bows, club, dagger/dirk, footman's flail, mace, or pick, hand/throwing axe, sling, spear, and swords); naturally, priestly restrictions may prevent him from taking some of these, depending on which god he serves.

Special Benefits: Barbarians are imposing and dangerous-looking. This tends to make others respect them or at least wish not to make enemies of them. Therefore, barbarian/berserker priests receive a +1 reaction adjustment bonus when encountering NPCs. This becomes a +3 among members of his own culture.

If the priest's culture has many Berserker warriors, as per *The Complete Fighter's Handbook*, the priest has an additional special ability. Berserkers normally take ten rounds to go berserk; in the presence of one of their own priests, then can do it in five. Additionally, if the priest, as part of his priestly class, has the *incite berserker rage* granted power, then berserkers of his culture in his presence can go berserk in *one round*. The priest is not required to use his power for this to take place; it just happens.

Special Hindrances: The barbarian/berserker priest has a problem in civilized lands: He doesn't respect the authorities and they have learned to be cautious of him. (This sort of priest keeps freeing his enslaved brethren, and, even if he worships a god known to this culture, he does so in a different way that the locals consider wrong.) Therefore, the barbarian/berserker priest receives a −3 reaction adjustment penalty when encountering NPCs in positions of power: Rulers, government officials, etc.

Wealth Options: No special requirements; this priest gets the usual 3d6x10 gp as starting money.

Races: There are no special restrictions here. Each individual DM has to decide whether or not his demihumans can live in what are considered barbarian cultures. If they can, then they will have priests among them.

Fighting-Monk

Description: This priest belongs to an order devoted in large part to the study of fighting styles, especially barehanded martial arts. These monks live and study in monasteries devoted to their orders. If, for example, they are priests of the god of War, these monks do not live and study in ordinary temples of that god; they have their own secluded monastery away from the normal temples.

These monks do not confine their war-training to the monasteries, however. They travel the wide world in order to learn the secrets of life, the world, magic and the gods. As an order, they sometimes volunteer their services to rulers in times of war, and act as elite forces against the enemy.

These monks are most appropriate for an oriental-flavored campaign and the DM may wish to decide that they cannot be used in his campaign. Before you create a Fighting-Monk character, consult your DM and ask if he is allowing the Fighting-Monk kit in his campaign.

In order to be a fighting-monk, the character must have a Dexterity of 12 or more.

If a fighting-monk wants to abandon this kit, he must go through a difficult process in order to do so. He must not use any of his unarmed combat techniques for three whole experience levels' worth of time. Once he's reached that third experience level, he has forgotten his unarmed combat techniques and may resume the wearing of armor; and, if he renounced some of his spheres of influence when he became a fighting-monk, may now resume those lost spheres.

As an example, a fighting-monk priest at 5th level decides to renounce his allegiance to the fighting-monk order. He adventures normally, still not wearing armor but otherwise performing as a normal priest of his priest-class. He abstains from using his unarmed combat techniques. At

8th level, he has abandoned his fighting techniques and may once again wear the armor appropriate to his priest-class.

If a character forgets himself and uses unarmed combat techniques during this process, he must "start over." It will be three experience levels from his *current* level, from the time he made the slip, until he can resume his priest-class.

Barred: A priest of any priesthood which starts out with Poor Fighting Abilities is barred from this choice.

Role: In the campaign, this priest is the philosophical warrior whose principal duty is self-enlightenment. He is less concerned with the ordinary priestly duties (such as guidance, marriage, community service) than those priests, but will still perform them; he just won't go out of his way to look for them, nor will he normally volunteer for them (NPCs must ask his help in these matters). Such characters are usually wanderers, which help make them appropriate for adventuring parties. They do periodically return to their monasteries, to pass on the learning they have acquired on the road, and to brush up on their fighting-skills; the rest of the time they spend out in the world.

Secondary Skills: This priest may choose or random-roll his secondary skill, if you are using the secondary skills system in addition to the weapon/nonweapon proficiencies system.

Weapon Proficiencies: Required: See under "Special Benefits," below. Otherwise, the priest may take any weapon proficiencies which his specific priest class allows him; he may not take any the class does not allow him.

Nonweapon Proficiencies: Bo-nus Proficiency: Tumbling. Recommended: Riding (Land-Based), Artistic Ability (any), Dancing, Reading/Writing, Religion.

Equipment: See "Special Hindrances," below.

Special Benefits: The principal benefit of being a Fighting-Monk is that the character receives *two free weapon proficiency slots* which he must use to take Specialization in one of the three styles of Unarmed Combat (Punching, Wrestling, or Martial Arts). These were described in greater detail in *The Complete Fighter's Handbook*, but that information also appears here, in the "Equipment and Combat" chapter. The Fighting-Monk is the only priest who can specialize in an Unarmed Combat style. He can specialize in any or all of the three styles, but he may only specialize in one of them at first experience level.

As a second benefit, regardless of what it says for the priest's class, the Fighting-Monk has a Nonweapon Proficiency Group Crossover with *all five* Proficiency Groups (General, Priest, Rogue, Warrior, Wizard). No proficiency he takes will cost double the usual number of slots.

The last of the Fighting-Monk's benefits is this: He doesn't have to spend all his starting Weapon Proficiency slots at first level. He can save his unspent proficiencies, and they do not "go away." Later, he can spend them at a rate of one proficiency per experience level to improve his martial arts or buy new martial arts.

Special Hindrances: This priest cannot wear any sort of armor. Additionally, if he's a priest-class with Medium Combat Abilities, he must "give up" some of his Spheres of Influence. He may have no more than *three* Major Accesses (one of which must be All) and *two* Minor Accesses. The player may choose from the accesses he currently has which ones the character loses and which he keeps.

Additionally, the priest may never own more things (weapons, treasure, money, etc.) than he can carry on his back.

Wealth Options: The Fighting-Monk gets the usual 3d6x10 gp as starting money.

Races: No special limitations. Humans, elves and half-elves seem visually more suited to this kit than dwarves, gnomes, and halflings, but the DM can allow those races to take this kit if he so chooses.

Nobleman Priest

Description: This priest was a member of a noble family and entered a priesthood. But even as a priest he keeps his opinions about the superiority of the ruling classes and his tastes for the finer things in life; he doesn't abandon his love of good food, good furnishings, comfort, the arts, intellectual stimulation, and so forth.

The Nobleman Priest prefers the company of nobles and is often appointed as an advisor to a noble family, a ruler, an important local governor, etc. He has less concern for the lives and welfare of commoners. When pressed, he will perform any and all priestly duties for commoners, but he usually seeks to avoid these duties; when he is a low-level character, he'll keep himself away from common folk as much as possible in order to avoid these inconveniences, and when he is higher-level he will assign a subordinate or a follower to attend their needs.

The Nobleman Priest is not necessarily evil or a bad person. In fact, he often adheres to a code of chivalric behavior much like a knight's. But he does have strong social prejudices which color his thinking.

Important note: A nobleman can become a priest and not take the Nobleman Priest kit. This sort of priest lives more frugally, like other priests, and does not have to have a disdain for the lower social classes; Nobleman Priests do not count him among their ranks.

There are no special requirements to be a Nobleman Priest.

If a Nobleman Priest player-character ever decides that he is wrong in his attitudes (which can occur in especially dramatic fashion if he is affected by the self-sacrifice of a commoner who has saved him, or if he falls in love with a character of the common social classes), he may choose to abandon this kit. If he does this, he will be ostracized by most of the nobles who were previously counted as his friends (the DM can have one or two more broad-minded nobles still count him a friend, and the player-characters can make up their own minds on the subject); he may even be exiled from his own family. As with any kit abandonment, he loses all other benefits and hindrances of the kit.

Barred: None.

Role: In the campaign, the Nobleman Priest is an aggravating snob (though he might not be aware of his snobbery). He is a fun role to play, but he'd better have some redeeming features if the other PCs are to continue to associate with him. If he does have redeeming features, it's very likely that some PCs will try to "reform" him to their own way of thinking.

Secondary Skills: Nobleman Priests may choose or random-roll their Secondary Skill.

Weapon Proficiencies: Required: None. Recommended: Long sword, bastard sword, lance, flails (all), maces (all), if allowed by the priest's actual priest class.

Nonweapon Proficiencies: Bonus Proficiencies: (General) Etiquette, Heraldry, Riding (Land-Based). Recommended: (General) Animal Training, Dancing, (Warrior, double slots unless the priest class has a nonweapon proficiency group crossover including the Warrior group) Gaming, Hunting, (Priest) Local History, Musical Instrument, Reading/Writing.

Equipment: The Nobleman Priest may spend his gold as he chooses — but he has certain minimum standards he cannot violate. Before starting play, he must buy:

(1) A suit of armor (if he is permitted to by his priest-class. . . and, unless his class limits him to lesser armor, he cannot buy armor less protective than brigandine or scale mail).

(2) At least one weapon larger than a dagger (again, if his priest-class so permits him).

(3) A horse (at least a riding horse), riding saddle, bit & bridle, horseshoes and shoeing, halter and saddle blanket.

Special Benefits: The Nobleman Priest starts with more gold than other priests; see below under **Wealth Options**.

The Nobleman Priest receives a +3 reaction from any noble of his own culture, and a +2 from nobles of other cultures. The DM can ignore this if there is a cultural hatred between those people and the priest's culture or the priest's god.

When travelling, he can demand shelter from anyone in his own land; he can demand shelter for two people multiplied by the priest's experience level (if he's eighth level, he can demand shelter for himself and a retinue of fifteen more people).

Special Hindrances: The Nobleman Priest is expected to live well. If he has enough money to do so, he may only buy high-quality goods, and so must spend at least two times the minimum necessary money for anything he buys. If a basic long sword costs 15 gp, he won't buy one worth less than 30 gp; the extra money goes into quality, engraving, etc. (He can't save money by having a friend or follower buy cheaper things for him; he's just not satisfied with anything less than good-quality merchandise.)

If the priest is broke and cannot spend this extra money, he can then settle for lesser goods. . . but the other nobles of his culture, if they see him with shabby accoutrements, will mock him, and he does not get his reaction bonus until once again all his goods are high-quality goods. In fact, if his gear and possessions look sufficiently shabby (DM's discretion), people may not believe him to be a nobleman at all, and may refuse him the shelter he could ordinarily demand. (This happens most often if a nobleman priest is robbed of all his clothes and goods and left to fend for himself.)

As he can demand shelter of others, other Nobleman Priests can demand shelter of him. This can be expensive if they decide to stay for awhile. This is also a good way for the DM to bleed extra money from the priest if he seems to have too much.

Wealth Options: The Nobleman

Priest begins play with more gold than other priests. He gets 225 gp plus the standard 3d6x10 gp. But he must spend a good portion of that on the Equipment required of him. If the priest abandons this kit, that money doesn't magically "go away," but as part of his social ostracization the character should suffer some sort of financial loss, equal to at least 225 gp, as determined by the DM. (Perhaps a malicious ex-friend destroys some of his property; perhaps a petty-minded business acquaintance betrays him on a business deal.)

Races: This kit has no special requirements for race. The DM may decide that not all races have the same kind of social snobbery that humans do, in which case that race could not take this kit.

Outlaw Priest

Description: This priest has decided to become part of some sort of outlaw community and serve that community's religious needs. The trouble is, for the character to take this kit, this group or community must be sufficiently outlawed that the priesthood in question does not approve of it. Alternatively, the priest may have decided that the god's priesthood is not serving him in an appropriate way, and he will have decided to create his own priestly order serving the same god. In this case, too, the regular priesthood does not approve of him. In either case, the priest must believe that he is still serving the god in a fashion that the god approves of. (The DM, obviously, must agree.)

Friar Tuck, the cleric who tended to Robin Hood's Merry Men, is the classic example of this type of priest.

This priest, in the pursuit of his duties, is opposed by other priests serving the same god. In addition, if he's identified himself with an outlaw or pirate band, he'll be wanted by the authorities as a member of that band.

There are no special ability-score requirements to be an Outlaw Priest.

A priest abandons this kit by leaving the outlaw band or opposing/disbanding the new religious order, whichever is pertinent. Additionally, by role-playing in the campaign, he must answer all the charges pressed against him by the authorities (he might do this by being tried and going to prison for a time, or paying reparations, or accepting tasks of penance from his temple); if he does not, he will continue to be opposed by his temple and wanted by the authorities.

Barred: Priests of the gods of Community may not take this kit. Priests of no Philosophy or Force may take this kit. (They can associate themselves with pirate or outlaw bands, but there is no censure within their orders because of it, and therefore no disadvantage to belonging to such a band.)

Role: This sort of priest has one of two roles, depending on the situation.

(1) With the first situation mentioned above, the priest has joined an outlaw or pirate band. In the campaign, then, he's the rogue priest who has decided that the band deserves his priestly guidance, and that this is more important than the demands of his priestly order. The priest either agrees with the band's outlaw activities or ignores them; his concern is that they receive the blessings of his god. Perhaps, too,

he thinks that they'll be a more ethical group with him around; he may be present to keep them from performing acts of brutality or rapine, which they might undertake were he not present.

(2) In the second situation mentioned above, the priest is a rogue visionary who thinks that he must serve his god in a way not approved of by the normal priesthood. This character is probably someone who went through the temple's normal priestly training, decided that there was something wrong or lacking in it, and set out to found his own order. A classic example of this is the situation where a priesthood has become corrupt and lazy, and a reformer priest has appeared to try to return the worship of the god to its former honorable state; the corrupt priests naturally wish to maintain the *status quo*.

Secondary Skills: The priest can choose his own secondary skill. If he's part of a pirate band, he may wish to choose Sailor, Shipwright or Navigator. If he's part of a landbound outlaw band, he might choose Forester, Hunter, or Trapper/Furrier. He may decide on none of these and make a decision based on his life before he entered the priesthood.

Weapon Proficiencies: Required: None. Recommended: If Pirate, cutlass*, belaying pin*, bill. If Outlaw, weapon choices appropriate for the outlaw band. (The "*" symbol refers to weapons introduced in *The Complete Fighter's Handbook*.)

Nonweapon Proficiencies: Bonus Proficiency: Religion.

Recommended Proficiencies (Pirate Priest): Pirate's Bonus Proficiencies: (General) Rope Use, Seamanship, Swimming, Weather

Sense, (Warrior, double slots unless priest-class dictates otherwise) Navigation, (Priest) Engineering (for shipbuilding), Reading/Writing (for mapmaking), (Rogue, double slots unless priest-class dictates otherwise) Appraising, Set Snares (in association with Rope Use skill), Tightrope Walking, Tumbling, (Wizard, double slots unless priest-class dictates otherwise) Engineering (for shipbuilding), Reading/Writing (for mapmaking).

Recommended Proficiencies (Outlaw Priest): (General) Direction Sense, Fire-Building, Riding (Land-Based), (Warrior, double slots unless priest-class dictates otherwise) Animal Lore, Bowyer/Fletcher, Endurance, Hunting, Running, Set Snares, Survival, Tracking, (Priest) Healing, Herbalism, Local History, (Rogue, double slots unless priest-class dictates otherwise) Disguise.

Equipment: No restrictions. Within the context of the campaign, if this is a pirate or outlaw band, it's a bad idea to wear metal armor (banded, brigandine, bronze plate, chain, field plate, full plate, plate mail, and ring mail). Metal armor drags pirates down to their deaths when they fall overboard; and it's noisy when worn by outlaws trying to ambush their prey. But this is just a factor the DM needs to remember, not a restriction on the kit.

Special Benefits: The main benefit of this kit is that the priest does not have any superiors. He takes orders from no superior religious authority (unless the god himself chooses to issue some).

Special Hindrances: The outlaw priest is opposed by the normal priestly order serving his god. When they hear of his plans, they try to thwart them (break up religious meetings, disrupt building of his temple, etc.). This priest never gets to build a temple at cut-rate prices; he must always spend the whole amount to build his temple. (If he ever abandons his kit, the regular priesthood may accept his temple as one belonging to the priesthood, but will never recompense him half the money it took to build it.) If the outlaw priest is part of an outlaw or pirate band, he is sought by the same authorities that seek that band, and will pay the same penalties under the law as they do if he is caught.

Wealth Options: Outlaw priests get the standard 3d6x10 gp for starting gold.

Races: No special restrictions.

Pacifist Priest

Description: This priest is devoted to the cause of peace. He is a champion of passive resistance, of achieving one's ends without resorting to violence of any kind.

There are no special requirements to be a priest of this sort. Nor are there special rules for abandonment of the kit, if the character eventually feels that he needs to be wielding force to achieve his ends.

Barred: Priests of the following gods, forces and philosophies may not be Pacifist Priests: Disease, Evil, Justice/Revenge, War.

Role: In a campaign, this priest can be a real aggravation to the more combat-oriented player-characters. Therefore, the DM should allow this priest in only the following situations:

(1) When he's an NPC, so that the DM doesn't have to work to contrive to keep him with the party all the time (they'll have an easier time of abandoning him if they wish);

(2) When he's part of a specific quest or mission (i.e., they must accompany him and guard him throughout the quest or it will automatically fail); or

(3) When all the PCs are pacifists (this would be a very unusual campaign or quest, indeed...).

Note, though, that just because the priest demands peacefulness of all around him, his allies don't have to obey. However, it is inevitable that in combat situations the player of the pacifist priest will feel left out (he can't fight); additionally, he'll feel compelled by his philosophy to argue with the other PCs, to chide them for their violence, which will get on their nerves. Therefore, the DM should keep such quests short, so that the pacifist priest doesn't drive the other characters to the point that they'll kill him.

Secondary Skills: This priest may choose or random-roll his secondary skill. It may not be Armorer, Hunter, or Trapper/Furrier (if he rolls one of these up randomly, he may re-roll).

Weapon Proficiencies: The Pacifist Priest may not know any Weapon Proficiency except bow and dart, and may know them only if his true priest-class allows them. The priest may only use these weapons in competition, as described below under "Special Hindrances." The priest still receives all his Weapon Proficiency slots, and if he ever abandons this kit may "spend" them at a rate of two slots every experience level.

Nonweapon Proficiencies: Bonus Proficiency: Etiquette. Recommended: Languages (Modern), Languages (Ancient), Ancient History, Singing, Musical Instrument, Reading/Writing.

Equipment: This priest may not buy any armor, and may not buy any weapon except dagger or knife (for eating only), and bow and dart (if he has proficiency with them).

Special Benefits: This priest is a very compelling personality. He receives a +2 to his Charisma score (his Charisma cannot exceed 18 from this bonus), and, in addition to any reaction bonus that his heightened Charisma gives him, he receives a +2 reaction from anyone who is not utterly opposed to his philosophy. (Beings opposed to his philosophy include priests and devoted adherents of the gods, forces and philosophies mentioned above under "Barred," and certain war-like nonhuman races like orcs, ogres and trolls.)

Special Hindrances: This priest may never wear armor, and may never use weapons, spells or any other tactics to harm a human, demihuman, nonhuman, or monster. If he ever violates this decree, his *god* will not punish him (because the pacifist's oath is one he took for himself, not for his god), but his own guilt will deprive him of all magic spells for the span of one month. (If the DM wishes, if the priest is a follower of the god of Peace, the god can instead punish him as a "Betrayal of Goals" from the **Role-Playing** chapter.) Naturally, if he later abandons the kit, he can resume the wearing of armor and use of weapons according to his priest-class.

Wealth Options: This priest gets the usual 3d6x10 gp.

Races: No special limitations.

Peasant Priest

Description: The Peasant Priest is the antithesis of the Nobleman Priest above. He's a champion of the common man, and prefers serving the commoner to any association with nobles. He has taken a vow of poverty; he believes he should sacrifice his worldly goods to the glory of his deity.

Note that the Peasant Priest need not have been born a peasant; he could have been born a nobleman and later abandoned that lifestyle and the privileges of his class.

There are no ability-score re-

quirements to be a Peasant Priest.

There are no special rules for abandonment of this kit.

Barred: Priests of the following gods, forces, and philosophies may not take this kit: Evil, Good, Prosperity.

Role: In the campaign, the Peasant Priest devotes himself to the needs of the common man. If he's part of an adventuring party, he won't support any plans which endanger or exploit the peasants or serfs, and will try to recommend plans which advantage them. (For example, if the party wants to use the locals to help lure the dragon out of its cave, so that the locals will be the first ones flamed and eaten, the priest will object. But if the locals are to be along as support troops, and have information and chances of success and survival at least equal to the player-characters', he won't have any such objection.) He'll insist that treasures be shared with the locals of the area where the treasure was found. (Assuming that the treasure is split into even shares among party members, he'll insist that the local peasant community receive two shares, for example.) In a greedy or tight-fisted party, the party might refuse his requests, which doesn't mean the priest has to attack them or steal from them... but this will inevitably result in the priest becoming disillusioned with the party.

Secondary Skills: The player may choose his priest's secondary skill.

Weapon Proficiencies: The player may choose his character's weapon proficiencies, subject to the limitations of the priest's actual priest-class. The DM may insist that the character start out the campaign only with proficiencies appropriate to a peasant, such as short sword, spear, bow, footman's weapons and the like; long swords (and bigger blades), horseman's weapons, exotic polearms, lances, tridents and the like are not. This should only be a restriction when the character is first created; afterwards, he can learn any weapon his priest-class allows him.

Nonweapon Proficiencies: Bonus Proficiencies: Agriculture *or* Fishing (player choice), Weather Sense *or* Animal Lore (player choice). Recommended: Any of the General proficiencies.

Equipment: The Peasant Priest has restrictions on the way he spends his money. Other than weapons, with which he has no monetary limitation, he may own only one object worth as much as 15 gp, and other than that one object may own nothing worth more than 10 gp. He may never own more than 75 gp worth of (non-weapon) property at any one time. If he receives money or gifts which put him above that limit, he must give away money and possessions until once again he is within the 75 gp limitation.

Special Benefits: The Peasant Priest always has shelter when he's in his own community; his own people will shelter him even from the land's rightful authorities. Among peasants of other communities, he cannot count on this benefit, but he receives a +2 reaction adjustment from all peasants.

Special Hindrances: The Peasant Hero's great limitation is described above under "Equipment."

Wealth Options: The Peasant Priest gets the standard 3d6x10 gp starting money. Of the money he receives, no more than 75 gp may be spent on goods other than weapons.

Races: No special limitation.

Prophet Priest

Description: A prophet is one who receives signs, dreams, or clues about the future from his god. Priests of the god of prophecy are prophets, but they aren't the *only* prophets. Priests of other gods can receive and pass along prophecies. However, since this is rarer, the DM has the right to approve or disapprove any character taking this Priest Kit.

To be a Prophet Priest, the character must have a Wisdom of 15 or better.

A character may not abandon this kit. As long as he is a priest, he is a Prophet Priest.

Barred: Priests of the god of Prophecy may not take this kit. All other priests may. (Priests of philosophies or forces don't receive their prophecies from a god; their prophecies are more like psychic impressions.)

Role: In the campaign, the Prophet Priest is partly a tool for the DM; the DM can use the character to supply clues and even red herrings to the characters. His is often a thankless job, and he is often a bit alienated from the normal folk (see "Special Hindrances" below).

Secondary Skills: The priest may choose his own secondary skill.

Weapon Proficiencies: Required: None. Recommended: Any that the priest's actual priest-class permits.

Nonweapon Proficiencies: Bonus Proficiency: Weather Sense. Recommended: None special.

Equipment: No special restrictions.

Special Benefits: The character receives the Medium Granted Power "Prophecy" from the **Designing Faiths** chapter. However, it's more limited than the Prophecy which is granted to priests of the god of Prophecy. With this power, priests may receive visions from the god at any time the DM decides, but may only deliberately sink into a trance in order to receive a vision once per day.

Special Hindrances: It's not normal for anyone but priests of the god of Prophecy to be prophets. Therefore, normal people are a little edgy around other prophets, and react to them at a −2 reaction adjustment. (This adjustment may never result in a reaction worse than Cautious, however.)

Wealth Options: This priest receives the normal 3d6x10 gp starting gold.

Races: No special limitations.

Savage Priest

Description: This is a shaman of a savage tribe. This character is a member of the tribe. The tribe itself is a technologically and culturally primitive one (by the standards and in the opinions of more "civilized" cultures), but is also one which is attuned to the natural forces of the world. The Savage Priest interprets the will of his god and acts as an advisor or leader to the members of his tribe.

This character might be an animal-totem shaman who assigns all the tribal warriors their animal totems. He might be the witch-doctor who insists on the deaths of the adventurers from the outside world. Take a priestess of a nature-god and give her the Savage Priestess kit, and you end up with something very like a nymph. Whether the Savage Priest is good or evil, filthy or clean-limbed depends on the nature of the tribe itself; the DM decides what the tribe is like.

To be a Savage Priest, a character must have a minimum Strength score of 11 and a minimum Constitution score of 13.

In abandoning this kit, the character is renouncing his membership with the tribe and accepting citizenship in some other culture. This frequently happens with Savage Priests who join adventuring parties, stay with them in travels through the world, and learn so much of the outside world that they no longer feel like part of their tribe.

Barred: Priests of the following god and philosophies may not take this kit: Disease, Divinity of Mankind, Evil, Good.

Priests of the following gods are *most* appropriate to this kit: Animals, Earth, Elemental Forces, Fire, Hunting, Nature, Sky/Weather, Vegetation.

Role: In a campaign, this character usually plays the role of the primitive who finds his world-view shattered by his experiences in the outer world... but who might teach his "civilized" companions something about simple truth and justice as he adventures with them. The DM should insist that the character role-play his tribal origins in the first four or five experience levels, until the character is more used to the outside world; this priest will be baffled by "high-technology" inventions (iron and steel weapons, boats made out of more than a single log, hourglasses, anything more sophisticated than the tools of his tribe), by civilized morals and ethics, and especially by the strangeness and unfairness of the laws of civilized men.

Secondary Skills: The Savage Priest character must take Fisher, Forester, Groom, Hunter, or Trapper/Furrier as his Secondary Skill (player choice, based on the activities of his character's tribe).

Weapon Proficiencies: The Savage Priest is limited to the weapons his actual priest-class permits him, and is further limited (when he is first created) to the following set of proficiencies: blowgun, long bow, short bow, club, dagger, javelin, knife, sling, spear. After he has adventured in the outer world, the character may learn other proficiencies.

Nonweapon Proficiencies: Bonus Proficiencies: (General) Direction Sense *or* Weather Sense (player choice), (Warrior) Endurance *or* Survival (player choice). Recommended: (General) Animal Handling, Animal Training, Fire-Building, Fishing, Riding (Land-based), Rope Use, Swimming, (Warrior, double slots unless the priest-class dictates otherwise) Animal Lore, Bowyer/Fletcher, Hunting, Mountaineering, Running, Set Snares, Tracking, (Priest) Healing, Herbalism, Local History, Religion, (Rogue, double slots unless the priest-class dictates otherwise) Jumping, Tightrope Walking, Tumbling, (Wizard, double slots unless the priest-class dictates otherwise) Herbalism. The Savage may *not* take Etiquette or Heraldry when first created.

Equipment: The Savage Priest, with his starting gold, may buy no armor other than leather armor and shield, and may buy no weapon not listed above under "Weapon Proficiencies." He must spend all his gold when he is created, or lose any "change" he has left over.

If you have *The Complete Fighter's Handbook*, use the Equipment rules for the Savage Warrior Kit instead.

Special Benefits: The Savage Priest has a special Detect Magic ability, resembling the spell of the same name, which he may use once per day per experience level he has (i.e., a 5th-level savage could use his ability five times per day). The rules for this power are:

Detect Magic. The Savage Priest is in tune with nature and can feel when there is something magical in the vicinity. As with the first-level Priest spell, he has a 10% chance per experience level to determine the sphere of the magic.

Special Hindrances: The Savage Priest is imposing and strange, and he worships his gods "all wrong" (i.e., civilized folk and priests recognize that his rites are different, unlike theirs). Therefore, he suffers a −2 reaction adjustment from all civilized folk (NPCs, that is; PCs can decide for themselves how they react to him).

Wealth Options: The Savage starts out with only 3d6x5 gp. After the campaign starts, he will encounter money, and the player may decide either that he likes the stuff or rejects it as a stupid city-human idea.

Races: No special limitations.

Scholar Priest

Description: This character is a researcher. He's most at home when he's poring over books, scrolls, papyri, clay tablets and other old writings. He's not forbidden from fighting, but is more likely to try to straighten out a bad situation with reason, personal charisma, or even trickery than with a weapon. His life is dedicated to the assimilation of knowledge (and, usually, the transmission of that knowledge to new generations).

A scholar priest must have an Intelligence ability score of 13 or better.

This kit cannot be abandoned. A scholar can break off correspondence with other scholars, can choose not to teach, can decide not to do any studying or writing for as long as he likes, but he can always re-enter the academic world.

Barred: Priests of the following gods, forces and philosophies cannot take this kit: Competition, Fertility, Life-Death-Rebirth Cycle, Strength, and War.

Priests of the following types are most appropriate for this kit: Arts, Crafts, Culture, Divinity of Mankind, Literature/Poetry, Music/Dance, and Wisdom.

Role: In the campaign, this priest is motivated by his desire for knowledge. He'll often be tempted by adventures where he's likely to be able to learn something. If an adventuring party is going to a ruin where a famous library once stood, he'll eagerly join on the faint hope that some scrap of that library still survives. He'll be part of expeditions to visit famous sites or ancient beings who might tell him stories of the past or solve old mysteries. He might be part of an adventure just so that he can chronicle it and preserve its events in history.

Secondary Skills: The Scholar Priest must take Scribe as his secondary skill.

Weapon Proficiencies: Required: None. Recommended: Any appropriate to the priest's actual priest-class. Note: See "Special Benefits," below.

Nonweapon Proficiencies: Bonus Proficiency: Reading/Writing. Recommended: (General) Artistic Ability, Etiquette, Heraldry, Languages (Modern), (Priest) Ancient History, Astrology, Languages (Ancient), Local History.

Equipment: The scholar-priest must always have writing material, quill and ink with him. If ever he loses them, he must regain or replace them as soon as possible, and in the meantime will be recording his experiences in any fashion he can find. Other than that, this kit makes no demands on the way he spends his money.

Special Benefits: The Scholar Priest can "spend" any of his Weapon Proficiency slots on Nonweapon Proficiencies instead. He doesn't have to; he can adhere to the normal pattern of proficiency choice that is appropriate to his priest-class. But if he wishes he may turn Weapon Proficiency slots into Nonweapon slots and thereby become a very skilled character. Also, the Scholar receives a +3 reaction bonus from other scholars, admirers of scholastic concerns, writers, journalists, and people who imagine that they are scholars. Because of this, when the party thinks it is in a situation when no one is willing to help, it may turn out that the mousy clerk, antagonistic king or homely witch they met is an admirer of or even correspondent with the Scholar Priest and will help them.

Special Hindrances: Many scholars are egotistical, and debates between scholars can become very heated and personal. Whenever the DM rolls a reaction check from another scholar, he should first roll 1d6. On a 1, the player-character scholar gets a -6 reaction adjustment instead of a $+3$, because at some time in the past (or even the present) he argued or disagreed with this scholar's pet opinion and offended him completely.

Wealth Options: The Scholar Priest gets the standard 3d6x10 gp starting gold.

Races: No special limitations.

Recording Kits on the Character Sheet

To record your priest kit on your character record sheet, do the following:

(1) When you write down the character's priest-class, also add the name of his priest kit there. If the character were a priest of the Norse god of thunder and also a peasant priest, you'd write "Priest of Thor/Peasant Priest."

(2) Where you write down the character's nonweapon proficiencies, add the ones you got free from the priest kit, and put an asterisk beside them to indicate that they are free proficiencies provided by the kit.

(3) Wherever you have space for notes, mark down the character's special benefits and hindrances, and any other facts you want to remember.

Multi-Class and Dual-Class Characters

Any multi-class priest can take one of the Priest Kits above. However, he can only take one kit, total. If he has several character classes, he can't take a separate kit for each class.

The same is true of dual-class characters. If a character begins play as a priest and takes one of the kits above, and then later changes to another class, he does not have to abandon the kit. However, he still may only have one kit. Also, if he chooses to abandon the kit when he changes class, he may not then take on a kit from the new class. The character may only have had one kit, ever, as long as he is played.

Abandoning Kits

A character created with a Priest Kit might, later in his adventuring career, decide that he has to abandon it. For instance, a Pacifist Priest might be crushed when his inaction resulted in the death of a friend, and might decide to abandon his pacifistic stance.

The player must tell the DM that he wishes his character to abandon the kit. If this choice is the result of some traumatic event, as in the example above, the character may simply wish to declare his intent. If the choice is a gradual one, the DM may want to work it into the storyline.

The priest abandoning his kit will have to role-play out his decision and its consequences. He'll announce his decision. . . and he must suffer the reactions of his allies (and the other members of his order!), whether good or ill.

He will give up all the kit's bonuses and hindrances. The character does not give up any bonus proficiencies, but they are no longer "bonuses." The character must "pay" for them by spending the next proficiency slots he receives on them.

Once he's abandoned a Priest Kit, the character may not take another Priest Kit to replace it. At this point, he's a normal priest of his specific mythos for the rest of his playing life.

Modifying and Creating Kits

The DM should alter the kits above in order to fit them better into his campaign world.

For instance, if there are no Savage races to which the PCs could belong, the DM should disallow the Savage Priest kit.

If you'd like to create all-new Priest Kits, refer to the kit creation rules in *The Complete Fighter's Handbook.*

There's more to role-playing priests than bashing miscreants, casting spells, waving holy symbols and making earnest pronouncements. In this chapter, we're going to talk about the differences between priests, even priests of the same orders, and about how they relate to the campaign world and their deities.

Priest Personalities

No two priests are alike in their goals, desires, quirks, and prejudices. It doesn't matter if they belong to the same priest-class, have the same Priest Kit, are at the same experience level and have rolled the same hit points. . . they're going to be different people.

Below are descriptions of several common type of priest characters. All of these personalities are drawn from priest character stereotypes common to the movies and fiction. Novice role-players should read through these descriptions and, if they wish, adopt one of these personality types for their priest characters or at least let these descriptions inspire them to work out the details of their characters' personalities. Experienced role-players, to whom the creation of personalities is second nature, should skip on to "Priest Adventures."

The Crusader

The Crusader is a priest with a mission. What that mission is, is up to the player and the DM; he may wish to convert the heathens, to restore a temple to its original glory, to clean up a corrupt priesthood, to crush the enemies of his faith, to destroy a powerful clan, or to gain special rights or privileges for (or merely a lifting of bad or prejudicial laws from) his people.

This is not such a bad thing when the Crusader's goals correspond to the goals of the adventuring party. That's easy to sustain for a multi-episode adventure. But when the other player-character heroes' attention turns to some other matter or enemy, the Crusader is less willing to go along. He may continue on with them for a time, but his attention always turns back to his personal crusade.

The Crusader is best suited to lawful alignments (lawful good, lawful neutral, lawful evil). He tends to be humorless, but certainly doesn't have to be stupid.

In combat situations, the Crusader is a straightforward fighter, all according to the limitations of his priestly class. But if the enemy is related to his Crusade, he'll become the fiercest and most energetic of fighters, sometimes taking dangerous risks and going all-out to rid himself of this most personal enemies.

In role-playing situations, he doesn't have to be a boring idiot who talks about nothing but his quest. He can have other goals and interests, too. But the further away he is from his personal crusade, and the less he is able to promote his goals, the more of his attention they will take up in his mind.

The Earnest Novice

This priest is a young fellow who has newly achieved his priestly rank. (Yes, all first-level priests are appropriate for this personality. . . but not all of them *have* to take it. Other first-level priests can be a little more sophisticated or worldwise than this fellow.)

The Earnest Novice is naive. He's easily tricked by smooth, polished liars. He is pure in his beliefs, especially those related to his priestly order. He serves as an inspiration for others; no matter how battered he is by life, he seems always just to stand back up and keep on going.

This character is best suited to the range of good alignments (lawful good, neutral good, chaotic good).

In combat situations, this character is prone to be a bit simple. He has very primitive combat tactics, such as "run at the enemy and hit him," or "stand where you are and shoot him;" such things as flanking maneuvers, feints, false retreats, and other military maneuvers are beyond his comprehension.

In role-playing situations, this character expresses cheerful optimism and, usually, a lack of understanding about the way the "real world" (that is, the campaign world) works. It doesn't occur to him to slip a waiter a bribe to get better service: That would be monstrously unfair and unprofessional! The ideas that a colleague might be corrupt, that a judge might render a decision based on how he felt that morning, that a beautiful young lady might not be absolutely virtuous are all alien to him. He'll accept them when his nose is rubbed in them. . . but they'll never occur to him naturally.

Most players who take this personality eventually abandon it; it's nearly impossible to play a character as remaining entirely innocent of the world through adventure after adventure. See "Changing Personality Types" below for more on this.

The Hypocrite

This priest is a smooth talker and an advocate of all the goals of his priesthood and all the virtuous behaviors there are. But, deep down, he doesn't believe in them. He's fooled his superiors in the priestly order, he's probably fooled his adventuring companions, he's certainly fooled his flock. . . but he himself knows the truth.

This is a pretty villainous personality type; when a hypocrite priest isn't a villain, he's merely weak-willed. Either way, such characters are rare among player-character heroes. And they never get away with it forever.

Here are some examples of this character's typical behavior:

He generously gifts coins to city beggars and earns their praise. But on the side, out of sight, he traffics in stolen goods, perhaps including objects stolen from temples of his order, and uses the respect accorded to priests to smuggle his stolen goods through city gates and inspection lines.

When a beautiful young member of the flock comes tearfully to him with problems, he arranges to see her privately to counsel her. Alone with the troubled young lady, he will seduce her, then abandon her, blackmailing her with the besmirching of her reputation to keep his own reputation clean. And should she, in her grief, decide to commit suicide, he'll be the most anguished of mourners at her funeral (perhaps he will officiate). . . and then begin to work on the young lady's better-looking friends the same way.

When sinners come to him after doing evil, they'll always find absolution. . . for a hefty price in gold pieces. Such sinners are almost always repeat offenders, and so they are also repeat spenders.

Obviously, this sort of personality is best-suited to non-player characters. But it is always an option for, and can be a challenge to, player-characters as well.

The Hypocrite is limited to lawful neutral, lawful evil, true neutral, and neutral evil character alignments.

In combat situations, the Hypocrite will tend to behave like the priest he's supposed to be. If he can find reason to get out of the way of combat, he will: For instance, if an ally is injured, the Hypocrite will drop behind the lines to heal or doctor him. The Hypocrite is also prone to directing the actions of his teammates in such a way that they take all the risks. If one of them is killed or injured, of course, he will appear to agonize over it.

In role-playing situations, the Hypocrite will be the smoothest and most concerned character around. However, his player will need to communicate, in private consultation with the DM or through secret notes, the Hypocrite's true motives and plans.

Eventually the other characters will catch on, and ultimately they will expose or even kill him. It's up to the player then to decide what the Hypocrite will do (assuming he survives): He could change his name and start over again elsewhere, or pretend to reform and become a little more sophisticated in his tactics, or he could even reform and change personality types.

The Motivator

This character is like a grown-up version of the Earnest Novice. He knows what the world is all about, but he intends to do his temple's business and see to it that his god's goals are met, with no complaints and no back-talk. He's a combination of cheerleader and drill sergeant. He leads by example, and he usually leads. He gets to know the minds of his companions and plays upon their own goals and desires to get his accomplished. This doesn't make him a villain like the Hypocrite; he probably intends this to be to everyone's benefit.

Like the Crusader, he performs best when he's headed in the direction of his personal goal; unlike the Crusader, he doesn't have just one goal that dominates his life, and can add the other player-characters' goals to their own. (But if he does take on someone else's goal, you can be sure that he'll be unceasing and maybe unbearable in trying to motivate that character toward that goal. He won't let the other character abandon the goal. He jut never gives up.)

This character is suited to any alignment. Obviously, if he's lawful good, his goals will be the goals of his god and his society; if he's chaotic evil, his goals will be his own, and very destructive ones, too.

In combat situations, the Motivator charges into the thick of things and tries to whip up his allies into a combat frenzy. He gravitates to the center of the skirmish line, and if he's fit for it will try to take on the biggest and baddest opponents.

In role-playing situations, he'll be a vigorous font of advice and helpfulness. He tends to be abrupt of speech and firmly set in his opinions (i.e., stubborn), but he's usually a good friend to have around.

The Philosopher

This character tries to fit each of his adventures and encounters into the grand scheme of the meaning of life. He's not a very exciting personality, being more thoughtful and reserved than the dynamic Motivator or energetic Earnest Novice. He often adopts a "Let's wait and see what happens" or "Maybe it was meant to be" attitude. He seldom initiates combat or aggression, but this doesn't make him a pacifist; once he gets into combat, he can be as formidable an opponent as any priest of his class.

The Philosopher is best suited to lawful and neutral alignments (lawful good, lawful neutral, lawful evil, neutral good, true neutral, neutral evil).

In combat situations, the Philosopher will often hang back for a round or so to gauge the situation and analyze things. In doing so, he may see something the other characters have missed (more enemies creeping out of a secret panel, an exit tunnel that would allow them to escape, or the stealthy motions of an enemy thief creeping around behind one of the heroes). But he won't hesitate long, particularly when it could mean life or death to his friends.

In role-playing situations, he tends to be very analytical, choosing his words carefully, thinking all the while.

The Politician

This is an ambitious priest. He wants to have political power within the community, within the temple, or both. This doesn't mean he's bad; he may be acquiring power because he believes he can wield it better than others and make the world a better place. But he goes out of his way to gather favors, advise powerful people (and to do so well!), to acquire treasure so that he can build great temples and influence the masses, etc.

The Politician has a weakness, though. Regardless of his motivations, he sometimes blinds himself to the truth so that he can continue acquiring power and influence. If two cities or countries are on the verge of war, and that war would benefit him and his power base, he might advocate that war be declared, and blind himself to the suffering this will cause among the people who have to do the fighting. If a woman comes to him with the classic dilemma where she is being told by her family to marry one man when she loves another, the Politician will first consider the influence he might gain from these respective matches first, and considers the lovers' and families' feelings second. He may not even realize this. . . but his advice will always be tinged with self-interest.

This is also a challenging role to play, especially if the character really is good at heart and is just concealing from himself the harm of his course of action. Eventually, the DM should confront him with the results of his selfishness: Perhaps one of his plans or pieces of advice results in tragedy, and the accusations of the PCs or NPCs who see through his motives convince him that he's been on the wrong path. When this happens, the Politician might wish to change to another personality type. On the other hand, sometimes the Politician is never caught at it, or never admits his culpability to himself, and just continues rising up the ladder of power and influence.

The Politician is best suited to lawful and neutral alignments (lawful good, lawful neutral, lawful evil, neutral good, true neutral, neutral evil). If he's Good, he'll probably eventually understand the damage he has done and can do. If he's Neutral, he won't go out of his way to harm people, but will not be truly touched by it when harm does occur. If he's Evil, this harm is merely another benefit of the job.

In combat situations, the Politician is like any other priest of his specific priest-class. However, if there's an important person around to impress, he may fight more vigorously or risk himself to save that person.

In role-playing situations, the Politician is continually ferreting out rumors and news, analyzing information, learning the personalities of important people, and looking at all situations and adventures in terms of the power and prestige they can bring him.

The Proselytizer

This priest's primary motivation involves converting worshippers of other gods to worship of his god. Nothing else matters. If someone is not according due to his god, that someone is going to experience a religious conversion attempt. (This doesn't mean that the Proselytizer necessarily believes his god to be the only god. In a land where many gods are worshipped, this is an uncommon belief. But if he finds someone who worships several gods but excludes *his* deity, the Proselytizer goes on the job.)

Proselytizers can be of any alignment, but most are dutiful priests of good alignment (lawful good, neutral good, and chaotic good).

In combat situations, the Proselytizer acts as any other adventurer. He might be more gullible when it comes to an enemy who pretends interest in his deity and professes a desire to be converted, but this will only occasionally take place in the campaign. (The enemy would have to know him and his motivations pretty well to make this attempt.)

But in role-playing situations, the Proselytizer talks about little other than his god, his temple, and his personal adventures in service to his god and his temple. He can be quite insufferable at times, in fact.

Ultimately, his adventures may convince him that there are other things to life than the ongoing conversion of non-believers; at this time, his player may choose for the character to take on a new, different personality. But even then, the character is likely to remain a bit more interested in religious conversions than other examples of his new personality are.

The Sage Counselor

This priest is primarily interested in acquiring wisdom and passing it on. He likes to help people. And since he's a priest, people often come to him with their troubles; he's always willing to advise them. (Depending on his experience and personal wisdom, he could be quite good at it, too.)

This personality is best suited to lawful good and neutral good alignments. (A chaotic good priest could also try to be a sage counselor, but his advice is likely to be more dramatic and less well-reasoned than that of the other alignments.)

In combat situations, the Sage Counselor is likely to try to persuade the enemy to surrender, to run away, or just to be reasonable. This doesn't mean that he's stupid, though. Confronted with danger, he can hit just as hard and defend himself and his friends just as fiercely.

In role-playing situations, the Sage Counselor goes out of his way to help people; if he sees a sad face and has some time available to him, he'll gravitate to the stricken person, kindly ask if he can help, and end up wrapped again in some other person's troubles. Incidentally, this is a great way to get the character involved on new adventures: The DM need merely run a tearful NPC past the priest, and another adventure is on its way.

Changing Personality Types

Sometimes, as mentioned above, it becomes necessary for a player to re-think his character's personality. Perhaps the character has outgrown that personality. (The Earnest Novice must eventually grow up, for instance.) Perhaps dramatic events have forced the character to re-think his goals and attitudes. (This often happens to the Crusader and the Politician.)

Since these Personality Types are not part of an official rule or game mechanic, the player can change them as he chooses. He shouldn't change his character's personality just because he's bored with it, though: Events in the campaign should be the factors which influence this change. Here are some ways it can come about.

The **Crusader** might achieve his life-long goal, or lead one party too many into death and disaster and realize that all he's doing is hurting people. In this case, he could become embittered and turn into a Hypocrite, playing on his good reputation, or could tone his approach down and become a Motivator, or could achieve a measure of wisdom and become a Sage Counselor.

The **Earnest Novice** could wise up and realize that the world is a more complicated and unfathomable place than he thought. If he becomes disillusioned by this, he could turn into a Hypocrite. If he simply matures a bit, he'd be a Motivator. If he acquires a specific goal, he could become a Crusader, Politician or Proselytizer. And if he simply acquires a bit of wisdom or perspective, he could become a Philosopher or Sage Counselor.

The **Hypocrite** could change his personality if he is confronted by the harm he causes and cares at all about it. (If he doesn't care, he won't change.) If he does change, he's likely to become a Crusader (trying to expose and eliminate other Hypocrites), a Politician (so he can gain enough power to weed Hypocrites out of his order), or even a Sage Counselor (who can possibly anticipate the tactics of other charismatic users).

The **Motivator** could run out of energy; after too many years of battering himself against the brick wall of an uncaring world, he might tire out. In this case, he's likely to become a more sedate Philosopher or Sage Counselor. He could conceivably become embittered and become a Hypocrite.

The **Philosopher** isn't likely to change. His personality comes with maturity, not before it. If he does change, it will probably be because he's grown tired of being dull and undramatic, and he's likely to become a Motivator, one anxious for adventure, combat and life in general.

The **Politician** will probably change only if he perceives that he's doing more than good (and if he minds that). In this case, he'll probably shy away from real responsibility in the future and become a Philosopher.

The **Proselytizer** is likely to realize that he is not serving his god best simply by converting others to that god's worship. He's likely then to become a Crusader, so that he can avidly pursue one of his god's specific goals; a Motivator, so that he can bring energy to other priests of his order; or a Politician, so that he can improve the stature of his god's worship through reorganization of the priesthood.

The **Sage Counselor**, like the Philosopher, isn't likely to change; this is a personality that is acquired with experience.

All Sense and No Brains

And now we're faced with one of the commonest questions about clerics and druids: How do you role-play a character who has a high Wisdom score and a low Intelligence score? How do you play all sense and no brains within an AD&D® game campaign?

Intelligence deals more with reasoning power, calculating ability, and memory retention. Wisdom deals with common sense, understanding of human nature, and judgement.

So when you're role-playing a character with a low Intelligence and a high Wisdom, try to break down the situations they face into the elements which the character's Intelligence and Wisdom would analyze.

Example: The characters have come to a rickety bridge which spans a gorge. They need to cross the gorge, but the bridge looks dangerous. Should they cross?

The character's Intelligence will evaluate the bridge's chances of holding up while they cross over. The character will look at the state of the wood, ropes, nails, how much and where it sags, where it's rotted through, and so on, and then will try to calculate the answer to this question: Will the bridge hold up if the characters cross over? If the character thinks it will, then his reply, regardless of the group's current situation and time available, is Yes: They should cross. If the character thinks it won't, then his reply will be No: They shouldn't.

The character's Wisdom will compare the risk to their need and situation. The risk is that the bridge will collapse and kill someone, perhaps a party member dear to everyone. What is their current situation? If the party has little time and is being pursued by a superior enemy force, then the risk is necessary, more or less regardless of what the Intelligence thinks of the bridge's chances; the character will say Yes, they must try to cross now. If the party has a good deal of time, then the risk is not necessary; regardless of how safe the Intelligence thinks the bridge is, Wisdom says not to risk it. A human life is not worth it.

This is the kind of decision-making process the character can undertake if he wishes to role-play a high-Wisdom, low-Intelligence character in a campaign. . . and obviously it can lead to great arguments between them and their high-Intelligence, low-Wisdom counterparts.

Priest Adventures

The DM may want to slant some of his campaign's adventures specifically to his priest player-characters. It's not hard to do that; he has only to build the adventure around one or more of the priest's duties or responsibilities.

The priest-oriented plot device we use to motivate the priest to action is called a *Hook*. To design an adventure around the priest character, the DM has to provide a hook that will bring the priest into the adventure, and do so in such a way that the adventure doesn't exclude the other player-characters.

The hook must address the priest in one of his priestly roles or duties. Below we present a variety of hooks and approaches to this sort of adventure.

Advisor of the Faithful

The priest provides guidance to the flock. Followers of the temple come to him for advice, and he's supposed to give it.

That advice can't be correct all the time, especially when the faithful come to him with no-win situations. When it goes wrong, the priest will probably feel guilty. When it goes disastrously wrong, and the injured party comes to the priest for help, the priest will probably be willing (if not anxious) to clean the situation up.

As an example of this hook, let's say a doting father comes to the priest with this story: His son has come to him and asked for money so that he can buy weapons and armor. His son has heard of a bandit encampment where there is much treasure to be found. The son is sure that with the right weapons and armor and a little luck he can sneak into the camp when most of the bandits are gone, defeat the guards, and make off with the treasure. The father doesn't know where the encampment is; his son won't tell him. The son is a good fighter and knows what he's talking about; on the other hand, he is youthful and a bit overconfident. The father asks "Should I give my son the money for this equipment?"

If the priest says Yes, the father does so. The son tries the raid but is captured after killing several bandits. The bandits send back his bloody, broken sword from their mystery encampment, with a ransom demand which the father (and even the PCs) cannot match.

If the priest says No, the father follows his advice. The son tries it anyway, and is captured because he was under-equipped; no bandits died. Again, the son is ransomed beyond the father's means.

If the priest says "Maybe, but my friends and I would like to get in on it," the father will take him to talk to the son. The son will sound agreeable to the proposition, but will sneak off at first opportunity. He doesn't want anyone else horning in on his adventure. And because he had to charge off prematurely, he doesn't know enough about the bandit encampment and is caught up in snares set around its perimeter. Here, again, he's captured and ransomed.

In either of these three cases, the father comes back to the priest to say, in effect, "Your lousy advice got my son captured, and I can't ransom him! Please save him!" Which the priest will be inclined to do. . . and he'll probably want to have his friends, the other PCs, along with him.

Incidentally, we don't recommend that you face your PCs with no-win situations such as the one above very often. It wouldn't be fair to do this time and time again; the players would (correctly) assume that they could never do anything right unless the DM arbitrarily wanted them to.

Agent of the Priesthood

When the priest is a low-level character, still near the bottom of the totem pole of the priesthood's hierarchy, his superiors will frequently send him on missions. A mission could be nothing more than "Take this letter over to the priest Aclastion in the next village," or it could be "There's supposed to be some horrible monster menacing our temple in the next village; do you suppose you could round up some of your more violent friends and go over there and destroy it for us?"

In the latter case, you have a situation where the priest character is the center of attention, and has ample reason and opportunity to invite his non-priest friends in on the action.

Defender of the Faith

When the followers of one faith make war on the followers of another, the priests get involved in the action. Since these wars tend to take place between entire cultures, the player-character priest will probably be an ally of the other player-characters. In this case, his temple superiors are likely to ask him to round up some capable allies and go on dangerous missions into enemy territories, or to hold a crucial mountain pass during a military campaign.

Defender of the Faithful

You read about Libels in the **Designing Faiths** chapter, under "Duties of the Priest," under "Vigilance." (If you didn't, you should now.)

When the faithful are threatened by such a libel, the priest must work against it; if he doesn't, or if he fails, his people will suffer more prejudice and be in more danger from people who believe the libel. (There will be enough who still believe the libel if it is proved false; if the characters *can't* prove it false, there will be many more believers still.)

In order to bring the other player-characters in on such a situation, try this technique: One fine day, the priest finds another priest (of the same temple) dead in his chambers. The dead man has been murdered, torn limb from limb. His chambers were barred shut from the inside; a thief could not have picked the bars. In the priest's hand is part of a page from his journal, and the rest of the journal is missing. The scrap of paper, written in his hand, is part of a longer chronicle: "in mortal danger. When the [insert the name of an enemy temple] summon the thing, it will kill him and *we* will be blamed. I know they work from the Citadel of Arbright, but could find out no more; I think perhaps they heard me as I listened to their talk. It is time for me to tell —" There the passage ends, obviously when the priest was interrupted by his murderer.

This puts the priest-character and his temple in a delicate situation. Obviously, the enemy temple will summon up some sort of monster to kill some person, probably an important person, and the priest's temple will get the blame.

Obviously, the summoned thing, whatever sort of monster it is, can penetrate locked chambers without violating the locks and bars.

The priest and his temple have to know more. But the authorities will not allow them to search the Citadel of Arbright, home of a powerful local family, on this flimsy and perhaps fabricated evidence. Therefore, the priest must sneak in, find out what is to be found out, and escape. He'll need the help of his friends. . .

And what they do find out, of course, is that the Clan Arbright is aiding the enemy temple. They together have found a way to summon an outer-planar creature into sealed chambers, and they plan to do this some night when the High Priest of the player-character's temple is closeted with the king. The being will kill the king and leave the high priest to take the blame, resulting in damage, perhaps permanent damage, to the faith. . . unless the priest-PC and his friends can thwart the plan.

Martyr for a Cause

The priest's god or the rules of the priestly order might force the priest to undertake some actions that the local authorities just don't understand or approve of. (See below, under ''Society's Punishments,'' for more on this.) If the priesthood is not protected against prosecution by the secular (non-priestly) authorities, then the priest might find himself on trial for any illegal action performed in the god's name.

Gods usually don't appear in court as defense witnesses. Therefore, the priest-PC must defend himself through legal means without the benefit of divine testi-

mony. If he's convicted, he might have to escape jail to avoid execution; he might even choose to accept execution in order to dramatize the injustice of his plight. Or, the court might sentence him to some suicidal mission to atone for the crime he committed. He isn't required by the court to go on the mission alone, but no NPC adventurers want to march with him into certain doom. Thus the priest character is again brought into an adventure because of his faith, and his friends the other PCs, if they truly are his friends, will accompany him on this quest.

Servant of the God

The god himself will sometimes send the PC on missions. Often, he will appear to the PC when he is alone, or will appear to him in dreams, and make his wish known: "You will travel to the wild lands of the Sylvan Curtain and there find the artifact known as the Eagle-Spear. Find it; take it from our enemies, who hold it; bring it back and install it in your temple. . ."

When he investigates the Sylvan Curtain and the Eagle-Spear, the priest will find that it's certain death to go there alone. He needs adventurers of all descriptions and abilities to help him if he's to pull off this adventure successfully. . .

Rites and Role-Playing

In a lot of campaigns, it's easy to ignore one of the priest's foremost functions: He's also the officiator at lots of rites, rituals, celebrations and ceremonies.

Every faith will have its own rituals and other special events; careful, judicious use of these will add

a lot of detail and flavor to a campaign.

The DM *shouldn't* sit down and work up a lot of rituals for each priesthood in his campaign, and then keep them juggling around in his mind until they emerge, one by one, during adventures. But what he *should* do is bring individual ceremonies and priestly events into his campaign as adventure and story hooks.

For example:

"Jeriash, your party arrives in the city on October 30th. Now, you could head on from there the next day, but November 1st is Vine Day, which commemorates your goddess stopping her work for the year, winter setting in, wine-making ceremonies, and so forth; it sort of behooves you to volunteer your help at the local temple for that event. . ."

The Vine Day celebration, a Mardi Gras-like costumed parade featuring wine-drinking excesses, is a good opportunity to inject some color into the current storyline, but that isn't all it has to be. The DM could wrap an entire story around it; for example, imagine trying to capture a group of ghouls as they roam these streets strewn with drunken, costumed celebrants.

Though the DM shouldn't work up all a priesthood's usual ceremonies in advance, whenever he does create one, he should make note of it. If he doesn't, and the right time of year rolls around again, the players will inevitably remember it and wonder why Vine Day isn't being celebrated this year. . .

Following are descriptions of a number of different types of rituals. Each of these can be adapted to the characteristics of different faiths and different gods. Not all cultures and not all gods will feature each of these types of rituals; the DM should decide which apply to which gods and to which societies.

Atonement

When the flock sins, or acts against the wishes of the god, the faith usually has a way for the sinner to reenter the god's good graces. This is an act of atonement. Usually, the bigger the sin, the more extravagant the act of atonement must be.

The first part of this process is usually the *confession*, a formal meeting of sinner and priest where the sinner confesses his deed. This puts the priest in the position of having to evaluate that sin and then charge the sinner with a course of action which will remove the stain of sin.

Remember that each different god will have different ideas of what constitutes sin. To the god of Love, for instance, the greatest sin is denial of love (particularly, growing old without having loved) or interfering in love (messing up someone else's romance).

Too, you must remember that in a pantheistic society (one which worships many gods), it is not usually a sin to do one god's will at the expense of another. If one culture worships both a god of Peace and a god of War, fomenting a war is *not* a sin directed at the God of Peace; it's a boon to the God of War.

To just about any god, an insult to the god (including verbal insults or desecration of a temple) is considered a sin.

Typical ceremonies of atonement include fasts and meditations where the sinner asks forgiveness of the god. More exten-sive sins require some sort of sacrifice (such as donation of a cherished object to the god's temple) or an act of expiation (the sinner doing his best to straighten out the bad situation he caused).

Calendar Ceremonies

Lots of gods have ceremonies based around the calendar, especially agricultural gods. Communities may have celebrations for:

The day that marks the start of spring;

The day when planting begins;

The day when harvesting starts;

The beginning of the grape-stomping season;

The official start of winter;

The day that the first trade-ship of the year is launched;

The day that some heroic figure, a worshipper of the god, is commemorated;

The day of thanks for the god's bounty;

The day commemorating some ancient tragedy;

The day of the dead (just before or after the night that the ghosts walk the streets);

The day commemorating some great battle in which the god participated;

And so on.

Communion

This is a ceremony where the participants try to commune with the god, to invoke a little of his spirit, to briefly become more like the god.

Here, too, each god will have a very different ceremony. Communion with the god of Competition will take the form of athletic games. Communion with the god of Prosperity will be a great, enor-mous feast. Communion with the god of Kingship will be a private little coronation where each household leader is acknowledged as the head of the household. Communion with the god of Peace will be a quiet meditation. Communion with the god of Love or Fertility is left as an exercise for your imagination.

Confirmation of Adulthood

The DM needs to decide when youths are considered to reach adulthood in the culture, and then it's possible to have Confirmations of Adulthood.

In a culture, this will be handled one of two ways.

Each youth could have a private ceremony on his birthday. Alternatively, all youths born in the same year could be confirmed on one specific day of the calendar.

Either way, in the ceremony, the priest will acknowledge the youth as an adult, and this will be marked by allowing the youth some activity which only adults can perform in the culture (for example, carrying weapons in public, wearing some garment reserved for adults, receiving a sword, etc.).

Confirmation of Birth

With this ceremony, the priest visits the newborn child and, in a simple ceremony, asks the god's blessings upon the child. This is always done in the presence of witnesses, because it's important in the culture for others to witness that the child has been born and that specific people (the parents) acknowledge the child as theirs. This becomes important regarding questions of inheritance or the succession of the titles of leadership.

Fast

This is a quiet sort of ceremony; the participants do not eat, usually for the period of a day, as a sacrifice to the god or a commemoration of some historical time of want.

Feast

The feast can be as small or great a feast as the DM cares to allow, and can celebrate just about anything within the faith. Feasts should be one of the most common sorts of celebrations within the faith, and a great feast is a convenient place to introduce all sorts of adventure elements (challenges from enemies, assassination attempts, mysterious clues left in the soup, etc.).

Funeral

Interment of the dead is also a common ceremony. Note that funerals don't have to be solemn affairs; all this depends on what the culture thinks happens to the departed spirit and how the culture feels about it. The funeral could be a time of mourning, a cheerful celebration of the departed person's life, a drinking-binge so that the mourners can forget their grief, and so on.

In any case, the ceremony can have several parts.

There is the Wake, which takes place before the funeral, where participants sit overnight with the body, exchange stories of the dead person's deeds, and (in some settings) protect the body from violation at the hands of evil spirits, who might try to inhabit and reanimate it, or to steal the not-yet-departed soul.

There is the Farewell, where the participants speak to the corpse of the departed and wish him well on his voyage; often, they present him with small gifts and tokens of their friendship.

There is the Interment, where the body is laid to rest, usually with the presents and a variety of the person's belongings. In some cultures of a type we consider cruel, the person's slaves and perhaps even his wife will also be laid to rest, even if they aren't dead yet. (Alternatively, the body may be burned, again depending on the culture's views.)

There is the Commemoration, where the mourners exchange stories of the dead person; this could be a very solemn or a very merry event. In any case, it's likely to accompany a feast for the weary, hungry mourners and participants.

Libation

Libation is the dedication of a little of one's drink to the gods. Every time a glass is refilled, the character pours a little to his god, either onto the ground or into a basin dedicated to the god.

Meditation

This consists of sitting, in private or with other participants, and trying to achieve a peaceful state of exalted awareness.

Mysteries

These are involved ceremonies which usually celebrate gods of nature or rebirth. Celebrated annually or semi-annually, they tend to have several elements and can go on for a full day or more, not counting the rituals which precede the actual celebration of the mysteries. Usually, the pattern is something like this:

In the days before the actual celebration, the participants go through *purification*. These rituals of purification involve fasting, ritual baths, and abstinence from physical pleasures.

On the day of the celebration, the participants dress in clothing appropriate to the ceremony, usually in featureless clothing of white (or a color preferred by the god), usually barefoot. They assemble at the temple of the god, and perform the *oath-taking*. A high priest administers the oath, where every participant swears that he will keep what he has seen a secret, and never discuss it with one who is not also an initiate into the mysteries. The participant swears in the god's name, and could suffer the god's punishment if he breaks his oath.

Next, there is the *procession*. All the priests and participants proceed in a parade to a site that is holy to the god. This is often a cavern or a very secluded glade, because there it is possible to keep the celebration hidden from the eyes of non-initiates. The procession is led by ranking priests, followed by lesser priests in charge of sacrifices, followed by musicians who play during the procession. Then come priestesses, who carry small caskets (or draw carts bearing those caskets); the caskets contain artifacts sacred to the god. (These artifacts aren't necessarily, or even usually, powerful magical items desired by greedy adventurers. They're more ordinary items: The rock sacred to the god, the fossilized stone showing the god's footprint, the bone from the feast in which the god participated, the statue the god himself blessed, the cast-off weapon used by the god in some famous event, and so on.)

Then, there are more functionary priests: Priests in charge of the upcoming feast, priests who lead sacrificial animals (if sacrifice is a part of this culture's worship), and priests who act as sergeants-at-arms (they carry non-lethal weapons such as staffs and use them to keep the disorderly orderly). Finally, the faithful (non-priest) followers come.

Once the procession reaches the sacred site, there may be a *sacred meal*. Sacrificial animals will be sacrificed and cooked, and then the feast eaten. The character of the meal depends on the character of the god: It could be stern and somber for a severe god, wild and orgiastic for a more free-spirited god. The sacred meal ends after nightfall.

Then, the three most important elements of the mysteries begin. They all take place at night.

First is the *recitation*, a series of songs or chants concerning the god, his deeds, his promises to the faithful, his demands on the faithful. The recitation sets the mood for the rest of the ceremonies; the listening followers are supposed to be reverential, at least, and the priests with the staves are still around to keep order and quell (or get rid of) troublemakers. Troublemakers tend to be rare.

Second, there is the *display*. The sacred objects carried in those caskets are displayed for the faithful. Since they actually are magical objects sacred to the god, they tend to inspire the faithful with the essence of the god.

Third, there is the *performance*. Priests trained as actors perform a play which commemorates the most famous of the god's stories, especially the one which most closely deals with the god's demands on and relations with his worshippers. Regardless of the quality of this play, it is performed at the end of a lengthy process of worship where the followers are exposed to many powerful forces of the faith, and the onlookers are all elevated to a state of rapture during the performance.

At the end, there is the *rebirth*. Once the performance has ceased, the lights are doused and the faithful are led in pitch darkness from the area where the play was performed. Once they arrive at the point of departure, where the procession home will begin, the torches or lamps are again lit, and among the faithful this journey in darkness is much like being born again.

Mysteries are an experience for the spirit, not the mind; this is not an educational event, but one which is intended to bring the followers closer to the nature of their god. Even in a culture which worships many gods, only a very few will have mysteries as part of their worship.

For the DM, the mysteries are an opportunity to introduce dramatic events into the story. During the mysteries, it is appropriate for the god to appear to one of his PC followers and charge that character with an important mission, for instance. Or it could be that during the celebration of the mysteries, one character will receive some sudden insight (a gift from the god) into some event which has been puzzling or confounding the player-characters for some time.

Naming

This ceremony is often a part of the Confirmation of Birth event: The child is given his name before witnesses. In some cultures, though, the child might be given a use-name when he is born, and won't be given his true name (or will *choose* his true name) years later, when he is old enough to understand its significance. It may be that in this culture the character's true name is supposed to be kept a secret, and the child tells it only to one priest, so that the god might know it.

Prayer

Prayer is one of the most common of rituals; it involves asking the blessing of the god, often through the recital of an ancient or famous prayer or part of a holy text.

Note that not all cultures demand that prayer be performed from a kneeling position or a pose of obsequience. Vigorous warrior cultures might perform their prayers standing erect and facing the skies, for example.

Purification

When a person comes in contact with some contamination (a taboo substance), he must be purified. In some cultures, whenever a person has killed another honorably, though he is not considered to have sinned, he must be purified of the killing. This ceremony involves a ritual bathing or washing of the hands (or other contaminated part) under the supervision of a priest, who invokes the god's blessing during the washing.

Sacrifice

In some cultures, animals are sacrificed to the glory of the god. One god may demand that the whole animal be destroyed; another will demand that the animal be killed for it and some part of it destroyed for him, but that the rest of the beast can be used as the worshippers see fit.

Obviously, human sacrifice is something demanded only by the most evil or unsympathetic of gods.

Priests and Punishment

Priests are servants of their gods, and therefore can't just do anything they want whenever they want. The DM must keep an eye on the activities of priest char-acters (including clerics and druids), and if the priest violates some tenet or commandment of his god, the DM should see to it that the god punishes the priest.

It's easy to be unfair when doing this, though, so the DM also has to keep an eye on *himself*. It's all too easy to say, "You should have *known* that your god doesn't want you to wear red; I've said repeatedly that his favorite color is blue!" That's not justification for a punishment of the priest, unless the DM has explicitly stated that the god's priests must always wear blue or face divine consequences.

Minor Offenses

Minor offenses which the god punishes include such things as:

Making a joke about the god (and even then, it must offend the god; some gods have a sense of humor);

Failing to perform all required priestly duties in a day (for example, "not having the time" to listen to the problems of one of the faithful and offer guidance); and

Becoming annoyed with the god's demands.

The god punishes such minor offenses by withholding some of the priest's spells on the following day.

Inappropriate Weapon and Armor Use

If a priest violates his order's restrictions on weapon and armor use, the god will punish him for it. There are two different types of violation of this restriction, and a different punishment for each.

If the priest deliberately violates the restriction because he wants to (for instance, if he puts on a set of metal armor when he isn't supposed to), this is a willful disobedience and makes the god very angry. He immediately does 2-12 (2d6) points of damage to the priest and takes away all the spells he granted to the priest today, and doesn't let the priest have any more for 1-6 (1d6) days. Even then, the priest must undergo rituals of purification and undertake an act of atonement if he's to have spells again.

If the priest violates the restriction for the best of reasons (for instance, if a gargoyle is strangling his friend, and he must use a forbidden weapon in order to be able to harm the creature), the god does 1-3 (1d3) points of damage to the priest (*after the fight is done*) and, if the priest does not undertake a ritual of purification at his earliest opportunity, will take away the priest's spells on the next day.

Betrayal of Goals

If the priest deliberately violates the goals of the god, then he's in real trouble. For instance, if a priest of the god of war advocates peace when war is in the offing, or if a priest of the god of love tells young lovers to wise up and forget about romance, then the god will definitely be offended.

The first time this happens, the god will give the priest an unmistakable warning. This could be a heart attack, costing 50% of the priest's current hit points. It could be a portentous destruction of a statue of the god while the priest is present. It could be an earthquake or other warning. The warning doesn't have to be *immediately* after the betrayal, but will be soon after.

The second time this happens, the god will appear to the priest. It doesn't have to be in person, right then; it might be in a dream, the

night following the betrayal. The god will sternly ask the character his motives and order him to return to proper worship.

The third time this happens, the god will immediately reduce the character to 1 hit point and change his character class. The priest will become an ordinary fighter at an experience level two lower than the priest's level (minimum first level); his normal hit point total and possessions will be unaffected. Until the character undergoes a severe ritual of atonement, the god will despise the character and plague him with little ills, diseases, and enemies. Once the character atones for the deed, the god forgives him. . . but the character will still be a fighter.

Sometimes, a god might deliberately confront the character with a test of the character's faith. For example: Part of the god's worship demands that anyone who tramples his sacred flowers be blinded. Then, the god befuddles the priest's wife or daughter, and that character stumbles across the sacred flowers where only the priest can see it. If he conceals the sin, he's punished. If, regretfully, he prepares to carry out the punishment, the god will be pleased. The god might interrupt the punishment, or wait until it has been carried out and then restore sight to the priest's loved one.

Divine Retributions

It could be that the priest will betray more than the god's usual dictates. The priest might turn on the god, betraying him utterly. This can happen when another deity, an enemy god, persuades the priest to serve him instead, and persuades the priest to steal some

important artifact from the god or reveal some critical information about the god.

When this happens, the god will punish the priest (assuming he survives the betrayal, which most gods will).

The minimum punishment the priest can expect is the character class change described above.

A medium punishment the god will bestow is instant death.

A greater punishment from the god involves the ruin of the character. The god can kill or merely take away the character's family and loved ones, curse him with afflictions such as blindness and lameness, see to it that all his enemies find out about his weaknesses, give extra power and weapons to his enemies, force the priest's loved ones to betray *him*, and so on. This doesn't happen all at once, but every episode for the rest of the character's life introduces some new, horrible calamity until the character is mercifully killed or kills himself. In any case, the character is no longer a viable one to play and the player should dispose of him as quickly as possible.

At the ultimate level, the god performs the greater punishment above, and then tortures the character's spirit forever in the afterlife.

Note that this punishment isn't just for priests. If a non-priest betrays the god in the same fashion, the god will visit the same sort of punishment on the character.

Society's Punishments

Unless the priesthood is the State Religion, priests are not immune to the law for their deeds.

If, for example, the priest of the god of Justice and Revenge hears about some great injustice, wanders over to the offender's house and kills the offender, then he's guilty of murder. There's no question. He'll be arrested, tried, and (the efforts of his priesthood notwithstanding) probably convicted; the only thing that could save him would be a declaration from the god, which is usually not forthcoming.

Therefore, when priests decide to do something which is illegal in the culture, they should do so circumspectly. If they wish to accomplish the desires of their god when those wishes are illegal, they'll have to do so in a fashion which protects them.

When Priests Renounce Their Faith

It's possible for a priest to renounce his faith — to declare that he is no longer a priest of a particular god. When that happens, he has one of two choices.

He can stop belonging to the priest-class and start over as a rogue, wizard, or priest of another god, according to the rules for dual-class characters. Naturally, he loses all his granted powers.

If his priesthood had Good Combat Abilities, he can lose one experience level and become a fighter; if Medium Combat Abilities, he can lose two levels and become a fighter; if Poor Combat Abilities, he can start over as a fighter according to the rules for dual-class characters. He'll never again be a priest.

When Gods Bestow Spells

Another effect of the fact that priests are servants of their gods is this: The god doesn't have to give his priest the spells the priest wants.

In most situations, when the priest prays for his spells, he gets the ones he desires. But if the god and DM wish, he could get different spells on some occasions.

There are two usual causes for this to happen:

If the god is displeased with the priest for some minor infraction, he might give the priest spells which dictate the priests' actions for the day. A fighting-priest might emerge from his meditation with only healing spells on hand, for instance, a clear sign that the god wants him to act in a supporting role today.

Or, if the god knows of a specific opponent that the priest will be fighting today, he might give the priest spells appropriate to defeating that enemy.

In neither case will the god send a telegram explaining why he's done what he's done. The priest has to accept what the god hands him that day, and has to do so without knowing why.

Priestly Followers

It's good to remember that the priest's followers, the ones who come to him around 8th level, are not mere spear-carriers or meat for the monsters. They haven't shown up so that they can be thrown to the jaws of dragons in order to give the priest more time to get away. They've shown up to serve the god and the priest.

That's why, in the **Designing Faiths** chapter, we talked about giving them names and personalities, and likewise talked about the priest getting fewer and fewer replacements if he wastes the followers he has.

Once again, this is a sign that the priest cannot act with utter impunity. He is dependent on the good will of his god, and his god will not look kindly on a priest who brings about the deaths of other followers of the god. The god who says, "Yes, my son, kill off my other followers so that you can have more gold" is a foolish god indeed.

Toning Down the Cleric

The cleric class is a very powerful one. He has access to sixteen Spheres of Influence (more than *any* other priest-class), good armor, and fair weapons. It's been a sign of the cleric's advantages that he is the preferred character class of many, many campaigns.

If this ultra-efficient character is too powerful in your own campaign, you might prefer to alter him. If you want to do this, tell all the cleric players well ahead of time and give them the option to convert their clerics to priests of specific mythoi provided in the **Sample Priesthoods** chapter.

Then, establish the following rules about the Cleric class:

(1) Keep his weapon and armor limitations exactly as they are.

(2) Establish that the Cleric has Major Access to only three spheres (one must be All; the other two are player's choice) and Minor Access to two spheres (player's choice). The player must choose his four sphere options when the Cleric is first created (or converted); it may not be changed afterwards. Each Cleric may choose a different set of spheres.

Naturally, you should only do this if you personally feel that the cleric class is too powerful in your campaign. If you don't, don't change him.

In this chapter, we'll talk about some of the gear that the priest carries and uses in the performance of his duties, and also about new weapons and combat styles used by some priests.

Priestly Items

The most common and important tools of the priest (as far as his culture is concerned, anyway) aren't his weapons and armor. They are the actual symbols of his priesthood.

Not all of these symbols are useful in combat situations, but they're appropriate for role-playing the priest. Let's discuss them briefly.

The Canon

Many faiths have a *canon*, or holy book. This work was written at some time in the distant past, either by the god or by a believer obeying the word of the god. This book usually describes important events of the past in which the god participated, explains the requirements the god makes on his followers, and explains the god's philosophy, goals, and concerns.

If the faith has a canon, then the priest will wish to have one. Books are expensive commodities: Assuming that it's a mere 200 sheets (400 pages) in length, according to the costs in the *Player's Handbook*, you're talking about 400 gp in paper alone (2 gp per sheet); binding will cost another 50 gp, for a total of 450. Sometime between 3rd and 5th level, the priest should have saved or accumulated enough money to commission a copy of the canon; perhaps, if he is lucky, someone will gift him with one, or he will in-

herit one. Regardless, a priest who reaches 6th level without having acquired a copy of the canon will be viewed with some suspicion by commoners and his fellow priests, who will question his devotion.

The priest should carry the canon wherever he travels, and if it is stolen should make every effort to recover it. The canon is not a magical work, and does not act as a Holy Symbol when used to confront vampires or similar monsters.

Not all faiths do have an individual, written canon. Some faiths share a common canon. Some transmit their canon orally; it is not written down anywhere. Some have none at all.

Holy Symbol

Most faiths have a holy symbol, some sign which serves as a representation for the god and his faith. This symbol is usually duplicated in wood, glass, or precious metals and carried by priests of the god. Ordinary followers of the god also can carry the holy symbol.

Every priest player should know what his holy symbol looks like. The DM can either decide, or let the player of the priest design it. (If he does allow the player to do so, the design of the symbol is still subject to the DM's approval.)

It's easy to create symbols for most deities, and there are suggestions for symbols for all the gods represented in the **Sample Priesthoods** chapter.

Holy Water

Holy water, that bane of vampires and many other monsters, is created in the following way:

In a temple of the god, three priests of second level or higher

stand over an empty water-basin and perform a ritual of prayer. They pray for the god's blessing and protection for an entire hour. At the end of that time, they each cast a spell, and do so simultaneously: One casts *create water*, the second casts *protection from evil*, and the third casts *purify food & drink*. Half a gallon of holy water is created.

(The *create water* spell can create up to four gallons of water, but the *protection from evil* and *purify food & drink* used this way can only create half a gallon of holy water. Therefore, for every two extra priests, one to cast each of those two spells, an extra half-gallon can be created. Nine priests together can create four gallons.)

The tremendous expenditure of magic and the time involved are the reasons why a single dose of holy water costs 25 gp to the adventurer. Obviously, any three priests can create holy water "for free" so long as they are second level or higher and are priests of the same god.

Holy symbols are enchanted in the same way. Each enchantment takes an hour, requires three priests (substituting *sanctuary* for *create water*), and requires a material component: Some object carved with the god's symbol.

Priestly Vestments

As mentioned in the **Designing Faiths** chapter, each priesthood has its own distinctive costume, and priests normally wear these priestly vestments whenever they perform their official duties. Some must wear them whenever they appear in public.

It adds color to a campaign when the players know what these vest-

New Weapons List

Item	Cost	Weight (lbs.)	Size	Type +	Speed Factor	Damage S-M	L
Bill*	5 cp	2	S	P	2	1d4	1d3
Lasso☆	5 sp	3	L	—	10	—	—
Maul☆	5 gp	10	L	B	9	2d4	1d10
Net☆	5 gp	10	M	—	10	—	—
Nunchaku*	1 gp	3	M	B	3	1d6	1d6
Scythe☆	5 gp	8	M	P/S	8	1d6+1	1d8

* This weapon is intended for one-handed use, and may not be used two-handed. In the case of nunchaku, two-handed flourishes are common, but blows are struck with one hand only at a time.

☆ This weapon is intended for two-handed use only.

+ The "Type" category is divided into Bludgeoning (B), Piercing (P), and Slashing (S). This indicates the type of attack made, which may alter the weapon's effectiveness against different types of armor. See the optional rule in the *Player's Handbook*, page 90.

ments look like. If the DM doesn't wish to design the priestly vestments for all the priest player-characters, he should allow the players to do so (subject to his final approval).

New Weapons

Several new weapons are mentioned at various times in this supplement. Below, we'll describe them.

New Weapons Descriptions

The **Bill** is a short hook on a short cross-handle, and is a weapon derived from the sort of hook used to spear and haul in fish or to carry sides of meat around.

The **Lasso** is a rope with a loop at the end; it's thrown at targets, and on a successful hit the loop settles around the target. The wielder can then pull the rope taut and seriously inconvenience his target. Extensive rules for the lasso appear in *The Complete Fighter's Handbook.*

The **Maul** is a polearm with a heavy bludgeoning head at the end. It is therefore a Bludgeoning weapon, and is appropriate for the use of clerics and specific priests who aren't allowed to use bladed weapons. When a priesthood allows the use of polearms, this includes the maul (and the mancatcher, for that matter); but when maul alone is listed, the priest cannot use the other polearms.

The **Net** is a weighted combat net on the end of a rope. Like the lasso, it is thrown to spread over a target; if it hits, it can be pulled closed, and the trailing rope used to pull the victim around. Also like the lasso, extensive rules for this weapon's use appear in *The Complete Fighter's Handbook.*

The **Nunchaku** is an oriental weapon and only suitable for oriental-based campaigns. It consists of two wooden handles connected by a short chain or short length of cord. It was originally derived from an agricultural implement, which is why so many

priests of nature-oriented gods can use it.

The **Scythe** is a large, curving blade that is sharp only on the underside of the blade (the concave edge); the blade is attached to a twisted pole some 5-6' in length. The wielder uses the weapon two-handed. The scythe is a harvesting tool used by farmers to cut down their grain; as a weapon, it is symbolic of gods of agriculture, time, and death.

Unarmed Combat

The following material is reproduced in part from *The Complete Fighter's Handbook*, so that players of Fighting-Monks will have access to the rules for martial arts combat.

Attacking Without Killing

Before proceeding, you should familiarize yourself with the "Attacking Without Killing" rules from the *Player's Handbook*, pages 97-98.

Knowing Punching, Wrestling, Martial Arts

As you saw in the *Player's Handbook*, *everybody* knows how to punch and wrestle. Any character, from the doughtiest warrior to the spindliest scholar, knows hot to twist someone's arm or punch him in the jaw. (Naturally, such factors as strength, dexterity and experience level have a remarkable effect on how often one hits and how much damage one does.)

Martial Arts are another matter. By "Martial Arts," we mean generic unarmed combat. This isn't karate, kung fu or tae kwan do: It's movie-style martial arts with no basis in real-world fighting styles.

A character may only know Martial Arts if the DM declares that this style is available for characters to learn. In many campaigns, it won't be. In most oriental campaigns, it will be. In campaigns where the occidental and oriental worlds have a lot of contact with one another, it could easily be.

To know Martial Arts at its basic level, the character must spend one Weapon Proficiency slot on Martial Arts. That's all it takes. Once he's spent that proficiency slot, he can use Martial Arts in the same way that other people use Punching and Wrestling, as we'll describe immediately below.

Martial Arts Results

At its basic level, Martial Arts skill is used just like Punching and Wrestling. Martial Arts combat occurs when a character attacks with his bare hands, feet, and even head. No weapons are used. (A character can hold a weapon in one hand and nothing in the other, attacking with his weapon one round and with his Martial Arts skill in the next.)

When attacking with Martial Arts skill, the character makes a normal attack roll against the normal Armor Class of the target. (If the attacking character has armor on, he *does* suffer the "Armor Modifiers For Wrestling" from Table 57 on page 97 of the *Player's Handbook*.) Any other normal modifiers are applied to the attack roll (from the attacker's Strength bonus, for example).

If the attack roll is successful, the attacker consults the table below for the result of the attack. If, for instance, the character rolls a 13 to hit, the result is a Body-Punch, doing 1 point of damage (plus the character's damage bonus from Strength, if any).

Martial Arts Results Table

Attack Roll	Martial Arts Maneuver	Damage	%KO
20+	Head Punch	3	15
19	High Kick	2	10
18	Vitals-Kick	2	8
17	Vitals-Punch	2	5
16	Head Bash	2	5
15	Side Kick	1	3
14	Elbow Shot	1	1
13	Body-Punch	1	2
12	Low Kick	1	1
11	Graze	0	1
10	Body-Punch	1	2
9	Low Kick	1	1
8	Body-Punch	1	2
7	Knee-Shot	1	3
6	Side Kick	1	5
5	Head Bash	2	10
4	Vitals-Punch	2	10
3	Vitals-Kick	2	15
2	High Kick	2	20
1*	Head Punch	3	30

* Or less

Descriptions of the Maneuvers

Body-Punch: This is a straight-forward punch into the target's stomach or chest.

Elbow Shot: With this maneuver, the attacker plants his elbow into the target's chest, side, or stomach.

Graze: This could have started out as any sort of maneuver, but it merely grazed the target; it wasn't landed firmly.

Low Kick: The attacker kicks the target in the leg or thigh.

Head Bash: The attacker slams his forehead into the target's face, which is a stout maneuver.

Head Punch: This is a good, strong blow with the fist to the enemy's head, particularly his jaw.

High Kick: The attacker kicks the target in the upper body somewhere: Stomach, chest, back, or shoulder.

Knee-Shot: The attacker brings his knee up into the target's stomach or thigh.

Side Kick: With this maneuver, the attacker has time to prepare and launch a very powerful sideways kick (which may be at the end of a cinematic leap).

Vitals-Kick: The attacker kicks his target at some vulnerable point: Groin, kidney, neck, solar plexus, etc.

Vitals-Punch: The attacker puts his fist into one of the vulnerable points mentioned immediately above.

Specializing in Punching

Any priest can specialize in Punching (or Wrestling, or Martial Arts). Of all the types of priests, though, only the Fighting-Monk can specialize in more than one

unarmed combat style. The DM may decide for his own campaign that Priests other than the Fighting-Monk may not specialized in any unarmed combat, or that certain types of priests (for example, of the god of peace) may not.

In order to do specialize in Punching, the Priest must devote a Weapon Proficiency slot to Punching. When he does, he gets the following benefits:

He gains a +1 bonus to all his attack rolls with Punching;

He gains a +1 bonus to all damage with Punching; and

He gains a +1 *chart bonus* with all Punching attacks.

The chart bonus is a reflection of the character's superior accuracy with Punching. When the Fighter-

Monk rolls and successfully hits, as you know, the roll itself determines which maneuver was made.

But on a successful hit, the Punching Specialist can modify that result. If he has a *chart bonus* of +1, he can choose the maneuver one higher or one lower on the chart.

Example: The fighter-monk Toshi punches an orc. He rolls a 18 to hit, and this turns out to be a successful hit. On the "Punching and Wrestling Results" chart, we see that this is a Rabbit Punch. But Toshi is a Punching Specialist with a chart bonus of +1. He can choose instead for the result to be a Wild Swing (which does less damage and has an inferior chance of accomplishing a knockout) or a Kidney Punch (which does the same

damage but has a superior chance of accomplishing a knockout). He changes the maneuver from a Rabbit Punch to a Kidney Punch.

Only if a character Specializes in Punching and thus has a *chart bonus* can he affect his punch results in this manner.

Specializing in Wrestling

The same rules given for Specializing in Punching also apply to Wrestling. If a Priest spends one Weapon Proficiency slot on Wrestling, he is a Wrestling Specialist:

He gains a +1 bonus to all his attack rolls with Wrestling;

He gains a +1 bonus to all damage with Wrestling (that is, all his maneuvers will do 2 points of damage plus his Strength bonus, and continued holds cause cumulatively 1 more point of damage for each round they are held); and

He gains a +1 chart bonus with all Wrestling attacks.

So if, for instance, he rolls a 9 to hit, and that hits, his result would normally be a Leg lock. If he chooses, he can change it to an Elbow smash or a Headlock.

Specializing in Martial Arts

The same rules given for Specializing in Punching and Wrestling also apply to Martial Arts, with one exception. No character knows Martial Arts automatically. Therefore, the character must first spend one Weapon Proficiency slot to know Martial Arts in the first place, and then must spend one more to become a Martial Arts Specialist.

As usual, when the character becomes a Martial Arts Specialist:

He gains a +1 bonus to all his attack rolls with Martial Arts;

He gains a +1 bonus to all damage with Martial Arts; and

He gains a +1 chart bonus with all Martial Arts attacks.

So if he rolls a 15 to hit, and the attack hits, he has performed a Side Kick. If he uses his +1 chart bonus, he can change that into an Elbow Shot or a Head Bash. He'll probably choose to change it to a Head Bash, for the improved damage and improved chance of KO.

More Than One Style

Only a Fighting-Monk can specialize in more than one unarmed combat style. A Fighting-Monk can only specialize in one of the three unarmed combat styles when he is first created. After first level, however, he may specialize in the other two.

As described in the writeup of the Fighting-Monk kit, the character can save some of his Weapon Proficiencies.

For example, at first level, he could specialize in Martial Arts, then spend another slot at second level to specialize in Wrestling, then another at third level to specialize in Punching.

However, if he first specializes in Punching or Wrestling, he cannot specialize in Martial Arts at the next experience level. He can only spend one slot per experience level, meaning that he'll first gain proficiency with Martial Arts at one level, then specialize at the next level.

Usually, the character, if he wants to specialize in more than one style, will take either Martial Arts *or* Punching, not both, and then take Wrestling. Martial Arts and Punching overlap one another somewhat, but Wrestling is useful when the character is being held.

Continuing Specialization

This is an option only for Fighting-Monks (and Warrior characters); other Priests *may not do this.*

If a Fighting-Monk continues to devote Weapon Proficiency slots to an unarmed combat style *after he is already specializing in it,* he gets the following benefits.

For each additional slot devoted to his art, as before:

He gains a +1 bonus to all his attack rolls with his combat style;

He gains a +1 bonus to all damage with his combat style; and

He gains a +1 chart bonus with all attacks in that combat style. With chart bonuses of +2 or more, the character can choose any maneuver within the range of maneu-

vers covered by his chart bonus (see the example below).

A Fighting-Monk, once he has specialized in a fighting style, can only devote one Weapon Proficiency slot to that style *per experience level.* Therefore, a first-level Fighting-Monk could specialize in Martial Arts by devoting two slots to it. He could not devote another slot to it until second level, and then could not devote another slot until third level, and so on.

Let's use that character as an example.

Example: Toshi the Fighting-Monk specializes in Martial Arts at first level, adds one proficiency slot to it at second level, and another at third level.

At third level, he has a +3 bonus to attack rolls with Martial Arts, a +3 to damage rolls with Martial Arts, and a +3 chart bonus.

Let's say he rolls a 17 to hit someone, and that the attack does hit. This would normally be a Vitals-Punch. But he has a +3 chart bonus. He can choose for the maneuver to be a Head Punch, a High Kick, a Vitals-Kick, the Vitals-Punch that was rolled, a Head Bash, a Side Kick, or an Elbow Shot. Assuming that he takes the punishing Head Punch, he'll do 3 points for the maneuver, +3 points from the damage bonus he gets for specializing, and any bonus his Strength grants him.

* * *

That, in brief, is the way Martial Arts works for the fighting-monk. You are encouraged to read the Combat chapter of *The Complete Fighter's Handbook* for more rules and guidelines on the use of unarmed combat in the game.

The following works were helpful in the creation of **The Complete Priest Manual**:

Lurker, Manfred, *Dictionary of Gods and Goddesses, Devils and Demons*, Routlege and Kegan Paul Inc., London and New York, 1987.

Meyer, Marvin W., editor, *The Ancient Mysteries: A Sourcebook*, Perennial Library (Harper & Row, Publishers), San Francisco, 1987.

Neugroschel, Joachim, *The Great Works of Jewish Fantasy and Occult*, The Overlook Press, Woodstock, New York, 1987.

Seltman, Charles, *The Twelve Olympians*, Thomas Y. Crowell Co. (Apollo Editions), New York, 1962.